THE OUTLIER

ALSO BY ELISABETH EAVES

Non-Fiction

Wanderlust
Bare

THE OUTLIER

A NOVEL

ELISABETH

EAVES

RANDOM HOUSE CANADA

PUBLISHED BY RANDOM HOUSE CANADA

 Published in 2024 by Random House Canada, a division of Penguin Random House Canada Limited, Toronto. Distributed in Canada and the United States of America by Penguin Random House Canada Limited, Toronto.

www.penguinrandomhouse.ca

LIBRARY AND ARCHIVES CANADA CATALOGUING IN PUBLICATION

Title: The outlier / Elisabeth Eaves.
Names: Eaves, Elisabeth, 1971- author.
Identifiers: Canadiana (print) 2023047392X | Canadiana (ebook) 20230473962 |
ISBN 9781039008045 (softcover) | ISBN 9781039008052 (EPUB)
Subjects: LCGFT: Novels.
Classification: LCC PS8609.A94 O98 2024 | DDC C813/.6—dc23

Text design: Kelly Hill
Cover design: Kelly Hill
Image credits: (palm trees) parinya, (woman) heitorjose / both Adobe Stock;
(house) imaginima / Getty Images

Printed in Canada

2 4 6 8 9 7 5 3 1

For Joe

"You people with hearts . . . have something to guide you, and need never do wrong; but I have no heart, and so I must be very careful."

—The Tin Woodman,
from *The Wonderful Wizard of Oz*
by L. Frank Baum

ONE

CATE

Twitchy after a long afternoon of meetings, I opened the closet in my office. I changed out of my workday uniform of jeans, white shirt, and black blazer, stepped into stilettos, and zipped myself into a snug black dress. Grabbing the same blazer and my purse, I took the elevator to the parking garage, where I unplugged my orange roadster. With the Seattle rush hour long over, I pulled up outside the Four Seasons on First Avenue less than ten minutes later. A cold February wind kicked up off of Elliott Bay as I handed my key to the valet.

I headed for the bar and took my usual seat at one end, from which I could see who came and went. It's a sleek place, all shiny wood and blown-glass lampshades, and it was just the right amount of crowded, full of people in expensive black fabrics. Men and women on quick trips, complication-avoidant but not immune to the seductive effects of a change of scenery. Outside the window, a rainbow of LED lights flashed from the Great Wheel, casting a glow over the dark bay. Jesse, my favourite bartender, was on duty, and as soon as he saw me, he brought me a glass of mineral water with a couple of ice cubes and a twist of lime.

Ignoring the jitter of the phone inside my purse, I sipped my water and watched the patrons while a dozen questions whirlpooled in my mind, surfacing people and events from my early teenage years. Old faces flickered briefly, dredged up by the report I'd read nine hours earlier. Needing to detach myself from the questions that had preoccupied me since then, I closed my eyes and took a deep breath. When I opened them, I spotted two prospects right away. A frisson passed through me, calming and exciting at once. One man, I guessed, was in his mid-forties. Dark-haired, a little shaggy, at ease with himself. The other was probably close to my own age, mid-thirties, and subtly out of place. His sandy hair formed a widow's peak and curled around his ears. He seemed overly alert, already glancing my way. Maybe noticing my long, bicycle-toned legs or the collarbone that had so fixated my ex, Gabriel. Though getting seen, I find, is mostly about behaviour. Being alone with good posture and open to the world, rather than hunched over a device. Meeting another person's gaze. Sometimes—sitting here or in a bar in some other city, after yet another meeting with investors—I imagined myself as a wizard with a wand, making those around me dance.

I ran my hand through my hair, irritated again that my business partner, Jia, had decreed I not cut it short again until after the sale of our company went through. It was chin-length, an accidental bob. I almost never wore my hair this long, but we'd had a recent spate of publicity, with lots of photos of me involved, and she said there was too much at stake for me to alter my image now.

The shaggy forty-something was the more obvious choice. He was handsome in a five o'clock shadow way, like Gabriel, who'd been gone for more than a year and now lived in Mexico City. The dark-haired fellow looked at ease, and the perfect age: young enough to still be taut under his shirt, old enough to have his own business to mind.

But the younger guy was sidling in my direction. His suit was cheaper than many of the others in this bar, but he wore it well. I could turn, rifle through my purse, make him go away with a simple movement. I could hold out for the other prospect, or someone else entirely. But I needed something easy after today, after my discovery up at the university in the morning and an afternoon of legalese.

Jia was no doubt at her lakefront home sipping a cold glass of white wine, and I deserved my relaxation no less. I tucked my stupid blond bob behind my ears and smiled.

"Which conference were you at?"

"I'm meeting a friend," I said.

He cocked his head like a dog detecting a sudden noise. Hearing my voice for the first time, deciding if he liked its low timbre.

"A girlfriend," I clarified.

"Can I get you another one of those?"

"That would be lovely."

He signalled to Jesse, who set another mineral water down in front of me with a wink. He ordered a fresh whiskey for himself.

"I'm Nate."

"Cate."

"Cate and Nate. That'll give us plenty to talk about."

"Should cover at least five minutes."

"Then we can move on to where we're from, favourite flavour of ice cream, and phobias." He had a crooked smile and a trace of an accent.

"Where are you from?"

Originally Melbourne, he said, but now he lived in the Bay Area.

"What brings you to Seattle, Nate?"

"Terribly boring things." He waved his hand vaguely around the room.

"Work?"

"Yes."

His reticence intrigued me. Men always wanted to talk about their work.

"What about you?"

"I live here."

"Meeting a friend. Right."

He looked at me and looked around. I looked back at him, willing him to challenge me.

"What do you do for work?"

I thought of making something up. Crane operator. Mortician. "Can I just say 'terribly boring things'?"

"Already used that line."

"I work in biotech."

"Very exciting."

"Sometimes."

"How did you get into the field?"

"I studied neuroscience."

"You must be very clever."

You don't know the half of it, I thought. I didn't need or want to talk about work; I had people with whom I conversed about work all day, who had vastly more interesting things to say about it than Nate possibly could. And Jia's cautionary voice inside my head told me to stay away from the subject.

He sat on the barstool facing me now, and I noticed the way his thighs strained against the fabric of his trousers. I imagined putting my hand on his knee. That would be premature, but it was titillating to think about. I uncrossed and recrossed my legs, forcing him to glance down.

"If your work is so boring, what else do you like to do?"

He said he played soccer. Though I find team sports beyond tedious, I encouraged him to talk about the subject for a few minutes. Weekly practice, good way to meet people, story about a missed goal.

"Must be how you stay in such good shape," I said, almost making myself laugh.

Nate blushed: sudden pink flare-ups in both cheeks. He was not experienced at picking people up in bars, so why was he talking to me?

I liked not knowing. It was like funnelling mystery elements into a beaker. Any kind of pop or fizz might result.

"We haven't covered phobias yet," he said.

"You go first."

"Terrified of sharp objects."

"Sounds like common sense."

"I get spooked just seeing a chef's knife on the counter. Like it can fly up and get me."

I wondered if this was true, unsure why someone would reveal such a vulnerability to a complete stranger.

"What about you?"

"Closed-in spaces. I'm claustrophobic." I jiggled the ice in my glass.

"Do you know why?"

The best fabrications are rooted in truth. "I had some bad experiences with closets."

He looked concerned, and I wanted to keep the mood light, so I said, "I went looking for Narnia and ended up trapped in a bunch of coats." This led to a discussion of children's literature, which made me think of Grandma Ida, who always made sure I was well supplied with books, sending me packages at the institute every month.

"You're not really meeting a friend, are you?" Nate eventually asked, and I silently cheered his boldness.

"No," I said, head down, false sheepishness. "I just wanted an excuse for an out."

"And the fact that you're telling me this is . . . promising?"

"Sure." I smiled up at him sideways.

Hesitation hung in the air, like he suddenly didn't know who he was.

"Nate, why don't you tell me about your hotel room."

"My hotel room?"

I imagined sweat beads flying off his head in surprise.

"Maybe I misunderstood—"

But he spoke before I could continue. "It's at the Ace."

Not of the managerial classes, then.

"Isn't that a glorified youth hostel?"

"Emphasis on the 'glorified.' I have my own bathroom and everything."

Outside in the Four Seasons driveway, I hugged my blazer around me against the salty breeze while we waited for my car.

"You're okay to drive?"

"I don't drink."

He fell awkwardly into the low bucket seat on the passenger side.

"This is stymieing my plan to put the moves on you in the back of a taxi."

"I guess you'll need a plan B."

We stepped into his dark-walled room at the Ace and I closed the door behind me. He stopped, turned, looked at me. That hesitance, like he wasn't sure what he was doing. A little fear. I like trying to read people's emotions. Sometimes it's as close as I come to feeling those emotions myself.

"I'd offer you a drink, but since you don't drink . . ."

"We're not really here for a drink, are we?"

I leaned against the door. He stood before me with a look of bewildered indecision on his face, so I met his eyes and took his hand. I slowly brought it between my thighs, and higher, until it touched the damp fabric of my underwear. As I studied him, something finally flipped. Blank desire dropped heavy over his pupils and erased whatever inhibitions he'd been wrestling with. Now he was all in, a partner in this adventure, as capable of leading as being led. He plunged his forefinger into me, and I felt the relief of intense sensation.

I dozed, as I tend to after orgasms. I awoke and looked at Nate, who was asleep now. So enthusiastic in the end, so just what I needed. I hadn't thought about the past, or the sale of my company, for hours.

But now that I was conscious, these subjects crept back into my brain. A used condom leaked onto the carpet, while another had made it to the rim of the garbage can. The bedside clock told me it was midnight, and I knew I'd have to face more contract discussions tomorrow. I found my clothes and purse, with my phone still tucked inside, and took them with me to the bathroom. I had multiple voicemails and texts from Jia, the most recent sent after eleven p.m. I sat down on the toilet seat to read them.

> Where are you?
> Please confirm you're at home.
> Call me back.
> PLEASE READ: Artigen leaked that they will offer. Numerous journalists seeking comment. DO NOT COMMENT. New LA Times tech reporter Nate Pryor is in town. Do not talk to him.

The anger surged up in me so completely, so physically, it was almost erotic. Speeding heart, coursing adrenaline, blurred vision. Who was *he* to try to derail me? I flung open the bathroom door with an image in my mind's eye of slapping him hard awake. Instead, I gripped the door frame. I couldn't give in to this. I took deep, slow breaths until my heart slowed down.

I found the trousers of his cheap suit on the floor, and in them, his wallet with his California driver's licence. Nathaniel Pryor.

I made myself return to the bathroom and closed the door. I started counting to ten, but decided at five that I was fine. I called Jia.

"I slept with him."

"Who?"

"Nate Pryor."

"When?"

"Just now."

Jia was silent, then, "Where are you?"

I told her and hung up.

I got dressed. I finger-combed my hair, once more cursing its excessive length, and put on my shoes and watch. I pulled a chair up beside the bed and sat down. I felt ticklish, like I had a wave inside me I couldn't quite catch. I nudged him in the neck with the tip of my heel.

"Nate."

He startled awake, feeling the sharp point against his throat without me even having to move. This moment delighted me. How much damage could I actually do, I wondered, with the heel of my shoe? Didn't they have metal inside them, these yet-again-fashionable stilettos?

Nate looked alarmed.

"You forgot to tell me something."

Eyes on me, he pulled gingerly away. "I'm sorry, what?"

"You didn't give me all the facts."

"I'm sorry, I don't like that—" He stared at my heel like it was a tarantula.

"I asked you what you did. And you asked me what I did, as if you didn't know."

"Ah."

"You're here under false pretenses."

He pulled the sheet more tightly around his naked body. "I was going to. But things—this—" He gestured around the room.

"You lied because you wanted to trick me into giving you information."

"I'm sorry, but I didn't mean to do this. I've never done this. I have a girlfriend."

"How did you find me?"

"Find you?"

"You didn't just accidentally run across me."

His brow perspired.

"Nate. How did you find me?"

"I heard a rumour."

"A rumour?"

"Just that—that you liked the Four Seasons. That you held meetings there."

The anger that coursed through me was directed at myself

this time. I did frequent the Four Seasons, but I didn't hold meetings there. Jia had warned me a dozen times that I wasn't some anonymous person. Today, feeling unsettled, I should have just gone home, or at least somewhere else. Some dive bar where no one would stalk me.

I'd made a mistake. Still. What did Nate think he was doing? How could he think he was justified?

"You planned this," I said.

"God, no. I just wanted to meet you and then—"

He backed off the bed, dragging the sheet with him and wrapping it around himself as he stood. I stared at his half-covered body to try to disconcert him further.

"This is bad for me too," he said.

"So this is bad for me? How exactly—are you planning to blackmail me?"

His face, neck, and shoulders turned pink with offence. "I don't do that kind of thing."

"My lawyer will be happy to hear that."

"Your lawyer?"

"She'll be here in a few minutes."

"No, no, no, no, no. This is crazy."

His eyes sought out mine, trying to make a connection. While we were fucking, we'd locked gazes, and the fear I saw in his—of vulnerability, of exposure—had sent me right over the edge.

He wanted connection? I would give him connection.

There was a knock at the door. I walked over to Nate. With me in my heels and him in his bare feet, we were the same height. I looked into his eyes, let him have what he was seeking. I lifted my hand to his face, slowly so that he wouldn't startle. I cupped my thumb under his chin in the spot where, a moment ago, I'd rested the tip of my heel, and pressed it into his jugular vein. He inhaled sharply.

"You're lucky I didn't hurt you," I said.

I went to the door. Jia wore her glasses, a sign that she'd rushed here from home. Her long black hair was in a loose bun, her face washed of makeup. She'd already looked tired this afternoon at work, with purple shadows under her eyes. The sale negotiations were getting to her.

Jia had with her a hulking man I recognized as one of our security staff.

"Are you all right, Dr. Winter?"

"Yes, thank you, Felix."

"This is my hotel room," Nate called out.

Felix turned to the journalist. "Sir, I suggest you put your clothes on."

Jia took me aside. I studied her face: angry. But her voice was calm. "Anything else I need to know?"

There was so much Jia needed to know. But all I said was "He has a girlfriend."

"That could be useful." She glanced over at Nate, who was trying to get into his clothes without dropping his sheet. To me she said, "Go home and pull yourself together."

"I'm sorry," I said, because I actually was.

I left Nate in Jia and Felix's care and drove the short distance to my apartment.

Normally, if I'm not consumed with research, I'm a champion sleeper. But tonight, I was bothered by the day's tumults and the evening's mistakes, so I drew a bath. My apartment is on the twenty-fifth floor and my floor-to-ceiling bathroom window faces west. On clear days, this gives me a view all the way to the Olympic Peninsula, but at this time of night, in this weather, I couldn't even see a star. I turned the light to its dimmest setting.

As I slipped into warm water in the near-dark, I reflected on what had just happened. From Jia's point of view, the worst thing I'd done was risk negative public attention. Yet Jia was missing critical information, things I should have told her a long time ago but never had. I kept thinking about how much I'd wanted to shove the pointed heel of my shoe into the journalist's neck. I hadn't felt such a violent urge in maybe a decade. That brief yet compelling thrill. I thought I'd channelled those desires into outdoor sports and one-night stands. And now the temptation had revisited me right when I had the most to lose.

If you considered just my accomplishments, you'd judge me a good person. Someone who's made a positive difference. All my therapists, doctors, and teachers helped make me this way. But none could ever tell me what to do with those exciting deviant moments that violate the rules. The urge to destroy even what I myself have built. Tonight, I'd played with that edge.

TWO

CATE

It was the study results that had really set me off, the day that ended with my spike heel on the neck of a journalist in his room at the Ace Hotel. A couple of dots on a simple scatter plot.

Jia was masterminding the sale of our company, and I wouldn't have had it any other way; I was the scientist, and she was the entrepreneur. But on some days, the process left me at loose ends. Impatient with all the strategizing and waiting, I'd slipped away to see Archibald Montrose, the man I called Dr. M.

Dr. M had always been open with me about his Cleckley research, and I was in touch with some of his graduate students, so I knew as soon as the new study was complete. I took the light rail to the University of Washington campus and found him in his book-lined office in the Health Sciences Center. His grey beard, which his late wife, Eden, used to trim, now touched his chest. He'd recently turned seventy, but his bright-blue eyes never seemed to age.

He rested his hand on a thick document with a plastic binding. "I've hesitated about sharing this one with you."

I nodded. He needed his moment to think, so I let him have it. I looked deliberately around the room, taking in books he'd written, books to which he'd contributed, books by other luminaries in the field of neuropsychiatry. For a time as an undergraduate, I'd been obsessed with Dr. M's work. I'd even thought of building my career around understanding psychopathy, of carrying on his mission. That was when he'd started sharing these studies with me, and promised I'd always have access to his future work. Even when I changed my mind and turned full-time to memory research, he kept letting me see the psychopathy studies before publication, and discussing background details with me, though I had no standing as a researcher in his field. I think he valued my perspective.

I fidgeted, wanting to grab the study from under his hand. Dr. M's round-bellied stone Buddha laughed at me from the windowsill. After several moments of silence, I reminded him that he'd let me see plenty of previous reports.

"This one makes me question our unorthodox arrangement."

"Why?"

He worried a hand along his desk, picking up items and setting them down: pen, paperclip, banana. Part of our job as scientists is to stay detached, and it looked like he wasn't quite succeeding. Sometimes, when I can't figure out what someone is feeling, I wonder whether my inability is due to my deficiencies, or if anyone would have a hard time in the same situation.

"Are they all in jail now or something?"

I meant this as a joke, but his beard quivered with annoyance.

"It's more complicated than that." He rested both hands on the document. I knew he didn't have to show it to me; if anything, ethical considerations suggested he shouldn't share it. But eventually he quit stalling and handed the report over, keeping the promise he'd made me long ago.

He said he had to deliver a lecture in Foege Hall, put on an old Gore-Tex jacket, and hoisted his daypack. I followed him out, then took the rain-slick brick pathways to Suzzallo Library, hugging the thick report to my chest, the wet cold penetrating my coat. Patches of snow clung to the lawns, and students moved in herds towards their classes. I climbed the grand staircase to the reading room where I used to study, a Gothic hall with vaulted ceilings and leaded-glass windows. The students seemed unchanged, concentrating, invisibly connected to their screens. I found a spot at one of the long wooden desks and settled in.

Children who entered the Cleckley Institute shared three traits. The first was a history of trauma or violence, which was usually how they came to Dr. M's attention. Second, they had all been diagnosed as "callous and unfeeling," which is what the medical community calls children with psychopathic tendencies, because no one wants to label a child a psychopath. Third, they had brains of a certain kind, which Dr. M determined the first time he scanned them, looking for less-than-normal activity in the prefrontal cortex, plus a shrunken amygdala.

The study in front of me looked at 110 former Cleckley patients who were now in their thirties. Dr. M and his co-authors, all former grad students and research fellows, had come up with a list of criteria to measure, among them: How much education did the subject obtain? Were they employed? With what income? Did they enjoy "significant family and social support," "some," or "none"? The questions covered whether they'd had major illnesses, mental health conditions, or addictions. Whether they'd been arrested, and if so, for what kind of crime and whether they'd been convicted.

On page 21, the case studies ended and the charts and graphs began, forcing me to face what I'd chosen not to visualize just yet. Forty-nine of the Cleckley graduates in the study had been arrested. Collectively, the Cleckley alumni had engaged in a great deal of fraud, as well as assault, rape, and, in four proven cases, murder. Extrapolate and nearly half the student body went on to a life of crime.

I wasn't shocked, exactly. But I was let down. Exasperated. I wondered why I'd been so determined to satisfy my curiosity. More than a decade ago, I'd reached the conclusion that there was no fix, no solution, no insight to be gained from this work. I'd moved on.

I kept reading.

The Cleckley subjects fell into two categories. First, the outright criminals. I didn't even finish scanning their lists of offences. The other, more numerous cohort somehow depressed me more, even though they performed "better" at life. They'd stayed out of jail. They'd attended some college, or random training programs.

They'd job-hopped and marriage-hopped. Collected food stamps, Medicaid. Declared bankruptcy. Tediously scraped by. But they'd avoided criminality, which made them the study's success stories. Left untreated, the authors believed 80 to 90 percent of these individuals would have committed crimes, but after their time at Cleckley, less than half did. This was why they reached their conclusion that Cleckley's program of treatment worked.

Just not as well as Dr. M wished it did.

I came to a page with two similar-looking scatter plots. In both, the dots made a slightly rising diagonal line from left to right: more time at Cleckley correlated with better outcomes on income and education. But that predictable success was not what caught my eye. On each plot, there were two dots separate from the rest of the pack, way up in the top right corner, millimetres apart. Two data points whose level of income and education were almost literally off the charts.

My mind went blank.

Two?

I flipped quickly to the case studies, which filled in biographical details, identifying each patient only by number. There was no easy way to tell which number corresponded to a given dot, so I just started reading. If a subject was so exceptional as to be way off in the top right corner, it would be evident from their biography.

I plowed through a litany of petty crime, dog-earing a few pages as I went. Number 24 worked for a car rental company in Eureka, California. Number 67, a software consultant in Spokane, had recently filed for bankruptcy. Number 73 was a pastor, married with five children. I kept skimming. Students studying near me left for class and others rotated in.

I came to Number 98, a boy who had arrived at Cleckley at the age of twelve. Son of a single mother, whereabouts of father unknown. He presented with the usual set of issues. Probable victim of physical abuse as a toddler. Later committed acts of violence against his siblings. When he shoved his brother out of a tree, their mother sought help, and eventually found her way to Dr. M. The boy's scans showed a brain with the telltale attributes.

So far, none of this made Number 98 substantially different in tendency or physiology from the other boys in the study. During his first months at the institute, he was a handful, attempting violence against staff and other kids. Later, in his teens, teachers described him as "charming" and "helpful," though these were not unique traits among students—the doctors tended to ascribe them to "strong mirroring skills." His grades were better than average but not wildly exceptional.

After he left Cleckley at eighteen, things got interesting. Number 98 completed college exactly four years later, with a double degree in economics and engineering from the University of Washington. He'd acquiesced to so-called extended monitoring, meaning he continued to talk to someone from Cleckley at least once a year. I turned the page and was surprised anew. After college he took a job in investment banking; several years later he enrolled in an MBA program. After his business degree, he began studying for a PhD in nuclear physics, once again at the University of Washington. Recently he'd worked in "energy finance," which was as specific as the report got on the subject of employer. It was an impressive resumé for anyone, let alone someone as unlikely to succeed as a Cleckley inmate.

I had goosebumps. He'd been right here in Seattle all this time. He'd never been arrested, had no major medical issues. He'd gotten married. I longed for more detail. Who were the people in his life? What did he eat for breakfast? What did his house look like? I read his whole case study twice and tried to find nuance between the lines. I noticed that the last date of contact with Number 98 was listed as two and a half years earlier.

I closed the study and put on my coat. I didn't search for the case history on the other peculiar dot on the scatter plot, the other callous and unfeeling child who'd attained a high level of education and income.

That one, I knew, was me.

THREE

CATE

I flew back across campus, almost losing my footing on an icy patch, and made straight for Foege Hall, where I slipped into the back of a small auditorium. Several dozen students occupied the theatre-style seats, and a spotlight bathed Dr. M in a warm yellow glow.

I looked at my watch and sat down in the back row. These would be seniors in psychology, this lecture part of the series they took on personality disorders and the brain. Dr. M knew its rhythms as intimately as an elder thespian performing *Macbeth* for the hundredth time. He didn't even opt for a microphone, instead projecting his voice with the skill of long practice.

"Psychopaths get a bad rap," he said. He paced to the edge of the pool of light and back to the centre. "If you went by television shows, you'd think they were all serial killers. But by most estimates, about a quarter of the prison population and one percent of the general population is made up of psychopaths. They walk among us. They are present amidst our colleagues, our neighbours, and others we interact with every day. There might be one in this very room."

I watched the backs of the students' heads. They'd be mentally flipping through people they knew, excited to have an explanation for some oddly callous acquaintance or vapid boss.

"Years ago, the psychologist Bob Hare came up with a way to identify psychopaths, a checklist of twenty qualities. Subjects are given a score of zero, one, or two for each quality, with a highest possible score of forty."

Here we go, I thought. Students scrawled or clicked their keyboards. Several had perched voice recorders on the front edge of their desks, as though those extra inches would ensure no word was lost.

"Serial killers do tend to score high. Ted Bundy scored thirty-nine, Clifford Olson thirty-eight, and Aileen Wuornos thirty-two. But clinically speaking, anyone who scores thirty or above is considered a psychopath. They are overrepresented among certain professions. Corporate chief executives, surgeons. As the scoring system suggests, it's a condition that exists on a spectrum—you can be a little or a lot psychopathic."

He picked up a black marker and turned to a large whiteboard, where he wrote down Hare's checklist qualities as he named them.

Grandiosity

Manipulativeness

Lack of empathy

Superficial charm

Impulsivity

Need for stimulation

Sexual promiscuity

Shallow affect

"Someone define 'affect'?" he asked the class.

Two students in the first row raised their hands.

"Feeling or emotion," said a young man in a red shirt.

"Yes. Note that 'shallow affect' doesn't mean zero. A psychopath may have feelings, but they are likely to be less intense, and of shorter duration, than those of a neurotypical person."

He started a new column and continued:

Pathological lying

Lack of guilt

Early behaviour problems

When he finished writing down all twenty qualities, he paused to look at his list, giving the students a moment to take it in. That was me, categorized, catalogued, pinned down in a box. Few zeros. Lots of twos, for instance on "need for stimulation" and "grandiosity."

I didn't know what my total score would be today, but I'd once scored thirty-one, putting me right up there in serial killer territory. I thought of jumping out of my seat and yelling, "Hey, sample psychopath, right here!" I was so tired of the checklist, of being a data point. It wasn't that I thought it was wrong, exactly. Just limited. And potentially dangerous—to me.

"We tend to think of the qualities on the checklist as negative. And many of them are indeed anti-social on a person-to-person level. An individual with a lack of empathy may, for instance, fail to recognize another person's pain as important. But some of the checklist qualities also confer advantages to society. A high degree of empathy could make one unable to cut into another person's body with a scalpel, but we need surgeons to do just that. High empathy might prevent experimentation on primates. And yet, if no one had ever dissected a macaque's premotor cortex, we would understand much less about human sight."

If I'd decided to study psychopathy after all, I'd pose this question for further research: What if you had empathy for the whole human race, just not for individual people? What were you then?

"Or consider so-called superficial charm," Dr. M said. "The person who glad-hands easily, who appears to listen to you so intently. We might also call this sociability. It serves a purpose in that it helps build relationships within and between communities."

Another question for further research: Don't my actions matter more than what I feel?

"And who can define 'grandiosity'?" Dr. M asked. He'd seen me, I knew, but showed no evidence of being ruffled. He pointed to a bespectacled student sitting near me.

"An exaggerated belief in one's own importance," the student said.

"Thank you, yes. Grandiosity is typically seen as a defect. Yet parents and teachers instruct children to chase their dreams, to aspire to be presidents or astronauts or championship athletes. By any realistic measure, we encourage an exaggerated belief in one's own importance, at least among the young. What social purpose does this serve?" He pointed to a woman in a grey sweater dress.

"We want at least some members of society to achieve major goals," she said.

"Why?"

"Because when they succeed, we all benefit."

"Exactly."

Dr. M turned to look at his whiteboard and paused for just a little too long. Maybe I'd ruffled him after all.

But then he faced forward again and dove into the lecture's next beat. He outlined how and why Hare had developed his checklist, as well as its uses, disadvantages, and ethical risks. He went over the pros and cons of predictive law enforcement, as it was already practised and as it might be in the future: What if you could lock someone up based on the high likelihood that they would offend? Another question I would want to research further.

After class, I went down to the front and hovered while students approached Dr. M with questions. Finally, the last one left.

"Shall we?" he asked, and we zipped up our coats.

Archibald Montrose and Eden Harrop met in graduate school in New England more than three decades ago. She'd started out in psychology, thinking she'd become a therapist, whereas he'd once planned to practise family medicine. They'd each known a psychopath. In Archibald's case, it had been a sergeant in the U.S. Army, and in Eden's, it was her estranged sister. By the time they met, they were both devoted to understanding the physiological reasons for psychopathic behaviour. They collaborated while they were still students, and married soon after receiving their PhDs. There was no dividing line between their home and work life, and colleagues came and went as they pleased from the Montrose-Harrop home in Cambridge, Massachusetts. This group eventually had a groundbreaking notion: Given that psychopaths take an outsize toll on society, what if you could identify them early and train them to be good, contributing citizens? A few years ago, at an academic conference, I met one of their friends from that time, and he told me Eden had been the true instigator. She did not want children of her own, having dealt with her psychopathic sister. But it had been her idea to focus on young people, to try to intervene. She kept prodding the rest of them to meet, and championed the idea of some sort of school.

Out of those meetings in a Cambridge living room, the Cleckley Institute was born. It had been my home for more than eleven years, and I was its most resounding achievement, or so I'd believed. Certainly, I was the only student-patient to evolve into Dr. M's confidant and protegé. Now, suddenly, I had a counterpart in success, a sort of sibling. I didn't know if I was more surprised that there was another one like me, or that Dr. M had never mentioned it.

We walked along Boat Street, past glass buildings reflecting masts and barren branches.

"Number 98."

"Yes."

"Why did I never know?"

"This is the first study covering such a long—"

"He did extended monitoring. I must have seen his brain scans."

"You did."

It occurred to me that our graduation dates were only five years apart. I might have met Number 98. Jumbled faces flashed through my mind. I thought of the farmhouse in the snow, of hiking through the woods in the spring.

"Who is he?"

"You've read the study," he said, gesturing to where I held it protectively in the crook of my arm.

"But you met with him and you never told me."

"Cate—"

"Who is he? Where is he?"

Dr. M shook his head.

"Why was the last time of contact two and a half years ago?"

"The subject chose not to continue to participate."

My curiosity felt like a violent wind at my back, but I held myself in check. Calmly, I asked him if I knew Number 98.

"He was some years ahead of you," Dr. M said. I could see his breath in the cold air. Though the institute wasn't large, fewer than eighty students at a time, we'd been siloed depending on our needs. But something about the careful way Dr. M delivered his non-answer made me think he was holding back.

"Tell me about him," I said. "Anything not in the report."

He took his time before speaking. Gulls cried and rigging clinked against spars.

"He came to see me when he was trying to choose a college major. Our meetings always left me hopeful—about him, and about our work. He told me he wanted to study business, because it struck him as the most reliable route to a secure income. He talked a lot about wanting to be safe."

Dr. M was looking at the sidewalk, not at me, but nevertheless, I composed my face to show merely clinical interest rather than burning fascination. A honk blared from a nearby watercraft.

"But I think his business studies bored him. He lit up when he talked about engineering." Dr. M smiled. "'Everything is engineering,' he would say. 'It's these walls, your car, your computer.' He wanted to invent something for the whole world to use. A creation that would save us from ourselves."

I nodded, willing him to go on.

"He was eloquent when he talked about these ideas. Sometimes he would sit across from me and draw sketches. A hydrogen fuel-cell car—that was one of them. Some sort of tunnel-based transit I never understood. Fusion energy—he wanted to use nuclear fusion to build power plants." I was struck as much by the tone of Dr. M's voice as by his words. Happy and nostalgic. I asked if he'd kept any of the sketches.

"Eden may have. I can look in her things."

"When was the last time you saw him?"

"It's been a few years. As I said, he quit extended monitoring."

"Didn't you want to see him?"

We stopped walking at the base of the stairs that led up to the Health Sciences Center.

"Very much so."

"Where is he? Where does he work?"

"I'm going to need that study back."

I handed it to him. "I want to know who he is."

"He declined to participate further. It would be wrong for any of us to contact him."

A surge of aggravation rose in my throat. "What if *I* declined to participate further? Would you just go on your merry way?"

He held the study to his chest and looked at me gravely. "My dear, I know this is a shock. But surely you see that I couldn't—can't—share his personal details. That would be quite different from sharing study data. Not to mention, it would go against"—he caught himself—"the subject's wishes."

The *subject*. I wondered how many times Dr. M had referred to me as "the subject."

"I thought I was alone," I said.

He frowned. "I caution you against seeing too much of yourself in this fellow."

"Why? What did he do?"

He shook his head. "It's not what he did or didn't do. It's that there are some things we never get answers to. Not just you—any of us. We all want to make sense of ourselves, but pinning our hopes to the idea that someone else has the solution tends to be fruitless."

"You're not going to tell me."

"It would be wrong, and it wouldn't help you."

"So why did you let me see the study?"

"If I'd refused, would you have let me hear the end of it?"

His smile reminded me I was being indulged. Dr. M thinks a lot about right and wrong, and tends to be immovable once he's reached a conclusion.

Except, very occasionally, where it comes to me.

FOUR

LUCIANA

The bright morning sun made Luciana's eyelids sting as she swung her pickup truck onto the strip of hard-packed sand in front of the lab. It was nearly ten—she was late—but that didn't explain why her assistant, Beni, was waving frantically from the front steps.

She had a slight headache. The night before, her husband, Dario, had thrown a surprise dinner in her honour, inviting ten friends to their home. The government had just officially established the Alvariño National Marine Park, which would protect three thousand square miles of the Sea of Cortez from fishing and dumping. The park's western border began just offshore, almost within sight of La Ventana, the Baja beach town where they lived and worked. In concert with many others, Luciana had made the park happen. She'd co-written the studies and testified to a federal commission about biodiversity loss. Last night, in celebration, Dario had poured her glass after glass of cava.

Beni was headed for the truck before she'd even turned off the engine. She gathered her wavy black hair, which had been drying during the drive, into a large clip. As she collected her purse and phone from the passenger side, she saw that Beni had also texted her twice. She hopped down from the cab of the truck as he arrived beside it.

"What is it?" she asked. He was a local kid, eighteen years old and a head taller than her, gangly in board shorts and a tank top.

He wasn't sure if he wanted to go to university, and had been cagey about his high school grades. But she trusted his mother, and his uncles had all been fishermen. A few still were, eking out livings up and down the cape despite the paltry takes. In his six months of employment, Beni had proven far more responsible than she'd been at that age, nearly twenty years ago now, as well as mechanically adept with the building and all their gear.

"Did you read my texts?"

"No."

"Have you been diving since Tuesday?"

He knew that she hadn't been.

"No. Beni, what's going on?"

"I'll just show you," he said, and turned on his heels. She'd never heard such urgency in his voice.

The lab was housed in a former shrimp-processing plant that her family had owned for three generations, a long, low building with chipped white plaster walls. Luciana had been a post-doc in marine biology at Woods Hole, tagging great white sharks off Cape Cod, when her parents started talking about selling the sandy old building to a hotel developer. Galvanized, she'd come home and claimed it.

Now she followed Beni through the lab's entrance, across the reception area, down the hall next to the conference room, and out the back door to the beach. The water sparkled turquoise. He crossed the sand towards their storage shed, a long, low building made of stone with a palapa roof, which sat perpendicular to the main lab.

"I always store the air tanks full," he said as they walked. Warm sand spilled into her sandals. "After the group from Scripps, I double-checked that they were *all* full." The team of professors from San Diego, who had been studying the migration patterns of sea lions, had been scuba diving every day.

Beni pushed open the shed door, which was made of heavy wood, and switched on the light. She glanced around the cool space. He kept it well organized, and had even instituted a labelling system for the spare wetsuits. Nothing seemed out of place. Regulators, buoyancy compensators, and neat rows of scuba tanks dominated one end. At the other sat two outboard motors and stacked drums of biofuels, which gave off the stink of used fry oil.

He gestured to the bright-coloured scuba tanks—twenty of them—stored on slanted shelves with their valves pointed out.

"When I came in, one was by the door. I checked it before putting it away, and it was nearly empty. I got worried maybe I'd forgotten to fill some of them—even though I always store them full."

"I know you do," she said, in what she hoped was a reassuring tone. He had a streak of anxiety, this boy. Someone must have gone diving, simple as that. She tried to think who.

"So I started checking the rest of them." He held up the regulator he'd been using to measure air levels, and it dangled from his hand like a robotic octopus. "At least thirteen tanks are empty."

"Thirteen?"

"Yes. I'm still checking the rest."

This didn't make any sense. Luciana stared back at him in bafflement.

"I could have forgotten to make sure the shed was locked," Beni said, almost to himself.

For a moment they both stood there waiting, as though the truth would reveal itself at any moment.

"It's not your fault," she said. "Let's just think."

Tighter security for the shed had been on her mind for years, but she hadn't gotten around to upgrading from what she thought was a decent combination padlock. Other than Beni, only Dario had the code, and he did sometimes borrow gear. But not in February, when he was busy with the hotel's kiteboarding guests and the water got so churned up by the afternoon winds that few tourists wanted to dive.

"Was it locked when you got here?"

"Yeah."

"And it looked normal?"

"Except for that one tank by the door, yeah."

She felt a building sense of unease.

"Is anything else disturbed?"

"Not that I can see. I was going to count everything."

Her unease hardened. No vandal would break in, open the valves, and let the air out of all their tanks. That meant someone had used the tanks and returned them. But why? If some person or group had the wherewithal to break in and take that many tanks, then they had a truck or boat on hand. They could have simply stolen everything in the shed and kept it.

"Go ahead and finish checking the tanks."

She went to stand next to Beni while he attached the regulator to one of the valves. The dial on the gauge lifted, wobbled, and settled firmly in the red zone that indicated it was nearly empty.

While Beni moved on to the remaining tanks, she paced the shed, running hands over equipment she'd paid for with hard-won grants and donations. This made exactly the wrong kind of sense.

"Fifteen empty, five still full," Beni called out.

"Which was the one you found by the door?"

He showed her. It was an old tank, its fluorescent-yellow paint chipped to reveal grey steel underneath. She heaved it out of the shelf, stood it on the ground, and squatted to inspect it. As she ran her fingertips over its curves and sides, she felt, and then saw, a "V" freshly scratched in the paint.

She straightened. The boy lifted the tank back into the shelf, then stared at her with big eyes. "What should we do?"

Luciana needed to calm and distract him, but she remained silent. Her eyes fell to the bone carving he wore at his neck, a stylized "V" for "vaquita," a species of small porpoise that had once dwelled in the sea here. Beni was too young to have seen a real one.

"Should we call my mom?"

Luciana shook her head. "First I want to check a few things. And I should be the one to call. If necessary."

She couldn't actually order him not to tell his mother, a friend she called Ursula but whom others called Detective Sanchez of the La Paz Police Department.

Beni nodded obediently, his face still scrunched in consternation.

"It's good you checked, Beni, otherwise we wouldn't have realized they were empty. Why don't you head back to your desk and open the mail. You can refill them this afternoon."

He looked uncertain at first, but then ducked out the door and loped off across the sand. Luciana watched him enter the main lab building, then turned back to survey her shed again, searching for items out of place. She found none.

Who would steal her compressed air but return the tanks, making sure she noticed one with a "V" for "vaquita" carved into the paint? Someone with a Robin Hood complex and a peculiar set of ethics. Someone who could guess the code to her padlock because he knew her family's birthdays. She felt a surge of anger, mixed with fear. And, somewhere deep down, a tiny bit of grudging admiration. This someone was betting she would look the other way.

Late that afternoon, Luciana locked the lab door and descended the steps to the beach. Dario stood waiting in shallow water, smiling, holding the gunwale of their old panga.

He'd texted an hour earlier with the single line *Evening cruise?*

Which meant he needed a break from hotel guests and kiteboarding students. She almost said no. After her late start and Beni's discovery, she'd been jumping from task to task all day. Paperwork, then a meeting with two dolphin researchers, followed by a phone conference with a professor in Veracruz. Around four o'clock, a journalist from *El Diario* had called and said he wanted to come up from Los Cabos to write about the new national marine park. All the while, she'd puzzled over the meaning of her empty tanks.

She didn't have time for a cruise. But she needed the calm she found on the water.

They brushed lips as she swung her legs into the hull, which Dario had stocked with their snorkelling gear, a picnic basket, and a cooler with a cold six-pack. She sat on the starboard bench and watched him start the outboard with a well-muscled right arm. His curls bobbed in his face as he yanked on the cord.

With the shoreline to their left, they cruised north, passing the campground, then the hotels and houses of La Ventana, then the fancier homes, until eventually the town was behind them and the beach almost deserted. The day's wind had died down and the sky was pink, the heat ebbing as the sun slid towards the hills. After about twenty minutes, Dario throttled down and steered them to the point at the north end of El Saltito beach, where there was a rocky outcropping and a group of islets. He cut the motor and dropped the small metal anchor at a spot they both knew well. Luciana cracked open two beers and handed him one. They sat on cushions facing each other, leaning against the hull.

"How bad?"

"Remember the time when there was no wind for a week, and that guy wanted his money back?"

"I tried to forget."

"This was worse."

She didn't know how her husband dealt with the public all day. Or she did—he was naturally gregarious and outgoing—but she couldn't imagine having to do it herself. They didn't even get exceptionally difficult tourists at Casa Azul. Their guests were the kind who took pride in a casual attitude, and left satisfied as long as they got to do their sports. But even so, they could be blithely relentless with their needs—for an extra pillow, an off-menu dish, another minute of conversation.

"This is perfect," Dario said. "I don't want to talk about it."

"Okay."

She knew he would change his mind, but in the meantime, she savoured the boat's gentle rock and her first sips of cold beer. Dario looked west, towards the shore, and she looked east, towards the sea's horizon line and the distant hump of Cerralvo Island. Everyone she knew still called it that, even though the government had renamed it Jacques Cousteau Island more than a decade back. As a marine biologist, she had nothing against Cousteau, but she didn't endorse this mania for renaming things to sound more tourist-friendly, as though the land itself were a marketing campaign. A calm inlet down the cape called the Bay of the Dead had been renamed the Bay of Dreams. Now locals called it the Bay of Dead Dreams.

"This guest wanted his money back because he got sick," Dario said at last. "He says he didn't know he wasn't supposed to drink the tap water."

"Naturally, you pointed out the signs that say 'Don't drink the tap water.'"

"Accept and blacklist."

It was Dario's new policy for dealing with unreasonable demands: give in, but then bar the guest from ever booking again. He'd got two other local hoteliers to go in on a shared blacklist.

They sipped their beers. Luciana heard a series of flittering splashes, the sound of flying fish. She remembered her missing air and felt a sense of foreboding.

"The group from Scripps is gone," she said, pushing the empty scuba tanks out of her mind.

"Too bad. They were great."

"They were *tiring*," she said. They'd come for dinner at the hotel, and Dario, of course, had had them all in stitches, even stern seventy-year-old Dr. Lozada, discoverer of a namesake arrow worm. Dario was a better participant in her work than she was in his. But that was because even scientists needed to be fed and entertained, whereas people on vacation didn't seem to need any skills she could provide.

She was tempted to tell Dario about the tanks, but held back. Her primary suspicion didn't entirely make sense. If she told her husband she thought Javier Sanz was involved, she would sound paranoid, and to make herself seem less so, she would have to clarify her past relationship with Sanz. If she did that, it would appear as though she had some sort of current relationship with him, which was not the case, but the prospect of Dario suspecting she did still made her apprehensive.

She told herself that the missing air was boring lab business, no more interesting to her husband than a stray invoice. Instead, she told Dario about the journalist.

"Does he need a place to stay?"

"I said we'd reserve him a room."

"In thirty years, they'll want to rename that island Luciana Gutierrez," he said, pointing over his shoulder.

"And we'll still call it Cerralvo."

Dario reached for the mesh bag that held their gear. He passed her a mask and snorkel. She felt relieved that they were about to be face down in the water, unable to speak.

They put on their fins, tumbled off the sides, and began a leisurely swim, following the edge of a reef that meandered towards the point. All her friends were there: cheerful yellow porkfish in a dense school, a trio of blue damselfish, two velvety speckled boxfish, and a silvery barracuda. She took a deep breath and dove down to peek under the reef. It was murky this late in the day, but there was a moray eel she liked to check on, and sure enough, it poked its head out and snapped its jaw. Eels were very territorial.

Luciana spewed water out of her snorkel as she surfaced, the taste of salt water on her tongue. Dario was kicking along near the outcropping. Even he needed human-free time.

As she headed for the outermost islet, she heard Dario's whistle and lifted her head. He signed that he was going back to the boat, and she gave him the "okay" sign before diving back underwater. Two sherbet-coloured parrotfish circled a rocky head. A school of sergeant majors flipped the late-day sun off their bodies like prisms, refracting it every which way, shooting rainbows.

Ten minutes later, Luciana did a languid backstroke towards the panga, her mask and snorkel around her neck. The beach was already in shadow, but the sun still shone on her. When she was almost to the boat, something floating in the water gently bumped her head, then her shoulder. She startled. Treading water, she looked.

She flinched.

She must have made a noise.

"What is it, love?"

It was, or had been, a foot-long huachinango, *Lutjanus peru* in scientific terms, also known as a Pacific red snapper, an ecological and economic staple. But something had happened to it. She looked left and right, as though the killer might still be in sight. She glanced over her shoulder at Dario, who was squinting at the thing in the water.

"Get the net," she called.

By the time she climbed into the boat, Dario had scooped up the fish and laid it down in the hull. They sat on opposite benches and stared at it.

The huachinango's head and tail looked normal. Between them, though, something had gouged four vertical lines deep into the animal's flesh. Each gash was a trench of oozing, wobbling tissue. She felt an unpleasant sense of recognition.

Luciana looked up at her husband.

"Shark?" he asked.

"A shark would just swallow it." She looked back down at the maimed corpse. "And look how even the lines are."

"An outboard motor, then."

"Could be." But she wasn't convinced. She picked up the dead fish by the tail and flipped it over. "Oh." To her surprise, the huachinango had an almost identical set of injuries on its other side: four deep gouges in a row. "How does that happen?"

"It could still be an outboard."

"I'm taking it back to the lab." She sat up and reached to open a locker, where she found a spare cooler.

Dario raised his eyebrows—at the prospect, she assumed, of a food holder being used for a lab sample.

"I'll wash it out."

He laughed. “I’m sure you will, but what’s bugging you? It’s just an injury.”

She felt self-conscious of her racing mind. “It’s not the first one I’ve seen,” she said. When she’d had Dr. Lozada and his colleagues out by Cerralvo, they’d come across another huachinango with similar injuries, but she’d left it to float away without further examination.

She placed the fish in the cooler and closed the lid, while Dario moved to the bow to pull up the anchor.

“I’m sure it was a motor,” she said. “But two in one week is odd.”

FIVE

GABRIEL

Gabriel no longer thought about Cate every day, but sometimes he'd let himself remember. Tonight, he'd had a pleasant dinner with three colleagues at a popular new restaurant in La Condesa. At dinner, Marta had mentioned that she'd always wanted to go fly-fishing in Idaho, and that was all it took. Following goodbyes on the sidewalk outside the restaurant, the others summoned rideshares, but Gabriel decided to walk home, the route now familiar after a year in Mexico City. He meandered, taking an extra loop around Amsterdam Avenue with the evening joggers and hand-holding couples, stretching a twenty-minute walk to an hour, letting his mind wander. He liked the gentleness of the February evenings here: dry and cool but never cold.

He'd met Cate in May nearly three years ago, as the pandemic tailed off. After so much cancelled travel, Gabriel was ready to go anywhere that would let him in. He web-browsed half the world—many places still closed, or roiled by war—but ended up on an outdoor-adventure tour in central Idaho, where he found himself standing at the base of a cliff in the Salmon-Challis forest, learning to belay. He was in the beginner's group, but his eye was drawn to the next group over, or rather, to a spot above it, high up the rock face, where a woman was sailing down the wall with the grace of an animal: a bird crossed with a gazelle, perhaps, arcing out and down before pushing off again, hypnotically, until she landed like a cat at the base.

"Is she with us?" a new acquaintance asked, equally transfixed.

She was, but Gabriel didn't answer, already protective. He'd first seen Cate the night before, when they were all introduced in a sprawling log cabin outside the town of Salmon. She was travelling with a friend, who was, like her, thirtyish and athletic. The two women had joked that they were on a corporate retreat. But despite that evening encounter, it was this vision of her soaring down the wall—red tank top, black shorts, grey helmet over her short blond hair—that he would think of as the first time he saw her.

The coincidence of their meeting, and the things they had in common, would take on significance for him. They both lived in Seattle. They'd overlapped as science undergraduates at the University of Washington, though they'd never met.

Over bison steaks the second evening, he scrutinized her, and she him.

"You wouldn't have wanted to meet me then," she said. She had an unusually deep voice—not husky or hoarse, but low and resonant.

"How come?"

"I was recovering."

"From what?"

"Being a teenager."

"Weren't we all."

He'd spent his adolescence in his hometown of Monterey, California, then come up to U-Dub on a rowing scholarship, already certain that he wanted to study marine biology.

"I was always training," he said, by way of explaining how they'd missed each other back then.

"I was always in the lab."

When the group parcelled itself into rafts the next day, he made sure to get in hers. The water was cold and churning, the sun brilliant. Dark evergreens and beaches of smooth rock lined the shore. In their second set of rapids, the bucking Middle Fork threw Cate up into the air and over the side. She disappeared for several long seconds below the river's swirling surface, and emerged laughing.

While the guide used his oars to keep the raft steady, Gabriel held out a hand to help Cate back in, ashamed of his own delight. He would have helped anyone, of course, but there it was.

The river chucked him off the raft next. He plunged into churning, icy blue-green water, tumbling with pebbles and twigs. After fifteen seconds in this wonder-world, he kicked to propel himself to the surface, but the river pushed him down. He kicked again, and the water shoved back violently. He grew conscious of his growing need for air, and the icy blue-green lost its beauty, became a terror. His chest grew tight and panic tickled his temples. *Not now, so stupid, when we've just met*. He thrashed and kicked but couldn't break the surface.

Then the river spat him out into calmer water, coughing and heaving. The frothing white rapids ended, and he floated on his back, sputtering, his orange life jacket now doing its job. The guide stroked the raft towards him. Tears poured from Gabriel's eyes and snot ran down his face and water spewed from his throat, but he was alive; the sky had never looked so bright. Cate reached down for him, and he flopped into the raft.

He felt wild and unhinged after that. The fear of death had entered and left him so quickly, and now it transmuted into outrage—how could he have let that happen?—as well as elation at this beautiful world that had readmitted him after all. He felt a kind of freedom from himself, like he might do anything.

That afternoon, Gabriel placed her. Cate had been a friend's crush. When he'd been a college freshman, one of his first non-rowing acquaintances, Marley, had invited him to an ad hoc dorm party, where he'd pointed her out. Gabriel had admired Marley's ambition. All the girls and a good number of the boys wore ponytails and T-shirts and Birkenstocks, but Cate had stood out. Something about her eyebrows, which were darker than the pale hair on her head, or her neck, or the confident way she held herself.

He didn't share this recollection with her. Gabriel had a good memory for faces, but also knew it might sound tenuous to claim he'd seen her once, so long ago. Almost like a wish to have shared a past. That night, after the whitewater descent, he was sure he'd never been so bold or charming. She laughed at his jokes—the ones about firefighting ducks and legless frogs and academic acronyms (PhD: "Piled Higher and Deeper"). When dusk fell, they put on long pants and slathered their wrists with bug spray. As they sat on the river shore with their fellow campers, he felt like everything was happening in extremes, and wanted that feeling to continue.

He turned onto Álvaro Obregón Avenue, and its honking cars and bright shops snapped him back to the present. He and Cate were friends now, the kind who texted or emailed once in a while. He thought of texting her, but decided he didn't need to. After their breakup, he'd gone travelling up and down the length of Baja in a mostly successful effort at self-healing. Shortly after he got back to Seattle, he'd been offered a new job, and he'd had coffee with Cate while trying to decide whether to take it. Motivated by the pandemic, the U.S. government had launched a global program to screen for animal disease, the idea being to catch it before it turned into human disease. The new agency was recruiting scientists like Gabriel, who until then had been a researcher at a federal fisheries centre in Washington State.

At a bakery in her Belltown neighbourhood, Cate had encouraged him to take the new position—to make a change, to move away—and he'd tried not to overanalyze why she was so enthusiastic for him to go. But she'd been right. Mexico City had lifted and changed him. His post-breakup depression, so frighteningly real at the time, had faded from view.

In his new role, he worked with scientists of different backgrounds—he was the fish guy, but there were also an entomologist, a virologist, a geneticist, and several others on staff. They worked out of an office belonging to the U.S. Department of Agriculture, in an annex on the grounds of the U.S. embassy. They all travelled frequently around the region. He loved it.

Gabriel passed a multi-storey café-bookstore, full of patrons, and turned off the busy avenue onto a quieter block. He was almost home. Mexico City was hellaciously polluted, and sometimes the ground literally shifted underfoot. It was more than seven thousand feet high, closer to the sun than he had been in Seattle, and by day he had to wear the patch that protected his permanently scarred, light-sensitive left eye. Yet the city also seemed to embrace him. There was the scent of his neighbour's climbing jasmine. The warmth of being around Spanish, which he'd spoken all his life but had rarely used in Seattle. The way his skin had darkened from the sun, despite the excess particulate matter in the air, as though he were an animal changing colour to blend in. The pink and orange flowering vines that spilled over walls, as they did in California. Somehow, Mexico City already felt more like home than Seattle ever had.

There was now also Penelope, the chef he'd met at a sustainable seafood event just two months earlier. He climbed the steps to his apartment building and the doorman buzzed him through. A dog barked tentatively at Gabriel from the courtyard, then quieted once it realized who had arrived: the neighbour who occasionally brought treats. Upon entering his apartment, he texted Penelope to say good night, and that he'd been thinking about her, though that was only minimally true.

SIX

CATE

Before I left the institute when I was eighteen, I didn't think a lot about the mask, a term Hervey Cleckley himself coined in his book *The Mask of Sanity*. The mask is how I pretend to be like other people. To be motivated by empathy, to have an ethical code that comes from deep within. Sometimes, if I'm not careful, I pretend too much. I take on another person's sports fandom or love of Impressionist paintings, mirroring them to the point where I seem untrustworthy. Keeping the mask in place while not overdoing it can get tiring, which is one reason I like to be alone.

When I got to university, I realized what a gift it had been to not have to think about the mask during my years at Cleckley, when I'd been surrounded by people who all knew exactly what I was. When I moved into a concrete-tower dormitory on campus, I was again surrounded, but now my job was to pass. I made no friends during my first year, having realized right away that the first thing everyone asked was where I was from. I told the truth only once. After I explained the Cleckley Institute to a guy from my freshman dorm, he told other students I was a "psycho." I'd had so many counsellors and therapists, you'd think someone would have prepared me to explain my past, but no. They'd taught me not to lie, but ultimately, in this situation, I had to. I'd spent more than half my life at Cleckley, and even a little bit of digging by a curious fellow student would reveal the institute's true purpose.

I tried telling classmates I was from Duvall or Cashmere, but those nearby places just prompted more questions. What high school? Did I know so-and-so? I soon realized I needed an identity that involved being from far away. I thought pretty carefully about this. It couldn't be a place that required an unsustainable accent. And it couldn't be anywhere that a lot of people knew. I settled on small-town Nebraska. When people asked me where in Nebraska, I said, "You wouldn't have heard of it," or "west of Lincoln," and if they really pushed me, I said I was from Burwell, a town I picked off a map because the syllable pairing struck me as immediately forgettable. (Unlike, say, Broken Bow.) I've still never been to Nebraska.

As adolescence receded, my peers became less fixated on high school, less likely to notice when I shifted the topic away from my past. Moving through the mossy sprawl of campus, I studied people like I studied cell behaviour and calculus, trying to grasp their nuances so I could emulate them. And I made friends, sort of. Not close friends, but students I could hang out with, whom I charmed through subtle flattery and a sprinkling of references to their favourite shows. I could never entirely shake the feeling that I was faking it. I thought this was a by-product of having been told my whole life that I had to compensate for my differences, but maybe it was because I actually was different. I couldn't tell. Sometimes I'd dodge a social event to go to the outdoor climbing gym, a group of craggy old slabs down by Portage Bay. I'd discovered climbing as a freshman, and the rhythm hooked me. The ascent made me narrow my focus, think of nothing but the next hold. The descent was a controlled fall, a simple thrill, the kind of feeling I understood.

While I was still an undergraduate, my grandma Ida began to succumb to Alzheimer's disease. First little bits of her mind disappeared, phone numbers and addresses crumbling away like pebbles before a volcanic eruption. Then whole tranches of long-term memory sloughed off. I'd always thought there would come a time when I could ask her more about my past, and why she'd made the decisions she did. No such luck.

She gave me her car, and every week or two, I drove out to see her in Roslyn, the foothills town where she'd lived my whole life in a well-kept Folk Victorian. She'd never remarried after my grandfather died, but she had close friends, and enough money saved up to pay for her own care. For a while, I had a home nurse come in. During that time, she still knew who I was, and I could sometimes uncover new tidbits. She said my grandfather had been so charming it got him into trouble, but she didn't say how. She often lost her train of thought. I wasn't like my mother, she told me more than once—I was smarter, more disciplined. I knew she wasn't just telling me I *was* those things, but also that I *needed to be* those things.

Once, after the nurse had left for the day, I was sitting by her bed, studying for a chemistry exam. She reached over and put a hand on my arm, met my eyes, and said, "I forgive you."

My spine tingled and I sat up straight. "What?"

"I forgive you."

"For what?" I asked, even though part of me knew. Her eyes went vacant. "Grandma, what do you forgive me for?" I put my hand on her arm and jiggled gently, but the moment of lucidity had passed.

We'd only talked about the fire once, amidst the blur of social workers and cops who came to call after it happened. But never since. Maybe that was something she'd meant to do before her brain deteriorated.

I thought of the fire as the reason I'd ended up at Cleckley. There'd been so many times when I convinced myself I didn't belong there. I believed I was not only smarter than the other kids, but better—as in, a better person. I understood the rules of society and how to function within them. I'd never mutilated animals, beat up a sibling, or committed the other petty atrocities common among my classmates. But my thoughts always came back to the fire. If I'd done that, I belonged at Cleckley as much as any of them. Yet the "if" had always lingered.

Now she forgave me, which meant she'd always known what I'd done. The fire had killed her daughter, my mom. Who had not been a good mother by anyone's account. But still, her child. Staring back at my grandmother's empty face, I was shocked that she would bring it up at all, confirming and absolving in one breath.

"I forgive you too," I said to the blankness. For sending me away to the place that had made me who I was.

When she became too much for one person to handle, I moved her to a memory care facility in the city, a tower on First Hill. On clear days, you could see the Cascades from her window, but I had no idea if she appreciated that. I often rode my bike to see her, even though she no longer knew who I was. I read to her from my science textbooks. The anatomy of the nervous system. Electrical versus chemical synapses. The nurses said she was calmer after I visited. Some lingering sense of recognition, they thought. But maybe that was a collective fiction, easier than telling families that the memory of a relationship could be erased.

It wasn't until I was a junior, working part-time in the campus pharmacy mixing drugs, that I internalized the fact that the people around me didn't care where or how I'd been raised. In fact, nobody thought about others in the analytical way I'd become so used to at Cleckley. In real life, people were too busy thinking about their own needs. At my pharmacy job, they just wanted to know whether I could concentrate long enough, and hold my hands steady enough, to combine ingredients. Later, when I was hired as a researcher by a lab studying proteins in mouse brains, all the director wanted to know was that he could trust my documentation, my memory, my attention to detail. My value lay apart from what my brain scans said. This realization came as a liberation, and it made dorm life easier too. If you give other people the attention they want and don't act too eccentric, they forget to wonder about you. The mask was finally clicking into place, feeling less like something I had to take on and off, and more like a part of who I was.

Dr. M and Eden always had a soft spot for me. I was seven when

I went to the institute, and they'd never enrolled anyone so young. Though I had a ward room like all the other kids, they made me feel welcome in their home, a rambling old wooden farmhouse inside the locked gates of the bucolic grounds. Once, I fell asleep on their couch. On the ward, Eden was elusive, always in her office, part of an adult world that required blazers and skirts. But when she woke me on her couch, she seemed like a different version of herself, wearing a soft sweater and smelling of honeysuckle tea. She walked me back to the ward wrapped in one of their quilts, which she let me keep. Later, the institute admitted more younger kids, and more girls. Other students got invited to the farmhouse, either because they lacked family or because they inspired some sort of fondness or interest. But Dr. M and Eden soon discovered that I had academic gifts, and so I remained special, their most intriguing and beloved specimen.

In addition to co-running Cleckley, Dr. M was a professor at the University of Washington in Seattle, two hours away over the Cascades. By the time I started there as a freshman, he was spending a couple of days a week at his office in the Health Sciences Center. Occasionally, I would drop by, and flop into a chair like I was in my own living room. Cleckley kept official tabs on me via extended monitoring, wherein a post-doc would ask me questions once a year. But my campus visits to Dr. M were informal. Our relationship was not quite teacher-student, not quite doctor-patient, not quite parent-child.

By the middle of my sophomore year, I was sure I wanted to study psychopathy. I craved a bigger picture. I wanted to see what I'd helped build with all my survey answers and visits to the MRI room. I told Dr. M that maybe, with my unique background, I could make real breakthroughs.

"Can I see the data?" I asked one day in his office.

He sat back. He liked clear, ethically correct answers, and this situation didn't have one. The occasional published study was one thing—anyone could read it. But Dr. M had data that no one outside of his professional world had seen.

"Are you sure this is what you want to do?"

"This is my life we're talking about. And I didn't choose it. I was too young to consent."

Grandma Ida had given all the permissions, signed all the forms. Of course, now that I was of age, I could withdraw, but I didn't want to.

He thought about it for twenty-four hours. I'm sure he talked it over with Eden. They decided that sharing with me was the right thing to do.

The data confirmed what I already understood. Popular entertainment loves the idea of the genius psychopath, but the truth is so much more banal. In practical intelligence, in fact, psychopaths are on average stupider than other groups, dragged down by a propensity for bad decision-making. It doesn't matter how high you score on an IQ test if you have no impulse control. Eden once said that to me, and I still say it to myself, regularly, lest I forget.

The more I learned about other Cleckley alums, the more I understood myself as a kind of walking proof of concept. I showed that what the founders were trying to do could be done. That you could take a child wired for anti-social behaviour and make them into—well, into me. But I was always looking for more evidence. I needed to know that my shrunken amygdala and traumatic early childhood did not mean I was destined for violence, prison, failure. I wanted there to be other Cleckley kids who could show me happy options, but as far as I could tell, they didn't exist. I was an n of 1. A random, a weirdo, an outlier. In a sense, I'd been searching for Number 98 before I knew he existed: someone who had overcome the same things.

Once, when I was a junior, I'd gone looking for a similar sort of affirmation. I'd been watching my dormmates getting ready to go out, envying their easy camaraderie. I wanted to feel what I thought they felt, and it made me think of Sissy. We'd been at Cleckley together for eight years, shared classes and toys and clothes. It had been two years since I'd seen her.

I texted her, and right away she invited me to her apartment in a brick building on Queen Anne, where she greeted me with a hug and her impish smile. She called me "Catie-cakes," set out a tray of papers and tweezers and little bags, and had me roll joints. Pot was still years from being legal. She wanted to drink shots of tequila too, and even though I don't have much of a taste for alcohol, I went along. When her wholesaler arrived, she made me hide in her closet, which I reluctantly did, down on the floor among her boots and belts, inhaling a familiar flowery smell off her dresses.

I heard a resounding smack.

I jumped up and raced back out into the hall, a boot on my left hand and a belt in my right, trying to stay ahead of the rush coursing up through my chest.

"Get the fuck out!" I screamed.

A short, lank-haired man in a denim jacket had Sissy pinned up against the wall, but as I charged, he pulled away from her. I landed the leather belt across his face with a ferocious crack.

"Who the fuck are you?" he yelled, reeling.

"I'm the person telling you to get out." My voice was a growl.

He scrambled backwards, almost lost his balance. I was disappointed he wasn't larger. I lunged while he was off-kilter and struck him hard in the head with the heel of the boot.

"Call off your fucking animal," he yelled, scrabbling for his back pocket and bringing out a switchblade. He twitched his forearm, trying to get it open, but I whipped it out of his hand with another crack of the belt, and it went flying across the room and hit one of the ceramic pots on the windowsill, sending it crashing to the floor. I shifted my weight from foot to foot, almost dancing, eager for more.

"Get the fuck out, Vic," Sissy yelled.

He cursed and backed towards the front door. As he turned away from me to leave, I cracked him with the belt again, this time across the back of his head. He wobbled. I kicked him square in the back and he fell to his knees, only halfway out Sissy's front door. I was about to kick him again, but she ran past me, lifted his feet, and heaved him over the threshold into the hallway, then slammed the door behind him and locked the deadbolt. She put an eye to the peephole.

I was shaking, still itching to kick something. Energy surged through me with no place to go. I felt like I'd just climbed a rock wall or had six cups of coffee, my mind so alert I could see the whole world.

After long seconds, Sissy took her eye from the peephole. "He's gone," she said. Then, to clarify, she added, "He walked away."

Chemicals still pinged around my body. I took a deep breath and thought: *Enjoy this, because it will end.* I threw the belt aside and let the boot drop to the ground. I shook my left wrist, which felt twisted and numb.

One side of Sissy's face was swollen and red. I found a tray of ice cubes in the freezer and dumped them into a plastic bag to make her an ice pack. I flopped down next to her on the couch, closed my eyes, and leaned my head on the backrest. As the rush dissipated, I longed for it to stay.

After a minute or so, I remembered the rest of my life. By any rational calculation, I should have stayed in the closet. By an even better calculation, I wouldn't have been here, gamely helping an ex-friend break the law out of a wish for connection. A thought began to form.

"Why did you tell me to hide?"

"Vic would have thought you were involved. And he has a temper."

"Is he going to come back?"

"He'll tell Lawrence some psycho bitch attacked him. But I'll tell Lawrence you were defending me. He's not supposed to hit us."

"Vic, Lawrence—Sissy, who are these people?" Struck by a sudden suspicion that I didn't sound normal, I concentrated on articulating my words.

"Lawrence is—"

"No, wait." I held up a hand. The thought forming on the periphery of my consciousness resolved itself. "I don't want to know."

Sissy looked at me in confusion, still holding the ice pack to her face. "You got him good, Cate. I've never seen that look on him."

This piqued my curiosity. How often did Vic come around? How often did he hit Sissy? And why did she put up with it? She was smart. She'd had a family who tried. But I stopped myself—I didn't need to know any of this. I needed to get out of here, in fact, because of how good it had felt to attack Vic. That deliciousness was gone, but my body held the memory of it.

Sissy and I looked at each other, and for just a second, I felt understood. But I chose to let her go.

"I know I got him," I said. "That's the problem."

That was the last time I reached out to a Cleckley classmate.

Some weeks after visiting Sissy, I told Dr. M that specializing in psychopathy felt like too self-referential and claustrophobic a path for me. I also feared professional dissatisfaction for another reason, which I didn't share with him: psychopathy isn't a disease, but a type of brain. It can't be cured, only dealt with. To find a cure for an actual disease, to contribute even a small amount of research to such an effort, seemed like a more straightforward undertaking. To find a place for wayward brains required a societal remaking I didn't feel equipped to tackle.

I cycled right from my bachelor's degree in biochemistry into a PhD program in neuroscience, eventually moving out of the dorms and into my own place, the third floor of a restored Victorian in Montlake, which I could just cover with my lab income and scholarships. It felt liberating to finally live so unobserved.

Ida was still in the memory care place on First Hill, far gone into her enigmatic self, surrounded by hundreds of warehoused, breathing bodies like her own, when I decided I would find a cure for Alzheimer's disease. That sounds grandiose to the point of delusion, of course. Nevertheless. By my third year of graduate school, I ran my own lab at the University of Washington. Then Ida passed away, and all her Roslyn friends and Eden and Dr. M came to the funeral.

I never slowed my pace of research. I'd known I wouldn't be in time to help my grandmother, but there were tens of millions more people watching their brains slide out of view. Most other labs were looking at amyloid, a kind of protein that builds up in Alzheimer's-afflicted brains like plaque builds up on teeth. The idea was that if they figured out how to clear out the amyloid, they could cure the disease. Not a bad theory, but I took a different path. My lab started making variations on a protein called angiotensin, which I knew from experimentation could stimulate new nerve cells and connections in the hippocampus.

I met Jia Koh at a campus biotech event while I was getting my PhD. She'd recently moved back to Seattle after earning law and business degrees from Stanford, and was working for a venture capital firm downtown. She gave presentations on campus from time to time, basically to troll for scientists like me.

After her talk on technology transfer, I approached her and told her I was developing a cure for Alzheimer's. She immediately took me for a drink at the Mountaineering Club, a rooftop bar near the university, more upscale than the older, scruffier U District spots that grad students liked. She looked chic in a sheath dress and blazer. In the old sweater and jeans I'd worn under my lab coat all day, I looked like I belonged in one of those other bars.

"When you say developing . . ."

"We know the compound works in mouse brains."

"You know?"

"One hundred percent. I need to start human trials. Now."

She asked me more questions, and I told her how my grandmother's illness had inspired my search for an Alzheimer's cure. We talked about less weighty topics too as we felt each other out: ski trails and running paths we liked, the pros and cons of Seattle versus Palo Alto. The subject of where I'd been before university never came up, just as it was never included in any biography or resumé or social media profile. I never actively intended to deceive Jia, I just never mentioned the Cleckley Institute to anyone.

Within a year, I'd finished my degree and Jia had left her firm. Based on my research, we hatched the idea for our drug, Nebusol, and founded our company, Alphaneuro. We started hiring and raising money. We moved from rented rooms on campus to our office building in South Lake Union—first just one floor, and eventually five more.

Like me, Jia can be manic, but unlike me, she can multi-task, whacking back an onslaught of distractions like the competitive tennis player she once was. As the chief scientist, I became the company's face, but there's no question that Jia made it run. Under the title of chief operating officer, she managed me along with everything else, letting me focus almost entirely on research. She hired people to contain me as needed: a battle-axe human resources manager to prevent unwise firings, an executive coach to get me to delegate, praise, and give the appearance of listening. I'm not one of those socially awkward quants; I can be quite charming. Set loose in a room full of investors, I'll work it like nobody's business. But most of the time, I'll choose an evening of checking my samples or reading new research over going to a party. Jia always chooses the party.

For more than a year, we had people in the lab around the clock, one of them usually me. By the time our drug entered clinical trials, we weren't the only researchers on the angiotensin path. But we did get to the finish line first. Nearly three years ago, the FDA approved Nebusol to treat Alzheimer's and several other types of dementia. That day, we held a party and press conference on the ground floor of our office building. The mayor came. The governor sent congratulations. I shook hands with trial participants, who gave public testimonials about their restored memories. Investors who'd ignored us showered me with pleas for lunch. Before that, we were just another biotech company, as far as the public was concerned. In the time since, I've been on the covers of *Forbes*, *Fortune*, *Wired*, and *Bloomberg Businessweek*.

Around the time we got FDA approval, Jia amped up our communications staff, and a woman named Ashley came to my office to take down my "narrative," as she called it, so that she could update my company bio. She asked me where I'd grown up and gone to high school, and I told her nobody cared about that, and stared at her silently until she moved on to the next question. Between the story of my grandmother, and me running my own company by the time I was twenty-six, she had plenty to work with. Ashley wrote speeches for me to deliver, along with press releases and talking points, and Jia signed off on it all. And somehow I managed to keep Cleckley unknown, even to Jia. She met Dr. M on a few occasions, but I just said he was my old mentor, a senior neuroscientist—true facts—and let her think he'd been my professor. He maintained discretion because you don't divulge people's confidential medical information.

Psychopaths are supposed to lie easily and with abandon, and many do, and it's certainly true that I can. Lying doesn't raise my heart rate. But I prefer to tell the truth. I like to live by rules that keep conflict at bay, because conflict consumes time and energy. So I don't, generally, lie or steal, and I don't physically hurt anyone, and I don't kill. You might wonder why I'd need a rule like "don't kill" when I don't work in a war zone or surgical theatre, where the opportunity tends to arise. It's not that I'm attracted to killing people. The occasional violent impulse notwithstanding, I'm truly not. I'm just concerned that I don't have the squeamishness, empathy, or fear that hold other people back when they're tempted. You know those people who don't feel pain? How without the proper signals from their nerve endings, they have to be extra careful not to burn and bruise themselves? I'm missing some of the proper emotional signals. My rules are my way of being careful. And since my earliest days at Cleckley, I'd believed that I needed to be careful because of the two deaths I already had on my hands.

When we decided it was time to sell the company, I realized that my grand elision represented a risk. Banks and would-be buyers would now scrutinize Alphaneuro even more closely, factoring everything they learned into their valuations. But it seemed too late to tell Jia about Cleckley. She was obsessed with controlling the narrative, and I feared that suddenly revealing I'd been raised in a psychiatric institution, and was technically a psychopath, and that any determined journalist could find this out, might shatter her nerves. Jia already had circles under her eyes and kept pulling on the hair on the left side of her head. It would have been irresponsible of me to dump a new headache on her. With my naturally lower blood pressure, I needed to keep my informational burden to myself, and hang on to my Cleckley secret until after the sale.

SEVEN

CATE

Walking to the light rail after leaving Dr. M, I veered off the footpath to sit on a cold concrete bench and check my messages. Behind me stood mist-shrouded evergreens, and in front of me, the concrete and glass rectangles of the medical school. I tried to summon the faces of Cleckley students, especially older boys, but the images that came into my head seemed like remembered dreams. Groups of students in classes and halls. Angles askew, rooms the wrong colour. Bowls of apples and pears from the surrounding orchards. Dr. M and Eden's farmhouse, with a fresh coat of white paint.

The campus was on the outskirts of the agrarian town of Cashmere, in the foothills on the east side of the Cascades. I remembered jaunts to the general store and canoeing on Lake Wenatchee. I distinctly recalled members of the staff—Nurse Bonamo, Nurse Chen—but among students, only Sissy was vivid. Others hovered just out of reach, circling a campfire, playing a board game. Who was Number 98? I'd come up to campus thinking I was motivated by intellectual curiosity. Evidently, I'd been deluding myself if all it took was one little dot on a chart to make everything personal again. I was tantalized by the scant amount more I'd been able to extract from Dr. M about Number 98. Someone who knew about finance and physics. An inventor, trying to *do* something. Like me.

I had four voicemails and three texts, all from Jia or her assistant.

"Could you try not to disappear on me again until we're done?" she asked when I got through.

Since I'd left the office that morning in search of the study, we'd had a new expression of interest, which meant more leverage to pit potential buyers against one another. That should have commanded my full attention, but it didn't.

"Have you ever hired a private investigator?" I asked.

"Due diligence hasn't turned up anything weird enough to warrant one."

"But say we wanted one."

"Are you worried about someone in particular?"

"Yes."

She was quiet for a moment, then said, "This isn't about the sale, is it?"

I admitted that it wasn't.

"Cate, I need you to focus, please. Where are you?"

"On the U-Dub campus. I wanted to see Dr. M."

She sighed. "Okay. But now we need you in the room here. And let's put off new projects until we get through the sale."

I said sure, of course.

I rode back to South Lake Union and took the glass elevator to my office, staring across the lake at the houseboats and office buildings on the opposite shore. We'd be handing over the commercial lease along with everything else, and I tried to imagine this view not being mine anymore. I made an effort to "sit with it" for a moment, as all my counsellors had advised, but I couldn't jostle up the right emotion. It occurred to me that I should go back to a therapist. Dealing with change and all that. I should find someone new—someone who didn't know my whole past. A fresh perspective.

As soon as I got to my desk, I pulled up a search engine, and then faced how absurdly little I knew about Number 98. His age, some academic institutions, a general field. Someone who worked in energy finance, whatever that meant.

I was contemplating my impotence when Jia arrived in my office in her two-tone slingback pumps and blazer, black hair draped down her back. Two lawyers from her team, Al and Wen, trailed her like baby ducklings, and the three of them corralled me for the rest of the afternoon as we scrutinized complicated offer sheets. I bounced my knee under the table and attempted to look serene. The dollar amounts were so high as to sound theoretical. More than ten billion, and I owned 40 percent of the company. It still felt abstract, but by the end, I was starting to think of what I might do with all that cash. My next grandiose goal. I wanted to cure other types of dementia, use memory drugs to treat PTSD, aerosolize more medicines, and find the genetic causes of brain disorders like my own. Beyond my own research, I could fund new companies, or give to non-profits and foundations. I would have to hire one of those consultants who tell you how to give away money. Life is so short. I wished I could clone myself so I could accomplish more. And people say narcissism is a bad thing.

Jia, Al, and Wen wanted decisions. How to value our many patents besides Nebusol, our crown jewel. Whether there were any patents we could exclude from the sale, minor discoveries I could take with me into a future venture. How to pay out our vested employees. Jia's assistant, Rebecca, interrupted us briefly, asking what we wanted for dinner: pork ribs for Jia, tuna poke for me, shawarma for Al and Wen. I gave Rebecca my best "I don't bite" smile as I ordered, because Jia so often reminded me that I could be intimidating to junior staff.

As we ate, Jia outlined her scheme to pit the three contenders against each other. But it had to happen quickly. We would make our first counter-offer the day after next, she said, and dismissed Al, Wen, and Rebecca for the night. Lights twinkled all around Lake Union, defining its misshapen triangle by their absence. A few nighttime boaters dotted the surface like stars.

"Have you thought more about what you're going to do?"

"It's getting real," I said, spinning around in my chair. Alone with Jia, my sprawling appetite for the future narrowed down to a single focus. In just a week, or maybe less, we'd have a deal. I only had to get through one more week without Jia or the public finding out about Cleckley.

"I'm going to start my own VC fund with the proceeds," Jia said.

She'd been in venture capital before we met, and now she was the genius who'd bet on Alphaneuro. She would excel.

"And Learning Adventures wants me on their board," she added.

"Learning Adventures?"

She looked at me with exasperation. "We always buy a table at their fundraiser?"

"Of course," I said, and I did remember her side passion, a non-profit organization that puts new tech into schools. I forget things sometimes, as though my brain does some automatic triage to help me stay focused. Which never seems to happen to Jia.

"What else?" I asked.

"I'll pay off my parents' mortgage."

She had a relationship with her parents that was both loyal and combative. I didn't entirely understand it, but then I'm no expert on having parents. She'd been raised in Belltown, but before it was slick and full of residential towers like mine. Her mom and dad had operated a hair salon, and she'd once described them as two oxen, yoked together by their burden. After launching Jia and her brother into lives along the lines of what they'd envisioned—degrees, incomes; they'd given up on hopes of marriage—they'd upped stakes and moved to the Eastside, way out where suburbia meets foothills. Gotten in touch with rural roots entirely alien to Jia.

"They're lucky to have you."

"I'm sure they'll find a new reason to disapprove," she said lightly. "What about you?"

"Angel investing," I said. I spun my chair. As the first investors in new companies, angels take flyers on wild ideas.

"In biotech?"

"Biotech, maybe energy."

"Energy? That's new."

The term "energy finance" pulsed in my brain.

"You want to tell me what's going on?" Jia asked.

"What do you mean?"

"Why did you ask about private investigators?"

I blinked at her. *One more week.*

"It can wait until after the sale."

"But why did you ask?"

I sighed. She sensed there was a situation that might require her control. Considering she dictated even my appearance now, I shouldn't have been surprised. I wished I'd told her about Cleckley years ago so that I'd have less to explain now.

"I need to find someone," I said with a shrug.

"This sounds important to you." She crossed her legs and her arms, and hooked her right toe around the back of her left ankle, like she was tying herself up in her own limbs.

"It is."

"Who is it you're looking for?"

I decided I could tell her without mentioning Cleckley.

"Dr. M has led an interesting neuropsychiatric study. I need to find one of the subjects."

"For angel investing? Why?"

I was still formulating an answer when she spoke again.

"Why can't Dr. M put you in touch?"

"There are confidentiality issues."

She narrowed her eyes. It occurred to me that maybe I didn't need a private investigator, just someone who could search reams of information for the right match.

"Don't we pay for some expensive databases?" I asked.

"Yes, but there are rules."

Soon after companies had started selling massive, cross-indexed troves of personal information, Congress had passed the Privacy Act, which restricted who was allowed to use them.

"But we must have someone on staff with a licence. Al or Wen?"

"Not them," she said, untangling her limbs. One of her pumps had come loose, and she reached down to put it firmly back on her foot. "But yes, we have someone."

"Who?"

"He's pretty busy."

"Honestly, this can wait."

"I don't want you hiring someone outside, and I don't want you distracted. Just give me a minute to figure it out, okay?"

"Absolutely."

"And don't go cyberstalking anyone."

"I won't."

She got up to leave, but at my office door she turned back. "Let's go somewhere when this is done."

"Like Idaho?" I asked.

"Like a vacation."

"I've heard of those."

After she left, I looked out at the lights around Lake Union for a few minutes, mentally replaying my visit to Dr. M. I didn't want to perseverate all night, though, so that's when I got changed and drove to the Four Seasons.

EIGHT

LUCIANA

Luciana poured herself a fresh juice, still warm from the oranges having basked in the sun on the counter. Their two-storey house sat on a rise at the east end of Casa Azul, the beach hotel that Dario owned and ran. From the kitchen window, she could see the domed roofs of the stucco guest cabins, and beyond them, a slash of sea. Her husband was reading the news on his tablet, their shaggy white mutt, Ricketts, asleep at his feet. She watched Dario push a curl out of his face, knowing it would fall back down within minutes. People always said the two of them looked alike, with their similar height, lithe builds, and dark hair. She didn't agree; he was prettier, with full lips and round cheeks. This morning, both of them had arrived in their kitchen in board shorts and blue T-shirts, an unintentional twinning so common that neither bothered to comment on it.

"They've finished building that resort out on Punta Arena," Dario said. He reached down to pat Ricketts, who lifted his head slightly, eyes obscured by overhanging fur. It had been two nights since their evening cruise and her discovery of the huachinango with gashes on both sides.

"Oh?" She kept her voice neutral. She and Dario didn't see eye to eye on the new development, which sprawled over a hundred acres of previously pristine waterfront, forty-five minutes southeast of La Ventana. For more than a year, the resort had been one of the chief subjects of gossip among local business owners, as they debated whether it would help or hurt them. Dario, who catered to kiteboarders and windsurfers, hoped to do business with the resort, offering lesson-plus-equipment packages to its guests. But Luciana had been dismayed by the construction runoff that obscured nearby reefs for months, blotting out the light they needed to survive. She'd been even more disappointed to learn that the resort was building a golf course—in the desert!—and an energy-sucking desalination plant.

"They plan to open next month," Dario reported, also striving to sound neutral. She liked that they did this with each other, treading carefully around points of contention. And she had to admit that the resort was not quite the ecological catastrophe she'd first feared. The owner had left swathes of land in an almost-natural state.

"I should try to meet him," Dario said carefully.

"Who?"

"The owner. Hunter Araya. It says he made his money in distilleries before moving out here."

She nodded, and Dario allowed himself a smile before returning to scrolling the news. A permission had been asked for and granted without either of them acknowledging that that's what had happened. Luciana turned back to the counter and split an avocado. She spread its yellow-green flesh on her toast and licked the knife.

"Christ," Dario said quietly.

"What?"

"Someone blew up a factory fishing ship. The *Bizan-maru*."

She paused with her piece of toast in the air. "Where?"

His eyes scanned the tablet. "Somewhere east of La Paz."

Here in their sea, too close to home. La Paz was just thirty miles to the north.

"When?"

"Three nights ago. Killed two crew. They're towing what's left to Guaymas."

"People were *killed*?"

Dario handed her the tablet. She put down her toast and skimmed the story.

"Weren't factory ships banned?" he asked.

How she wished that were the case. They were like industrial islands, catching, processing, and freezing fish without discrimination.

"They're phasing them out. We don't go to zero for a few more years."

She reached the last paragraph of the story like an anchor hitting the seabed: *The environmental organization Reef Pirates issued an announcement claiming responsibility for the attack.*

"Reef Pirates." Luciana looked up at her husband. "They don't—they've never—I mean, they've boarded ships, but they've never blown one up."

Dario looked at her with compassion. "You know some of those folks, don't you?"

Stricken, she didn't want to elaborate, and he didn't ask her to. Suddenly she wanted to get out of the kitchen, to flee this information. But she couldn't escape the fact that Beni had discovered the emptied tanks the morning after the attack on the *Bizan-maru*.

NINE

GABRIEL

Gabriel and Cate had been together for more than a year when a co-worker at the Fisheries Research Center lent him a sailboat for a long weekend. The two of them navigated the teak-decked, fibreglass-hulled, thirty-five-foot vessel around the San Juan Islands, anchoring at night near state parks, waking up with a salty mist on their skin. On their third day out, they decided to dive one of the shipwrecks dotting the floor of the Salish Sea, a cargo ship that had sunk in the 1960s. It was supposed to be 120 feet down.

After tying off the boat, Gabriel removed his eye patch. His sensitive left cornea, so vulnerable to sun on the water, was well adapted to the undersea world. They suited up, checked each other's equipment, and stepped off the stern one at a time. After regrouping at the buoy, they released the air from their vests and floated downward, following the line to the sea floor, united in exploration. On the descent, Gabriel felt the initial peace that always came over him underwater.

The light dimmed quickly as they went down. At about 100 feet, he checked his wrist computer and turned on his flashlight, which beamed into green nothingness. They both held tight to the line, undulating like human flags in the strong current. At 120 feet, he could not see the bottom, nor a shipwreck, nor anything but the translucent void. They made "don't know" gestures at each other and continued down. They got deep enough that they risked narcosis, a kind of drunkenness brought on by the seepage of nitrogen into one's blood. And that's when, in the beam of his dive light, he saw a sort of pole, then a structure, too square to be natural, but so covered with shells and seaweed it barely looked man-made. They descended farther, still holding on to the line. There was a gravitational pull—he swore he could feel it whenever he got close to the seabed. Then—bump—the sandy bottom. They shone their lights around, and he was astounded by what he saw. A wall towered above them, high as a three-storey building and covered with swaying white sea anemones: fluffy, pale treelets united in one enormous cloud. This was the hull of the wreck, he realized; the deck, if it remained, must be far above them. The sunken ship had become an ecosystem of its own, and as he moved his beam around, it picked up sea life: cruising ling cod, an eel, a curled pink-and-grey octopus staring back at him with one eye, as though annoyed to have been disturbed. He turned to Cate, but she was gone.

Still holding the line, he shone his light all around and found her clinging to a rock ten yards down-current. She pointed up. Digging one gloved hand at a time into the sand, she made her way back to him, and slowly, safely, they ascended the line until they were at the height of the deck. They saw shapes—a squarish cabin, railings, lifeboats—all of them tilted and covered with life, kelp and urchins and darting small fish that made the scene look dreamlike and organic, as though the whole wreck had grown from the sea floor instead of having been forged from steel and sunk in a storm.

Cate wanted to explore the deck, he knew, and he did too, but he had a sense of foreboding. They were too deep, the water too dark, the current too strong. There was no one else on their boat if things went awry. Reluctantly, he signed to her that they should ascend. She pointed two fingers to her eyes and back to the deck. He tapped his computer. Time and depth were of the essence. She opened her palm at him: five minutes. And then she swam away. Upon reaching the deck, she held on to a piece of railing. Cautious, tempted, he followed. Amid the wonky, creature-covered structures on deck, the current was weaker, and they were less out in the open than they had been on the line. He began to explore. There was something hallucinatory about being around man-made things underwater, the objects familiar but the perspective jumbled. He held as carefully as he could to a stanchion, using just the fingertips of one hand, plenty of leverage in his buoyant underwater state, and chased a scooting ling cod with his light beam. He checked the time and looked for Cate.

His feelings for her always oscillated, but no more wildly than at that moment, as he swung from the delight of doing his favourite thing with his favourite person to wondering where she was and cursing her for not paying attention; when they were underwater together, it was every bit as incumbent on her to keep track of him as vice versa. Wait, there she was. Down-deck, near the door to the wheelhouse. He swam to join her. They both peered in through the door, beaming their flashlights. Intact metal instruments, now green-grey, would once have been shiny yellow brass. The table would have held charts. Small fish darted in and out a porthole. They signed to each other, and he thought they'd agreed to ascend.

He was back at the line when he sensed, then saw, that Cate was not with him. He returned to the deck with gentle kicks, letting his anger suppress the fear that something had happened to her. He swam from stanchion to stanchion, searching, aware that his heart rate was rising and trying to keep it steady because if his heart pounded, he would breathe more heavily and use up his air. He swam down to the lower side of the deck and began making his way along the railing, a fuzzy attempt to be systematic. How long had he been searching for her now? His computer told him nearly ten minutes, which meant that either it was wrong or his judgment was off. He suspected he was not thinking clearly, which drove him to do the right thing, or at least the standard-protocol thing: separated from his partner, and having searched for her, he should surface.

He swam back to the line, ascended a few feet, and held tight, watching the screen on his wrist to count the minutes. There was no way to ascend quickly from this far down without giving himself a deadly case of the bends. He turned off his light. He closed his eyes and counted his breaths to try to distract himself from fear for Cate. She was experienced, she was sensible, she would ascend. He turned his light back on so that she, somewhere in the depths above or below him, might see the beam and feel reassured. He counted off three more minutes and climbed another twenty feet, loosely holding the buoy line. The water was lighter and greener here, but still confusing to the eye in its blankness. With no point of reference, he had no sense of how far he could see. At each stop on his way up, Gabriel entered a sort of self-hypnosis, his way to endure the eternity of waiting.

The water grew lighter around him, until he could see the sky, warped by the crystal-clear slosh of ocean. His air gauge was in the red, but he was almost there.

When he broke the surface, he inflated his vest and looked all around. The sun had come out. He could see their boat, but no one on deck. He kicked rapidly towards it. He yelled her name. But the only sound he heard in response was the splash of water against the hull, and then his own breathing as he rolled out of his vest and hauled himself and his gear onto the stern. He removed his mask and his left eyeball immediately ached. Standing on deck, he scanned the surface for bubbles, or objects, or Cate. If she had decided to surface but couldn't find the line, the current might have carried her far from here during her ascent.

He saw nothing. He would contact the Coast Guard. As long as he had steps to take, he could keep his fear at bay. Standing on the cabin stairs, radio in hand, he looked to the buoy one last time. He lifted the radio to his face.

There! She surfaced, her hooded head like a seal's catching the light. She raised her hand and gave the sign for "okay." He hung the radio back up and felt the onrush of blood to his face.

They didn't speak while he lifted her gear onto the deck, casting a glance at her air gauge, which was also in the red. Didn't speak while he accepted her weight belt and fins and stowed their tanks. But once they were sitting awkwardly on deck, both still in their wetsuits, he grabbed her in a hug and held tight. He pressed his face into her wet hair and cursed with relief. She twisted to hug him back, and his sanity began to return.

"It's okay, it's okay," she said. To him. Soothing him.

He felt confused. How was it okay? He felt nauseous, and it wasn't due to the bobbing boat, but from awareness of just how acute his fear of losing her had been. An image flashed in his mind before he could banish it: Cate's kelp-tangled, white-faced corpse hovering above that sunken deck. Even as they clung to each other in their thick neoprene, he knew she was calmer than he was.

"Let's get warm," she said.

They peeled out of their suits and rinsed off using the sun shower that lay like a jellyfish on the cabin roof. They towelled and dressed, and the cotton and fleece felt good against his chilled body. They sat on opposite bench seats in the small cabin.

"What happened?" he asked, taking both of her hands in his.

"What do you mean?"

His sense of alarm twitched.

"Down there. You disappeared. I thought—I was worried. I looked for you."

She hesitated.

"What?" he asked.

"I went into the wheelhouse."

"But I thought we agreed to go up. You gave the okay." He suddenly felt shaky, torn between being upset and wanting to calmly find out what had happened.

"I thought we agreed to go in."

Miscommunication. Okay. It happened sometimes when you were down deep and narced.

"You must have been in there a long time."

"My fin got caught in some old line tangled with kelp."

Gabriel's heart rate rose. He was appalled that she had been alone and stuck, but why had she gone in? They didn't know this wreck. The structure could be unstable, could trap a diver with a fallen beam or blind them with kicked-up debris.

"Jesus Christ, you could have—you could have—" He couldn't bring himself to say it. He didn't feel the delicious relief of other post-close-call moments with Cate. He didn't feel the usual desire. Instead, he felt sick.

"It's okay. I just cut myself out."

He was horror-struck, imagining what would have happened if she hadn't been carrying a dive knife.

"You did the right thing," she said. "We both did the right thing."

"I didn't! I didn't know you were stuck!"

She looked serious for a moment, then laughed in a deflecting way. "It's okay, Gabriel. I'm here. Shouldn't we move the boat?"

They were still tied off to the buoy, bobbing in the Haro Strait. They would want to find an anchorage, somewhere sheltered where they could stay for the night, eat, and rest. And so they raised the sail, talking little, and for an hour or so, with him at the tiller and her at a winch, Gabriel felt the smooth, comforting groove of them working together. They anchored in a cove at Moran State Park, where for dinner they heated soup on the little rocking stove and ate it with buttered bread and chopped fruit. Gabriel had half a bottle of wine, and Cate drank one of her juices. Afterwards, wrapped in warm clothes, they lay on the cabin deck and watched the stars come out. But he couldn't let go of their earlier adventure. Incident. Near-drowning.

He tried not to sound judgmental when he asked her why she'd gone into the wheelhouse.

"I was curious," she said.

"But you know the risks."

"Yeah."

"Weren't you afraid?"

"No."

"There's something I'm not getting."

"There is."

This answer surprised and intrigued him.

"What is it?"

"I don't feel much fear."

"What are you talking about?"

"I do a little, sometimes. Just not a lot. I don't feel a normal fear response."

He rolled on his side to look at her, trying to process what she'd just said. Her words were oddly clinical, yet they were usefully precise. He thought back on his time with Cate. She was daring in that way certain athletes are. People called her kind of behaviour "fearless," but he'd never actually thought the term was literal.

"What do you mean?"

"My brain works differently."

She meant that literally too.

His questions cracked open a world. She told him a strange history stretching back to a rural road in Duvall and a ramshackle house. Her stepfather had regularly locked her and her stepbrother in a closet—to protect them from her mother, Cate had figured out in retrospect. Her mother had been wildly erratic, prone to disappearances and fits of rage. Gabriel found this upsetting, but it turned out to be the least of what she had to say.

Cate had started fires. One particular fire when she was six, and the resulting death of her mother and stepbrother, propelled her to the mint-coloured halls of an institution. He tried to put that fact in some frame of reference, but found that he didn't have one. Surely a six-year-old was innocent? Or was she? He knew a few children, had nieces and nephews in the single digits, but he had never thought to imagine their potential for malevolence.

At the institution, there were doctors and counsellors and teachers. She climbed in and out of a white metallic tube that took pictures of her brain. Dr. M presided over it all; her grandmother hovered stern and angelic in the background. Cate told Gabriel what the MRIs and PET scans showed, notably that her brain bore disturbing similarities to a serial killer's.

"Hold on, did you say Dr. M?"

Gabriel had met him only twice, but Cate talked about him often.

She nodded.

"You said he was your mentor."

"He was. Is."

"You said he was your professor."

"He advised on my thesis."

Gabriel thought of the erudite, avuncular man he'd met at brunch at Cate's apartment. He'd been charmed by this quasi father figure. Dr. M was one of those bright-eyed old professors who are genuinely curious about the world, inquiry a bedrock part of their personalities. He had asked Gabriel questions—about growing up on Monterey Bay, about marine biology. Gabriel had felt better knowing that, though Cate had no close family, she had Dr. M. Now his impression of the man became tinged by something sinister.

"You were his subject?"

By this time, they were lying on their sides, twins in the womb-like forward berth. He shuddered as though he were freezing, as though he'd been trapped on the sea floor. Cate seemed like she might talk all night, as lucid and voluble as he'd ever seen her, behaving in exactly the way he'd thought he wanted her to. She could be too cool sometimes, which gave him an anxious craving for more. Now here she was, sharing and open and honest, and dear God, why hadn't she told him any of this before?

She was talking about empathy, or her lack thereof.

"But you are empathetic," he said.

"It's not necessarily a bad thing not to be. It makes me a better decision-maker."

"You're making my mind melt. Of course you're empathetic. If I was hurt, you'd help me. Even if it put you at risk. Even if it cost you. Even if it wasn't the rational thing to do."

Seeing in her eyes that she was about to deny it, he placed four fingers firmly over her mouth. She remained silent. Nowhere in his welter of emotions did he feel the reassurance he thirsted for. He felt conflicting things, a desire to protect her and to get away, to run to the opposite end of the boat. He couldn't place the heavy, cold feeling in his chest, because it made no sense lying here in the berth with his beloved.

Later he would recognize the feeling as fear. That night, though, he made himself swallow it. He couldn't hear more. He took Cate in his arms, and she burrowed into him, her head on his shoulder. They rocked to sleep that way, and the next afternoon sailed back to the mainland.

On a sunny Sunday afternoon a few weeks after their sailboat trip, Gabriel drove to see Dr. M. Cate's revelations about her past had left him mentally revisiting their entire relationship, swinging between hope and dread. Bees animated the flower beds in front of the professor's house, a Craftsman bungalow in Ravenna. Gabriel parked his car but didn't get out. He sat there for a time, wondering if he should do what he planned. Then he climbed the steps to the covered porch and rang the bell.

Dr. M seemed bemused to find him on his doorstep.

"Hi, Dr. Montrose," Gabriel said, then suddenly felt tongue-tied.

"Is Cate all right?"

"Oh—yes. At least, I think so. I was wondering if you could talk, actually. About her."

Dr. M's grey beard was even longer than Gabriel remembered. "We can talk, but you must call me Archie. Deal?"

Gabriel nodded. He followed Dr. M across a living room with an enormous faded Turkish carpet, to a kitchen with black and white countertop tiles. An electric kettle was already boiling.

"Will you have some tea?"

They sat down in a breakfast nook that bumped out into the backyard, which looked just as prolific as the front yard, only more oriented towards fruits and vegetables. The tea tasted mainly of ginger, and Gabriel felt hot with culpability over everything he wanted to ask. Dr. M stared penetratingly at him from above his spectacles.

"Cate told me about you and the institute and how she grew up."

Dr. M nodded slowly. "Does she know you're visiting me?"

"No." Gabriel felt his face burn.

"I see."

There was a long pause as Gabriel thought about how to ask what he wanted to without violating Cate's confidence further.

Dr. M spoke first. "She doesn't share that history very often. If ever. She certainly must trust you."

Gabriel took a deep breath and expelled a rush of words. "I feel honoured by that, really, but I also feel terrible because—" He faltered. "I feel disturbed, to be honest. She told me she's a psychopath. Is that true?"

Dr. M looked down at his tea. "You're the first romantic partner she's ever told me about, let alone introduced me to."

Gabriel's cheeks grew even hotter.

The doctor regarded him steadily, then seemed to take pity on him. "I will address what she told you," he said, and paused again, as though bolstering his resolve. "By the measures we use to identify psychopathy, which include behavioural traits as well as brain physiology, she has met the definition, yes."

Gabriel felt as though his chest were imploding.

"But it's important not to get hung up on definitions."

"Isn't that what you do, though? Define these things?"

"That's useful in the clinic, but not in day-to-day life. Half the people in the world"—he waved his arm in a circle—"could be described as one thing or another from the DSM." He meant the *Diagnostic and Statistical Manual of Mental Disorders*, the bible of psychiatric assessment. "That's constructive for devising ways to help them. And help society. But these are just categories. They tell us how groups of people are alike, but not how the individuals within those groups are different from one another."

"Does she love me?"

Dr. M looked just as surprised at the question as Gabriel was at himself for asking it.

"Does she say she loves you?"

"Yes."

"It's not productive to second-guess people's expressed feelings."

That was not a helpful answer as far as Gabriel was concerned. If Cate was really a psychopath, did he love a person who couldn't love? Vestiges of his maternal Catholicism reared themselves, things he hadn't believed since childhood. Could someone be damned from the start?

"I'm not going to say more specifically about Cate," Dr. M said. "That would be unfair without her here. But I can answer general questions."

"Can they change?"

"Some of them, yes, in some ways."

"Is that why you decided to study psychopathy? To see if they could change?"

Dr. M set down his mug. "That does take me back."

"To what?"

"A long time ago, I encountered an extreme psychopath. He had a total absence of empathy. A very destructive person."

"Where?"

"Vietnam, in the early 1970s. He was an American soldier, a sergeant named Krist. I was a medic."

"What did he do?"

"Executed innocent people. Up close. Another soldier and I witnessed what he'd done." Dr. M paused heavily. "The other soldier—Jackson—started praying, right after what we saw. He was praying for us to be delivered from evil, which was the best explanation at hand. Some people still think it's the best explanation, but that's not how I understand the world. I wanted to know the cause. Why a human brain does this. How you stop a Krist from becoming what he was."

"But they're not all like Krist."

"Correct. Psychopathy is a spectrum disorder. Like autism or OCD. He was a severe case."

Gabriel took a deep breath. "Cate told me about your research. She said a high percentage of the Cleckley students had . . . bad outcomes."

"In our longest study to date, nearly half went on to have criminal records, if that's what you mean. And most of the rest face other challenges."

"And she shares their characteristics."

"Physiology, brain chemistry, aspects of background trauma, some behavioural traits—yes."

"So why is Cate not like the others?" Gabriel was trespassing again, and he expected the old professor to shut him down.

"This is a question I've studied for decades," Dr. M said. "You're a marine biologist, correct?"

"Yes."

"I read about a study of coral reefs. In Micronesia, it may have been. Vast areas of coral reef are dying as the ocean acidifies. But in Micronesia, they've found a coral population that's thriving, adapting. They're studying it to try to understand why it's surviving while the others are not."

"It's in Guam, but yes, I've read that study."

"Same basic organism, same circumstances. So why do some remain robust? This is what I'm trying to determine. But I need more Cates."

Gabriel was chilled by the sudden transformation of Cate into a data point, but Cate *was* a data point to Dr. M, after all, even if she was also a beloved protegé.

"So are there more?"

"They can be hard to find. And then, of course, human subjects are wigglier than plants and animals. You can't just put a bunch in a tank and change the pH balance."

Yes, Gabriel thought, there was a big difference between studying non-human animals and human beings, but an even bigger one between studying human beings in general and one you knew personally.

They didn't address whether they'd tell Cate about this conversation, but when Gabriel left, he had a feeling neither of them would.

In the weeks after her self-revelation on the sailboat, Cate and Gabriel's moods moved in opposite directions. Cate seemed relieved, even lighthearted. Gabriel tortured himself over what she was really feeling. He asked her, once, to describe her love for him. "I'm the same person I was before I told you about Cleckley," she replied. He came to hate that name. What if the Cleckley Institute had taught her falsehoods about herself? He wanted to liberate her by showing her that she was wrong, that it had somehow all been a big mistake. But the more upset he became, the calmer Cate got.

He castigated himself over his own lack of compassion. If she couldn't help the way she was, she didn't deserve to have him turn on her. But in those weeks of late summer and early fall, he also realized that her confession had clarified an unease he'd already felt. It was all highs and lows with Cate. Even their first twenty-four hours together had set the pattern. That night on the riverbank after rafting, kissing her had been like merging into the universe. But earlier that day, he had, for a minute, literally thought he was going to drown. At the time, he didn't see these two experiences—near-death followed by transporting passion—as connected, but now he could only see them that way. Every high he felt with Cate outdid the previous one. Lifetime peak upon lifetime peak. But between the highs lay valleys of anxiety and fear, each one worse than the last.

He understood her sense of a calling, because he felt it too. He could get so absorbed in work that he missed a meal or two, and at first he'd thought they were alike this way. But as well as her episodes of total obliviousness to life outside the lab, which could go on for weeks, she was extreme in her appetite for risk. And now he understood that she wasn't going to change. He conceded to himself that the relationship might have been unhealthy all along.

He broke up with her one fall evening in her apartment as the sun set over the Olympics. He'd prepared himself with reasons, but she didn't ask for any, let alone cry. "I thought this might happen," she said, and that was it.

Afterwards, as he gathered his things from her bedroom and bathroom, he felt even more dismal. He was the first person she'd ever told about her past, and he'd affirmed her worst expectation.

TEN

CATE

The morning after I slept with Nate Pryor of the *Los Angeles Times*, I blended a chia seed breakfast smoothie, feeling exasperated with myself. Here I was, practically counting my gains from the sale, imagining my future good works, and I'd put it all at risk. I wondered if I should take up prostitutes, men I could pay to perform and then discreetly go away. Yet that would eliminate half the fun.

Jia came early to our meeting. Some office angel had set out pastries and a thermos of coffee to sustain the lawyers, and the weak February sun streaked in across the lake.

"He has some leverage, we have some leverage," she said, flipping her hair back. "Pryor could write a tell-all essay about his night with Cate Winter, put it online. That would be embarrassing. It could inspire a bunch of 'erratic CEO' stories. As of yesterday, we basically had them in a bidding war."

"But," I said.

"I made him go away."

"Thank you."

"Don't get too excited. Once he got his clothes on, he drove a surprisingly hard bargain."

"What do you mean?"

"I made promises. He did too. His end of the deal is that he's not going to write anything before the sale."

"Good."

"And if he does, we'll spin it. Predatory journalist deliberately attempted to seduce and blackmail would-be source. He preyed on you."

"Ick. That makes me sound like a victim."

"It's better than coming off as the aggressor," she said. "Fortunately, I think he's still attached enough to his career, and his girlfriend, that he won't go public. One call to his editor and he would lose his job."

"And our promises?"

"Your next venture—whatever it is, whenever it is—he gets the first interview."

"Jesus."

"You do not get to complain."

"I have no idea what that will even be."

"With any luck, he will have gotten out of journalism by then."

"But—"

"Cate, this could have come out much worse."

She was right, of course. I blew out my breath, realizing as I did so that I sounded petulant.

"I'm sorry about—" I started this sentence without knowing how it was going to end. "About causing stress."

"Stress? You mean, because of the literal billions of dollars on the table? For all of us?" She vibrated with sarcasm.

"I really am sorry."

"You're messing with people's futures. And I know you know that. That's what I don't understand. I'm trying to steer this ship into harbour, and you're out looking for someone to fuck."

"It was stupid."

I wondered what she would think of the gigolo idea. She did appreciate efficient solutions.

"Where's Gabriel, anyway?"

Jia had loved me having a boyfriend. She thought it kept me calm and made me an easier sell. And because she didn't know about Cleckley, she couldn't understand why we'd broken up.

"You know he moved to Mexico City."

"Doing what again?"

"He works for that new agency that screens for wildlife disease."

"You're still in touch."

"Barely. Stop."

"I wasn't thinking anything."

"You were."

"I liked him."

"You liked having a CEO in a nice, committed relationship with another scientist."

"But I also liked him."

"I did too."

She got up and poured herself coffee, a sign that she was done rebuking me for now.

"Felix is going to work on your search," she said.

"Felix from last night?"

"He's a wizard with the databases. But he's going to need information from you. Someplace to get started."

For the last twenty-four hours, my memory had tossed up more faces from Cleckley. Terry, bushy-haired with braces. Hunter, with that scar on his forehead. Calliope's red curls.

"Okay."

"And when you finish work today, and tomorrow, and every day until this is done, please go home and nowhere else. Don't communicate with anyone, and don't go on social media. Just do nothing. Okay? Until we're finished?"

"Absolutely."

Al and Wen arrived for our meeting, which passed tediously. Afterwards, I held my usual Tuesday session with our lead researchers in the sixth-floor lab. Everyone had heard rumours of corporate manoeuvring, but the scientists were less interested in speculating about the fate of the business than they were in their research, which currently involved studying the effects of a virus on transgenic mice.

The sixth floor was getting low on mice, and I said I would personally order more from the supplier.

For the next two days, I followed orders. I stayed late at work, went straight home, and caught up on reading journals. In the mornings I worked out on my stationary bike with the machine interface, increasing my daily mileage to twenty.

On Thursday, Felix came to my office. He settled gingerly into a chair that was, for him, a tight fit. He wore a goatee and a cornflower-blue shirt.

"I hear you're a database wizard."

He tilted his head. "Patent holders can be surprisingly hard to track down."

"Thank you for your help the other night."

"You let me know if that reporter gives you any more trouble."

That reporter had, in fact, left me a rambling voicemail, but it didn't rise to the level of trouble.

"I will."

Felix removed a notebook from his breast pocket with a flourish. "Now. What can you tell me about this gentleman you're looking for?"

I faltered, suddenly uneasy about sharing. If I started here, where would it end? Would Felix find out about the fire? Would he report back to Jia?

He saw my hesitation. "Dr. Winter, my mother had Alzheimer's disease," he said. "She got into the Nebusol clinical trial, and now we have her back. It's an honour to work with you."

I was thanked a lot in general terms, handed laurels by organizations. Less often one-on-one, like this. I was surprised, my cynicism disarmed. I also understood what he was trying to tell me: that he was loyal. You don't co-run a company for eight years without recognizing the value of loyalty.

"This will have to remain confidential," I said. "Just between you and me."

"Of course."

This was my moment. I could allow Felix into my world or turn my back on the whole affair. I took a deep breath.

"He's a subject in an unpublished neuropsychiatric study," I began. I detailed everything I'd learned about Number 98, while Felix took notes. I explained what the Cleckley Institute did.

"But you have no name? Not even a first name, or an initial?"

I'd thought about how to make this search easier. "Would it help if I gave you several names that *might* be correct?"

"Definitely."

"I don't know for sure if any of these are him," I said, tempted to backtrack on the whole thing again. But I needed a detached eye, and I needed to know where to look. "These are just names I remember."

The words slipped out before I could catch myself. Thankfully, Felix didn't ask, *Remember from what?*

I closed my eyes and thought of Cleckley. Images of its classrooms and wards guided me to faces and sounds. To older boys whose names I knew.

"Prescott Beecher," I said. "Two 't's." Felix wrote it down. "Elias Franklin." I envisioned hallways, the nurse's office. "Jon Partikian—he went by Jon-Jon." Camping trips. "Terry—" A flap of red cloth on a branch. "Actually, not him."

In the end, there weren't many names I'd ever known in full, even fewer I remembered now. Finally, I said the name I'd been circling, as it pulled me and pushed me away. "Hunter Brandt."

ELEVEN

LUCIANA

Luciana arrived home after dark, weary. For the last two days, she'd gone through all the appropriate motions, but she couldn't stop thinking about Javi and what he'd done. As she unlocked the door, she wondered once more if he'd known that people would die. People just earning a living, like fishermen everywhere. It must have been a terrible miscalculation. Those death-star ships were so automated, they had surprisingly small crews. As Javi and his fellow divers swam up on the giant hull to place explosives, using her tanks, he must have thought the crew would all escape in lifeboats.

In the newspaper this morning, a government spokesperson had called Reef Pirates domestic terrorists, which crushed her. They'd just been kids when they started out, angry they'd never get to see a vaquita.

Dario texted that he'd be another half hour at the restaurant, and that the dog was with him. She sat on their sofa and opened her laptop, and hesitated only momentarily before typing "Reef Pirates" and "Javier Sanz" into a search engine. The internet hurled up a video.

Javi strutted and looked into the camera like a motivational speaker. His backdrop, a blue screen with a Reef Pirates logo over his right shoulder, gave away nothing about where he might be.

"Thank you to everyone who has reached out to express support. Your donations and words of encouragement make our work possible."

She hadn't seen him in the flesh in a year, and even then, they'd only nodded at each other from across a crowded room at a fundraiser for a wildlife rescue organization in La Paz. While he was just a guest, showing his face as a matter of respect, he'd attracted a phalanx of admirers who would have made him hard to talk to even if she'd wanted to.

"We didn't take this decision lightly," he said to her now—or it seemed like he did, so direct was his gaze into the lens. His hair was sun-streaked, and he wore a black T-shirt, suggesting a vague militancy she supposed was intentional. Everything about his image was intentional now.

"We founded Reef Pirates fifteen years ago in the belief that strategy matters as much as goals."

Just as she'd gone off to graduate school in Massachusetts.

"The pressures on the Sea of Cortez have only grown more extreme. At the same time, the government has become an active participant in enabling its destruction."

Nonsense, she thought. *What about the Alvariño National Marine Park?* But the suggestion that the government was essentially a fumbling neutral party, capable of both good and ill when it came to conservation, would have been far too nuanced a point for Javi's rallying cry.

"The loss of human life that occurred during our most recent action was regrettable, and not our goal. However, up against what we face, disabling the factory ship the *Bizan-maru* was essential."

No, no, no, she thought, wanting to snatch the video off the internet before anyone saw it, as if that would make the whole event less real. But the counter already showed 1.2 million views, a number so absurd it gave her another stab of panic.

"More factory ships exactly like that one are in the Sea of Cortez at this moment. Even more are scheduled to enter our waters, making their way here from north, south, and west. Our so-called government has abandoned us."

Had he gone around the bend, or was he pandering to extremists?

Once you started pandering to extremists, what did that make you? And why was she still reluctant to think of him as an extremist when he was right here on her laptop, trying to justify the death of two people? He kept talking. And talking. This was a show, meant to display stamina and charisma as much as convey information. Wherever he and his comrades had recreated their studio—because they must have abandoned the Reef Pirates office in La Paz—they had brought their clever lighting, which bounced flatteringly off Javi's wide forehead and broad chest.

"If no action is taken, sea life will continue to disappear. There's no more time to talk about it. No one is coming to our rescue. It's down to us: Reef Pirates and our hundreds of thousands of supporters. An increase in donations since we disabled the *Bizan-maru* shows how many of you are ready for new tactics. Ready for more actions."

Molten alarm spilled from her skull. She could no longer tell if her anger was rooted in their personal history of joys and wounds, or her ex-lover's newly repulsive moral stance.

"We will not apologize for defending our sea."

"Oh, Javi," she whispered, and just then heard Dario and the dog at their front door. She swiftly shut her laptop.

The next morning, Luciana made a point of leaving before Dario was up. Deception exhausted her, yet she couldn't seem to abandon her loyalty to Javi. And she was infuriated to realize that he'd counted on this. He'd trusted that while she would figure out how her tanks had been drained, she would keep his secret. It said something about how well he knew her. Worse, he knew a version of her she didn't like anymore, one she didn't want Dario to see.

Arriving first at the lab brought her some serenity. Morning sun poured through the slatted windows into her office, and she began to answer her emails and texts. After she and Dario had found the dead huachinango off El Saltito beach, she'd asked a few contacts if they'd seen anything similar. Now a dive operator from Cabo

Pulmo had emailed to say he'd found several near the Outer Islands. He'd attached a photo of a fish with four coagulating cuts.

Beni appeared at her office door with a large silver cooler on a hand truck.

"What's this?"

"I went to see my uncles last night. I asked them to keep specimens, like you said."

"How many?"

"Eleven."

"Eleven?" She could hardly believe it.

"Over two days."

"Did they record locations?" She came out from behind her desk.

"Yes."

"Let's get these catalogued," she said. She'd been intending to focus on a new study measuring biomass within the national park. But these fish with the deep gouges were now more than a random oddity. She had to at least satisfy her curiosity.

She followed Beni down the cinder-block hall and used her swipe key to open the door to the main laboratory, a pristine room full of stainless steel surfaces. After they'd washed their hands and put on gloves and lab coats, she opened the cooler and removed the top fish from a macabre pile. It had three gashes on one side, four on the reverse. She mentally ran through the possibilities again. Predator? Outboard motor? Disease? She looked back down into the cooler.

"All huachinangos?"

"One bluechin parrotfish."

The dive operator had found a parrotfish too. Luciana asked Beni to photograph, measure, and store each deceased fish, then returned to her office. She began to make notes, devising a more systematic plan to find out if there were more specimens out there. She'd reach out to her network of researchers, fishermen, and tour guides. She'd revisit any location where more than one wounded fish had been found. She'd look at the current charts.

Her phone pinged with a reminder: she had to go back to the hotel to meet the journalist. She briefly contemplated fobbing off the welcome duties on Dario, who would surely say yes. But no, she had an important first impression to make, so she got up and headed for her truck.

Luciana parked in the shade of a date palm at Casa Azul and walked to the palapa-roofed stucco hut that served as the reception area. As she arrived, a drab black sedan pulled into the parking lot. The man who got out had wide, tawny features and straight black hair, and was dressed more formally than anyone in La Ventana ever did, with closed leather shoes and a button-down shirt tucked into khaki trousers. She went to meet him.

"Tenoch Gomez?"

He gave her a firm handshake and then looked around at their landscaping, which was made up of many types of cacti and a few palms, like he was trying to confirm to himself where he really was.

After introducing herself, Luciana offered to show him to his cabin. "You can get settled, have lunch, and then come down to the lab," she said. "Can I carry something?"

She cast a glance into his car and noticed a wad of damp towel with a dark reddish stain on the passenger seat. She dragged her eyes away to look at him, and realized that he'd seen her notice it. She tried not to look alarmed.

"If you don't mind taking the suitcase, I'll get the rest," he said, and walked back to his trunk, from which he hoisted a cardboard box. "My travelling office."

She lifted his black suitcase onto the flagstone path. The hotel complex was built into a dry arroyo, the path sloping downward from the road to the beachside building that housed the restaurant and Dario's office. White stucco guest cabins were scattered up and down the arroyo, and the one they'd reserved for Tenoch was on their right, halfway down the path.

"How was your drive up?" she asked, still thinking of the dirty towel in his front seat. She only made the long drive to Los Cabos if she had to pick someone up at the airport there.

"Strange, to be honest."

"How so?"

She gestured to his cabin and they climbed the front steps to the porch. He didn't answer right away, so she unlocked and opened the door. Tenoch walked through and set his box down on the floor next to the bed. She was prepared to give the standard spiel about the faucets, fridge, and Wi-Fi, but Tenoch came back out onto the porch and sat heavily on one of its two pink Acapulco chairs.

"I'm sorry," he said. "I'm a little shaken." He balled his left fist into the palm of his right hand.

She took the other chair.

"When I was leaving my house in San José, I found a dead bird in my car."

She pictured a small songbird, some confused creature that had flown in an open window. "I'm so sorry. That must have been disturbing."

"It was a turkey vulture."

"A turkey vulture?" The image was absurd. The turkey vultures that perched in the cardón forests all over the peninsula were hefty creatures, with wingspans of nearly six feet.

"Murdered, actually. Well—is that what you call it, if it's an animal? What I mean is, it wasn't just dead, it had been killed. Throat slit, plus a bullet."

Her mind flashed to her dead huachinangos.

"I threw it in the garbage, and then I tried to clean up my car seat," Tenoch said. "Hence the mess you saw."

"No wonder you're upset."

"It's a threat."

"Do you know why?"

"Some story I wrote, no doubt."

"Did you call the police?"

She heard in her own question the echo of Beni suggesting they call his mother about the empty tanks, which she still hadn't done.

"That's what I was thinking about on the drive. Whether to report it. I don't even know what to call it. Cruelty to wild animals?"

"You should report it."

"I've met some police officers through my work, but—" He broke off with a shrug. "I've only lived here a year."

She understood what he was wondering: Could he trust the police? Would filing a report be worth it?

"I know a detective in La Paz. Ursula Sanchez. I'll give you her number."

He looked at her dubiously.

"You can trust her."

"Okay," Tenoch said, but he didn't sound convinced.

"Her son works for me. And she's a friend."

Tenoch nodded then, and Luciana texted him Ursula's number. She sat with him in silence for another minute, to give him room to say more, but he seemed lost in his own thoughts.

At last, she asked, "Where did you live before Los Cabos?"

"Chiapas." It was their country's southernmost state, some 1,500 miles away. "I had two colleagues who were killed. I changed my byline when I moved."

"You came to Baja to be safer?"

"Yes."

A mutilated bird would have upset anyone, but in Tenoch, Luciana saw, it had also penetrated an existing substrata of dread.

"And have you been safer?"

"I thought I was. Maybe not anymore."

"Call Detective Sanchez," Luciana said.

TWELVE

CATE

EZRA AND I ARE on the muddy bank of the creek behind our house, with metal buckets we copped from the garage. I've upturned one to use as a chair, and so has Ezra, and we've thrown sticks into the bottom of a third. I have a pack of matches I took from the box on top of the fridge, where Wayne and Sabrina keep cigarettes, pipes, and spoons. All of which we're forbidden to touch.

We take turns swiping the match heads along the strip on the outside of the box, just like we've seen our parents do. At first, they don't light, but we're curious and patient. Eventually, a flame erupts from my fingertips with a hiss. I stare at it, entranced, and drop it into the bucket just as I feel the heat. The tiniest twigs catch fire. I light another match and drop it in, and this time, more sticks light up with a crackle. Ezra and I look at each other, then into the bucket. I'm dazzled by the dance of colours, orange and blue and white.

In the following weeks, Ezra and I repeat our ritual with the buckets on the creek bank. We think of new things to burn. Paper blackens and turns into air. Pine branches fizz and smell like Christmas. We try an old plastic toy car, which melts into blue goop, the stench hitting our nostrils with an alien sting. We try a couple of dead bees, which blacken and shrivel. Then a dead mouse from a trap in the basement. It becomes a skeleton and then nothing, invisible amid the ashes. We collect more dead mice and a robin's carcass, and we burn them all up in funeral pyres. I keep my eye out for bigger corpses. Out in the truck with Wayne, I've seen roadkill—raccoons, a dead deer. I mull over how Ezra and I could set one of those bodies on fire, but the logistics evade me.

My eyes hurt and I can't stop coughing. A big man wraps me in a blanket and carries me off. I can't see anything but grey smoke and wonder if I've gone blind. Then I see flames reaching out of the smoke like arms. I'm too hot. I sweat and cry, and the liquid burns my face. I hack and hack, one cough beginning before the last one ends.

Suddenly we're under the night sky. I feel noise and heat and chaos behind me, but I see stars and treetops above. In front of me is a row of ambulances and fire trucks, lit up by flashing lights. The big man hands me to two other grown-ups. They set me on a kind of bed and shine lights in my eyes. They put a plastic thing on my face. It's full of delicious cold air, and suddenly I'm not coughing anymore. I'm staring at our house. I can barely see its crumbling shape inside the biggest fire I've ever seen, a roaring orange monster.

THIRTEEN

LUCIANA

Luciana went for a walk on the beach after dinner, the full moon lighting her way. A hundred yards north of Casa Azul, she pulled up the encrypted messaging app she'd installed that morning while hiding in the bathroom with the door locked. She wondered if these things worked, or if she was incriminating herself by using it. She'd become a scientist to make sense of the world. To solve problems through systematic thinking. Now Javi had introduced chaos.

A few days after the attack, the government had officially designated Reef Pirates a terrorist organization and declared it was seeking the arrest of the group's founder, Javier Sanz. Today, a week after the explosion, while she and Dario were having breakfast, she'd received a text message from an unknown number. "Spam," she'd remarked, even as a cold feeling in her gut told her she was the intended recipient. On closer examination, the message contained a link to download something called Neofone.

She'd spent the rest of the day fighting a rising sense of panic. She'd gone to the lab, knowing no one else would be there on a Sunday. She'd lain down on the floor of her office with her fingertips pressed to her eyelids and tried to articulate to herself what she feared most.

Javi had used her tanks to assault the *Bizan-maru*, and she hadn't reported it. So, however tacitly and retroactively, she'd supported the action. Given material aid to a terrorist organization. She could go to jail. Not see a living fish for years. She wondered if it made her selfish, that she feared imprisonment above all. But her fear wasn't purely self-interested. If the Gutierrez Centre for Marine Studies was discovered to have aided and abetted terrorists, all its work would be tainted. The reputation of any scientist who'd ever based a study at her lab would suffer. The centre would have to close.

Her nerves buzzed like faulty wiring as she walked north along the beach. In the last week, she'd had dozens of imaginary conversations with Javi, ranging in tone from plaintive to furious. Now she stabbed her phone with her forefinger.

"Lulu," he answered.

"You call me that like you care." She was shaking with anger.

He sighed, deep and heavy. She heard church bells on his end of the line. A town square, a Sunday evening Mass. She pictured him: sun-streaked hair, bone carving at his neck, T-shirt faded and thin.

"I do. That's why I sent you the link." His voice was so familiar, it could have come from inside her own head. She'd heard it deliver a hundred speeches and even more intimacies.

"What you did could destroy the lab. It could get me sent to jail."

"Let's talk in person."

A part of her had still hoped he would deny it, even though he'd taken responsibility for all the internet to see. He was a wanted man.

"Like hell," she said. The church bell tolled. Her mind flickered to an oasis, a campground. "I don't want your secrets."

They were both silent. She realized how fast she'd been walking as she approached the hot springs. A couple of small groups sat around pools they'd dug, feet in the warm water. At a distance, their headlamps bobbed like fireflies in the dark. She gave them a wide berth.

"So you only called to berate me?"

"You deserve it."

"Maybe so."

His calm needled her—he was too canny now to be baited. That was one way he'd changed since they'd met as teens, shortly after his family moved to La Paz. Then he'd engaged in every fight—personal, familial, environmental—and both girls and boys loved him for it. Now he picked his battles. He thought in terms of strategy and alliances. Even, apparently, when it came to her. She realized then that he wanted something more from her. Some favour in the future, or maybe just her silence. His calm in the face of her fury, and his mollifying words, meant that in some small measure, he feared she could turn on him.

But she also wanted something from him, and it had nothing to do with the *Bizan-maru*. Reef Pirates, she knew, had been amassing satellite surveillance equipment for years. It had hacked foreign fishing fleets. It now had a better ability than any organization outside the navy to track ships in the Sea of Cortez.

She sat down on a rock at the surf's edge and watched water wash over her sandalled feet. "I need information."

"I want to help."

"Are there any factory fishing ships within a hundred miles of La Ventana?"

He was silent.

"I know you track them. Since the *Bizan-maru*, everyone knows you track them."

"Lulu!"

"Suddenly so cautious with me," she said, unable to contain a spike of sarcasm. "I just need to know if there are any around here, and how long they've been in place."

He didn't answer. With wonderment, she understood that he really thought she might betray him.

"If your bullshit with my shed was some kind of loyalty test, I think I passed."

"Why do you need to know?"

"I'm finding these dead huachinangos with an injury. Or maybe a disease. Gash marks, usually four or five, on both sides of the body."

The quality of his silence shifted.

"Have you seen what I'm talking about? Or heard about it?"

"Go on."

"I've found thirty-four in just over a week, and I wasn't even looking. A few here in Ventana Bay, a few near Cerralvo, more by the Outer Islands. The current's moving them around."

"You think they're discarded bycatch," he said.

"At first, I thought maybe an outboard. But the pattern of injuries is odd. And why this many?"

"Could be a factory ship," he said slowly. "Their machines are disgustingly wasteful. They spit out all kinds of bycatch."

"Exactly."

He was delaying. Maybe he'd chosen the site of his next attack. Even as she wanted him to trust her, she wasn't sure if he should. She waited him out in silence.

"I only know of two ships," he finally said. "One's been in the far north for a month. Almost to San Felipe. The other is off Mulegé."

Luciana toed the damp sand with her rubber sandal. Both sites were too far for their discards to show up here. Unless there was a closer ship, her theory looked weak.

Javi had decided to trust her, though. She considered asking after his well-being, as though this was a normal conversation. She wondered if his parents knew where he was. For a foolish second, she almost offered to be a go-between.

But she would do no such thing. She had to protect her lab and her work. Javi now had two human lives on his hands. And because of him, so did she. She did not want to have the conversation in which he justified their deaths as the cost of protecting something bigger.

"What are you going to do?" she asked at last.

"Keep going."

She imagined his defiant expression. "I shouldn't even be talking with you."

"Lulu."

She felt an unwanted surge of warmth in her chest. "Don't call me that."

"We still want the same things."

"But we haven't been stronger together in a long time."

FOURTEEN

CATE

I made myself an espresso and waited impatiently for Felix, who had messaged to say he had my answer. Out the window, across the sound, the Olympic mountains made a jagged outline on the horizon. When I'd first come to Seattle, they'd always been snow-covered in the winter, but now, only the highest peaks remained white.

When Felix arrived, I took him into my home office, where he propped a tablet on my desk and brought it to life.

"Number 98 is Hunter Brandt," he said. "Would you like to see a photograph?"

My skin prickled. In the lab you learn not to trust a guess, no matter how true it feels. Get too attached to a theory before it's proven, and it could bias the research.

I'd wanted it to be Hunter, and also hadn't. In the days since Felix had started digging, I'd remembered a hike, and a group of us in the woods. An accident. Worried adults—Dr. M, Willow, Eden, the nurses—herding us back to our places. Hunter somehow at the centre of it all.

Felix took my silence for a yes. He swiped at the tablet and a face appeared, a professional portrait scavenged from the dead web link of a venture capital firm. Neat black hair, prominent cheekbones, a winning smile. A touch of grey at his temples, tie knotted at his throat. It was the boy I remembered, now a man in his late thirties, with crow's feet and looser skin. I looked for the scar and spied it, a pale line running from eyebrow to hairline. I studied the grey eyes as though I could find some feeling in them, as though they were animate.

"Do you have more?"

Felix swiped to a collage. A photo from a university yearbook showed a lanky young man. There were athletic shots—he'd windsurfed, run track. I asked where Hunter Brandt was now.

"Until two and a half years ago, I have his employers, his company, his ISP server."

I told Felix what Dr. M had told me: two and a half years ago, Number 98 had pulled out of extended monitoring.

"Monitoring?"

The study he was part of, I explained. He told the study supervisors he didn't want to be contacted anymore.

"Did something happen to him?" I asked.

"There would be records if he'd passed away."

I felt inordinately relieved. Then I asked myself why I cared. When Sissy had emailed to let me know that Calliope had been killed in a car accident, I'd felt nothing. But Calliope wasn't like me.

"So where was he two and a half years ago?"

"Around here. He lived on Capitol Hill, and his company was in South Park. They were developing nuclear fusion."

I was pleased and impressed that Hunter had had a grand ambition, which caught me off guard. I remembered what Dr. M had said, that the young Number 98 wanted to invent *a creation that would save us from ourselves*. I was unsettled at how near to me he'd been, building up his company while I built up mine.

"I wasn't familiar with fusion," Felix said. "Are you?"

"Just the headlines."

I knew that in fusion, multiple atoms merge together, giving off a burst of energy in the process. Fusion is what makes the sun shine. But though many companies and governments were trying, no one had successfully harnessed fusion for practical use.

"This is what Hunter Brandt was trying to do. He had

investors, even a client." Felix hesitated, then went on. "He seems to have overpromised."

Almost three years previously, Felix explained, a client and an investor had launched lawsuits against Hunter's company, and Hunter, in turn, had declared bankruptcy. This made me think of the moment, about four years after launching Alphaneuro, when Jia and I thought we wouldn't get another round of funding. Investor after potential investor told us we were too far from our goal, that it was taking too long, that it sounded to them like amyloid was the better path. I remember thinking that four years of my life might as well have evaporated. It angered me when one of our funders made it clear that we were just another bet in his portfolio. When I told him he lacked the vision to boil water, much less advance human knowledge, Jia temporarily banished me from investor meetings. My deficiently emotional heart went out to Hunter again when I learned of his company's troubles.

After the bankruptcy, Felix said, Hunter took down all his social media profiles. Closed his bank accounts. Ended his leases. And legally changed his name to Hunter Araya.

"Araya?"

"I don't know where he got the name. He may have pulled it out of thin air." Felix paused, brow furrowed. "He officially changed his driver's licence to the new name, and then—"

"What?"

"Then I couldn't find anything more. Not in New York or California or here."

"Maybe he hasn't bought anything?

"You can't hide from the databases. I should have been able to find something. A lease, a phone, a health record. He seemed to have just disappeared."

I picked up on the way he phrased it. "Seemed?"

"Since there was no record of Hunter Brandt or Hunter Araya being deceased, I looked farther away. And I found something."

I was jittery with impatience.

"Assuming it's the same man, he's registered as the owner of a business," Felix said with an air of triumph.

"Where?"

"A resort in southern Baja."

I thought of Gabriel, who had gone to Baja after our breakup and waxed beatific about it the next time we spoke.

"That makes no sense. Why would Hunter go from a fusion company to a resort?"

Felix turned up his hands. "It's possible it's not the same man."

But how many men named Hunter Araya could there be?

"I have a theory," Felix said, sounding hesitant.

"Tell me."

"I have family in Tijuana. Baja has problems getting enough electricity, and this guy was in the energy industry. Maybe he had business down there."

I suddenly felt more focused than I had in months. Brandt, Araya, whoever he was, hadn't merely survived Cleckley. He'd been trying to transform our way of life.

"Do you have an address for this resort? A name?"

"Dr. Winter, if I may ask . . ."

"Yes, Felix." I tried to appear patient.

"Who is he to you?"

I was awash in discomfort. By inviting Felix to research Number 98, I'd invited him to examine me too.

I explained that Hunter and I had a connection dating back to when we were kids. That we'd shared a teacher.

"Archibald Montrose," Felix offered.

I felt exposed. "Yes."

"When someone wants someone else found, if it's not money or revenge they want, it's something personal."

"I'm not seeking money or revenge."

"Dr. Winter," he began again. Felix was inside my perimeter now, like the forward party of an invading force. "He's trying not to be found. He erased his whole background. In my experience, it's best not to contact people who do something like that."

If Number 98 hadn't turned out to be Hunter. If Hunter hadn't been the only other Cleckley alum to live a life like mine. If I hadn't been on the brink of change, my attention ready to be captured by something new.

If any of these factors had been different, I might not have become quite so consumed. But as it was, hemmed in by the pending sale and Jia's admonishments, I had plenty of time to search for more information.

In the week after Felix gave me Hunter's new name, I found a couple of stories that mentioned him on Baja news sites. One included details about the number of rooms (120) and amenities (swimming pools, docks, golf course) at his resort. The stories called him an entrepreneur "from the mainland," but I couldn't find any record of Hunter Araya prior to him buying the land.

I read everything I could find about the surrounding area. Places with names like Cabo Pulmo, Punta Arena, La Ventana, and Los Barriles, clustered around the east side of the southern end of the peninsula, where the Sea of Cortez meets the Pacific Ocean. I set up search alerts to find more stories. I began to imagine this place where Hunter now lived, its sandy roads and turquoise water.

I went to the office. I met with Jia, Al, and Wen, and displayed the requisite interest in the negotiations. I went to the lab to check progress on a study of proteins in organoids, which felt pointless since I knew I would soon pass oversight to my company's new owners. I went home and searched the internet.

When our deal to sell Alphaneuro was all but publicly announced, one of my search alerts popped up a new piece. It said that in the Alvariño National Marine Park and thereabouts, fish were turning up dead with unusual frequency, apparently from some kind of disease. Mostly red snappers. The story was by a reporter named Tenoch Gomez, and it quoted a local marine biologist, Luciana Gutierrez, who was investigating the phenomenon. She pleaded for the state government and a nearby university to help fund "urgently needed" research. She referred to the fish die-off as a "scientific mystery."

In the early stages of discovery, some instinct and guessing are always involved. You have to come up with a hypothesis to test. And sometimes your brain is working towards something before you even know it. During those fervent internet searches, I was subconsciously working towards something. At least, that's how it seems when I look back now.

FIFTEEN

CATE

A WOMAN SITS IN the back of the car with me, while a man drives us along a highway through the mountains. We're going to my grandmother's house, the woman says, but that doesn't bring up any image or feeling, so I don't reply. I look out the window at all the evergreens passing by, thinking about how far we're going. I should keep track of where I am, but it's hard when I keep getting handed around.

The town is called Roslyn. The house is painted a pleasant shade of yellow and has a garden in front. A slim woman with steel-grey hair comes out, and I think, *Yes, I've met her before.* When she crouches down to look at me, I see that she has tears on her face. She stands up and takes me by the hand.

After the man and woman leave, we sit on the blue couch in my grandmother's very neat living room,

"You can call me Grandma or Ida," she says.

She shows me pictures of the last time we met, and I try to remember, but I was only three. We were in a playground.

To my unspoken question, she says, "Your mom had a sickness in her brain." She puts the album down on the coffee table. "She didn't want you and me to see each other."

Over time, I go through all the drawers and cupboards in the kitchen, but Grandma Ida doesn't seem to have any matches. Then it's Thanksgiving, and she's having friends over, and she sets out candles on the dining room table. I'm staring at them when she reappears with a box of matches.

"Can I light them?"

She looks at me, pauses. "Do you know how?"

I nod.

"Okay, then." She watches me as I light a match on the first try. Afterwards, she puts the matchbox in her pocket.

Grandma Ida has a room where she does her bookkeeping work. She's never told me to stay out of it, but I know it's her private space. One day she goes outside to water her flower beds, and as soon as she turns on the hose, I march up the stairs to her office door and twist the knob. I think it's just sticky at first, and give it a jiggle, only to realize it's locked. I'm so surprised I almost run outside to ask her why. Now I'm sure she keeps the matches in there.

When she's working, she usually leaves her office door open. I take to lurking nearby for a minute or two before I announce my presence. This is how I hear her say, "She set a fire that killed two people." Explicit and mysterious, they seed a vine that will wind through everything else.

When she gets off the phone, I step into the doorway, and she looks up at me.

"I miss Ezra," I say.

"Oh, honey," she says, and comes and gives me a hug.

Two women take turns coming to Grandma Ida's house to talk to me about the fire, which neither Ezra nor my mother survived. One of the women wants to put a lot of specific facts in order, and I try to help her do that. She asks me the same questions over and over. The other one is much less clear about what she wants, and I find her lack of direction frustrating. I don't know how I'm supposed to please her.

There's a third grown-up who has questions. He asks me if there's anything good about the changes that have happened in my life, and I say I got out of that house, at least, and so did everybody else, even Ezra, in a way.

My questioners, and their questions, start to blend together.

The more I repeat an answer, the more confidently I speak. I understand that we're creating a story.

But when I'm alone after our conversations, thinking about what I said, I realize I no longer know if I remember certain things, like why Ezra and I got locked in the closet, or if there were really two smaller fires at the house before the big one. On some facts, I'm clear, but others seem malleable. My memories are like the dots in a dot-to-dot puzzle. I can follow the order of the numbers and get the picture I'm supposed to get. But I can also ignore the instructions and instead connect the dots in a completely different way. I can turn what was supposed to be a whale into a starfish, or a wolf into a bear. Without the connective tissue, I can assemble the dots into anything I want. What I want right now is to please, and be praised, and not have to move again.

SIXTEEN

GABRIEL

Paseo de la Reforma was even louder than normal during his walk to work. Election vans had burst into the city seemingly overnight, with garish blow-ups of candidates' faces plastered on their sides and loudspeakers blaring promises that drowned one another out.

Gabriel ordered a large coffee in the back of Cuauhtémoc Market and carried it with him as he checked through security in the embassy annex and climbed the stairs to his office. He started most days by reading new reports from around the region, which extended south through Central America and east through the Caribbean. They all focused on dangers affecting animals, typically pathogens that were behaving in a new or vexing way. Before putting his phone in a drawer, Gabriel sent a text to Penelope wishing her an excellent day, so she would get it when she awoke, as was now their morning routine.

He was about to close the drawer on his phone when it rang. Penelope was awake early, he thought—then looked at the name that popped up, one he hadn't seen in months. In surprise and confusion, he answered.

"How's Mexico City?" Cate asked.

Why had he answered the phone? Yet why shouldn't he have? Gabriel's startled thoughts tumbled over one another. Since he'd moved away a year earlier, they'd been in occasional touch by email. The last time he'd seen her in person, over coffee in Seattle, he'd felt consciously grateful that the drama of his Cate-inspired highs and lows was behind him. Now they could just be normal. Friends.

So why did her voice still have this bracing effect?

"Gabe?"

"Sorry, just surprised. It's great here. Really great. Just great." He urged himself not to babble.

"I found a scientific mystery for you," she said.

"Oh really?" It was just the sort of thing she would consider a gift: a difficult puzzle.

She launched into a story she'd read online about a researcher in Baja and some deceased fish. The Sea of Cortez had numerous problems with overfishing, many of which Gabriel was familiar with, and few of which had anything to do with his work, which focused mostly on disease. Having recovered from his initial surprise, he listened to Cate to be amiable. He'd seen her do this, become briefly possessed by some phenomenon that happened to cross her radar. Like space debris, or the first computer to beat humans at Go.

"They're just turning up dead?" he asked. Typically, a species faded more quietly.

"She's found hundreds of them. Read the story."

To appease her, and because hundreds of unexplained fish corpses did sound peculiar, he said he would.

"How did you end up reading about it?"

"Do you want the long version or the short version?"

"Let's have the short one. I've got a lot on my plate."

"We're going to this town called La Ventana. I'm reading up on the area."

"We?"

He couldn't help it. The word made his stomach lurch.

"Jia and me. We're renting a house."

He exhaled with a relief he refused to examine. But he was still perplexed.

"Like a vacation?" he asked. A beach-town vacation sounded unlike her.

"Mostly. Partly. We sold the company, so we're taking a trip. To celebrate."

"Wait, you sold? Congratulations! You two worked so hard for this." He felt genuinely glad, and the uncomplicated purity of this emotion pleased him. He didn't want anything from her, except for her to be well. And so he didn't push on the "mostly, partly."

Still, her fish story interested him. After he got off the phone, he clicked on the news link she sent. After reading that, he searched Luciana Gutierrez, the scientist reporting the die-off, and then reviewed several papers about the Pacific red snapper. In the middle of the afternoon, he called and spoke to Dr. Gutierrez herself. And at the end of the day, he composed a memo to his boss, Marta, detailing a surprising onset of fish mortality off Baja's East Cape.

SEVENTEEN

CATE

After the deal to sell our company closed, I had my hairdresser come to the kitchen of my apartment, where she did away with my bob and left me with a shiny blond cap. It was my first act of extravagance as a wealthy person. After she left, a florist arrived and placed tall ceramic vases with curling white branches around the place. Jia's assistant, Rebecca, turned up at four, followed by five caterers, a DJ, and a three-piece jazz band. I changed into a black jumpsuit and pointy gold sandals. Jia got there before any of the other guests, to help, but Rebecca and the caterers already had things handled, so we hid out from all the activity in my home office. It had a view of a construction crane, which, though it was nearly March, was still decorated with blue and white lights that spelled out "Happy New Year."

I'd proposed Baja for our celebratory jaunt, and Jia was easy to persuade once I showed her photos of the beaches and the shrimp tacos. I had a ticket for ten days and she had one for six. Now that we'd made it all the way through the sale, I wanted to tell her the truth about my past, for the same reason I'd eventually told Gabriel: I wanted to be known. I planned to finally fill in that moat of missing knowledge while we were hanging around our rented beach house. I didn't expect it to be easy, but I thought it would be less difficult now that my past wouldn't affect her future.

Our colleagues—former colleagues—arrived with spouses and friends, and with cards and gifts, dressed in suits and slinky dresses

I'd never seen before. Jia spoke, I spoke, and board members made toasts. After the speeches, the DJ took over. Shareholding scientists cut loose, much richer than they'd been three days earlier. Some planned to give themselves sabbaticals or reconnect with their families. Some wanted to keep right on working. Dr. M, chatting in the corner to a husband-wife pair of physicists, bobbed his head to the music.

Everyone wanted to talk to me. People told me it must be bittersweet, and I said yes, of course. A half dozen asked me what was next, which frankly seemed a little premature. As drug developers, they knew better; you couldn't just whip up a new medicine. For the first two years after launching Alphaneuro, I'd studied a single molecule that had turned out to be a dead end. But being asked what was next also frustrated me because I wanted to know the answer too.

I had feared the evening might feel interminable, but it was over in an instant. The caterers transitioned from pouring glasses to collecting them, and the DJ ceded sound back to the jazz musicians. Our guests started to leave. I had just said goodbye to the new sixth-floor lab director, wishing him good luck with the mouse supply, when I turned around to find Dr. M. He'd arrived early with a bouquet of white lilies, which was entirely in character, but it was unlike him to stay so late. He was waiting to get me alone, I realized. I beckoned him into my office and closed the door.

"Jia mentioned that you're looking for someone involved in one of my studies. She seemed to assume I would know what she meant."

While this sunk in, I motioned for him to sit down. I should have considered this angle.

He bent his tall frame into a leather easy chair and put his head in his hands, while I took the seat opposite him.

"You're looking for him," he said.

"What did you expect?"

"Dammit, Cate, it's not right."

"You've spent all this time studying our lack of empathy. But what about empathy for us? Didn't you think knowing about someone like Hunter"—he flinched at my use of the name—"might have made me feel less alone?"

He looked stricken. "It very much crossed my mind. But there are so many factors." He examined his hands. "There are things I'm responsible for." He stood up and paced to the window, through which he observed the Happy New Year crane and the towers beyond it. He returned to his chair. "You needed to satisfy some curiosity, and I presume you have. Hunter exists. For reasons of his own, he chose to cut off contact. Please let that be enough for you."

"How much do you actually know about him?"

He hesitated, so I went on.

"Did you know he had a fusion company that went bankrupt? That he was living in Seattle?"

Dr. M shook his head, not a denial but a refusal to hear more.

"What if he also thinks he's the only one?"

"He *asked* not to be contacted."

"What if I asked you not to contact me? Would you just abandon me?"

"Of course not."

"I haven't contacted him," I said. True statement. The house I'd rented was less than an hour's drive from Hunter's resort, but I didn't have a plan for beyond when I arrived in Baja. "What's wrong with just knowing more?"

"You won't leave it at that. And you don't know what he does or doesn't know."

"About me? How would he know anything about me? Unless you shared data with him too." The accusation tumbled out.

"Nonsense."

"Then what's the big deal?"

He rubbed his forehead. "You're seeking Hunter because you think he's like you. I take some blame for your feelings of isolation. Maybe there are ways we could have handled that differently at Cleckley, some kind of program of social support . . ." He trailed off. "And I let you study your own classmates. That was my decision." Another pause. "But you're not going to learn what you want to learn by contacting Hunter."

"Do you even understand what I want?"

"You want to know that your biology and background are not your destiny."

"He inflicted violence on people when he was a child, like me. But he overcame his past, like me. He started a company, like me. He's advancing fusion. Fusion! Or at least he was. I want to know what happened."

Dr. M looked at me quizzically. And then his blue eyes became unfocused, and he paused for so long that it became uncanny. Finally, he snapped back.

"Cate, we're here celebrating because you've done something extraordinary. You don't need someone else to prove what you are or are not."

But what if I let go of the controls? I wanted to ask. Who would I be then? Would I be Sissy, with her pointless petty crimes? Calliope, dead from her own stupid decisions? I needed to see Hunter up close to understand how he reconciled his past actions with his life now. To expand my own mental range of possibilities.

Dr. M broke into my thoughts. "You need some kind of break, obviously. Can't you go somewhere else?"

I looked at him. I felt the realization as a jolt in my body before I logically understood the implication of his words. He didn't just know I was looking for Hunter. He knew where I was going, and why.

"Somewhere else?"

"Jia said you're going to Baja."

"I thought you didn't know where Hunter was," I said, hearing the tone in my voice. Judgmental. I crossed my arms and waited for him to speak. There was a babble of voices outside my study door. The caterers leaving. Rebecca taking their invoice and saying good-bye. This was wealth, I supposed. Having people to manage people, even in your own home.

"It's easier not to keep secrets," I said. "Isn't that what you always taught us?"

"The Biennial Conference on Cognitive Neuroscience."

"What about it?" It was an academic conference I'd attended a couple of times.

"It was at a hotel in Los Cabos last year. One year after Hunter disappeared."

I felt impatient.

"My talk was on long-term outcomes for adolescents treated for psychopathy. It was well attended, which I mention because it made the hall very crowded. During the question session, there were lines at both microphones, and the lights they point at the stage are rather bright, so I couldn't see who was next in line until it was his turn to speak."

We looked at each other.

"I nearly jumped when I saw it was him. I barely had time to compose myself. He asked if there were any subjects left out of my final conclusions. I was a bit stunned, but given the large audience, I tried to answer in a normal fashion. I said that of course there were some outliers, but I'd eliminated them from the results, as there were too few to be of statistical significance. He left the microphone. I wanted dearly to follow him, but there were more questioners in line, so I stayed put.

"After the presentation I went to the conference registration desk, but they wouldn't give me a list of attendees. I walked through the poster board presentations, the dining room, out to the swimming pool, all over. I even asked the concierge if he'd seen a man of Hunter's description."

I waited for him to go on.

He opened his palms. "I didn't find him. He didn't try to reach me in any other way. It was"—he paused—"unsettling."

I felt sure that Dr. M was leaving something out.

"So that made you think he's living in Baja?"

"You tell me."

I owed him better than games. "It seems that way."

"Then you know more than I do at this point," Dr. M said wearily. "Do you remember him as a boy?"

"Yes. He sometimes came to dinners at your house." I remembered the night after a snowstorm, everything soft and shimmering.

"That's right. Do you remember field week?"

"Yeah." It had been an annual week of outdoor skills for "good" Cleckley students. I must have gone three times. We canoed and hiked and built fires and had to get ourselves from the woods back to our cabins using a compass. And my favourite activity, easily the top memory of my Cleckley years: jumping off a rope swing into the lake as many times as I wanted, until I was waterlogged and shivering.

"Cate, I have obligations to our former students that you don't have. That includes my obligations to you."

"And to Hunter."

"Correct. There are also things I just don't know. Because I can't know. Do you understand? We want facts, but sometimes we don't get them. Do you remember the field week during which there was a terrible accident?"

It took me only a moment to recall. The memory wasn't buried. It was just sitting there, filed in a mental cabinet I never bothered to open.

"Terry," I said. "He died."

"Yes."

"Hiking, right? Did he fall down a cliff?"

"Yes."

Terry had had stiff brown hair that never seemed to lie down, a bow-legged gait, and a silver charm of some saint that he always wore around his neck. He'd died two decades ago. I tried to remember what I'd felt then. I felt nothing now. It was as though Dr. M were narrating a documentary that I happened to be in.

"The thing is, Cate, I can't be sure of what happened." Dr. M rested a palm on each thigh. Eventually he looked away, back out the window, then down at his hands. "I don't know. Not for certain."

"What are you trying to tell me?"

The bowl that contained my adolescence seemed to crack.

"That I have a feeling. Please don't go."

"My plane leaves in thirty-six hours."

We met each other's gaze, and his blue eyes exposed him. He wanted something too: information.

"Maybe I can fill in some of those holes."

"I would never ask you to do that."

I think I knew then that an irreversible shift had occurred. I'd been warned, or invited into some sort of pact. I didn't yet understand the meaning of our conversation, but I couldn't pretend it had never happened.

Neither of us were in the habit of hugging, but for some reason he gave me a long squeeze when we said good night in my foyer.

I thought he wanted to protect me from a merely psychological blow.

EIGHTEEN

GABRIEL

The morning after flying to Baja, Gabriel piloted his rental car, a retrofitted electric Bug, along La Ventana's main road. The morning sky was already a surreally bright blue. The air seemed to contain more oxygen than Mexico City air, and probably actually did, between the lower elevation and the lack of air pollution.

Many of Gabriel's happiest moments, as well as the one that had cost him clear vision in his left eye, had been on, in, or around the sea. When he was nine years old, snorkelling not far from home off of California's Point Lobos State Park, a juvenile white shark had bitten him in the face. Its teeth had penetrated his eyeball. The scarring on his iris and cornea were permanent, and Gabriel had forever since worn a patch in bright light unless he had on sunglasses.

But the accident never deterred him from enjoying the water. And this particular shoreline, along the Sea of Cortez, was where he had come back to himself after his breakup with Cate. Once, up near Mulegé, he'd slept in a cave that overlooked the water, and woken to a trio of grey whales spouting mist from their blowholes. A pair of fishermen had come along and warned him to get back to the beach before high tide cut off his egress.

After he'd talked to Dr. Gutierrez on the phone, she'd emailed him photographs, numbers, and dates. When he reported his findings to Marta, she told him to go find out what was happening—if nothing else, to assure themselves that this ailment, whatever it was, wasn't going to spread. Cholera in humans, she reminded the team, had originated as bacteria in coastal waters. And Gutierrez, operating as she did on a tenuous scaffold of grants, was grateful to have another expert set of eyes on her conundrum at no cost to herself.

As Gabriel waited to turn left off the main road, a van with a megaphone whined by, exhorting everyone within hearing range to vote for Francisco Iguaro on March 12, only ten days away. By the sound of it, Iguaro was running for governor of the state of Baja California Sur. Red letters on the side of the van said "Light Up Baja!"

The ear-crackling noise receded, and Gabriel pulled the Bug onto a sandy patch in front of a one-storey white building near the south end of town. A modest metal plaque indicated that this was the Gutierrez Centre for Marine Studies.

A teenage receptionist in board shorts, a tank top, and a carved bone pendant introduced himself as Beni and led Gabriel down a dim corridor with concrete floors and white walls. He settled Gabriel in an office where slatted windows admitted slices of bright light. A large monitor dominated the desk in the middle of the room, and one wall was covered with a poster showing "Fish Species of the Eastern Pacific." As he took a seat, he heard a torrent of words coming down the hall. Then she was in front of him, small and loud, deeply tanned, in a slicked-back ponytail and neoprene shoes. He felt like a giant next to her. She took him in, thankfully showing no reaction at the sight of his eye patch.

"So, this is your job?"

"To look for novel animal pathogens, yes. Mostly marine, in my case."

"We don't know if it's a pathogen yet."

"Fair enough. Consider me a resource."

She raised her eyebrows at him as though to ask, *You're all I get?* Then her eyes went to the door, as a man with a smooth face and straight black hair edged into the room.

"Perhaps you've met?" Luciana asked. "Tenoch is staying at Casa Azul as well."

But Gabriel didn't recognize the other man, who was dressed in khakis and a tucked-in madras shirt.

"Tenoch is a reporter with *El Diario*."

Gabriel shook his hand, quickly making the connection. "I read your story about the die-off. That's how I first learned about it."

"I'm glad someone did. Now I'm working on a longer piece on the subject."

"He came to write a happy story about the national park, and did so, very nicely," Luciana said. "Then I saddled him with this mystery."

Gabriel had mixed feelings about seeing Tenoch here. For the kind of frontline work he did now, media reports could be essential, alerting the scientific community to strange phenomena. But he was leery about making journalists privy to the messy middle of scientific research, given that they were so likely to emphasize the dramatic example over the data.

Luciana gathered the two men behind her while she sat down at her desktop screen and pulled up a map. The town of La Ventana lay along a bay the shape of a cradle in the bottom left quadrant of her screen. Punto Arena marked the bay's southeastern limit. North of there, Cerralvo Island floated in the sea, while to the south, towns and villages dotted the cape like a string of pearls: Cabo Pulmo, Los Barriles, San José del Cabo. To the east, in the Sea of Cortez, bobbed a scattering of smaller islands. Dominating the centre of her screen was a lopsided triangle, superimposed on the water in a darker blue.

"The new national marine park," Luciana said.

Gabriel knew that she'd been instrumental in its creation. Something about seeing its thousands of square miles laid out on a map, every life within it newly sheltered, was very moving.

She clicked and several clusters of red dots appeared on the screen, both within and outside the national park's boundaries.

"The sites where we've found the dead fish."

Gabriel bent to scrutinize the screen. "What are these?" he

asked, pointing to several yellow shapes towards the eastern side of her map.

"We call them the Outer Islands," Luciana said. "We wanted to make them part of the national park, but they belong to private owners. It's a political issue, actually. The incumbent governor, Villalobos, wants to take them out of private hands and give them over to the park."

"Is there anything on them?" Tenoch asked.

"No permanent human habitation. Fishermen build camps and use them for a few nights at a time. But mostly the inhabitants are wild animals. Here"—she pointed to a barely visible speck—"there's a colony of sea lions. And here"—she pointed to an island shaped like a boomerang—"nesting pelicans."

"The dots," Gabriel said.

"One for every ten specimens found in a location. After I realized that outboard motors didn't make sense, I thought we were looking at some kind of parasite."

"But?"

"We began to find more types of dead fish. Wrasses, barracudas, pufferfish. All within a certain size. I didn't think a single parasite would afflict so many species."

"What about hypoxia?" Gabriel asked. Global warming was reducing the amount of oxygen in wide swathes of ocean.

"We're running chemical tests to be sure, but the markings don't make sense."

Gabriel looked at the clusters of dots, but they made no real pattern. "What do the locations say?"

"We don't know. I need to do an analysis with current charts to see how the corpses are moving."

Luciana stood to her full height, which put her several inches shorter than Tenoch and a full head shorter than Gabriel. "I'll show you the lab."

They walked down the concrete hall to a heavy-looking door, which she opened with a swipe card. The air-conditioned space inside was lined with shiny white tile and stainless steel. One wall contained a series of computer monitors and another was dominated by a row of glass-front refrigerators. Beyond a glass partition, a man and a woman in white lab coats worked at side-by-side biosafety cabinets.

"We began photographing each example," Luciana said as she moved across the room. "We're aiming to necropsy at least one of each species." She swung open the heavy door to one of the refrigerators and removed a foot-long Pyrex box, which she carried to a stainless steel table and set in front of Gabriel and Tenoch. She removed the lid and the astringent, familiar, slightly sickening smell of formaldehyde stung Gabriel's nostrils, underlaid by something salty and rotten.

The box contained a single foot-long huachinango, its bright-pinkish hue faded by death. Four vertical gash marks lay parallel on the corpse as though put there by a giant claw, each a mosaic of congealed blood and ripped flesh. Any single cut that deep could have killed the fish; with four, it didn't stand a chance.

Gabriel stared at it, his mind flipping through possibilities, coming up with nothing that matched his experience.

"Gloves?"

She held out a box of latex gloves and he snapped a pair on. He picked up the fish and carefully turned it over to study a similar set of gash marks, less deep but just as unnaturally symmetrical, on the reverse. He studied these for a minute and then turned the fish back to its original position, slipping off the gloves.

"Still no viruses or chemicals?"

"None. And internal organs look normal."

"Could they be discarded bycatch?"

She hesitated. He looked up and saw consternation pass over her face.

"As far as I can establish, there aren't any factory ships near enough."

"How many are you up to now?"

"We've collected four hundred and eighty-two."

She put the lid back on the Pyrex box and replaced it in the fridge, then with a flick of her hand, gestured for the two men to follow her to a computer monitor.

"A catalogue," she said, as a colour image of another dead fish appeared on the screen. A small parrotfish, rainbow-skinned when alive but greyer in the photograph. Three parallel gash marks. She clicked and another image appeared, this time one of the myriad kinds of boxfish that inhabited these waters. Speckled, with four gash marks. Some of the bigger fish had five.

"What do you think, Doctor?" Tenoch asked Gabriel.

But he didn't think anything yet. It had been a long time since he'd been confronted by something so mysterious. He turned to Luciana. "I think," he said slowly, aware of the journalist's poised pen. "I think this bears further investigation. Do you have a place I can work?"

NINETEEN

CATE

DR. M BRINGS ME into a room full of toys. He sits with me at a child-height table, long legs outstretched, while Grandma Ida and another doctor watch us through one-way glass. I'm wearing a blue smock dress. There are wooden cars, a fire truck, and dolls in the room, but I'm most drawn to an abacus with bright-coloured beads.

Dr. M doesn't ask me anything about my mom, Ezra, or the big fire. He shows me drawings of a panda bear family in various situations and asks what they make me feel. Then he shows me photographs of children's faces and asks me what those kids feel. He puts a cookie out and tells me that if I leave it alone while he leaves the room, I can have a second cookie upon his return. As soon as he explains this, I seek a third way: I go around the low table and stick my hand in his jacket pocket. It's empty.

When Dr. M leaves the room, I ignore the cookie just fine. I pick up a doll with brown wool hair and a sailor outfit on its floppy body. I take the head in one hand and the body in the other, and twist with so much determination that the threads holding the head onto the torso tense and fray and ultimately snap. White stuffing spills out of the doll's throat. I'm not a screamer or a crier, but this is my scream and cry. It's my vengeance on myself for the fire.

Dr. M comes back and folds down into the child-high seat.

"Why did you remove the doll's head?"

I don't answer.

"Are you mad?"

I nod.

"You're not a bad kid, you know. You're not in trouble."

He sets the promised second cookie on the plate, next to my first. But I ignore them both just to show him I can. To show him I have some control over this whole situation, which of course I don't. I'm performing, trying to manipulate, with no idea where it will all lead.

The doll decapitation is not the grounds for my diagnosis. Nor is the way I respond to the face photos or the panda family, nor my preoccupation with the abacus. It's that calculating quality, a watchfulness with the aim of seeking my own advantage, that catches his attention.

He and a nurse take me into a blindingly white room. I have to lie down on a platform and hold very still. They give me headphones that play music, but I can still hear the mechanical screech. The platform moves, and my body glides headfirst into a tube. The brain scan seals my fate.

TWENTY

GABRIEL

Gabriel stifled a yawn and reached for his beer. He'd changed time zones by only an hour, but Dario, Luciana's husband, had been talking for the last thirty minutes about local realtors and hoteliers and ranchers, punctuated by can-you-believe-it facial expressions.

He, Luciana, and Dario had just finished dinner in an alcove off the Casa Azul restaurant, an indoor-outdoor space with terra cotta floors and a palapa roof, scattered with athletic gringos eating fish tacos. Dario, who wore long shorts, black two-day stubble, and a dark-blue Casa Azul hoodie, was a Madrileño who had come to Baja for the kiteboarding, fallen in love with the desert-meets-sea landscape, and also fallen in love with Luciana, a prodigal daughter returned from her studies abroad. Now they worked in symbiosis. Luciana put up visiting scientists at Casa Azul, and husband and wife borrowed boats and dive gear from one another.

"And now this," Dario said. He reached into a pocket, pulled out a piece of paper, and slapped it onto the wooden table. "It was on the bulletin board outside Oscarito's."

"The grocery store," Luciana filled in.

It was a flyer. In red and black text accompanied by drawings of green fish, it said:

¡Si! a un futuro sustentable
Para La Ventana y su ecosistema
¡No! A Palacio Pericú

"Yes! to a sustainable future for La Ventana and its ecosystem." It was hard to argue with that. The last line said "no" to Palacio Pericú, a new resort. Gabriel leaned down from his chair to pat Ricketts, the hotel's white-furred, long-bodied mutt.

"You've seen these?" Dario asked his wife.

"Yes, love."

"You probably agree."

Instead of answering her husband, Luciana explained to Gabriel: construction runoff from the new resort had damaged the coral and its dependent critters.

"This"—Dario waved the flyer around and slapped it back down—"is like throwing a bomb at the economy. No, thank you, we don't want any jobs here."

"Dario is hoping to work with the resort," Luciana said.

"What do you think, Gabriel?"

As a conservationist, Gabriel's instinct was to side with Luciana, but he had no wish to get between husband and wife.

"I think the chicken mole was delicious."

"Very diplomatic," Dario said with good cheer. He crumpled the flyer and shoved it back in his pocket.

Ricketts turned in a circle and settled himself on Gabriel's foot.

"And what do you think of Lucy's fish mystery? Is it another nefarious capitalist plot?"

"I doubt a plot. But it is mysterious."

"The last thing I need is one of these sports influencers hearing about dead fish," Dario said, and gestured to the main part of the dining room. "We can't live on science alone, right, darling?" He winked at his wife, who scowled. "I'll tell you what it is. It's that fishing ship out of Shizuoka. It has ten times the capacity of the old ones. A literal factory. But the little fish, they're bycatch. If they're under twenty inches, it spits them back out."

Gabriel looked to Luciana, but she crossed her arms and looked away. He knew that she doubted the bycatch theory.

"That's what's happening to these poor huachinangos," Dario went on. "So wasteful. On the bright side, they're phasing out the giant ships. Right, love?"

"Wasn't one of them attacked?" Gabriel asked, remembering this from the news.

But a frost had come over his dining companions. Something was off between them, or between them and himself.

"I have to go," Luciana said, standing up just politely enough that he couldn't be sure she was unhappy, but also couldn't be sure she wasn't.

Gabriel walked on the moonlit beach after dinner, then returned to his cabin, a white stucco cube with a domed roof and a palapa awning over the deck. He planned to watch something, then go to sleep. But when he sat down in the cowhide easy chair and opened his laptop, a message from Dr. M caught his eye.

> Archibald Montrose here. Would be grateful if you could give me a call.

A zing of alarm shot up Gabriel's spine. Dr. M had never contacted him before. The only time they'd associated outside of Cate's company was when he had driven to the older man's house, looking for answers. He picked up his phone.

"Gabriel. Good of you to call so quickly."

Dr. M didn't sound as urgent as Gabriel had expected.

"Is Cate okay?"

"Ah—I didn't mean to alarm you. No immediate danger, as far as I'm aware."

Gabriel exhaled. How was Cate still able to make him feel afraid for her?

"It's just that . . ."

Gabriel wondered if they'd been cut off, but no, he heard faint classical music on the other end. Maybe this call had nothing to do with Cate after all.

"You're someone I believe she trusts," Dr. M finally said. "And you're aware of her upbringing. That puts you in a highly unique position."

Gabriel fiddled with the heavy linen curtain at his window and peered out into the arroyo, wondering how to respond. "She's a good friend," he said at last.

"You have her best interests at heart."

He suddenly understood that Dr. M was about to ask him to do something, and that it would be payback for the time Gabriel had visited his house.

"She's going to Baja to look for someone."

Confused, Gabriel thought maybe Dr. M meant him—that Cate was coming to look for him. But Dr. M didn't know where Gabriel was.

"She's taking a holiday," Gabriel said. "With Jia."

"Yes," Dr. M said. "But she also intends to look for someone. That's why I'm calling. She's trying to find a man named Hunter Brandt."

"Doctor—"

"Archie, please."

"Archie. She didn't tell me she was looking for someone. That makes it no business of mine."

"Still, I'd like your help."

Gabriel waited.

"Hunter Brandt is, like Cate, an alumnus of the Cleckley Institute." The older man paused. "However, he's declined to further participate as a subject in our research. Which means that none of us must contact him, and Cate is one of 'us,' so to speak. She's been privy to all the studies."

Gabriel actually laughed. "Doctor—Archie—you want me to stop Cate from doing something she wants to do? I *know* her."

Another silence. Then, "I do see your point."

Gabriel did not see Dr. M's point, though.

The doctor went on, "It's not just a question of ethics. I'm concerned for her safety. I've tried to discourage her from seeking the man out, to no avail. As you know, she tends to disregard risk, and on this issue in particular, I fear I've lost her trust."

"What's the problem with her finding this guy?"

"Cate thinks he holds the key to understanding something about herself. Her history, our school. I can't blame her. But she's going to be let down."

"I'm sure she can handle a letdown."

There was a long pause, during which Gabriel heard the older man breathing, the strains of classical music still playing in the background. Brahms, he was pretty sure. Gabriel walked to and fro between his bed and the cowhide easy chair.

"Cate's pursuit of him is potentially dangerous. Whatever you may think of my relationship to Cate—"

You don't want to know, Gabriel thought. He'd considered Cate's faith in Dr. M misplaced ever since he learned how their relationship really began.

"—I wouldn't ask if I didn't think this was important. You have her trust, you care for her well-being. I'm asking if you would please try to persuade her to seek adventure elsewhere."

Who was Dr. M to ask Gabriel to protect Cate, who they both knew was unprotectable? If this person, this situation, was in fact dangerous to her, why put Gabriel in the middle of it? Weren't professionals needed? Psychiatrists? Police? And yet it had to be serious, or Dr. M wouldn't have contacted him.

So Gabriel knew he would try. Cate would loathe him for meddling. But the thought of inspiring such strong feelings in her motivated rather than dissuaded him.

TWENTY-ONE

CATE

The morning after Jia and I arrived in Baja, I took a kiteboarding lesson from Dario, the owner of Casa Azul, which was a few minutes down the beach from our rental house. Almost immediately after I entered the water, the kite—a bow of fabric stretched taut over a frame—pulled me off balance and dragged me across a rocky reef, abrading my right leg below my short wetsuit. Salt water stung my broken skin.

The next time I tried, the wind caught my kite just so and lifted me into the air. At the zenith of my arc, I had that where-have-you-been-all-my-life feeling, the buzz coursing through every part of my body as I sailed down, skimming the sea like a flying fish, board connecting with water. Adrenaline blanked out thought and I was all thrill.

I did this for a couple of hours, erasing past and present, alternating injury with ecstasy pretty much one for one.

Afterwards, I sat on the beach in my wetsuit and sunglasses, in the lee of the hut where Dario kept his equipment. I observed an angry new bruise on my knee, and blood trickling down my calf.

Gabriel found me there. "Don't get up, you're hurt," he said.

I smiled up at him. He looked appealingly tanned and healthy. Maybe Seattle had never suited him, and maybe I hadn't either. He had a deepness of feeling—for animals, people, me—that I'd always wanted to absorb and channel. But he deserved someone who shared that depth.

Gabriel crouched to give me a hug of hello, and as I leaned towards him, he almost lost his footing in the sand and tumbled into me. We caught one another's elbows, and for an instant it was like we were truly embracing, and I remembered his calming warmth. But then the moment passed, and he took a seat at an appropriate distance. He'd told me on the phone about his new girlfriend, Penelope, who I imagined gave him the sincere affection he craved.

"Have you tried it?" I asked, nodding to the water.

He shook his head. "Dario offered, but I've been in the lab."

"It's amazing."

He gave me a look with his good eye. Impressed, maybe, or bewildered. "I'm not sure I can take the broken bones."

We sat side by side on the sand, watching the dozens of kite-boarders. Each bright-coloured kite made an arc against the blue sky, so that together they looked like a flock of giant psychedelic birds. Below their kites, attached by long, tense lines, the boarders leapt and twirled. I understood them better than I understood most people. They were motivated by nothing more emotionally complicated than a desire for pure sensation.

"When you told me you were coming to Baja, I thought maybe it had something to do with my influence," Gabriel said.

"You told me how much you loved it."

"Mmm-hmm."

"And I was curious after reading those articles."

"You didn't come here to see dead fish, though. Or even to take a vacation."

He sifted sand with one hand while I looked at him, wondering how he knew.

"I *am* on vacation," I said. *This is Gabriel*, I reminded myself. *Just tell him*. "But I'm also looking for someone."

"I know."

I had that feeling of being invaded. Wary.

"Dr. M contacted me," he said.

I felt an internal lurch. This was not supposed to happen in my compartmentalized world.

"That's weird," I said, keeping my voice and face calm. "Why?"

"He said you're looking for a guy named Hunter."

I said nothing.

"Who, I'm guessing, is the same Hunter who owns the new resort out on Punta Arena that Dario and Luciana keep talking about."

I looked out to sea. The wind was dying. Kiters were coming into shore.

"I don't see why Dr. M would bring that up with you."

"I'm not sure I do either."

"There's no law against looking for someone."

He muttered something.

"What?"

"Like that would stop you."

"When do I ever break the law?"

Once, I'd nearly misled lab inspectors from the CDC, but Jia had stopped me just in time.

"I just mean, you do what you want, when it suits you."

That's what you used to like about me, I didn't say.

"I'm curious about Hunter."

"The problem is, Dr. M asked me to try to stop you. Obviously, I told him you were unlikely to listen to me. But here I am, making the effort, because I said I would. So here we go. Here's my pitch. Dr. M cares about you. I think we can agree on that, yes?"

"Sure."

"He wants to protect you. So why not let yourself be protected? He knows this guy, and he thinks this is a bad idea. Such a bad idea that he reached out to me, which was strange. Why don't you just do some more kiteboarding and go home?"

My thoughts became detached from the conversation. I'd once had control over Gabriel. I don't mean that in a hostile way. You can love what you control. But it's a fact: I'd known what I could elicit in him, how my actions would make him behave. I'd walked a line between exciting him and upsetting him, which always kept him slightly off balance. Right up until the night when I told him everything, I'd had that power. Now I didn't anymore, which was probably healthier in some sense—that's what my last ex-therapist would have said. Maybe Gabriel was really my friend now. That was certainly what we'd been playing at.

"He's being totally inappropriate, asking you to interfere."

"I agree. But here we are."

"Tell him you tried your best."

He laughed at that and got up to leave.

"It's good to see you, Cate," he said, looking down at me with his hands in his pockets.

I looked at him, squinting up into the bright afternoon light. "It's good to see you too."

I hadn't settled on how to approach Hunter, except that I wanted to do it in person. I didn't know whether I would pass off our meeting as coincidence or simply tell him who I was. I wondered if he would recognize me, more than twenty years on. I was still deciding how to engineer a meeting when Dario showed me the way.

Our white stucco rental house overlooked the beach and wrapped around a courtyard on the inland side. It had terra cotta patios and a roof deck that was alternately too breezy and too hot during the day, but perfect for stargazing. Two nights after we arrived, thanks to Jia's initiative, we hosted a small dinner party, inviting Gabriel, Dario, and Luciana, whom until then I'd known of only as the scientist who'd discovered the spate of dead fish. Compact and energetic, she held my shoulders firmly when she air-kissed my cheeks.

After devouring Jia's pan-fried garlic shrimp, the five of us gathered on the bright-yellow sofas in the living room, which surrounded a glass-topped coffee table. I sat at ninety degrees to

Luciana, such that our knees almost touched. Beyond the big windows, the moon rose over the sea, super-engorged due to some atmospheric trick.

"You're the reason Gabriel's here," I said to Luciana. She had an interesting face, faceted like a jewel.

"I hear you're the reason."

This struck me as concerning, and I was about to deny it when she continued: "You sent him the news story about the die-off. How did you find it?"

"Oh, right. I knew we wanted to come here," I said, gesturing at Jia, who was talking to Dario. "I was reading up."

"My husband would be upset to know that's the first thing people find when they're looking for a hotel in La Ventana."

"It wasn't the first thing. I tend to over-research."

"I can confirm that," said Gabriel, who sat to my left.

"Did you two work together?" Luciana asked.

"No," we said at the same time, then looked at each other, and Luciana looked at us, but neither of us volunteered further information.

Dario entertained us with stories about hotel guests. A husband who became surly when his wife bested him at kiteboarding. A twelve-year-old who accidentally caught a reef shark off his paddleboard. A tourist who sat on his taxidermied pufferfish, requiring Dario to delicately remove the spikes from his behind.

Dario knew all about the new resort, Palacio Pericú, forty-five minutes to the southeast. He hoped to do business with the owner, providing kiteboarding services for guests.

"Tell us more about the resort," I said.

Gabriel looked at me and looked away, with a shake of his head. Then he asked if anyone wanted another drink and went to the kitchen.

Hunter Araya, Dario said, had arrived in the area a couple of years earlier, permits and contractors in tow, and begun to build a lavish spread. There were competing rumours about where the man and his money came from; as Dario understood it, he'd previously made a fortune in distilleries. I wondered how Hunter had managed to put that story about.

"Oh—and there's the party!" Dario said. "You must come, both of you. Luciana and I will be there. It's the night after tomorrow." He squeezed his wife's hand and she rolled her eyes.

Araya was throwing a big party to celebrate the resort's opening, a private affair, Dario explained, but he was sure he could invite two extra guests. Jia thrives on people, so I knew she would say yes.

"I'd love to," I said. And just like that, I had my way in.

With my goal suddenly closer, I felt the cautionary tug of Dr. M's voice inside my head. But this was the perfect set-up. In a crowd, I could observe Hunter from afar before deciding how to proceed.

I went to the kitchen. Gabriel had cut a bowl of lime wedges and was now chopping up an orange to put in the sangria. I put a hand on his forearm. In the dim evening light, he'd removed his eye patch, so I could see his left iris and the ragged, off-centre black square that he had instead of a pupil. He glanced at my hand, then up at my face. I removed my hand. I was taking liberties, treating him like I had some kind of right. It was hard to shake a habit.

"Come back," I said.

The two of us carried beers and the sangria pitcher to the living room and retook our seats. Luciana was telling Jia about her objections to the resort while Dario shook his head. I wondered how deep her disapproval ran. I felt an impulse to defend Hunter, whom I didn't even know yet. A kind of atavistic feeling, as though he were family.

"What did people say about that attack on the factory ship?" Jia asked.

As Dario began to answer, Luciana glanced around, full of tense energy, the way some people get when they're telling a lie and aren't very good at it. I picked up the sangria and was beginning to refill her wineglass when suddenly every light in the house went off. I was so startled that I sloshed liquid onto the coffee table and set the pitcher down with a clank. "Dammit."

"Welcome to Baja California Sur, my friends," Dario said. "You're not really here until you experience your first power outage."

I grabbed a napkin and wiped up the splashed sangria as best I could in the dark.

"The house info said something about candles," Jia said.

I crossed to the dining room, my bare feet guiding me across warm tile. Groping my way, I opened the splintery credenza, where I felt around until I found candles, a box of matches, and kerosene lanterns. When I returned to the living room, the other four were bathed in milky moonlight, talking about electrical power.

"Baja is the only area not connected to the mainland grid," Dario said.

"Can it get connected?" Jia asked.

"There's a plan to run a line under the Sea of Cortez. There's a politician—"

"Aye, not politics," Luciana said.

"Francisco Iguaro," Dario went on. "He's the challenger for governor. His campaign slogan is 'Light Up Baja.'"

"When's the election?" Jia asked.

"A week from today."

I lit the candles, which made me think of Grandma Ida. *Schwick, schwick, schwick.* How she'd let me light the candles at her Thanksgiving table not even six months after the fire, despite the qualms she must have felt.

"This is so peaceful," Dario said, glancing around at our faces, lit only by candles and moonlight. "Everyone has gas generators now. The power goes out, and two minutes later, someone turns one on. They sound like truck engines."

"But you're going to turn ours on as soon as we get back," Luciana said.

Dario looked at his watch, then leaned back on the sofa and scooted closer to his wife. "Let the guests wait, love. This is the adventure they don't know they need."

"I don't know this man," she said, and leaned her head on his shoulder.

But it was late—or Baja-late, as Dario called it, nearly ten p.m.—and the darkness encouraged us to wrap up. I struck matches again to light the two kerosene lanterns and handed Jia one to take to her room. Luciana, Dario, and Gabriel had brought headlamps. Gabriel told them to go on without him—he was going to help clean up. I said goodbye, then followed the sound of clinking glass to the kitchen, where Gabriel, wearing his headlamp, was loading the dishwasher. Out the window, a shimmering white V extended over the blackened water to the horizon.

He closed the dishwasher.

"Do you know your way back?"

"I'll just take the beach."

"I'll walk you to the top of the stairs."

I opened the sliding screen door and we went out onto the patio. Looking southeast along the curve of the bay, we could see that all of La Ventana was dark. In the far distance, though—far out on the peninsula that formed the southeastern arm of the bay—there was a small, pulsing glow of light.

"You see that?"

"Someone has a very powerful generator," Gabriel said.

We stood there with crossed arms, staring at the puzzling light.

"Cate," he said, in a tone that signalled he hadn't stayed behind just to help clean up.

"Yes?"

"I don't really mind Dr. M contacting me about you. He's concerned."

"I mind."

"I know."

There was another pause while we stared across the starry bay to the distant light.

"Do you trust him?" Gabriel finally asked.

"Of course. He's like family."

"Strange kind of family."

"We take what we can get."

Gabriel's relatives were distributed among close-knit pods in California. His siblings, parents, and even a grandmother were alive. I'd been matter-of-fact, but I saw on Gabriel's face that he was worried his words had hurt me.

"Okay, I trust him, but he's not right about everything," I said. "And I've come to see that our interests are not always the same."

The light, way out on the point, was too bright to be a lighthouse. Was it a cruise ship, lit up like a Christmas tree?

He turned towards me while I stayed facing the distant light. I spoke before he could.

"There's a gate at the bottom of the stairs." I pointed to the landing that led down to the beach. The garden was lush; some talented horticulturalist had made the desert bloom. By day it was shades of green, and at night all glints and shadows. "Just be sure to bolt it behind you."

Gabriel looked down, arms still crossed. Images popped into my head. How easy it would be to just take him, strip him, mount him, right here, feeling the scrape of tile on skin. I remembered how his emotion became my emotion, how I used to steal it and feel it gush through me. I wondered if he'd resist, with his new life and all. But self-discipline was the only reason I was anything. Tomorrow or the next day, I'd ask after the girlfriend.

Finally, he moved off towards the stairs, descending into the grey-black rustle of plants. I looked again to the southeast, to where the pulsing dot of light still glowed.

TWENTY-TWO

CATE

ONE NIGHT AFTER A blizzard, six of us go to dinner at the farmhouse. We put on snow pants and duffel coats to make the ten-minute walk from the ward. Nurse Chen marches us along the shovelled path, where the white banks on either side rise taller than me.

After supper, Eden makes us hot chocolate and sends all the kids into the living room, where we play Monopoly. There are red plastic hotels all over the Park Place and Boardwalk corner of the board. Terry wins, which means he's supposed to get to choose the next game. He fingers the saint's charm at his neck and says he wants to play Balderdash.

"Do you guys want to jump off the roof?" Hunter suggests instead.

No one speaks.

"How?" I ask.

We all put our outerwear back on. But the others just go out the front door to throw snowballs, while I follow Hunter up the smooth old wooden staircase to the second floor. A few feet from the top of the stairs, Hunter stands on his tiptoes and reaches up, and to my astonishment, grasps a sturdy wooden ladder that is attached to the ceiling. He unfolds the ladder and sets its feet on the floor. He looks at me, amused. I'm grinning wildly.

He climbs the ladder. At the top, he pushes on a wooden panel that lifts into the void above. He climbs a few more steps, then hoists himself out of sight.

I scamper up, and when I get near the top, he reaches down and pulls me easily into the attic. I stand unsteadily on a plank that's been laid across the joists in place of an actual floor. I try to get my bearings in the dark, inhaling the cold, musty air. There's a big arched window ahead, through which I see the faint glitter of moonlit snow on pine trees. I hear the other kids' muffled shouts.

"How did you know this was here?"

"Sometimes I explore. Stay on the planks. If you step off, you'll fall through."

"I can't see."

"Your eyes will adjust."

I do as instructed, waiting, listening to us breathe. Sure enough, I'm soon able to make out the line where the last plank meets a darker blackness. Hunter is a man-sized shadow, moving away towards the window.

By the time I get to the window, he's opened it and hopped his butt onto the sill. The others are hollering at each other in the snow down below. I use both hands to lift myself up. Once I'm seated, I swing around so that I match Hunter, straddling the windowsill with one leg braced against the sloping roof and the other hanging into the attic. We're barely a foot apart. I look out and down, dizzied by our height, feeling a surreptitious thrill that, though we can see the others, they haven't noticed us yet. We have a secret. We are a secret. Something wells in my chest at the thought of jumping.

I don't think I've wobbled, but Hunter touches my shoulder as though to steady me, which sends even more electric waves pinging around my chest.

He smiles. "You okay?"

"Yes."

"You excited to jump?"

"Yes."

He points down the sloping roof to where the eaves jut out over the porch. "We'll slide down to there. Then jump out. Away from the house. Are you scared?"

"No."

Maybe I am. I feel shaky and eager. I want to feel whatever I'm going to feel on the way down. Something else is going on too, dizzying me. I feel a physical pull towards Hunter that I've never felt before.

"How old are you?" he asks all of a sudden.

"Thirteen."

"Are you ready, Catie?"

I nod and swing my leg from the inside to face fully out, with both legs extended down the sloped roof.

The two of us slide slowly down to the very edge. I don't know if I can control my speed, feeling the gravity, sensing the air opening up just beyond. I ignore the shouts as Terry, Jon-Jon, Calliope, and Sissy spot us coming down the roof. I push out and away.

I fly. I feel wild sensation, limbs pulsing, heart pumping, brain exploding in chemical delight. I'm aloft.

TWENTY-THREE

LUCIANA

The journalist wanted to speak to Luciana again. One last interview, he said, before he went home to Los Cabos. He'd published his feature about the national park during his first week in town, and then, a few days later, his piece about the dead fish. And then, to her surprise, he'd stayed on at Casa Azul for nearly a month, taking advantage of the long-stay discount. Some days he worked in his cabin or came by the lab, but he also disappeared for long stretches in his car. Luciana's theory was that he was spooked, afraid to return home after finding the slaughtered turkey vulture in his passenger seat. That for him, La Ventana, at the end of a road along the sea, felt comfortably distant from the tourist metropolis of Los Cabos, two and a half hours away.

At Luciana's urging, Tenoch had reported the turkey vulture to Detective Ursula Sanchez. He'd told her that he'd covered criminal gangs back in Chiapas, and that, since coming to Baja, he'd published a story about corrupt construction deals in Los Cabos.

"I don't think she was interested in my hypotheses of the crime," Tenoch had told Luciana. "But at least there's a record."

Tenoch now seemed to be every bit as interested as Luciana and Gabriel in finding an explanation for the fish die-off. This morning, he'd taken one of the lab's pangas out by himself, following careful instructions from Beni on how to change the gas cannister and lift the outboard. He'd returned in one piece, the boat undamaged, and, according to Beni, had then gone back to the hotel to change.

When he arrived in her office, she poured him a glass of hibiscus juice from the pitcher on the credenza.

"How was your boat trip?"

Tenoch glugged back most of his juice and set the glass on her desk. "I think I found something," he blurted. "But I can't be sure yet. I need to check some things and go back."

"Did you find samples?"

"Dozens in one spot. I didn't collect any, I'm sorry. I couldn't manoeuvre the net and the outboard at the same time, and there was a current . . ."

"It's okay. But how many dozens? And where were you?"

Luciana had yet to visit a location where she'd seen more than five or six of the dead fish at once.

"One of the Outer Islands."

"You got all the way out there?"

"There were waves coming back. I thought I was going to capsize."

"It kicks up. Can you show me on a map?"

"I'd like to show you in person. Could we go back out there tomorrow? I need to corroborate some things first, otherwise I might sound crazy."

"All right, we'll go. But did you see any ships out there?"

Tenoch said he had not, and pivoted the conversation. "This party at Palacio Pericú tonight. Are you going?"

"Yes. Best to make nice with the neighbours."

"I'd like to come."

"Oh?"

"I need to talk to the owner, Hunter Araya. There could be another story there. A case study in environmental impact."

The opportunity to help pressure the resort's owner about his environmental footprint was irresistible to Luciana.

"I'll ask to put you on the guest list. Gabriel also wants to go, so I was going to call anyway."

"I appreciate it. And one more thing," he said, pulling a notebook and pen out of his pocket. “My editor wants a follow-up on the Reef Pirates story. The *Bizan-maru*?”

His tone of voice was so casual that, for a moment, she wasn’t sure if he’d actually said those words. She froze, like an animal sensing a predator.

“How can I help you with that?” she asked, managing a smile.

“After we ran the national park story, a few readers pointed out that you were on record as supporting Reef Pirates. So some sort of comment would be helpful.”

“Obviously I don’t support killing people.”

“But in the past you supported the organization?”

A sense of injustice fuelled her next words. “Look, Reef Pirates wants to reduce pollution and overfishing. I want to reduce pollution and overfishing. That’s why I used to support them. But that was long before they did anything like the *Bizan-maru*. I don’t condone violence.”

“So can you publicly say that you no longer—”

“I don’t know how I could be any clearer.”

She knew she sounded snappish.

“What’s your relationship with Javier Sanz?”

“Who?” she asked, and felt her cheeks become hot.

“Javier Sanz. The head of Reef Pirates. Do you know him?” Tenoch pressed.

“He’s from La Paz. So am I. It’s not that big a city.”

“You’ve met him.”

“Sure. Parties, events.”

“What’s he like?”

“I don’t know. Tall. People say he’s charismatic.”

“Did you find him charismatic?”

She’d hardly met anyone more so. “He started Reef Pirates. He got people to do what they did. So he must be, right?”

Easy, she told herself. She’d gotten along so well with Tenoch until now. But his questions triggered a sense of alarm.

"I'd better get back to work," she said, softening her tone. "I'll make sure to call about the party."

She dislodged the journalist from her office, telling him he was welcome to go work in the conference room. She called Palacio Pericú and asked the party organizer to put two more names on the guest list, friends of her lab. On the spur of the moment, she added that she would no longer be able to attend herself. Dario would be annoyed, but he would survive.

Deciding not to go to the party brought temporary relief, and she tried to work but was soon caught up in what-ifs again. What-ifs like closing the centre, and going to prison.

She closed her window and locked her office door, then opened the encrypted messaging app, which she'd thought many times about deleting. She called Javi.

"To what do I owe the pleasure?"

"Have any journalists tried to contact you?"

"They're always trying to, but we're not giving interviews."

"Who in particular has tried to contact you?"

"Maria has a list. Why?"

"There's a reporter for *El Diario*. He's been here writing about the national park and the huachinangos. I think he knows something about us."

"What about us?" Javi asked slowly.

"He might know about you stealing my tanks. And the fact that I didn't report you."

"There's no way anyone could know that."

His smug confidence exasperated her.

"Of course there is! How many people do you need to get in and out of my shed with fifteen tanks? Four? Five?"

Javi was silent.

"Any of them could have talked! One of them carved a 'V' onto a tank!"

"My people don't talk."

"You don't understand journalists. They're persistent. They

find a weak spot and they go for it. This *El Diario* guy started asking me how I knew you, what you were like. He might find out about us. Back then."

"Did he ask you anything about the incident of concern?" He was too careful to say "*Bizan-maru*," and his caution aggravated her further.

"No. But he can get there if he keeps looking. What if he goes after Beni? I'm not made for this. I'm not good at this. I can't leave my community—" She felt a rising fear as she put it all into words.

"Lulu," he cut in. "You're going to be okay. No one knows, and no one is going to know. I'm going to make sure."

She didn't answer, but she let herself be calmed.

"Now. Tell me the journalist's name."

TWENTY-FOUR

CATE

WE STAY IN LOG cabins on Lake Wenatchee, girls with Nurse Chen, boys with Nurse Bonamo, twelve or so kids in total. Not everyone gets to go. I'm one of the "good" kids, and I take the privileges as my due, not wondering what it means to be a good bad kid. Cleckley is all about creating microcosms for its students, little subunits of society where we can practise being normal.

We have two outdoor instructors, Willow and Todd. Willow matches her name, tall and strong, with long brown hair in a ponytail. Todd is spry like a mountain goat, and wears tooled-leather wrist cuffs. They both carry Swiss Army knives, objects very much forbidden at Cleckley and therefore fascinating. I study the way Willow unfolds her knife to prepare food, ties her hiking boots, and tucks the occasional pebble into her pocket.

They take us canoeing and hiking. They teach us how to use a compass and coat a match in wax to keep it dry. Todd shows us how to bundle up our food and hang it from a tree branch by a rope, to keep it away from bears and bears away from us. Willow is a plant expert, always pointing something out: ferns and mushrooms you can eat, poisonous berries, bark you can easily strip and use to make a shelter. One night we practise making fires, and Willow compliments me on my skill.

There's a rope swing over a cove near the dock that we can only use with supervision. I sail out over the water and drop with a splash, so many times that I get rope burns on my hands and thighs. I keep going until Nurse Chen herself comes down to the dock and tells us it's time for dinner. I'd been testing Willow's authority, but I know better than to mess with Nurse Chen, whom I've never seen without her hair in a tight black bun.

There are six of us in my wilderness overnight group: Hunter, Terry, and Calliope, who are older, as well as Jon-Jon, fifteen, Sissy, fourteen, and me, thirteen. Plus two adults, Willow and Dr. M. A good ratio, you'd think. We hike with one adult in the front and one in the rear, but whenever we come to a fork in the trail, Willow encourages us kids to make the choice: look at the trail map, use our compasses, look at the sun, and decide as a group. Considering the battles kids get into on the ward—sometimes actual fisticuffs, but more often protracted cold wars in which possessions get defaced or go missing—we're saints during our overnight, as though fresh air and bear awareness make us more responsible. What seem like high-stakes issues on the ward, like earning screen time or beating Sissy at chess or showing off the shoes Grandma Ida sent, have all receded in importance. I see the smallness of my life behind walls, but also that there's something beyond them. The others must feel like this too. Sissy and I roll our eyes at each other when we think Calliope is being flirty with the older boys, but that's as mean as anyone gets. Dr. M is quiet, neither instructing nor interrogating, just watching.

Among the kids, Hunter emerges as de facto leader. When we're deciding where to set up camp, he asks all of us what we think of the site, just like a teacher would do. He digs the latrine mostly himself. I'm walking back from it after dinner when I hear talking. Hunter and Terry have just strung up the bear bag and are standing under it, Hunter still holding the end of the rope. Terry's hair makes me think of a squirrel's tail. I stop to listen.

"Did she let you?" Terry asks.

"She basically made me."

"No way."

"Yes way."

"Then what?"

"Then it was curfew. Bonamo was there in like thirty seconds."

"Why don't you just break out?"

"Too much hassle. I'm trying to get out of here, not get stuck."

"Go back to the part where you had your hands on her tits."

They're talking about Calliope, with her curly red hair, her eyeshadow, her grown-up curves. Jealousy surges through me. Since our leap off the roof, I've nursed intense fantasies of kissing Hunter, but our actual relationship hasn't progressed beyond hallway hellos. To Hunter, I'm a kid in a snowsuit. If he remembers our moment at all.

What if Calliope were gone, I wonder. What if she got lost in the forest or fell off a cliff or got sick from the red baneberries that Willow warned us not to eat. Then I would present myself to Hunter in the woods. I would unbraid my hair and he would kiss me like he could have that night on the windowsill, and put his hand on my chest, which was nothing like Calliope's but not completely flat.

I stand quiet just feet from the boys, enjoying my invisibility. Hunter ties off the rope holding up the bear bag to a wide tree trunk, and Terry checks the knot and declares it safe. The boys move off, and I move on.

Later I climb into my sleeping bag in the small tent I share with Sissy.

"Who do you like better, Hunter or Terry?" she whispers, her face inches from mine.

I'm surprised my answer isn't apparent. Besides Hunter's obvious virtues, Terry is obsessed with hand-painted figurines, and saliva pools around his braces.

But Sissy feels differently. "You can have Hunter, and I'll have Terry, and that way Calliope can't have either of them."

She doesn't define "have," and I'm not sure what this divvying-up plan means we're supposed to do, but Sissy is savvier than me.

As I fall asleep, I imagine sidling up to Calliope on a clifftop, bumping her with my shoulder, and watching her fall away into the tree canopy below.

In the morning, we have oatmeal with salmonberries we gathered ourselves. We've built fires and put them out. We haven't gotten lost or been bit by anything more serious than a mosquito. Our little group is celebratory. Now all that remains is a hike back to our canoes and a paddle back to the cabins. The weather is dry, our campsite cast in a warm green glow. I feel a new sense of possession about Hunter, as though Sissy's pronouncement has given me permission to fully indulge my crush. I contrive ways to be closer to him, for example by volunteering to pull up the pegs as he takes down one of the tents.

Early in the hike out, Sissy and I hang close to Hunter and Terry, separating them from Calliope, who's behind us. But after a while, our group spreads out along the trail. Hunter is ahead of me, Jon-Jon behind me, and then we become even more attenuated, like the particles of the universe moving farther away from one another. The trail is steep and narrow. It drops to a stream bed, then climbs. Way up ahead, I can just make out Hunter's red backpack through the trees, and then it bobs away and I'm alone with the sound of my breath and swishing leaves. I climb higher, feeling calm and absorbed. It's the way I sometimes feel when I get lost in a math problem, following the logic until I emerge victorious and hours have passed. Except here, the challenge isn't abstract, but about putting my feet in the right place.

After a long upward stretch, the path flattens out, running close to the edge of a cliff. A rock wall rises above me to my left and another one drops to my right. I stop at an outcropping and stand on the edge to look down. I study the shadow shapes on the rock wall below, diamonds and triangles, elongated by my vertical perspective. Halfway between the clifftop where I stand and the dense trees below, I see a flapping piece of red fabric caught on a branch, like one of those ribbons used to mark hiking trails. Beyond the knotted forest canopy, the lake is deep blue in the late-spring sun. Near my feet I notice a root pulled up and freshly snapped, pale and ropy, and the bed of pine needles disturbed by fresh damp-dark dirt.

I don't know how long I stand there. Sissy catches up with me, then Calliope and Jon-Jon. We line up like birds on a wire, not speaking but smirking and jostling as we compete to see who can stand closest to the cliff. Jon-Jon almost loses his footing but manages to fall backwards to safety.

"Away from the edge, please," bellows Dr. M, bringing up the rear.

A half hour later, we catch up with Hunter and Willow, who are waiting for us in a clearing between several enormous pines. Calliope, Hunter, and Jon-Jon link hands to try to put their arms around one of the trunks, but it's still much too big.

"Where's our Terrence?" asks Dr. M.

We sit on rocks, pull granola bars from zippered compartments.

"Yeah, where's Terry?" Sissy chimes in.

We drink water. I watch Willow and Dr. M confer, then Willow asks, "Did Terry tell anyone he was going to pee?"

When none of us respond, the adults get worried. They ask us when we last saw him, and we all say some variation of the same thing: before the last big hill climb, where we became strung out along the path.

"I'll go back and look for him," Hunter says.

But the adults decide that Willow will be the one to search, while the rest of us stay with Dr. M. She's away a long time, and when she comes back, her tan is gone. She and Dr. M speak in whispers, then they come speak to us.

"Terry has suffered a terrible accident," Willow says.

We stare at her in silence. She tells us she's called for help, and that park rangers and paramedics are coming via boat to the base of the cliff. Dr. M will lead us the rest of the way to our canoes.

"Is he dead?" Jon-Jon asks point-blank.

Willow glances at Dr. M, and he nods gravely. Her voice is shaky. "I wasn't able to reach all the way to his"—she swallows—"to Terry. I climbed down partway, until I could see him between the trees. He was unconscious. I don't know. I'm sorry, I don't know."

"He probably broke his neck," Jon-Jon says, matter-of-factly.

Calliope elbows him.

"No," shouts Sissy, then "no, no, no, no, no, no, no," her words merging into a howl.

Dr. M walks over to try to soothe her. Then Hunter does a very grown-up thing. He goes to Willow and puts a hand on her shoulder, which I think is weird, but he looks like a man next to her and she lets him hug her. I feel jealous again.

Everyone is acting crazy. I'm going to be the calm one in all this, I decide. I'm going to help Dr. M. He's standing two feet away from Sissy, speaking to her quietly, while she kicks at a tree trunk in fury. I go to them and she stops kicking as I ease in beside her. I take her firmly by the shoulders from behind, as the nurses did to us when we were small and enraged. Sissy lets me guide her to sit on a rock, and flops over herself, exhausted and incoherent.

TWENTY-FIVE

CATE

I put on the only dress I'd brought to Baja (black), touched up my pedicure (silver), and shook my hair into place, still pleased by my post-sale shearing. Ready before Jia, as usual, I flipped up my laptop screen on the old wooden desk in my bedroom. The early-evening sky was pink, and the white curtains billowed inward on a breeze. I opened the file Felix had compiled for me, which I'd already pored over dozens of times. I looked at the most recent photos of Hunter, the ones from his defunct company website where he wore neat black hair and a salesman's grin. I wondered if he would recognize me. I'd been baby-cheeked, long-haired, not nearly my full height.

Jia's voice penetrated my consciousness like a far-off alarm clock. She was right beside me, dressed in a pink-and-orange minidress.

"Who's that?"

"Our party host. Hunter Araya."

She bent down to get a better look, then smiled at me. "Look at you, googling our host. That's the kind of thing I do."

Before she left Baja, I planned to tell her exactly who Hunter was, and that he was the one Felix had helped me find.

As we rolled through La Ventana in my rented SUV, we passed hotels scattered down to the sea on our left, and on the right, taco restaurants, a gas station, a tortilleria, and a tire repair joint. At the south end of town, I took a left and drove down the short slope to the lab. Dario had asked us to give Luciana a ride, as he'd gone early to meet with someone about kiteboarding affairs. A man I didn't recognize stood at the entrance, short and sturdy in slacks and a tucked-in shirt, his shoes and hair a matching shiny black. He shifted an old satchel and came towards us.

I rolled down the driver's side window and told him we were looking for Luciana—just as she appeared in jeans and a T-shirt. She introduced the man with the satchel as Tenoch Gomez, the journalist whose story I'd sent to Gabriel.

"Tenoch is going to the party instead of me," she said. "Can you do me a little favour and drive him there?"

Jia leaned out the window to tell Luciana we could wait while she got changed.

"No, no, you go without me. Tenoch is going in my place."

"I think there's a guest list."

"Yes, all very exclusive," Luciana said, a little huffily. "I phoned the resort for both of them."

"Both?"

At that moment, Gabriel bounded down the front steps of the lab in black jeans and a floral shirt. *No*, I thought. When had Gabriel ever chosen a big bash over fish specimens? Except he wasn't choosing the party, of course. He was choosing to keep an eye on me for Dr. M.

"Are you sure you want to come?" I called to him, injecting an edge into my voice that I hoped he would understand meant *Seriously, fuck off*.

But he just said, "You bet," and climbed into the back seat after Tenoch. There was no way to eject him without getting into an inexplicable argument in front of everyone else.

I gunned the engine too hard and vaulted us from the dirt drive onto the paved road. Jia grabbed the dash and gave me a look. The road away from town cut through a forest of cacti, each a gnarly giant, with turkey vultures perched on the highest branches. At the highway I turned left. I sulked and Gabriel grinned stupidly out the window, refusing to meet my glare in the mirror, which left Jia and Tenoch to make conversation.

"You work for the laboratory?" she asked brightly, but he said no, and explained that he was a reporter.

I felt a protective surge towards Hunter.

"Are you writing about the party?" Jia asked.

"About the resort. Did you know the owner built a desalination plant to get water for irrigation? It's very innovative."

"Are you interviewing him?"

"If I can."

We passed through the tidy town of San Juan de los Planes, nestled among date groves and palm oil plantations. I spotted a corner shop and fantasized about asking Gabriel to pick us up some bottled water, then taking off while he was inside. I would have done it if we'd been alone. The sky turned from pink to black in what felt like an instant.

"What did you cover in—where did you say you were from?" I heard Jia ask.

"Chiapas. I wrote about crime and human rights."

"Why did you move here?"

"Several colleagues were killed."

We all muttered how sorry we were.

"It's calmer in Baja," Tenoch said. "Beaches and tourists and rich people, like a telenovela. But it's not as calm as it looks."

The road was silvery grey in the early dark. The route passed gently upward through neat rows of palm trees until we reached a chiselled stone sign that read "Palacio Pericú." Tenoch read the words aloud and guffawed. Jia glanced back at him.

"Pericú was the name of a local tribe," he explained. "Killed centuries ago by the Spanish."

Over the next rise, a stone guardhouse came into view, and when we pulled up in front of it, a black-uniformed private security guard took our IDs to check them against a list. A second guard sat inside with a machine gun across his chest. Jia looked pointedly at the weapon, then at me. I shrugged, preoccupied with what lay ahead: how to get rid of Gabriel, how to get Hunter alone.

The guards let us go, and a few minutes later, we saw the resort spread out below us, and beyond it the moonlit sea. I drove under an arched stone gate into a well-manicured landscape of tall coconut palms and oasis-like ponds with little bridges. I thought: *Hunter's domain*. Low, discreet lamps lined the winding road, guiding us to a flagstone driveway in front of the entrance to the main building. A black Mercedes had pulled up just before us, out of which emerged a woman in a purple sheath and a man in a royal-blue dress shirt.

"You see? A telenovela star," Tenoch said. "Rina Uribe."

I parked behind the Mercedes and got out, leaving the key in the ignition. After the others exited, one of a team of boys in matching polo shirts took the car away. The actress had been waylaid by another guest a few paces ahead, and Tenoch gave her a little wave, to which she nodded back curtly.

I moved closer to Gabriel as we headed for the entryway. "I don't need a babysitter," I said. We entered an airy lobby, open to the night air on two sides, with a long ornamental pool at its centre.

"I'm just here to party."

"You're never anywhere to party," I said.

The women wore diaphanous fabrics, the men pressed linen, and everyone had glowingly good skin. Waiters circulated with sunset-coloured drinks, and soon Gabriel, Jia, and Tenoch each plucked one from a tray. I hoped they got sloppy.

The curvilinear, modern space was made of stone and wood, echoing the land's contours. Nothing so obvious as a check-in desk was evident. I'd expected the resort to be ostentatious, but this was subtle in its elegance. Live cumbia music floated up from one of the patios, which were lit by strings of yellow bulbs. Several large yachts, white in the moonlight, floated at nearby moorings. I scanned the room, checking every face.

"That"—Tenoch pointed to a man in a Western shirt—"is the candidate for governor. Francisco Iguaro, the one whose slogan is 'Light Up Baja.'"

"Like, literally, illuminate?" Jia asked.

A black moustache dominated Iguaro's face, which I now realized I'd seen on the side of election vans in La Ventana. Flowery white embroidery emblazoned his black shirt.

"It has a kind of double meaning," Tenoch said. "Turn on, like you would turn on a light, but also, turn on the ideas, turn on the imagination."

"There was a power outage two nights ago."

"Everything grows—more people, more roads, more business. But the electrical system gets worse."

The incumbent governor, Samuel Villalobos, was in the lead, but he was vulnerable on this issue of electricity, Tenoch explained. For years, politicians had promised a new electrical connection from the mainland to Baja, to run under the Sea of Cortez, but they hadn't delivered.

"Iguaro doesn't like me very much," Tenoch said.

"Why not?" Jia asked.

"When he was mayor of Los Cabos, he gave a construction job to shoddy builders, and a residential tower collapsed. I wrote about it."

"Did you know he'd be here?"

"I had no idea."

He tilted his glass towards Jia and knocked back a slug of the orange beverage. They kept talking, but I tuned out. Gabriel, thankfully, went to explore a table of hors d'oeuvres. I looked around the room for someone tall with black hair and a forehead scar. Someone with the air of a king in his kingdom.

"Cate!" cried Dario from across the fountain. Waving, he made his way over to us. It was the first time I'd seen him in anything other than board shorts. His pink short-sleeved linen shirt was open to show his chest hair, and he wore pressed trousers with leather sandals.

He looked confused. "Where's my wife?"

"Luciana asked us to bring Tenoch in her place."

"She's not here at all?"

I wasn't sure why I'd ended up in this role, but I gave him her reason. "She wanted Tenoch to come instead."

Dario grabbed my elbow and hissed with frustration. "I give her such an opportunity, and she blows it off. She still thinks the rich are the enemy of the people or some communist bullshit they teach in the universities here."

"I'm sure Tenoch is okay. These people have seen journalists before."

"He will want to attack Hunter. Like the man needs more headaches."

At that moment, Dario looked up like a predator sensing his quarry, and locked eyes on a point across the room.

TWENTY-SIX

CATE

I felt a jolt as Hunter turned his head. His prominent cheekbones and black eyebrows exactly matched the photos. Underneath, I could still see the adolescent, past and present rolled into one. For a moment I was thirteen, camping, unburdened by my future, and the exhilaration caught me off guard.

From across the crowd, I watched him move. He was handsome from certain angles, too gaunt from others, depending on how the light caught him. Dressed in tropical-formal style, linen trousers and a short-sleeved shirt, he beamed a smile at the couple he was talking to, the soap opera star and her date. I savoured the moment, and wanted it to go on. I felt powerful, seeing but unseen, knowing I could hang back and choose when to strike.

Suddenly he looked straight at me. I was thirty feet away, through shifting bodies and bobbing heads, so he couldn't have sensed me watching him. I held his gaze until a nudge from Jia pulled me away.

Dario led us across the room. Just the three of us, as we had somehow lost both Gabriel and Tenoch. Time sped up, a swirl of noise and colour, and suddenly I was shaking Hunter's hand, which was dry and too strong, a forceful grip like men use on other men. I gripped back hard.

"Dario said he'd invited two brilliant friends."

There was something about his voice, smooth and faintly familiar, that put me at ease.

"Was your wife able to join us?"

"She's not feeling well," Dario said.

"I'm sorry. I'd have liked to meet her. She was so important to the marine park."

"Her great pride." Dario sounded wistful.

"And you're the mastermind behind Alphaneuro?" Hunter asked me.

A bolt of alarm crossed my frontal lobe. But he was just talking, making a connection.

"You follow biotech?"

"Your sale was front-page news."

"Jia's the actual mastermind," I said, turning to my friend. "I just did what she told me to."

"She did what I told her to *after* she invented a cure for Alzheimer's," Jia said.

He showed us the smile from the corporate photo. "Congratulations to you both." His expression took us in equally, but I thought I felt a special current directed at me.

"How did you find our little corner of the world?"

"It was Cate's idea," Jia said.

"Dario's teaching me to kitesurf," I said, deception launching itself as easily as a bird.

"I hear he's a great instructor." He spoke easily, but I could feel him scrutinizing me, trying to figure something out.

"I haven't scraped my leg across a bed of sharp rocks in at least two days."

"She's fearless," Dario said.

"Is that so?" Hunter asked.

"Nonsense," I said.

"Truly," Dario insisted. "There's a moment some students can't get past, when they have to trust their skills for the first time. Cate doesn't hesitate."

I felt exposed. I was sure Hunter was trying to place my face.

"Tell me, Cate, what was the breakthrough that made Nebusol such a success?"

His use of my name felt intimate, but this was a routine Jia and I had polished.

"Breakthroughs are built on the backs of many others."

"Your modesty is charming. But someone has to make the last leap."

"It was two-fold, one part complex, one simple. The hardest part was to build the right compound. We created one—similar to angiotensin—that could stimulate the growth of new nerve cells. From that new growth, the brain can start to build a scaffold of retrieved memories." A dramatic pause, to let the momentousness of that discovery sink in. Then: "But by the time we had an effective compound, other labs were actually very close to us. One of them would have caught up within a year."

"And the simple part?"

It sounded so basic now, but it was a major part of the drug's success. Jia gave an encouraging nod, even though she'd heard what I was about to say dozens of times, standing in front of investors or colleagues or the press.

"The delivery system," I said. "My grandmother had Alzheimer's disease, you see, so I knew that people suffering from dementia can be very difficult to calm. Even violent. Some of them have to be restrained. I watched my grandmother as her disease advanced. She could no longer communicate with words, but I could see that she was suffering. And the greatest battle each day was convincing her to take her medication. To get her to swallow."

Hunter shook his head in seeming sadness. I had the sense that we were actors on a stage, each performing for an audience of one.

"It turns out this is a common problem. And if we'd gone the route of a standard oral medication, it was going to be a large pill. So we aerosolized it," I said. "Then we worked with a device manufacturer to create an inhaler." Pause. Both Dario and Hunter looked rapt. "When Nebusol went on the market, nurses were thrilled. The fact that the drug re-established memories was the breakthrough that got the most attention. Understandably. But it also calmed patients. They suffered less. And there was no battle to administer the medication."

"Sometimes engineers don't think of the most important thing," Hunter said. "Will people want to use their invention?" He no longer had that look behind his gaze. He'd either placed me or given up trying.

"Yes," I said, meeting his eyes. I wanted to take him by the shoulders and tell him that I understood him, just as he understood me. We were members of the same church.

"You changed the world," he said, as though he knew those were the exact words that would gratify me most.

What passed between Hunter and me felt so electric I was sure it must be visible, but I don't think Jia or Dario even noticed. I wanted to talk to him alone, but there were easily a hundred people here, nocturnal butterflies flickering down to the sea. He was liable to be pulled away, perhaps by the bespectacled man in the white shirt who had just materialized at his elbow. I had to ensure a future conversation.

"I understand you're involved in the energy sector," I brazened, conscious that I risked outing myself as a stalker. How would he react to someone who knew he wasn't Araya from a distillery on the mainland, but Brandt from a fusion company in Seattle?

His smile didn't change, but he paused before speaking. "Modestly. A few projects to support the resort."

"What sort of things?"

"Anything that doesn't emit carbon."

"I'm looking for investment opportunities in green energy."

Jia gave me a look. Hunter studied me, skeptical. I rode out both of their stares until Hunter said, "This is Octavio," introducing the guy at his elbow. The hand-off was so deft that it took me a few moments to realize I'd been passed to an assistant. Octavio took my information down on a small tablet, incrementally interposing himself between Hunter and me as he did so. Behind him, Hunter kept chatting with Jia and Dario. He asked her something about intellectual property law, and Dario about the newest kiteboards. As he methodically bestowed focused attention on each of them, I remembered a definition I'd once heard: a charming person is one who makes you feel like you're the most interesting person in the room.

"What?"

Octavio was speaking to me. He had a slight build and deep crow's feet. I was tempted to elbow him aside as Hunter drifted away into a new group of party guests.

"What types of energy are you interested in?"

"All renewables."

"And are you positioned to lead an investment round?"

"Isn't that question a little premature?"

"There are so many demands on Mr. Araya's time. Knowing some particulars helps speed things along. For both of you."

He gave me a smile that suggested he doubted my time was worth as much as Mr. Araya's. I hadn't felt so patronized since before Nebusol, and I would have found it amusing had he not been blocking my path to Hunter.

"How long have you been with Mr. Araya?"

Octavio adjusted his spectacles. "More than two years. Since he came over from Guadalajara."

"Guadalajara? That's where he was? Before moving here?" I thought about the several years I'd told people I was from Burwell, Nebraska.

"Indeed."

"Tell Mr. Araya I'm interested in discussing his time in Seattle. With a view to investment opportunities, of course."

"Seattle?" Octavio suddenly looked less self-assured.

"Indeed."

"Is there anything else I can convey?"

I shook my head. He made a little "hmm" noise and walked away. I looked around the crowd. Jia and Dario were still close by, but I could no longer see Hunter.

Suddenly, though not as surprisingly this time, the lights went out.

The moment after the terraces went dark, gasps and exclamations rose from the crowd, like a gently cresting wave, then they settled back into the same rhythm as before. The band slowed, musicians fell out of sync, and wayward strains floated over the guests. Then the bandleader called out, and the players reunited in an acoustic marimba. The moonlight bounced off the sea and reached up to where I stood, and the crowd took on a ghostly appearance. A cheerful group gathered around the politician, Iguaro. A few cried, "Light Up Baja!" and Iguaro's voice rose above theirs in response: "Twenty-four-hour electricity for all!"

"Satisfied?" Gabriel asked me. In the shadowy moonlight, I hadn't seen him approach.

"I should ask you the same. I met him, and the world didn't explode." I ran a hand through my hair and softened my tone. "You don't need to keep an eye on me. It makes me feel watched."

He took a sip of his tropical drink.

"It makes me feel watched by *Dr. M*," I added. His face turned serious. "Anyway, mission accomplished. Let's try to have fun."

In the moonlight, Dario spotted some people he knew from Los Cabos, a bejewelled realtor and her elegant friend. Seeing an opportunity, I took Dario's arm and put my mouth to his ear. I needed to talk to Jia alone, I said. Could he look after Gabriel, introduce him around? I had barely turned away before Dario had Gabriel air-kissing his friends.

Jia and I descended from one tiered patio to the next until we reached the water's edge. A pier provided parking for a handful of small powerboats, dinghies to the yachts moored farther out. We sat down on a bench at the end of the pier, facing back towards the party. From this perch, the bay spread away in a dark sheet to the north and west. Across it, we should have been able to see the lights of La Ventana, but the far shore was entirely dark, meaning the power outage had hit there as well. Directly in front of us, the resort stretched south along the shore in a series of round-roofed wooden buildings and stone terraces.

The lights came back on as suddenly as they'd gone off, and the buildings glowed from within once more. Dock lights illuminated the pier, and strings of yellow lanterns lit the patios. I realized we were sitting in roughly the spot where I'd seen the mystery light from across the bay two nights before.

But Dario had talked about how loud the gas generators were when the power grid went out. I heard only music and voices. Which might have suggested that the grid was back online. Yet northwest across the bay, the far shore was still dark.

"No generator," I said to Jia.

"Maybe the grid is on here but not there."

A waiter passed with a tray of peach-coloured drinks.

"To world domination," she said, grabbing another glass and raising it, and I raised my fist to meet it.

"To world domination," I said. As always, neither of us meant it entirely ironically. It felt odd not to have a mutual obsession anymore.

"There's something I've been meaning to tell you," I said.

I was finally going to do it. But just then, Hunter reappeared on the main terrace above us, with the candidate for governor and a microphone. As he began to speak, the crowd quieted. I started to calculate how quickly I could get to him.

"Many of you are familiar with our special guest, Francisco Iguaro." Hunter held up Iguaro's hand and the audience applauded. "The future of the world depends on how we use our energy resources. And so does the future of our home, right here. But here we have different choices. Baja has never been connected to the national electrical grid, and we thought our isolation was a liability. Not anymore. I would like to tell you tonight"—he paused and gazed at Iguaro—"that what we thought was a liability is an asset. Just as the sea gives us fish and our oases grow food, our location makes a different form of energy possible. To power Baja, we don't have to rely on fuel brought on tankers from Guaymas. We can make our own energy. Francisco Iguaro"—another pause—"is not telling you to wait for an undersea link to the mainland. He has a plan to generate power right here at home."

Cheers and more applause from the crowd.

"What is it?" Jia asked. She'd been staring out to sea, sipping her drink.

"What?"

"What did you want to tell me?"

"I need a favour," I said, turning to face her on the bench. No way could I tell her now, not when a plan for the rest of the evening was coming together in my head.

She turned to me. "You need to tell me that you need a favour?"

"No. I'll tell you the thing I was going to tell you tomorrow. I need a favour tonight. Can you get a ride back to La Ventana with Dario, and make sure Gabriel comes with you?"

"Yeah, but why?"

"I want to get some more time with our host. But I don't want Gabriel to—you know. Worry."

"I see."

"It's not that."

She held up her hands. "I'm not the boss of you. Anymore."

"It's really not that. I just need you, Gabriel, and Tenoch to hitch a ride back with Dario. And not worry about me."

"Part of my job description was worrying about you."

"Worrying about whether I'd torpedo the company, you mean. You must be relieved you don't have to do that anymore."

"A little." She smiled. "Maybe a lot. But there's other stuff I'll miss."

"Like what?"

"Looking out over Lake Union, plotting to take over the world."

Up on the terrace, Hunter wrapped up his speech and the guests clapped. The name "Iguaro," repeated so many times, hung in the air like an echo until the band resumed. I watched Hunter as he moved off to his right, quickly obscured by other people.

"I have to go," I said to Jia, and squeezed her hand.

I wove through the crowd and took the stairs to the main terrace two by two. When I got to the top, I turned left. I paused to stand on tiptoe, looking over heads, and glimpsed Hunter's black hair and shirt collar at the edge of the crowd. He turned and disappeared from sight. I headed to where I'd caught my last glimpse, took the same turn I'd seen him make, and found myself on an empty flagstone landing between two elevators, suddenly away from the crowd. An outdoor staircase led down to the water.

After a moment's hesitation, I took the stairs. At the bottom, a long walkway paralleled the building on my right, with a rocky breakwater on my left. The building had doorways but no windows, suggesting these were not hotel rooms for guests. I was in some more utilitarian part of the facility. I glimpsed movement at the far end of the walkway and quickened my pace.

One of the doorways on my right was open. I looked inside and was startled to see a roomful of men in the all-black uniforms the guards at the resort gatehouse had worn, right down to the dark metallic machine guns. The men were at ease, a few looking at screens, two tête-à-tête in a corner, six or seven in all. One saw me and came towards the door. I moved along the walkway and heard the click of a lock behind me. I returned to thinking about what I was going to say when I found Hunter. How I would introduce the subject of our shared past.

At the end of the building, I had a choice of turning right, going up a set of stairs, or following a paved path that led over a small headland. I turned right and found another door into the building. I felt sure Hunter must have gone in this door, but when I tried the handle, it was locked. Frustrated, I turned back towards the walkway and smacked right into Tenoch. I stepped on his foot; our shoulders crashed.

"Ow!"

"Sorry!"

We backed away from one another and laughed.

"Are you looking for something?" I asked.

"Our host, as a matter of fact. Have you seen him?"

"I thought he came this way, but I don't know where he's gone."

"You're looking for him too?"

"Sort of. Yes."

"Popular guy."

We both shifted our weight. He seemed to be waiting for me to get out of his way, while I was hoping he'd abandon his quest so I could pursue my far more important one.

"Were you going in there?" I asked, pointing my thumb over my shoulder. "Because that door's locked."

He hesitated, then walked past me and tried it anyway. He turned back to me. "Sorry. Journalists. We have to try doors ourselves."

"So I've learned."

Exasperated, I abandoned the chase. I needed to be more patient.

Bumping, cologne-scented bodies still crowded the dance floor. Jia was salsaing with someone almost her height. Gabriel was still talking to Dario's friends from Los Cabos. Across the terrace, Dario gestured elaborately with his hands, deep in conversation. I felt detached from all of them, and prowled the edge of the crowd, scanning and restless, avoiding eye contact.

"Dr. Winter?" came a voice from my left.

I turned, and there was Octavio.

TWENTY-SEVEN

LUCIANA

After the partygoers left for Palacio Pericú, Luciana stayed on at the lab, first organizing data from the die-off study, then checking on the two dolphin researchers, then sharing a beer with them. Her colleagues kept her restlessness at bay until the power went out. She apologized for the inconvenience and switched the lab over to the generator. Then, since Dario was at the party, she drove back to Casa Azul to get the power back on there.

After turning on the insistent rumble, she let herself into her house, where Ricketts greeted her, wagging his long body. She was about to get ready for bed when a Neofone bubble appeared on her phone.

Javi was at the hot springs. He wanted to know if she could come meet him. Now.

She almost said no. But something primal in her thought he could quell her agitation, even though he was largely the source of it.

There was no one else on the beach, and shifting clouds obscured the little light cast by the crescent moon. All the homes up on the ridge were dark. Walking northwest along the water's edge, she spotted his panga first—he'd come by boat, from who knew where, risking God knew what. By the time he stood up, detaching from the shadows cast by several large rocks, she was shaking. She didn't know if it was from anger, or fear of the consequences that trailed in his wake, or a purer form of anticipation. She turned off her headlamp and put it in her pocket.

"I'd tell you you're crazy, but you'd take it as a compliment."

"Hi."

He was a grey-scale painting in the dark. She studied him intensely, checking and rechecking that it was really him. He wore a threadbare sailing jacket over his T-shirt and rolled-up jeans. She did not let herself hug him, but it gratified her to be so physically close. In addition to the tumult of anger and frustration he elicited in her, she feared for him, and it reassured her that he was right there. Her shaking stopped.

"I'm glad you're safe," she said, and it was a relief just to say those words, but even as she did, she knew that he probably wasn't really. "Why are you here?"

He glanced at his panga and displayed his irresistible half smile. "I was in the neighbourhood."

"Don't joke."

He made his face sober. "You're right. But I actually was, sort of. And I may not get more chances to see you in person."

The implication alarmed her. "Of course you will."

"Not for a while."

"Don't tell me where you're staying."

"I won't."

"Did you just want to see me to see me?"

"Let's sit down."

They each found a smooth rock and sat, facing the sea. Right in front of them, a depression showed where someone had dug a hot pool. Luciana touched the damp sand with a bare toe, testing for temperature. It was warm from geothermal activity, as though a blood vessel throbbed just under Earth's surface.

"You don't need to worry about the journalist," Javi said.

"Oh." She almost regretted having told him about Tenoch on the phone that afternoon. She'd probably sounded paranoid. And she'd put herself in the position of being taken care of by her criminal one-time lover, which seemed wrong. Her husband might be home at any minute. Being here with Javi felt both intimately familiar and wildly out of line.

"Let's leave it at that," Javi said, although, unusually, he didn't sound sure of himself.

She looked up at his face, which she could see better now that her eyes were more adjusted to the dark. His expression was open, vulnerable, indecisive—nothing she associated with him. And she did leave it at that. As with Javi's location and intentions and everything he did now, the less she knew, the better.

"Did you learn any more about the dead fish?" he asked.

Another way in which she'd asked him for help.

"We keep finding them," she said. "A lot towards the Outer Islands, the east side of the park." She wondered how much she could really trust him. "I'd understand if you thought you couldn't tell me the location of a factory ship."

It seemed farcical, this dance they were doing. Colluding in her ignorance so that she wouldn't be tempted to betray him.

"I would tell you."

"So there are no ships near the Outer Islands?"

"No. The one in the north moved east. The one near Mulegé is still there. And there's a new one coming around the cape in a few days. That's it."

She sighed. "Then I don't know what's going on."

"You'll figure it out, Lulu. You always do."

He shifted on his rock. She really needed to get back.

"I don't support what you did."

"I know."

They stood. This time, they put their arms around each other. He felt bigger and more enveloping than her husband, which also felt wrong. But she held him tight for five, eight, ten seconds before they broke apart. She helped him lift the panga into the water and waited while he climbed in, then she turned and walked back towards home.

TWENTY-EIGHT

CATE

Octavio's golf cart made a low hum as he zipped us along dimly lit landscaped paths.

"Why do you have so many armed guards?" I asked.

He glanced at me sidelong. "A resort like this has to have security. It's just a reality."

Most of the buildings we passed were dark.

"Do you have a lot of guests?"

"Just a few. This is our soft launch."

We came to a Y and he took the left branch, buzzing past aloe and bougainvillea.

"Almost there," he assured me, and a half minute later, he swung the cart between two tall banks of eucalyptus. He parked and led me past date palms and up a flight of stairs. Beyond a heavy door made of dark tropical wood, we passed through a vestibule and arrived in a living room with screened windows overlooking the sea. On a low table between two sofas sat a carafe of water, a plate of lime wedges, and a bowl of almonds. Octavio gestured to one of the sofas and left me alone.

I felt like I'd swapped roles with Hunter. I'd pursued him this far, but now he was setting the scene.

The room was decorated with artwork, each piece in its own pool of light, and to amuse myself during this prelude I examined them. On one wall, there was an orange-and-green abstract painting that in its depths hinted at objects: a flagpole, a car. On the opposite wall, an austere geometric photograph resolved itself into a row of empty swimming pools, a tiny gardener with a hose standing to one side. In the middle of the room stood a twisting sculpture made of black tire treads. I was studying this last one when I heard him.

"It's by Martín Castro," he said, his voice filling the room, resonant in a way it hadn't been against the party noise. "Some say he's derivative, but it has a special meaning to me. He collects the rubber from the tire repair shops you see up and down our highways."

He said "our highways" so convincingly, like Baja was in his blood. I suddenly wanted to explain that I understood his charade more deeply than he could imagine, but also, that he didn't have to perform for me.

I knew this was my last moment of potential retreat. I could play myself off as an investor, or even a seductress, and slip back into the night with him none the wiser that I was, in fact, his other.

"What about this one?" I asked, gesturing to the photograph of the swimming pools. I still had the feeling that I could watch him from afar, an illusion that was rapidly slipping away.

"Xeno Montoya," he said. "I'm very fond of it, and I'd be happy to tell you more." He turned away from the photograph and took me in with the same appraising gaze. "But I don't think that's why you're here."

He looked me up and down in a way that would have offended a normal person, but I figured he was trying to unsettle me and just waited for him to be done.

"Why don't we sit?"

He poured me water and we sat down on opposite sofas.

"I'd like to know what you're doing here," he said with a smile.

You won't leave it at that, Dr. M had said.

"Let me spare you," Hunter said. "You said you were, quote, 'looking for investment opportunities in green energy,' but I don't believe you."

"Yet you invited me here."

"I may have an ego on me, but I know that beautiful young billionaires don't just turn up and throw money my way, however much I might wish that to be the case. Nor does anyone just happen to have *heard* about my energy projects." He ate an almond. "And you told Octavio you were interested in my time in Seattle. So. Who are you and what are you doing here?"

I couldn't put it off any longer. "Back at the party, you looked at me like maybe I was familiar to you."

"Yes."

"We've met before."

His eyes flickered as he calculated possibilities. "Are you with one of the environmental groups? These anti-resort protestors? Because if you are, out with it. No cloak-and-dagger required. Our interests are more aligned than you think."

"The Cleckley Institute."

He froze. Soft waves, the chirp of a gecko. "What did you say?"

I knew he'd heard me from the way his face had gone rigid.

"Cleckley."

He remained frozen. Struggling to keep the mask in place. "He sent you?"

"Nobody sent me."

"They—you—you're hounding me *here*?" Anger drove his voice. "You have absolutely no right."

"Nobody sent me."

"You're one of his study-mongers, chasing up his mice."

"No." I'd gone too far not to lay out my cards, but still I hesitated, as though I could pull back.

"Then why are you here?"

"I was also a patient."

A blood vessel throbbed at his temple and his pupils grew wide.

I spoke slowly, giving him time to calm down. "I was sent to Cleckley when I was seven."

This time, when he stared at me, it fell into place. "You're Catie."

There was wonder and surprise in his voice, and I wanted to bask in it. I wanted to know what he was thinking, what he remembered about me. But instead, he asked questions.

"How did you find me? *Why* did you find me?"

"I saw study results."

"My name isn't in those studies. They're anonymous. Archibald Montrose may be twisted, but he wouldn't do anything to screw up the integrity of his precious work."

"He didn't share your name. He shared studies with me because"—I put it as simply as I could—"I became a neuroscientist. And because I asked."

Hunter guffawed.

"He didn't give me your name."

"Then what?"

"I just saw that there was another outlier."

"An outlier."

"I saw your case study. You'd been to graduate school, founded a company, had no criminal record. I wanted to know who you were. Dr. M tried to stop me. He said you'd left the study, that it wasn't right to contact you."

"The fact that you're here makes it very hard to believe you're not one of his minions."

"Call me what you want, but I'm not his grad student, or a study director. I'm not here on his say-so."

Hunter's initial wave of anger appeared to dissipate as his body relaxed. "You're his protegé."

"You could say that."

"And you're rebelling." A conspiratorial smile spread across his face.

"You could say that too."

Back at Cleckley, the nurses had put up posters to help us identify other people's emotions. On the left side there were clusters of faces, and on the right side, labels that explained their expressions, like "angry" or "surprised" or "joyful." To this day, I tend to study people's faces for slightly too long when I meet them, which they sometimes find unnerving. But Hunter didn't seem unnerved. He looked skeptical and amused.

"Why would you want to dredge up those years? Surely you weren't fond of them?"

"I have questions."

He squinted at me.

"You came when you were twelve. I'd been there a few months already."

"I was locked up for my first six months. They certainly wouldn't have let me near the small children." He fondled an almond. "With good reason."

I laughed at his frankness.

"What?"

"I want to be able to talk like that. Without judgment, without causing shock. To someone who isn't a therapist."

"Psychopath seeks friend?"

"If you want to put it that way."

"Can I pour you something stronger?" he asked, walking over to a sideboard.

"No, thanks."

He opened a beer and took a long swig before coming back to sit down. "I gave up on the shrinks, myself."

"Why?"

"I found it quite boring, to be honest. All that chatter. Do you still see them?"

"Not in the last couple of years," I said. "I got busy. And everything seemed on track."

"Who was your favourite nurse?"

"Mapes," I said, realizing he was testing me, still not quite believing who I was. "She always explained what she was doing."

"Mapes sussed out that I stole syringes from the nurse's station. But I never felt like she held it against me."

"What about you?"

"I should say Bonamo, just for what he put up with."

My dreamscape past felt more real, hearing someone else talk about it.

"How did Montrose get you into the tube?" Hunter asked, meaning the magnetic resonance imaging machine—the MRI—a claustrophobic white tunnel that emits piercing noises.

"I made him explain what he was going to look at. I wanted to see my scans."

"And?"

"He kept his word. He showed me pictures of my brain."

"Weren't you the genius baby. He bribed me by promising extra video game time. He was so good at bargaining with kids, wasn't he? Isn't there something odd about that?"

"There's a lot that's odd."

"Do neuroscientists really know what it means when electricity flows this way or that in the brain?"

"Not the way we want to."

A doorbell chimed and Hunter went to the vestibule. While he was gone, I stood up and walked to the windows. The moon was no longer visible to the east, meaning it was past midnight.

"Octavio," he said when he returned, "to tell me the party is wrapping up."

I could have made some remark about not wanting to keep him from his guests, but I didn't bother, feeling that we were already beyond pretense. He joined me at the window and we stood side by side, looking out. I felt that electricity between us, like anything could happen. Like the universe was suddenly bigger, the range of my emotions more expansive.

He asked me more about Dr. M, and about my memories of Cleckley, and even about my life now. I asked him questions too, but I deliberately didn't ask why he was here in Baja, or why he was now Araya and no longer Brandt. That could come later, during the many hours I believed we were going to spend together. It was around three in the morning when Octavio picked me up in his golf cart, shuttled me across the quiet resort, and dropped me at my car.

When the sun came up, it felt as though the white curtains in my room were designed to accentuate light rather than block it. I put on my eye shades and went back to sleep. When I awoke a couple of hours later, I had a text message from Hunter: *Let's continue the conversation.*

I replied, *Many notes to compare.*

I also had a text message I hadn't previously noticed from Dario, sent the night before. *Is Tenoch with you?*

I puzzled over that. The curtains wafted inward on the breeze, and pelicans flew in formation outside the window. I was still sitting in bed when I heard the sound of the cowbell from the courtyard gate, followed by a knock on the door. I got up in my pajamas, a silk T-shirt and shorts, to go answer. I saw no sign of Jia and wondered if she was still sleeping.

It was Gabriel.

"You couldn't get enough of my coffee?" I asked, a reference to an old joke about who made it stronger.

But his face was grave. "Something happened. I said I'd tell you."

We stood in the doorway in the morning sun.

"The journalist, Tenoch?"

"Yeah?"

"He drowned last night."

TWENTY-NINE

CATE

I stood there, trying to squeeze the meaning from Gabriel's words. How could the journalist be dead? Gabriel took my elbow, closed the door behind him, and guided me towards the sofa.

"Where?" I asked.

"At the resort. Off one of the breakwaters. Is Jia here?"

"I don't know."

The details of the evening came back to me. My machinations to make sure Dario drove the others home. Crashing into Tenoch outside the building with the locked door. His search for Hunter, my search for Hunter.

"I thought he went home with the rest of you," I said.

"Yeah. And we thought he went home with you."

"Why?"

"You were gone, and we couldn't find him. The place was emptying out, so we would have seen him if he was there. Neither of you answered texts."

"I just saw it."

Gabriel took a deep breath. "A detective from La Paz called Dario this morning. She's coming by the hotel, and she wants you and Jia to be there."

"Why? You said he drowned."

"I guess they have to—you know, eliminate possibilities." Gabriel spoke slowly, as though puzzling over his own words.

I didn't know how to act. I could put on sad, no problem, but the issue was one of calibration. How sad were you supposed to be about the death of someone you'd just met? How would I know if I was overdoing it, or underdoing it? Gabriel reached out tentatively and squeezed my shoulder, then let his arm drop. I replayed the very short amount of time I'd known Tenoch. He'd chatted with Jia in the car while I glowered at Gabriel. Chatted more with Jia at the party while I plotted how to approach Hunter. Then gone looking for Hunter himself. I should have paid more attention.

"Why was he in the water?"

But Gabriel had no answers. I thought of Luciana, how she'd placed the journalist in our care.

"Oh, God. Luciana."

"She's pretty cut up."

We heard the courtyard gate, and then Jia came in the front door. Earlier, I'd envisioned how I was going to make her coffee and come clean about Cleckley. I'd been looking forward to the relief.

"I think I can eat two avocados and two mangos before my last day, don't you?" She held up a cloth shopping bag. Then she saw our faces. "What?"

Gabriel had her sit down on the couch and told her. She was so shocked that tears leaked from her eyes. *I should have cried too*, I thought.

When we descended to Casa Azul, we found Luciana first, glum and teary. I hugged her, then Dario, because that's what I was supposed to do.

Dario had given over his office to a pair of officers from the La Paz police. I hadn't been waiting long when they called me in. The detective in charge was Ursula Sanchez, matronly and middle-aged. The black wisps escaping from her bun gave her a harried look, and the file she held looked absurdly thick for an incident that had just happened. With her was a boyish man with a beaklike nose, who hung back and took notes. It occurred to me that this was my first time encountering a police detective as an adult. Some of the grown-ups who had interviewed me after the big fire had been police, and an officer had come to Cleckley after the hiking trip where Terry died. The institute was meant to change my life so that I wouldn't have such run-ins in the future, and it had succeeded. How strange that I was meeting a detective now, far from home, after the string of coincidences that had put me at the same party as Tenoch Gomez.

"How did you know him?" Detective Sanchez began.

I explained that I didn't really. That I'd given him a ride to the resort the night before.

"Luciana Gutierrez had agreed to attend the party. Why didn't she go?"

"I don't know. She said Tenoch was going instead."

"She must have given some explanation."

"I have the impression that she doesn't approve of the resort. She thinks it's caused pollution." I tried to remember my conversation with Luciana outside the lab. "All she said was that she had work to do."

"Gabriel Cuellar also decided to come at the last minute. Why?"

"I think Dario invited him. He must have thought it sounded fun." Not plausible. But the real explanation, that he was keeping an eye on me, wouldn't have sounded plausible either.

She asked what we'd discussed during the drive and at the party. I felt wary. I said that Tenoch had talked about his background, his move to Baja, and his interest in the resort's desalination plant.

"What else?"

"There was a politician at the party, the guy running for governor."

"Iguaro."

"I think he said that Iguaro didn't like him. Because of a story Tenoch had published." I tried to remember exactly what Tenoch had said, but I'd been half checked out of the conversation. Had he said he was going to interview the politician?

Sanchez looked at her young deputy, who made an asterisk in his notes.

"Did you see the journalist speak to Iguaro?"

"No."

"Did you see him speak to Hunter Araya?"

"No." Was it wrong not to volunteer information that Sanchez hadn't asked for? About crashing into Tenoch as we both searched for Hunter?

"When was the last time you saw him?"

"A little before eleven."

"Dario thought he got a ride back to La Ventana with you."

"I heard that."

"But you drove home alone?"

"Yes."

"What time did you leave the resort?"

Keep it simple, I told myself. *Truth is simpler.* "Three in the morning."

Her eyes snapped from her notebook to my face. Even the younger detective lifted his beak to look at me.

"Where were you between eleven p.m. and three a.m.?

"At the resort."

"Where at the resort?"

"With Hunter Araya in his quarters."

I weathered a raised-eyebrow look, but I didn't care if she thought we were having an affair, as long as I didn't have to explain our connection.

"So your friends thought you'd left before them, but in fact, you stayed very late."

"Apparently, yes."

"Did Mr. Araya leave your company during the time you were visiting him?"

"No."

I wondered how much detail she was going to demand, but instead she changed tacks. She pulled a piece of paper from her folder, a protest poster I'd seen outside the grocery store.

¡Si! a un futuro sustentable
Para La Ventana y su ecosistema
¡No! A Palacio Pericú

"What do you make of this?"

"Someone is upset about the resort. Thinks it's bad for the ecosystem."

"Had you seen these signs?"

"I saw one at Oscarito's."

"It didn't disturb you?"

"Not that much."

"Why not?"

Because everything upsets someone, I wanted to say. *You can't live your life by protest posters.* I shrugged.

"Did you discuss it with Tenoch Gomez?"

"No."

"Did he share his views about the resort with you?"

"No."

"Did he mention an organization called Reef Pirates?"

"No."

"But you've heard of them?"

"They're like Greenpeace?"

She snorted. "Their leader is wanted on terrorism charges."

"Different, then."

"The journalist didn't mention whether he was writing about them?"

"Not that I remember."

"Ms. Winter, why are you in La Ventana?"

I could see that her abrupt changes of direction were purposeful.

"I'm a tourist."

"But why here in particular?"

I saw myself in the vaulted reading room of the Suzzallo Library, poring over the study.

"I heard it was good for kiteboarding."

"You kiteboard?"

"I do now."

"You just take up a dangerous sport like that?"

"I suppose I do."

I was lying to the detective, I realized, but it felt entirely necessary and natural.

THIRTY

GABRIEL

Shaken and dismayed by Tenoch's death, Gabriel was reluctant to entertain the possibility that the journalist had been killed. It was simply more likely that the guy had drowned: one drink too many, a stumble on the rocks. Detectives, he felt, were susceptible to confirmation bias, bound to see criminal behaviour because that was what they looked for.

When Gabriel joined Detective Ursula Sanchez and a birdlike young sergeant in Dario's office, she first asked him to outline his movements over the previous evening, then probed what he knew about the dead man.

"Tenoch Gomez spent a lot of time at the lab," the detective observed.

"That's why he was here. He was writing about the national park and the fish die-off."

"Not about Reef Pirates?"

"Not to my knowledge."

"But you know who they are?"

"Of course."

"What about Luciana? She's worked with them, no?"

Gabriel paused to think. He did not want to do wrong by anyone in this conversation—not by the detective, nor by Luciana. "I read that in the past she's spoken supportively of their aims," he said slowly. "I don't think that's the same as 'working' with them."

"And that didn't bother you?"

"Why would it? Her documentation of the deceased huachinangos is very sound, and it's concerning. That's why I came. My agency investigates unusual—"

"Animal disease and mortality, yes. Did Tenoch Gomez know that Luciana had 'spoken supportively,' as you say, about Reef Pirates?"

Gabriel felt buffeted by the implications flying around. "We didn't talk about it."

He fell silent while the detective studied him. The afternoon sun poured in through the window, and it felt surreal to him that he was being interrogated about a possible murder.

"Do you have any guesses as to who would want to hurt Mr. Gomez?"

He shook his head. "The main thing we talked about was the fish die-off. He wanted answers we don't have yet."

"And where does that mystery stand?"

Gabriel sighed, relieved to move into more comfortable territory. "We've eliminated some possibilities. Tested the flesh for different substances."

"Mr. Gomez told Luciana yesterday that he'd found a large cluster of these cut-up huachinangos."

"Yes. We were going to investigate further," Gabriel said. He felt a wave of sorrow as he remembered that Tenoch wouldn't be doing anything anymore.

"My brothers have seen them," the detective said. "They're fishermen. The men they work with have strange theories."

Gabriel said nothing at first, unsure if it was appropriate for him to pose questions. But after a silence, he asked what those theories were.

"Everything from the factory ships to divine punishment."

Gabriel had heard people blame animal disease on godly intervention before. They could credit supernatural beings all they liked, he felt, but that still didn't solve the problem of explanation. That was his job.

"It's hard enough for fishermen to make a living when everything goes right," Detective Sanchez went on. "Then you get one new law, one too many hurricanes, or something like this—what are they supposed to do? All their money is in their pangas and nets. You need land to ranch, and believe me, my brothers are not cut out for tourism."

Gabriel nodded sympathetically, unsure if he was still being interviewed. The young sergeant stared out the window.

"If you had to guess?" she asked.

"You're a detective," he said. "You can't go drawing conclusions before you have conclusions, right?"

"Maybe I can help."

"Maybe." Local lore tended to be a mixed asset, in his experience. Fishermen, hunters, and backcountry campers were frontline eyes and ears but more than once had led him astray.

"I used to go to the Outer Islands," she said. "Before they were privatized. All the fishing families did."

Gabriel thought of the yellow shapes on the east side of Luciana's map.

"We grilled fish on the beach. The children climbed up the hills to hunt heron eggs. We'd sleep under a palapa, or in one of the caves."

"It sounds lovely," he said.

"You can go now, Dr. Cuellar. Let me know if you learn anything helpful to our investigation, and I'll do the same for you."

After Sanchez dismissed him, Gabriel joined Dario, Luciana, Jia, and Cate—all of whom seemed stupefied by the death and the investigation—around a wooden table in the Casa Azul restaurant. From this perch, they were sheltered from the wind but could see the afternoon kiteboarders. Dario went behind the bar and poured shots of mezcal, which he brought out with a bowl of sliced lime.

"Why would someone kill him?" Jia finally asked.

There was a long pause, during which their gazes all settled on Luciana.

"Why are you looking at me?"

"You knew him better than any of us," Gabriel said.

Luciana scowled.

"He wrote about the disappeared back in Chiapas. Made a lot of enemies," Dario said.

"Are you saying someone could have followed him?" Jia asked.

"It's not a place where journalists are very popular."

"Or," Cate said, "he just drowned. A few drinks, no railings."

Gabriel thought she sounded impatient with it all, but he was inclined to agree. "Did the detective search his things?" he asked.

"Not yet," Luciana said. "She's coming back with a forensic specialist."

"They put police tape across the front door of his cabin, and the sergeant is guarding it," Dario said. He shook his head, seemed about to say more, then decided not to. He was no doubt worried about what guests would think.

"What about his family?" Gabriel asked.

Luciana wiped tears from her cheeks. "I phoned his editor. He's going to call them."

Jia sighed and the men looked down at their drinks.

"Did he tell *you* why he wanted to go to the party?" Gabriel asked Luciana.

"He said he wanted to talk to the owner."

Gabriel glanced involuntarily at Cate.

"Didn't he want to talk to the politician with the moustache?" Cate asked. "Jia—didn't he say that?"

"No," Luciana interrupted. "He wanted to talk to Hunter Araya."

THIRTY-ONE

CATE

The night after we learned about Tenoch's death, I dreamt about my stepbrother, Ezra, for the first time in years. He escaped the fire but floundered in the stream that ran behind the house. That's what I heard the adults say. At first, they were afraid Ezra had died in his room, inhaling smoke. But what his father had been hysterically trying to tell the firemen was that Ezra wasn't there—wasn't in his bed when Wayne went to look for him. Maybe he'd gone outside to pee. Maybe he saw the flames and ran. The fire spread quickly across the dried-out grass, right down to the water's edge, and then a spark jumped across and ignited the neighbours' orchard. Ezra was stuck in the middle, disoriented. He knew how to swim; we'd learned in tandem, competing to hold our breath longest. But the undulating orange walls of fire confused him, or so I imagine, and Ezra drowned.

I woke suddenly. He was five when he died, a secret thumb-sucker with straight brown bangs who could hit a moving squirrel with a rock. I tried to remember the texture of his skin, his smell when we shimmied across the dirt to sneak up on the ducks. I tried to feel something. I tried to remember setting the fire. Ezra was lost in the blur of all that happened right afterwards. So many adults interrogated me about our lives out there on the farm, about the various sheds and machines, and most of all about Wayne and my mother, Sabrina. Then Grandma Ida claimed me, moved me fifty miles away, put me in a different school. I remember a sense of having mastered my fate. Not long after I was delivered to her care, Grandma Ida took me for a psychological evaluation, and that was when I met Dr. M.

Lying in my bed in La Ventana, I watched the white curtains puff inward in the darkness. I pictured a thirty-something man with straight brown bangs, the person Ezra never became. Tenoch had straight hair and looked about the same age. I tried to summon up some sentiment for him. Tenoch Gomez, a byline in the newspaper. Was I callous for not feeling more? But this wasn't like Ezra's death, that buried scar that I'd grown around. This was like the death of a seatmate on a bus, just another passenger in life. I'd made my face sombre down at Casa Azul, but now, away from anyone watching me, I could think about what, if anything, came from inside me. I tried imagining who his family members might be, to see if that would elicit emotion. But no: nothing. I remembered that Tenoch had come to Baja for a safer life. That did arouse something. Not sadness. Anger, at the stupid unfairness of his death.

After I left Cleckley—all throughout college and grad school—I kept seeing the same therapist at Dr. M's insistence, Dr. Letitia Gottlieb. But the fakery crept in. She asked me so many times what I felt that I began to perform even for her. Which maybe was the point: not to quit performing, but to learn to do it everywhere. To do and say the right things at the right times. What I've never figured out is to what extent other people are performing too. Maybe everybody just follows the rules about how they're supposed to behave in certain situations. Maybe they're not really feeling what they express, or not feeling anything at all. It's a thought that makes me feel less alone.

Jia and I drank coffee on the sea-facing patio, with her already dressed for her flight back, in ankle boots and a cashmere scarf, while I wore shorts and a T-shirt. It was just twenty-four hours after we'd learned of Tenoch's death. We revisited what we remembered about him, but it wasn't much, and we fell silent.

"When we were sitting on the pier at the party, you said you were going to tell me something," Jia said.

Why did I keep thinking this was going to be easier for future me than for present me? I didn't need a shrink to pinpoint where my reluctance came from: I would tell Jia, and she would pull away like Gabriel had.

"You remembered," I said.

She looked at her watch. White enamel, elegant against her slim wrist. Her flight was in five hours, and the drive to the airport would take two.

"Does it have to do with why you wanted Felix's help?"

I met her eyes.

"It's too complicated to explain before you go."

She gave me a long look. I thought of just spewing it all out, but then she would leave, and I would have no way to monitor her reaction. With my complicated feelings about everything else at the moment, or my feelings about the feelings, or my feelings about my lack of feelings, I needed stasis with Jia for a little longer. I wanted us to be exactly as we had been.

And this morning, somehow, she knew not to push me further.

I walked her out to her rental car and rode with her up to the gate so that I could lock it behind her, and she bumped away along the unpaved road in a cloud of yellow dust. I was heading back down the driveway when I heard the crunch of a vehicle easing to a stop outside the gate. I returned and found a courier truck with a package addressed to me. Standing in the shade of a giant cholla, I read the sender label: *Archibald Montrose, Health Sciences Center, University of Washington.*

That afternoon, I was hosing off after a swim when Hunter texted that he was nearby. I had just enough time to finish rinsing, change into a T-shirt and skirt, and comb my hair before I heard the cowbell jangle from the courtyard gate. I went to open the door, but just before I did, I noticed the unopened package from Dr. M on the dining room table. I hid it in a kitchen cupboard behind a stack of plates.

In a T-shirt, shorts, and rubber sandals, with sunglasses pushed back, Hunter could have been any snowbird wintering in Baja. I ushered him in and invited him to sit on the yellow sofa.

"You heard about the accident?"

I nodded, and told him about Detective Sanchez coming to talk to us.

"I gave you a hard time about seeking a friend."

"Yeah, you did."

"Finding other Cleckley patients was never something I wanted to do."

"Neither did I, until I saw that study."

"But it seems like you arrived just in time."

"How so?"

"This drowning. On my property. I feel like I don't have to pretend with you." He glanced up, looking almost shy, to gauge whether I understood.

"You mean you feel like people are watching to see how you react."

"Exactly."

"I felt that way too, when I was with the others yesterday."

He looked out the window at the cruising pelicans. "We were looking at putting a railing on that path along the breakwater. That could have made a difference." Quietly he added, "I feel awful that we didn't."

I couldn't help wondering: Did he feel awful?

"Apparently he wanted to interview me. He'd asked Octavio about setting a time."

I let my hand rest on the back of the sofa, near Hunter but not touching him.

He turned my way and said, "You never asked why I changed my name."

My innards tightened. "When I started college," I said, "everyone constantly asked where I was from. So I made up this story about being from a small town in Nebraska."

He smiled for a moment, wide and natural, but then his face turned dark. "This is the kind of thing I've always been afraid of."

"What do you mean?"

"We're too easy to blame."

"No one is blaming you."

"Not yet. But if they knew my background—that's Dr. M's big accomplishment. He's enabled psychological profiling. That's the entire point of it."

"No one allows predictive policing."

"Not yet, but it's coming. They already use it for parole decisions. People with bad brains are next. Why else keep records on a bunch of psychopathic kids who've never broken the law?"

I'd had these qualms too. Dr. M's research could have unintended consequences for people like me.

"Anyway, that's why I changed my name. And left the studies. I want to be a person *without* a psychological profile, without a bunch of doctors chasing me around, making pronouncements on what I'm capable of."

There was something beguiling in Hunter's words. Something deliciously liberating. I'd been a lab rat so long, I could barely conceive of not being one.

"All those studies are out there, published, and we never had a say. It's prejudicial. And when a terrible tragedy occurs"—he choked up, recovered himself—"it ends up compounded. They'll look at me."

"Only because it was on your property. That's just bad luck."

"And Dr. M will be a witness for the prosecution."

"He's never wanted that. He wants to protect us."

Hunter snorted.

"Detective Sanchez is hardly going to track down your childhood medical records."

"What if someone reaches out to her?"

"Who? Dr. M? Why would he? He doesn't know about any of this."

Hunter looked at me. Questioning. I felt a frisson at the back of my neck. It occurred to me that we were one another's alibis for the time of Tenoch's death.

"*I'm* not going to tell him."

He kept searching my face. "You're still close to him," he said.

"Sure."

"I used to go to dinners at the farmhouse," he said.

"I know. I remember." *Drink me in*, I thought.

"But later too. I'd go visit him and Eden."

"Sounds familiar."

"I was his protegé, like you. No, not a neuroscientist. That must really be the cherry on the sundae. But they had high hopes. He wanted to keep me close."

We were special, just the two of us.

Then he said something that startled me. "I'm afraid, Cate."

We faced one another, each with an arm on the back of the sofa. I felt like a taut rope ran between our rib cages, tugging us closer. I felt his fear of me, or, if it wasn't fear, his knowledge of his vulnerability to me, because of what I knew. I was a potential threat to him, and that, in turn, meant I should be afraid of him. What would he do to silence me? The question put my body on alert.

He had a tear on his cheek. I brushed it away and felt that remarkable cheekbone, susceptible under my thumb. I moved my hand to his forehead and traced the white line that ran from hairline to eyebrow. His grey eyes looked right into my own. He took my wrist and moved my hand over his face, inviting me to read it by touch, and I imagined expressions I couldn't see.

"Do you remember those posters with the facial expressions?" he asked.

"Yes." Once again, his memory made my own past real.

"They should have taught us like this."

His face was warm, hard, soft under my fingertips.

"What do I feel?" he asked.

"You want me."

He took my thumb in his mouth, and the trap door fell open in my belly. His eyes went a shade darker, and moving with certainty, he took my hips and stood me up in front of him, then reached under my denim skirt. He found my panties, warm and damp, and pulled them down so that they hung around one ankle. He wet his fingers in his mouth, then brought his hand up between my legs. His forefinger stroked and slid, and I moved rhythmically against his hand, one of my palms on his shoulder to steady myself.

His undid his shorts and wriggled them off, and his cock sprang up from the folds of his boxer shorts. He looked from me to it and back, like *What are you going to do about that?* I thought about resisting my desire, but instead I put a knee on either side of his hips, took his cock in my hand, and guided it in.

I rode him like that, enthralled, insides gripping, until I came. My body curled over his. He stroked my back while I caught my breath, and then, once I was relaxed, he flipped me onto my back, held me down by my shoulders, and rocked into me, deep and relentless. Time slowed down as he came, and I reached up to touch his face again. I watched him, lost and possessed, feeling the completeness and brevity of my control.

We moved into the bedroom, where we fucked with more deliberation. Afterwards, I tied on a sarong and he found his shorts, and we drifted to the kitchen as the sky turned the pink of pre-dusk. I got out pico de gallo and corn chips. I was about to open a cupboard to get glasses when a tiresome note of caution reasserted itself like a corset suddenly pulled taut. Dr. M's package was back there, to the right of the glasses and behind the plates. For one liberated moment I thought maybe I would grab it and show it to Hunter, and we could rip it open like children with a birthday gift and see what was inside.

Instead, I turned from the cupboard to the glasses in the dish rack. I poured water for myself and found a beer in the fridge for him.

"Sit," I commanded, not wanting him to get helpful and open the cupboard himself.

"Do you not drink alcohol?"

"Not in ages."

"Did you have a bad experience?"

I sat down across from him. I was going to give him my standard answer, that brain researchers get protective about their brain cells. But a wish to share suddenly tempted me like a narcotic. "I did, yeah."

His face was sympathetic.

"I don't like to lose my inhibitions, in case—"

He looked at me with anticipation.

"Just in case."

"What happened?"

"It was a long time ago."

He looked so intent, so sincere, he could have been yet another therapist.

"Do you remember Sissy?"

"Your little pal."

I told him about going to Sissy's apartment, all those years back. How she'd wanted to do shots before we rolled joints. Then about the guy she called Vic turning up, and how I'd kept kicking him even when he was on the floor.

Hunter was quiet for a moment, and when he spoke, his voice seemed thicker. "He attacked your friend."

"I liked it, though. *Really* liked it. I wanted him to come back at me just so I could hit him again."

He gazed at me and sipped his beer. "You like to be in control."

"Absolutely."

I enjoyed seeing the smile bloom across his face.

"Cleckley tried to stuff us full of guilt for who we are."

"I don't feel guilty."

"But you don't feel free."

"Maybe not." The burden of the fire had shaped me, after all.

"Look at everything you've done. You goddamn cured *Alzheimer's*." He jumped up from his seat, raised his beer in the air. "Have you really let that sink in? You're a fucking hero! You should be the freest person in the world!"

I laughed. "I don't even know what you mean."

"You beat up one asshole drug dealer and felt good about it? Big deal! You're saving lives!" He sat back down triumphantly. "That's what they got wrong at Cleckley. They want us to fit in, but we're not supposed to be like everyone else."

Now was the moment I'd been half-consciously waiting for. "What about you?"

He was lit from within. "Fusion."

"Tell me more."

"Fusion has the potential to be an infinite energy source. The raw ingredients are literally everywhere. They're in seawater. That means no more burning fossil fuels. No more global warming. No more poverty, even. Imagine cheap energy for everyone that doesn't wreck the planet."

"But does it actually work?"

"For a long time, no one could build a plasma that was stable enough, that could be sufficiently contained."

"What does the plasma do?"

"It heats. You have to put two hydrogen isotopes together, deuterium and tritium. The plasma raises their temperature enough to make the fusion reaction occur. Then you use magnetic fields to control the plasma."

"This is still experimental."

"Not anymore."

His tone was confident and conspiratorial. I could see how he'd convinced investors. Inspired them with their chance to help stop climate change. To do good and get rich. But I still wanted to know what had happened to his business, how he'd ended up down here. What pin had been pulled?

"This is what you were doing before you came to Baja?"

He continued to smile, but his eyes went blank, and I knew he was weighing what to say. Balancing a desire to win more of my admiration with prudence.

"I had a company back in Seattle. We hit some setbacks that probably shouldn't have surprised me." He swigged his beer. "Funding was a constant challenge. We just had one more scientific hump to get over: keeping the plasma stable. I knew we would get there, but my investors lost patience."

He was slipping towards caginess, and I would have preferred him to say nothing rather than lie. Tasking Felix with investigating his life now seemed like a gross violation.

I put my hand over his and said, "I thought my company was toast at least twice. That we weren't going to get more funding and would have to shut down. I don't know what I would have done without Jia."

His confident expression came back. "I haven't left it all behind. It's not going to invent itself."

"But ninety-nine percent of people act as though things *will* invent themselves," I said. "Like someone else will take care of solving problems. *They'll* do it, this magical 'they' in the sky."

"We're the they."

"Exactly."

He finished his beer and stood up again. He came over and cupped my cheek in his hand, so that I looked up into his face and he looked down into mine. His thumb played over my cheekbone.

"I'll show you what I'm doing."

"When?"

He gave his whole-face smile and said, "Very soon."

The crunch of tires on gravel faded. I thought of joining Gabriel and the others down at the hotel, but the package in the cupboard nagged at me like the insistent beep of a dying smoke detector. *Not yet*, I told myself. In the shower, I sat on the tiled bench and let the water wash over me. I hadn't thought about what to do after I actually found Hunter. Now I wanted to savour this feeling, which was better than I'd dared to expect. Peaceful yet energized. Except for that distant warning beep.

I put on a sweatshirt and leggings, checked my email for no reason but to delay, and made my way back to the kitchen. I retrieved the package from behind the dishware, cut it open with a pair of scissors, and carried it to the sofa. Inside there was a stack of paper, bundled into an accordion folder and held together with a rubber band. There was a note on Dr. M's letterhead, written in that looping longhand that reminded me of his gait. It said, *The trouble with being an atheist is, there's no one to ask for forgiveness.*

I slipped off the elastic band and eased the document out of the folder. It was a collection of patient notes, the first entry dated 1998.

THIRTY-TWO

GABRIEL

The moon had waned in recent nights, but it still cast its path upon the sea like something from a children's storybook. Sleepless, Gabriel lay in the hammock on the deck of his cabin. He could see directly across the arroyo to where Tenoch had stayed. Police tape still criss-crossed the front door of the cabin, which awaited forensic inspection, but the young sergeant was gone.

Gabriel felt a sudden and strong urge to talk to Cate about Tenoch's death, this event that was not about them but had happened around them and felt like an emotional conduit. He wondered if Cate, just up the hill, might feel the same way. He still sometimes wondered how she experienced emotions. When the question began to obsess him too much, he reminded himself that he could never experience other people's feelings exactly the way they did. He couldn't feel what Penelope or his sister or his father or anyone felt for him. Not being able to know the hearts of others might be maddening, but it was the human condition, and therefore, he told himself, he shouldn't fixate so much on not knowing what Cate felt.

And Cate shouldn't self-analyze so much either, he believed. Her knowledge of herself as an object of study had made her too prone to do that, and he wished she could just let go of it all and experience her feelings for what they were. Whatever they were. He regretted that he'd never found a way to say that to her. She'd told him her attachment to people was utilitarian, that if someone stopped being useful to her, they would stop being an important part of her life. Gabriel didn't believe it.

He reached for his phone and called Penelope instead. He felt a moment of guilty relief when she didn't pick up, and resolved to write her an email. It would be easier to explain in writing that someone had died. In a minute, he would get up to fetch his laptop.

The arroyo was all moonlight and shadows. From a few cabins, interior lights glowed dimly behind linen curtains, but mostly they were dark. The sports enthusiasts went to bed early. Over on Tenoch's deck, distinct features were lost in the gloom, but he stared long enough to make out shapes: two chairs, the arch above the doorway, the stairs leading down to the ground. There was a glint on one of the windows.

He was getting tired. Just the email to send, and then he would go to bed. He swung his feet to the ground and was about to stand when the glint on Tenoch's window moved. Someone with a flashlight must be coming up from the beach. But he saw no one, and the wide flagstone path that ran along the bottom of the arroyo, quite visible in the moonlight, was empty. He lifted his feet back into the hammock and stared at Tenoch's window. The glint bounced and darted. Gabriel realized with a start that he wasn't looking at light reflected off the window, but rather a light coming from within. Someone with a flashlight was inside Tenoch's cabin. A shiver passed over him, and he willed himself to stillness as he groped for explanations. A cleaner? But why at night, with a flashlight, when the police tape was still up?

The pinprick of light disappeared, then reappeared in the window on the other side of the door before going out. Gabriel, motionless in the hammock, continued to stare. He stared for so long, with no more sign of the light, that he grew drowsy. He must have been imagining things.

Gabriel swung his feet to the ground, ready to go inside to bed—he'd write Penelope in the morning—then froze as the door to Tenoch's cabin opened. Heart revving, Gabriel crouched so he could peek over his railing without being seen.

A figure set down something large and square and shoved it out the door, then ducked under the police tape and came out onto the deck. The shadowy form closed the door and stood hunched for a few moments, then picked up the large object and balanced it on one hip. A dark-coloured hoodie frustrated Gabriel's attempt to glimpse a face. The person descended the stairs, but instead of heading for the moonlit flagstone path, disappeared behind the cabin.

Gabriel ran down his own stairs and sprinted across the arroyo. He broke left around the side of Tenoch's cabin. Behind it, he stopped and quelled his breath to listen. A narrow dirt trail ran up towards the road and down to the beach, but it was dark, with cacti and boulders and the steep side of the arroyo blocking the moonlight. He looked left and right. He heard the sound of feet on gravel up towards the road, and set off in that direction. But his right foot landed on a loose rock and his ankle twisted painfully, so that it was all he could do not to cry out. He stood to catch his breath and gently tested his ankle, and an aftershock shot up his leg.

The pause gave him time to consider the absurdity of what he was doing. Did he plan to tackle the mystery figure, and if so, then what?

He turned and limped back to his cabin. Once inside, he thought of calling Dario or Luciana or the front desk. But he was so tired, he doubted his own judgment.

His thoughts returned to the hoodie. He hadn't seen the front, where the logo would have been, but it could have been a Casa Azul sweatshirt. Dario wore one all the time, but so did other staff, and they were popular with guests as well.

He made sure his screen door and his wooden door were both locked. He decided not to turn on a lamp and thereby signal to anyone watching him (who would be watching him?) that he was awake. He removed his shorts and shirt and draped them over the cowhide chair, and gave his pillow and sheet a routine shake. After he was stretched out in his boxer shorts, his mind went back to Cate, up the hill, whom he now wanted to talk to even more. His thoughts spiralled out like the arms of a galaxy, reasoning and wondering, growing more confused, until finally, near dawn, he fell asleep.

4/21/98

PATIENT NOTES

Completed intake for Hunter, a boy of 12. Tall for his age (5'7"), skinny, black hair, grey eyes. Has an old scar running from left eyebrow to hairline. Gave two versions of how he got it (fight at school; bear encounter). Tendency to lie.

Hunter is from Portland, where his mother, Sarah Brandt, and two younger siblings reside. Ms. Brandt says the forehead scar was a result of abuse by Hunter's father. Parents separated when Hunter was 5 and other children 3 and 1. Siblings R (10) and M (8) present as sociable but cautious.

INCIDENTS PRECEDING REFERRAL

AGE 4–8: Violent tantrums. Ms. Brandt constrained him with backward hug technique, received bruises.

AGE 8: Sharp increase in dead birds on porch, not attributable to feline.

AGE 8–9: Ms. Brandt observed less physical violence from Hunter. May suggest that he was learning to control his behaviour, or that he was learning to hide it.

AGE 9: Hunter had a dispute with a neighbour boy over a video game. In reaction, Hunter took the other boy's bicycle, partially disassembled some components, and returned it to the boy's garage. When the boy used his bike, it collapsed, leading to scrapes, bruises, and a sprained wrist. The neighbour boy's father examined the pieces, concluded bolts and screws had been loosened.

Shows forethought, sustained malice.

First known incident of Hunter trying to twist his brother's forearm. When confronted, Hunter said he "wanted to see what would happen." Similar incidents occurred about six times.

AGE 10: Held his sister's head underwater in the bath.
AGE 10–12: Teachers reported Hunter making verbal threats to other students, including "I'll kill you."
AGE 11: Neighbour's dog (chihuahua) disappeared.
AGE 12: Hunter pushed younger brother from a tree, resulting in a broken arm and hospitalization.

SUMMARY

I won't forget the look on Ms. Brandt's face while she readied herself to go over Hunter's history. Haunted grey eyes. Exhaustion.

She left her husband, she said, to spare her younger children his violence, but she feared she had waited too long, and that his actions had made Hunter "the way he is." It's a sadly common phrase among the parents we see, one they come up with before they begin to understand their children's brains. I told her, of course, that we couldn't be sure. Hunter's external environment—the abusive father—most likely interacted with internal traits over which no one had any control. Genes may play at least as great a role as the father's behaviour. Tomorrow we'll have the results of his MRI.

These parent meetings always fill me with mixed feelings. The parents are grateful to have found some respite—both practical, in that we will care for their children, and the emotional release of finding doctors who understand their predicament. It gratifies me to be able to provide them with that much. But the hope in their voices fills me with concern, because of what we can't promise.

4/28/98

PATIENT NOTES

Week 1. Hunter occupies room 10 on the west corridor. He threw most of his small belongings (books, cups, pens) at staff via the hatch in his door.

Threw urine twice.

Tried to assault Nurse Bonamo during room check.

In the last two days, he has turned book pages into paper airplanes and sailed them out the hatch. He may be experiencing more calm, or perhaps ran out of other projectiles.

He attended his first session with me on Monday. Did not appear agitated. I asked him if he understood why he was here. Transcript follows.

TRANSCRIPT

HB: My mom and my teachers think I'm bad.
AM: Why do they think that?
HB: I pushed Robbie out of the tree.
AM: Why did you do that?
HB: I thought I would feel something.
AM: Feel what?
HB: Feel good.
AM: Did you?
HB: Yes.
AM: What about Robbie?

HB: My mom was mad.

AM: How did Robbie feel?

HB: I don't know.

AM: How would you feel if someone pushed you from a tree?

HB: Angry.

AM: Do you think it's possible that Robbie felt angry, then?

HB: Yes.

AM: Are there other things that make you feel good or excited?

HB: Other than what?

AM: Other than hurting people.

HB: Yeah.

AM: What are they?

HB: Stuff people don't know about.

AM: Things adults haven't learned about.

HB: Uh-huh.

AM: Like what?

HB: Sometimes I'll take an animal.

AM: Like the chihuahua—Poppy?

HB: Uh-huh.

AM: What did you do to Poppy?

HB: I killed her with a knife. I cut her neck. She bled.

AM: And how did that make you feel?

HB: Excited. Just for a couple of minutes.

AM: And then?

HB: I had to get rid of her or Mrs. Bayliss would find out, so I dug a hole.

AM: Did you think about how Mrs. Bayliss would feel?

HB: Mad.

AM: How else might Mrs. Bayliss feel, losing her dog? What if you lost your dog, how would you feel?

HB: I dunno.
AM: Hunter, what else gives you enjoyment?
HB: Shawn took me hunting a couple of times.
AM: And Shawn is?
HB: He was my mom's boyfriend.
AM: What did you hunt?
HB: Deer.
AM: What did you like about hunting?
HB: The way it fell.
AM: How did it fall?
HB: Fast. Then a big thump. Breaking branches.
AM: Mmm-hmm?
HB: Also its eyes. When we got up to it, I looked at its eyes, and they changed. They became less shiny.
AM: Do you understand the difference between hunting and hurting someone's pet?
HB: Yeah. Shawn explained it.
AM: Did he know that you killed Mrs. Bayliss's dog?
HB: He never said, but I think so.
AM: What's the difference?
HB: If you get a hunting licence, you're allowed to kill a certain number of deer at certain times. But if you kill someone's pet, it's breaking the law.
AM: And what happens when you break the law?
HB: You can go to jail.

SUMMARY

In my judgment, Hunter answered my questions honestly to the best of his ability. I believe we have something to work with here. Eden has told me I'm too prone to optimism with our newest patients, but she watched our meeting through the one-way, and even she agrees that the boy seems promising. In any case, without my optimism, how could I do this work?

8/1/98

PATIENT NOTES

Ms. Brandt informed us that she is moving with her new partner and younger children to Northern California. We strongly encouraged her to continue monthly visits.

8/7/98

PATIENT NOTES

Hunter said he had "no feelings" about the rest of his family's move to California, and that it's "probably good." Calm demeanour.

8/15/98

PATIENT NOTES

New room-inspection protocols instituted as of August. Under Hunter's bed, shoebox found containing:

-a syringe
-a lighter
-a paring knife
-a light bulb

Items can only have been obtained through theft. The

syringe is from the medical ward; must have been taken during a routine appointment. The light bulb was an opportunistic swipe from the janitor's cart. The knife and lighter are clearly from the kitchen and probably required the most forethought. Hunter would have had to leave and return to his room during the half hour before the ward is locked. Transcript follows.

TRANSCRIPT

AM: Why did you have these items?
HB: I like collecting stuff.
AM: What do all these items have in common?
HB: They're sharp. (Laughs)
AM: A light bulb isn't sharp.
HB: It is if you break it.
AM: What did you plan on doing with these things?
HB: Just keeping them.
AM: Is that all?
HB: Self-defence.
AM: What do you need to defend yourself against?
(SILENCE.)
AM: Hunter?
HB: People.
AM: What people?
HB: Like Terry.
AM: Terry?
HB: I've seen him threaten some kids.
AM: You wanted to protect others?
HB: Yeah.
AM: Let's focus on you. What did you plan to do with these items?
HB: Be ready.
AM: You stole them.

HB: I know.

AM: There are consequences. You'll lose computer time and free ward.

HB: I know.

SUMMARY

It's so difficult, with these children, to know when to keep the pressure on and when to let up. But I of all people should understand their capacity for deception. I work so hard to remind myself that they are not irretrievable, like Krist was. As a result, I sometimes go too far in the other direction and begin to believe they possess some sort of inherent morality. Eden is more clear-eyed. But then, horrific as Krist's actions were, I only knew him for a short period. Eden had to live with her sister for her entire childhood.

Hunter was very calm during our interaction, giving no indication that he cared about losing privileges. The literature, and our experience, suggests a conundrum: psychopathic children and adults have a stronger positive reaction to rewards than neurotypical people, but a lesser negative reaction to punishment. Essentially, carrots work, but sticks do not. But how do you develop a behaviour modification system based entirely around carrots?

1/10/04

PATIENT NOTES

We have achieved a major first: Hunter has been offered early acceptance to the University of Washington. When he came to us six years ago, I defined success as simply preventing violence. So much has changed. We must dare to have high hopes for our children. We have to imagine careers and relationships for at least the brightest among them.

In total, eight students, all 17 or 18 years old, will leave the institute this year, our first cohort to enter adulthood. I feel as though we're in a race against time. What if, when they take over their own lives, we haven't done enough?

1/17/04

PATIENT NOTES

Hunter was always tall for his age. Now he's filled out in the shoulders, and his acne has cleared up, and he walks like a man. I sent him to pick up Drs. Peck and Mendoza, visiting scholars from Florida. They want to open a similar institute in Tampa and have followed our studies closely. Hunter escorted them right to my office and said he would put their suitcases in their rooms. Playing bellhop was a nice touch; Hunter has never stayed in a hotel, but I suppose he's seen them onscreen.

Peck has a face like an inquisitive rodent, and Mendoza has a rich black beard. He asked if Hunter was one of our post-doctoral fellows, as apparently Hunter chatted extensively about which staff does what and who resides where on campus. "Hunter is one of our patients," I explained, at which both doctors went pale. It reminded me of how far we've come. A few years earlier, had I known nothing about Hunter but his diagnosis, I might have had a similar reaction. Peck seemed delighted once he got over his initial shock, but Mendoza remained suspicious.

"How does he know so much about your work?" Mendoza asked.

I explained that Hunter is bright and has been here for six years—and that, besides, we're not trying to hide from our patients who they are.

"He was quite charming," Peck said.

"His charm was superficial," Mendoza said. Easy for him to say in hindsight.

As the presence of our visitors suggests, we're beginning to gain notice, and I've rarely felt so assured of our mission. If, based on what we've achieved, a network of clinics can be opened, the opportunities seem boundless. I envision a world in which every child can be channelled towards a career most suited to his or her neurological profile. Not long ago, colleagues regarded our project as little better than a warehouse, a place to keep violent youths until they become dysfunctional adults. We know we can think bigger.

1/18/04

SUMMARY

Today Officer Ziegler gave his talk to the seniors on how and why one might become a police officer. Our visitors from Florida sat in.

Not surprisingly, the students used the opportunity to ask questions about the law, some quite cheeky. Calliope asked whether, if you commit a crime when you're under 18, it stays on your adult record. Answer: no. Peck gave me a meaningful glance, but having witnessed Ziegler's talk when he gave it at the local high school, I know neurotypical teenagers ask the same question. The idea that we can hide facts about the world from students is, in any case, a foolish one.

Officer Ziegler had asked to speak with me once his talk was over, so I sent our visitors to their next observation and invited him to my office. He wanted to make me aware of several shoplifting incidents around Cashmere. The hardware store, the liquor store, and a hair salon have all been hit. He said he was just informing me as a community member, but I'm quite sure he was letting me know, in his not-so-subtle way, that he suspects some of our students.

I pointed out that only our best-behaved older teens get any off-campus time, and even then, just a few hours a week. I fear Officer Ziegler is looking for an easy target rather than investigating what's actually going on, and frankly, I'm disappointed. We've fielded community suspicion ever since we opened, and none of it has ever been borne out.

1/20/04

PATIENT NOTES

Hunter is preoccupied with whether he'll have enough money after he leaves us. He's received his own support payments ever since his mother moved out of state, and we kept them in an account that he may access now that he's 18. Eden has taken it upon herself to talk with him about financial choices; I suppose she feels a special desire to protect him. For all the difficulties the parents of our children have been through, Hunter's mother is the only one to have cut ties.

Part of Hunter's college tuition will be paid by the state under a mandate to help students with disabilities. He doesn't much like this, as he thinks he'll be stigmatized. Eden assured him that no one needs to know where the money comes from.

1/21/04

PATIENT NOTES

The seniors' counsellors are preparing them for their upcoming transitions. Dr. Mendoza and I watched Hunter's session with Steve Yurman today. Transcript follows.

TRANSCRIPT

SY: Have you considered reaching out to your mother?

HB: No.

SY: Why is that?

HB: She cut me off.

SY: Is that upsetting?

HB: She's of no use to me.

SY: Do you think there's any value to being in touch with family members, even estranged ones?

HB: Sure, if you want to find out if you have a genetic disease or something. Otherwise, no.

SY: We've talked about support networks. What about your siblings? Extended relatives?

HB: Siblings, no way. I wouldn't go near them.

SY: Why not?

HB: That would be useless.

SY: Mmm-hmm.

HB: My mom had an uncle. She would talk about him like he was this rich guy who could solve all her problems when he died.

SY: Solve her problems—do you mean with money?

HB: I guess.

SY: So you're interested in this uncle?

HB: I don't know. I wouldn't be able to find him without asking my mom.

SY: Are you worried about financial challenges?

HB: I know I'm supposed to say no. School is paid for, blah, blah, blah. But if you look at the real world, money solves a lot of problems.

SY: What would you like to study?

HB: Engineering with a minor in chemistry.

SY: What makes you interested in engineering?

HB: It solves problems.

SY: Tell me more.

HB: Don't you read about what's happening in the world? We need a source of energy that doesn't pump greenhouse gas into the atmosphere. That's really messing things up. It's making the shoreline totally unstable, it's causing more storms, it's causing more fires. We have to take carbon out of the atmosphere—carbon capture and sequestration. And we have to create ways of making energy that don't emit carbon. Like nuclear power. They can literally save millions of people's lives, and they're not doing it.

SY: Who's not doing it?

HB: The adults. Anyone. They're just indulging themselves. They should go to jail.

SUMMARY

When Hunter spoke about his ambitions with such animation, I could tell Dr. Mendoza was impressed. It was a glimpse into how we might channel our patients, rather than suppress them. The key that Mendoza and most of the others are still coming to understand is this: the goal should not be to stop these children's urges, but to direct them. We may never be able to teach them the kind of empathy we value most. But we can teach them to use their rationality and intellect to embrace *cognitive* morality. Instead of fighting their need for a reward system, we must encourage them to see society as a reward system, and themselves as able to reap its benefits. Work with their natures rather than against.

1/30/04

SUMMARY

Officer Ziegler sent me evidence from the surveillance camera at the Cashmere Hardware Store: Jon-Jon, face clearly visible along with his self-administered spiky haircut, in the act of pocketing a package of drill bits.

This was disappointing.

Officer Ziegler asked if he might come interview Jon-Jon. All very polite, but of course I had no real choice, and felt rather grim. Until now, none of our patients have had encounters with law enforcement while under our care.

While we waited for Officer Ziegler, we settled Jon-Jon in an observation room and searched his bedroom. No drill bits. Then Nurse Kimball called from town: a security guard had caught Calliope stealing a bottle of lotion from the drugstore. Kimball had talked the guard into relinquishing her, but he was calling the police.

I joined Jon-Jon in the observation room and confronted him. Almost immediately, he confessed to stealing the drill bits, which I suppose is something. We strive so hard to instill honesty. We try to make them see its usefulness, make them understand that their lives will be simpler if they don't lie. But when I asked him where the drill bits were, he became vague. "You'll have to return them to the store," I said. He said okay, he would "get them." I asked whether he could take me to them. No, he said. I told him a police officer was going to talk to him, but this did not make him more forthcoming.

Calliope displayed contrition but, similarly, provided little information. She has spending money from her family. Were there things she needed that she felt she couldn't afford? No. Why was she trying to steal the lotion?

"I'm sorry, I won't do it again."

"Have you stolen other things?" I asked, thinking of Officer Ziegler's various implied accusations of recent weeks.

"I really feel uncomfortable talking about this."

I told her Officer Ziegler was coming here to talk to her, and that I would be present while she was interviewed.

"I can do it alone," she said.

"It's for your protection. So that you have an advocate."

"No."

I wished I could offer up Eden, but she was packing to leave on one of her fundraising trips. I explained to Calliope that she had to have an adult, and she finally chose Nurse Kimball.

If there's a bright lining to this sorry state of affairs, it's that Calliope and Jon-Jon did tell Officer Ziegler the truth. They'd both committed multiple thefts over the previous four weeks, which, between the two of them, accounted for eight of the ten incidents Ziegler was aware of.

Unfortunately, they both said they did it all at Hunter's behest. He'd persuaded them he could sell everything online and distribute the gains.

I admit, I was skeptical. Hunter's status as future university student has, I've noticed, upset the balance between him and the others. It made me feel ill to search his room with a police officer present. In his closet we found the drill bits, two cannabis pipes, a bottle of scotch, a bottle of ammonia, bolt cutters, zirconium earrings, and a power drill.

I did not feel I had the strength to be the one present when Ziegler interviewed him. Nurse Bonamo, who has a great deal of fortitude, agreed to do it while I watched through the glass. When Hunter passed me on his way into the observation room, I told him I'd tried to protect him from this.

He confessed to Ziegler. Yes, he said, he'd asked two others—both under 18, as it happens—to steal the items.

Calliope hadn't wanted me in the room because she believes Hunter is my favourite, and as she told Ziegler, she was afraid I wouldn't believe her.

While Officer Ziegler worked to establish culpability, I tried to understand why. For their resale value, Hunter told Ziegler. He said he was trying to save money for college. It was all I could do not to interrupt. Hunter stared straight at me through the one-way glass, as though he knew precisely where to gaze. He's spent too much of his life in these observation rooms.

I'm quite certain Hunter didn't concoct this scheme

for the money. He convinced the others to steal for him to demonstrate that he could. Perhaps I should marvel at his powers of persuasion. I was chagrined to have to recognize that I had been persuaded by him too.

6/1/04

SUMMARY

On May 21, Terrence Zimmer died of a broken neck and other injuries after falling from a cliff during a backpacking trip in the Okanogan-Wenatchee National Forest. He was 17.

Of all my fears for our students, I never contemplated this. I had hopes for Terry. I thought he might find a place in the world.

Of course, it's the "how" that bothers me most. Was he pushed off the cliff by another student? There, I said it. I don't see how I can possibly discuss this with the sheriff. He seems a decent sort, but he gave me a blank look when I told him our children have atypical brains. I know just how little support and sympathy our children will find in the world. That leaves us as their only champions. Our legal advisor said it's possible that if one of them were brought up on serious charges, a court could insist on psychiatric records. If that happens, these children, and our work, are doomed.

How can I be honest, knowing the ways my words can be twisted? That one of them could be sent to juvenile detention because of my documentation? That their mental health records will cause the stigma that convicts them?

I will NOT condemn any of them based on hunches. I need evidence, something more than my own cold fear.

I don't feel confident that the sheriff will find it. He hasn't told me all the details, but the coroner said Terry's injuries were consistent with a fall. The sheriff's team has, I assume, studied Terry's clothing. They spent some time sifting dirt and twigs from the top of the cliff. But what if they learn nothing?

What if we are building psychopaths who are simply better at hiding it?

6/15/04

PATIENT NOTES

We were conducting the full quarterly room inspection. I don't know what compelled me to do Hunter's room myself; Bonamo and the new orderly were doing a fine job on their own, and I'd just stopped by to check in. I suppose I thought I was showing respect, de-institutionalizing the process.

In his bedroom drawer I found a Saint Christopher charm—silver, size of a nickel, fellow holding a staff. On the other side, the words "Saint Christopher protect us." I asked the orderly to finish Hunter's room and took the charm back to my office. I found some photos of Terry and enlarged them. I suppose I wanted to discover that I'd misremembered, that Terry's charm actually bore a likeness of Mickey Mouse. No such luck. The artifact from Hunter's drawer is the Saint Christopher pendant that Terry wore on a chain around his neck every day that we knew him.

9/28/16
Subject completed extended monitoring.

SUBJECT NOTES

He has returned to Seattle, and to school: a nuclear physics PhD program at the University of Washington. This morning he came to my office for the first time in eight years. He's 30, looks well, and seems pleased with his new direction.

"Ultimately they just want to make money," he said, talking about his most recent employer, a venture capital firm in the Bay Area.

"Isn't that their raison d'être?"

He shrugged, reminding me of the exaggerated way he would shrug as a boy.

"These guys, though. They talk such a good game. They say they're up for long-term bets, but when it comes to fusion, they defer to the number crunchers."

He's older than the average student in his program, but also better off financially. He said he's buying a townhouse in Capitol Hill.

9/15/17
Subject completed extended monitoring.

SUBJECT NOTES

No apparent new developments based on the survey. I suggested we meet, but he didn't respond.

9/18/18
Subject completed extended monitoring.

SUBJECT NOTES

Having heard no response to my invitation after two weeks, I didn't expect to see him. I was surprised when he appeared at my office door this morning.

Hunter has had an eventful spring and summer. He left his PhD program without completing it and launched a business with others he met there. I can't help seeing in this decision the same warring impulses we saw in him as a boy: he was inventive and ambitious, but always impatient. He's building a prototype nuclear fusion reactor in a rented warehouse, down on the Duwamish Canal in South Park. His company is called Terrawave.

He said his design will produce no greenhouse gases or radioactive waste, and will run on tritium and deuterium, making it a true no-carbon energy source. He's managed to attract some capital and is hiring people—scientists, engineers, managers.

He asked after Eden, and I told him she passed away. I've been 11 months without her now, and I wish she could see him. For a moment he looked blank, without affect at all. Then he told me how sorry he was. He even shared a memory of her: at dinners at the farmhouse, if he hung around the kitchen after washing the dishes, she would offer him an extra helping of dessert. I couldn't help being touched, despite myself. He performed his grief and empathy well. Eden and I can take some small credit for that.

9/24/19
Subject completed extended monitoring.

SUBJECT NOTES

We met in my office this morning. Could this be an annual tradition?

His mind is largely occupied with work. Terrawave has thirty-five employees and a major investor, Maris Capital. He showed me photos of a prototype plasma stabilizer, a silver thing the length of a bowling lane. His current challenge involves sucking water from the Duwamish Canal and building a large heavy-water reactor to isolate the deuterium, which the city seems not to want to authorize, though he says he's on the verge of a bureaucratic breakthrough.

"In the survey you mentioned a life partner," I said.

Her name is Joelle. She leads kayaking tours for a travel company.

"She's the only one who gets me out of the warehouse," he said.

He offered his phone for me to see her: compact and dark-haired, smiling, with a number from a marathon pinned to her top. Bright eyes, light freckles. Pulsing with life. I felt a happiness for him, a feeling Eden would have shared. I also felt misgivings, looking at Joelle. What was being with him like for her? I felt a sense of responsibility—misplaced, perhaps, but nonetheless.

I handed back the phone.

"She keeps me grounded."

"Grounded?"

"We go away for the weekend. Go out for dinner. Normal stuff."

"Have you shared your background with her?"

He shook his head emphatically. "What's to tell?"

9/23/20
Subject completed extended monitoring.

SUBJECT NOTES

There was no preplanning for today's visit, but I've come to expect his annual arrival.

He and Joelle married at Seattle Municipal Court in July and celebrated with a kayaking trip to the Sea of Cortez. She moved into his place in Capitol Hill, and they have a second home she already owned on San Juan Island.

"Family money," he said, by way of explaining the second home.

"Do you talk about your own family with her?"

"I told her I never knew my father, and that my mother is dead."

"Is she?" I asked. We track our former Cleckley subjects as much as possible, but we don't keep track of their family members.

"I don't know."

"You never did see her again."

He shook his head. "She's been dead to me since I was 12. As far as Joelle knows, that's when she died. What's the difference?"

I wanted to ask him more about his wife. Certainly, most of our subjects have been partnered, many in fact married multiple times, yet the nature of being in an intimate relationship with someone on the psychopathy spectrum is still something of a mystery to me.

But he was more interested in talking about his work. His South Park campus has grown. Terrawave's machine can stabilize a plasma for a full half second. He even has a client, a company called Esperanza Development Associates, which specializes in building zero-carbon-emission communities. Esperanza has hired Terrawave to provide all the power for a mini-city in Eastern Washington, which is being built on the site of a town destroyed by fire.

I also learned today that nuclear power operators are required to meet considerable regulatory requirements, with any new type of design facing special scrutiny. Terrawave has submitted mountains of paperwork to the Nuclear Regulatory Commission, Hunter said, and he himself has had several meetings with officials.

"See, doc? I'm being patient."

9/15/21
Subject completed extended monitoring.

SUBJECT NOTES

He didn't answer my email inviting him, but again he showed up. I observed that he'd done this several times.

"I don't always know if I want to come. It's better if it's spur-of-the-moment."

"Why do you think you might not want to come?"

"To avoid the feeling of being under the microscope."

When I asked him about his home life, he answered in generalized superlatives. Everything was "great," Joelle was "great." Though she had recently "dragged" him away to go kayaking off Vancouver Island.

He regretted being pulled away from his work, which he speaks of with great intensity. His team hasn't overcome its technical challenges. Their machine can generate energy, but only in unpredictable bursts. The plasma needs to be more effectively corralled.

"We're almost there. I can feel it."

But he needs another investor. Or another client. One way or another, more money to achieve the final breakthrough so he can commercialize the product.

"Esperanza is waiting," he said.

I was startled. "On . . . the product? I didn't realize you were so advanced."

"We promised installation this year, and it's September."

"Sounds stressful."

"I'm good," he said, and he did seem at ease.

9/6/22

Subject declined to complete extended monitoring.

SUBJECT NOTES

I feared this day would come.

Typically when this happens, we try to conduct a final debriefing interview. I asked him, in a voicemail and emails, if he would speak with me. He never replied.

9/16/22

SUBJECT NOTES

NOT FOR CLINICAL USE

I've done further research based on public sources: newspapers, websites, legal filings. This is an unorthodox undertaking, but I felt there should be a record. A more complete picture of his life may eventually have some medical value. The material below should not be considered of clinical use, until and unless the subject chooses to resume contact with the Cleckley studies and discusses these events.

In April, Esperanza brought a lawsuit against Hunter's company, Terrawave, alleging that their contract was based on false assertions. It appears that, prior to signing the deal, Terrawave had assured Esperanza it would soon have both regulatory approval and a fusion reactor to deliver.

Maris Capital, the investor, subsequently scrutinized its own dealings with Terrawave and determined the company had made false claims about both regulatory approval and the speed of its progress. In May, Maris Capital also brought a lawsuit, alleging fraud.

After extensive negotiation, Hunter agreed to settle the Maris Capital lawsuit, but on difficult terms: Terrawave would be liquidated and its physical assets sold. Furthermore, Maris would become owner of Terrawave's intellectual property, including the fusion reactor design that Hunter had brought to life and refined.

A court ordered Terrawave to make annual payments to reimburse Maris for its investment, an arrangement that helped Hunter avoid a fraud conviction. Maris will also take possession of Terrawave's physical assets.

He is left with nothing.

9/24/22
SUBJECT NOTES

NOT FOR CLINICAL USE

Yesterday morning I received a call from a woman named Lee Barrett, who identified herself as Hunter's lawyer. My mind went to his business troubles, but she clarified that she was conducting research in preparation for a possible criminal defence.

She explained that last Saturday, Hunter placed an emergency call from a remote beach on Waldron Island, reporting that his wife, Joelle, was gone, swept away after they were both caught in a storm and her kayak capsized.

There is a recording of Hunter's 911 call, in which he sounded shocked and distraught.

The Coast Guard found Joelle's kayak and its contents, and a part of the subsequent investigation focused on the question of how she could have been separated from her vessel if she was wearing her spray skirt. Police seem to have concluded that the waves were violent enough to rip her from the hull.

The sheriff's office in Friday Harbor held Hunter for two nights and questioned him exhaustively, then let him go with a caution that they would need to interview him again. He retained Ms. Barrett and gave her a list of potentially helpful people, which included me.

In response to her questions, I confirmed that yes, I had been Hunter's doctor and known him since childhood. When she asked if I could be a character witness in court, should one be necessary, I said I would need to think about it.

I do wonder if Hunter included me on that list by mistake. When I got off the phone, I thought of him at 18, gazing insolently at me through the one-way glass after being caught for his shoplifting scheme.

Poor Joelle.

10/15/22

SUBJECT NOTES

NOT FOR CLINICAL USE

Hunter's lawyer, Lee Barrett, called me again today.

A Coast Guard team found Joelle's body caught in a rocky channel between two islands in the San Juans. Bloated and partially decayed, it provided no forensic evidence about the moment of her death, except insofar as she had no broken bones.

Authorities have found no evidence that would lead

them to charge Hunter with wrongdoing, Barrett said, yet she asked me again about being a character witness. I asked why that would be necessary. She said Joelle's sister, Nomi, is pressuring the San Juan County attorney to bring a criminal case. I told Barrett again that I was undecided.

A new fear has assailed me. What if there's a murder case and I'm called by the prosecution? What if I'm asked for my views on Hunter's capabilities? I would have to testify honestly. I would have to say that Hunter scores high on the psychopathy scale and has very low empathy. And that as such, he is more psychologically capable of murder than the average man. Significantly so. Perhaps I might even say that the stress of his professional troubles could have reduced his capacity for good judgment.

No one is going to ask me, of course.

10/19/22
SUBJECT NOTES

NOT FOR CLINICAL USE
The riddle of Terry's death has always haunted me. Now it's happened again. I can't stop trying to envision the sequence of events that led to Joelle's death.

10/30/22
SUBJECT NOTES

NOT FOR CLINICAL USE
I decided to contact Hunter; I owed him a conversation at least. Lee Barrett said she'd "pass the request along." Later I tried to email him, but my message bounced back. I tried calling; his phone number has been cut off. Terrawave has

shut down its company website and removed all the content. Hunter also closed his two social media accounts.

He is erasing himself. It gives me a peculiar feeling of helplessness.

1/11/23
SUBJECT NOTES

NOT FOR CLINICAL USE

We had his home address in the study files. He'd never invited me there, but I knew he lived in one of the townhouses on the east side of Cal Anderson Park. I know the neighbourhood, and could imagine him and Joelle walking to buy groceries at the QFC, or in this or that local restaurant. She made him do "normal" things, he'd said.

Last night I drove to his home. It's a modern brick building with an iron gate leading onto a plant-lined courtyard. The grey furniture and potted palm in the upper window looked anonymous. Most notably, a "For Sale" sign hung on the outer wall. I rang the doorbell, but nothing stirred.

Later, at home, I went on the realtor's website and scrolled through the rooms, looking at beds and sofas that belonged, presumably, to a staging company. Though I felt foolish playing detective, I called the realtor this morning and ascertained that the seller no longer occupied the home.

Never since Hunter came to us at the age of 12 have I not known where he was.

2/1/23
SUBJECT NOTES

NOT FOR CLINICAL USE
At the beginning of this grand venture, we had certain fears. What if we couldn't get funding? What if we raised hopes we couldn't fulfill? What if our treatment methods simply didn't work?

I didn't know, at the outset, how attached I would become to our subjects, how invested in their futures. Nor did I know how our research at Cleckley might influence the evolution of the law.

I hired my own lawyer, Jayden Park, to try to understand what could happen. He learned why Joelle's sister is so sure of foul play, and why the county attorney is still seriously considering a murder charge: Hunter, as his wife's primary beneficiary, inherited $300 million upon her death.

This fact shattered my last hope of his innocence.

Park also told me that if the county does bring a criminal charge against Hunter, I could be subpoenaed to provide medical testimony. It saddens me to think that the next time I encounter him in person, we could be in a courtroom. I do not know how I will bear it.

3/4/23
SUBJECT NOTES

NOT FOR CLINICAL USE
Jayden Park called late yesterday. The San Juan County attorney's office has closed its file on Hunter. It will not bring a charge. Despite the suspicious circumstances of

Joelle's death, it simply can't find any evidence of murder.

For the first time in weeks, I slept all the way through the night.

THIRTY-THREE

CATE

By the time I turned the last page, I understood what Hunter meant by betrayal. I went out to the patio. It was so late that the moon was in an unfamiliar spot, directly above me, halfway across the sky between the eastern horizon and the dark line of the mountain ridge in the west. Stars sequined the sky. I wished there were light enough to run or bike or paddle, shake out my body while I processed all this information. Joelle and Hunter were adventurers, out at sea. An accident was possible.

Hunter had never asked to be tracked. And when, as an adult, he'd asked to withdraw from monitoring, Dr. M had continued to keep tabs. I'd never tried as hard as Hunter to separate from my past. I hadn't probed the walls of my prison the way he had. Now I saw that even if I had, I wouldn't have succeeded. We both remained Dr. M's subjects, completely.

I was chilled by the way Dr. M had laid out what he would say if asked to testify. I could have been in the same position. What if something had happened to Gabriel while we were out diving? What if there had been an accident and the police had sought me out? What would Dr. M have done—told them I was "more psychologically capable of murder than the average"? Of *course* Hunter had changed his name and moved to Baja. I thought of all the times someone had implied there was something wrong with me. I was too callous, too risk-taking, too breezy in my dismissals of other people's ideas. Now the same kinds of judgments could close in on Hunter.

Dr. M was trying to warn me about Hunter. But I took Hunter's story as a warning about something else: what Dr. M could do to me too.

I waited for the sun to come up. Waited for the wind.

I needed to kiteboard. Needed to be wind-whipped and salt-stung. But by ten a.m. it was clear that, in a rare occurrence for a winter day in La Ventana, the wind wasn't going to come. I heaved open the door to the garage, where I crashed around until I found a serviceable mountain bike and helmet. I pedalled northwest on the dirt road that ran past the house, and a mile along, turned left onto a hard-packed trail that wound upward through the cactus and scrub. I pumped my legs and lungs until they burned. Every time I came to a fork, I took the path that led up, wondering how far into the hills I could climb, whether I could actually reach the mountain ridge. Branches and cactus spikes scraped my skin. When the ground turned sandy, I left the bike behind and kept climbing, following a path that snaked between elephantine boulders. The sun touched its apex. Sweat poured from me as I finished my water bottle. I welcomed the brutality of the oven-like heat. Every year or two, someone died of heat exhaustion in these hills, Dario had said.

But before the sun could thoroughly crisp me, the geography changed and I entered a canyon. First I smelled it, then I saw it: a trickle of water coming down from the hills. Bright-green algae and tiny frogs. I climbed higher and the creek widened. The path ended at a rock wall, down which spring water seeped in thin streams. I leaned against it and refilled my bottle, then drank.

I ran back along the trail as far as my bike, remounted it, and raced down the hill like I was being chased, twisting the handlebars left and right to avoid crashing into the cacti. As I skidded from the bike trail back onto the dirt road, the chain broke and I fell. Pain shot up my left side, ankle to skull, and I relished the punishment.

When I sat up, nothing felt broken, but my skin seemed to be on fire, and I saw that the flesh of my upper left arm was embedded with tiny bits of gravel. I walked the bike the rest of the way back to the house, sunburnt and squinting.

THIRTY-FOUR

LUCIANA

Beni offered to help as soon as he saw Luciana lugging the cardboard box through the front door.

"No, no," she insisted, "pretend I'm not here. I have a phone meeting."

Thankfully, he didn't ask what was in the box.

When she got to her office, she set down her load and locked the door. She sat and removed the lid, now able to clearly see what was in it, after having hastily added items in the dark the night before. Three hard drives, a stack of notebooks, and a laptop.

She worked fast, suppressing her many qualms by telling herself she had to save her lab. She had to protect her work, that of every researcher who'd passed through the centre, and the credibility of the science behind the national park.

She went through the notebooks first. Most were full of unfamiliar subject matter, but one contained Tenoch's notes on her, the lab, and the fish die-off. She skimmed it and set it aside.

Next, she tried to log into his laptop, but couldn't get past the password request. She turned to the hard drives and plugged the first one into her desktop. She held her breath while she clicked on the drive's icon, but it opened right away. Better yet, it contained a gargantuan amount of information, organized into files labelled by subject and date. But she soon realized that all the material was at least a year old.

On the third hard drive, she finally found what she was looking for: a set of files backed up the day of the party. Tenoch had organized photographs, maps, notes, recordings, and transcripts into folders with headings like "Marine Park," "Politics," and "Whales." She ran a series of name searches and found plenty of mentions of her own, as well as files referencing Gabriel Cuellar, Hunter Araya, and the gubernatorial candidate Francisco Iguaro.

She found nothing, though, for Javi or Javier Sanz.

She retyped her search. Still nothing.

She tried "Reef Pirates" and found a document by that name. Her stomach clenched as she made herself read through it, twice. It was just a few paragraphs long, and Tenoch's information was no different from what had already been in the news.

The document contained two quotes from her. She'd given the first to a television reporter five years previously: "I understand why some people see Reef Pirates as their only hope, when the government has done so little to prevent this calamity of extinction." The other she'd given to Tenoch Gomez the day he'd died: "I don't condone violence."

She exhaled. But her relief was brief, because as the urgency of her immediate task washed away, guilt took its place. She'd taken police evidence and abused Ursula's trust.

She jumped out of her chair and started pacing.

She'd done it to protect the lab, yes, but now it was clear that Tenoch had presented no threat. And that led to an even worse realization, one she'd held at bay since learning of his death. In her last conversation with Javi, he'd told her she didn't have to worry about the journalist anymore.

He could have meant any number of things. Like he'd talked to Tenoch, or he'd talked to his fellow Reef Pirates to make sure they wouldn't leak. She'd deliberately not asked for details. Now she saw that he could have meant only one thing. She grabbed her phone and jabbed in a number with a rising sense of trepidation.

Her call complete, she began copying all the files from Tenoch's third hard drive onto her own computer. While she waited for them to transfer, she liberally photographed pages from his notebooks.

She stacked everything neatly back into the cardboard box. When she sped past the front desk, Beni tried to stop her. The boy was too diligent.

"Gabriel wants to see you," he said. "Can I tell him you're free?"

"I'm not here, remember?"

"Should I tell him when you'll be back?"

But she was already outside. She stowed the box in the bed of the truck, between a cooler and a plastic crate, and covered all three with a tarp.

She took the back street that led to the beaches south of town. After a series of sandier and sandier roads, she came to an open area surrounded on three sides by cactus forest. On the fourth lay a giant sand dune. There was just one other vehicle there: Ursula Sanchez's SUV. Luciana pulled up beside it.

They both got out and walked up a path to the top of the dune, from which they could see all of Ventana Bay, pure aquamarine in the sun. Nearby sat the charred remains of a bonfire.

Luciana's heart raced as she envisaged what she was about to do. Was this it? Was she going to tell all? Would she really betray him? She plunged in.

"Javi Sanz."

Ursula looked at her with interest. Luciana went on.

"Someone used and returned fifteen of my tanks the night of the *Bizan-maru*. I didn't realize—" No, this wasn't about defending herself. "Well, I did realize, obviously, once I knew the timing. I don't know who else would do that to me."

"You said you wanted to talk to me about Tenoch Gomez?"

"I told Javi I was worried that Tenoch might hurt the lab. That he had damaging information."

How much to tell? She gulped a breath and was about to speed ahead, but Ursula stopped her.

"You have a way to reach Javi?"

"He calls me sometimes."

Why, why, why had she said that? She was not built to lie. Ursula held her gaze alarmingly, but then turned and looked out at the water.

"Go on."

"Tenoch started asking about how I knew Javi, which doesn't have anything to do with anything." She heard the defensiveness in her voice. "I didn't understand what he was looking for. I got very worried he was going to write something that would hurt the lab. If he associated us with Reef Pirates, after what they did, that would destroy us."

Ursula was losing patience. "My girl—"

"When I spoke to Javi, I told him how worried I was. He asked for Tenoch's name, and I gave it to him. The day of the party. The day he died."

She felt an immediate sense of respite, then remembered she had one more thing to say.

"Later that night, Javi told me I didn't need to worry about the journalist anymore. But I didn't know what he meant. At the time."

Ursula glanced at her and looked back at the water before speaking. Why was she so calm? Luciana had just betrayed Javi and solved the detective's case.

"What time did you speak to Javi that night?"

"About eleven."

"On the phone?"

"In person. At the hot springs."

She winced as she admitted this to Ursula, who gave her a look of profound disappointment.

Ursula sighed. "Javi Sanz is a criminal."

Even now, it was hard to hear it stated so baldly.

"I've wanted to arrest him since he was twenty-one and blockaded La Paz Bay with kayaks," Ursula said. "And many have joined me in this ambition since Reef Pirates started boarding ships."

Now all Luciana could think was that Javi was going to prison and she would have put him there.

"But right now, I'm trying to find out what happened to the journalist, and I don't like to see you so distressed."

These kind words did not relieve Luciana's pain. But the detective went on.

"No one saw Javi at the party. No one saw any of his known associates. And now I have two sightings of him during our window for the time of Gomez's death. Yours in La Ventana, and another in La Paz."

As Luciana absorbed this, she felt an inkling of comfort. La Paz was even farther from the resort than La Ventana—some two hours by panga.

"He had a lot of gall, showing his face. Did he tell you where he's staying?"

Luciana thought of the tolling bell she'd heard when Javi called her after going on the run. It brought an image to mind. But there were towns up and down the peninsula with mission bells, she told herself. He could be anywhere.

"He didn't tell me," Luciana said.

Ursula studied her for a moment, then looked back to the water.

"In any case, we have another suspect. Someone threatened Tenoch Gomez a month before he died," Ursula said. "They put a mutilated turkey vulture in his car."

As Luciana remembered Tenoch telling her about the dead bird, relief ballooned inside of her. If whoever did that had killed the journalist, it couldn't have been Javi, who would have had no motive before Luciana gave him one.

"Then who was it?"

"Probably associates of Francisco Iguaro. They've done this kind of thing with animals before. It's tiresome, but it can scare people quite effectively."

Luciana took a moment to remember what the date was. The election was two days away.

"Iguaro could be our new governor."

"Yes. He was angry over Gomez's reporting about that tower collapse in Los Cabos. Iguaro gave out the construction contracts."

"Can you arrest him?"

"He's kept himself untouchable. I could pick up one of his people, maybe, but I need more time."

Both women gazed at the bay, still unusually smooth and dotted with a few paddleboarders. Then they turned and walked back down the sand dune to their vehicles. Luciana felt more unburdened than she had since Tenoch's death. She was climbing back into her truck when Ursula said, "I've arranged the forensic inspection."

Tension crept up Luciana's neck again, and she forced herself not to glance towards the bed of the truck. She settled herself in the driver's seat. "Great. When?"

"We'll be there first thing tomorrow morning."

Another reprieve. After Casa Azul was asleep tonight, Luciana could return the box to the cabin, and this adventure in duplicity would be over.

"We'll have coffee for you in the restaurant," she said to Ursula, and started her truck.

THIRTY-FIVE

GABRIEL

He spent the morning in a spare office at the lab, ostensibly reviewing the global literature on sudden fish die-offs, but in fact summoning up the nerve for a confrontation. He saw only two options. Either he went straight to Detective Sanchez and told her about the hooded figure he'd seen leaving the dead journalist's cabin, or he talked to Luciana first. Since she'd shown him nothing but professionalism and generosity since his arrival in La Ventana, he decided he should alert her before he informed the cops.

Frustratingly, she'd come and gone before he could speak to her, and Beni didn't know when she would return. Gabriel took refuge in the white-walled containment area, where he pulled out several Pyrex boxes. He hoped that re-examining the specimens might spark an intuitive understanding he wouldn't get from numbers, descriptions, and photographs. He was just getting absorbed in his task, working on a stainless steel table under a vent hood, when Beni buzzed to tell him Luciana was back. Maybe there was a perfectly good explanation, he told himself as he washed his hands and walked to her office.

He closed the door behind him and threw himself into a seat in front of her desk. "I saw someone come out of Tenoch's cabin last night around midnight. I was on my hammock."

Her face froze.

"I know it's got nothing to do with me, but I'd like to know what's going on."

Luciana glanced at the door, but it was just as shut as he'd left it. She looked at him gravely. "It was me," she said.

He felt a wave of relief that she wasn't denying it. "I thought maybe you or Dario."

"He doesn't know."

"Know what?"

She crossed her arms and looked out her window, so he went on.

"Look, Luciana, I'm not going to hide things from the police. Did you have something—do you know something—about how Tenoch died?"

Her words were calm, but her voice quavered. "I thought maybe I knew something. But I just told Detective Sanchez, and it's not what I thought it was."

Gabriel was still confused. "Why were you in his cabin?"

"I copied his files and notes."

Dread landed with a thud in Gabriel's chest. "Why?"

"I was worried he had information that could hurt me. Not just me—the centre. All our work."

Gabriel could think of only one thing that would have pushed her to tamper with police evidence. "Your connection to Reef Pirates."

"I don't condone their tactics. I don't support them at all anymore. But Tenoch was asking questions, and they're designated a terrorist organization now. I was afraid he was going to write something that would send me to jail."

She looked sad and raw. He wanted to trust her.

"It turns out I was wrong. He wasn't planning to write anything like that."

"But you still copied his files?"

"Yes. And we need to look through them."

A trill of alarm leapt up his throat. "We?"

"The day of the party he'd found a huge cluster of dead fish, and he was so charged up when he came back from his boat trip. Plus, he'd done reams of research. I need help going through it all."

Gabriel wondered how he'd become so tangled in this mess. Animal problems very often turned out to be people problems, but this was the first time he'd been asked to rifle through the contents of a dead man's hard drive.

"We can decipher whatever he found faster than the police," Luciana said. "Don't you want to know?"

"Of course I do." This was, after all, why he was here. But it wasn't just playing fast and loose with the police that bothered him. He blurted it out. "Look, if Tenoch was killed, it might have been for something he knew."

"Yes."

"So if we go diving into his files, then we're going to know that thing too."

"Yes," she said, and looked at him like she'd been waiting for him to catch up.

The afternoon sun streamed in through the slatted windows. Luciana worked at her desk, and Gabriel at an old computer they'd wheeled into her office on a cart. Amid the journalist's research on the fish die-off, there were a half-dozen files named for individuals. She opened the one on Francisco Iguaro, the political candidate, and he opened the one on Jean Lavalier, a name neither of them recognized.

Gabriel scanned a paragraph of notes that left him perplexed. "He's a physicist," he said.

"Why would Tenoch consult a physicist?"

"No idea. Maybe it will become clear."

But it didn't. Lavalier had once owned a company called Dynamic Fusion. Four years earlier, his team had been on the verge of commercializing nuclear fusion, close to "capturing a star in a bottle," as he'd told a reporter. The chief technical challenge that remained was to create a stable plasma, a super-heated state of matter, hotter than the core of the sun.

Gabriel scrolled through the transcript of an interview Tenoch had conducted with a professor who explained how to fuel a fusion reactor. Of the two substances required, tritium and deuterium, tritium could be purchased cheaply on the open market and deuterium existed abundantly in seawater. If you had a tritium supply, plus a heavy-water separator to extract deuterium from the sea, then you had the fuel to create fusion.

Gabriel shifted to a set of news stories about Lavalier, one of which included a photo of the scientist, bearded and solid, forty-nine years old, surrounded by a team of men and women in matching lab coats. Behind them lay an enormous silver cylinder, covered with portals and protrusions. The caption identified the location as the Dynamic Fusion laboratory in Vancouver. Gabriel did a quick web search and discovered that Dynamic Fusion had run out of funding and shut its doors three years earlier. He couldn't find any information about Lavalier since, nor any indication of why Tenoch was interested in the man.

He told Luciana what he'd learned, and asked her what was in the Iguaro file.

"Just the story he published months ago. Basically, when Iguaro was mayor of Los Cabos, he took cash under the table to permit development projects. One of them was a housing complex for hotel workers, built on unstable land. When one of the buildings collapsed, it killed a hundred and three people."

"Jesus."

"Everyone around here knows someone who died there," Luciana said.

"Hunter Araya sang the man's praises at the party, saying Iguaro has a plan to generate power here in Baja. I wonder if he knows."

"Tenoch has a file on Araya too. I've just started to look at it," Luciana said, scanning her screen. "Looks like he's given a lot of money to Iguaro. Campaign donations over the last two years." She looked up. "Dario told me that when Cate met Hunter, she told him she wanted to invest in energy companies."

Gabriel's solar plexus tightened. "That doesn't make sense. That's not Cate's field of expertise."

"That's why Dario remembered. We thought she was in drug research. Did she say anything to you about what she discussed with Hunter?"

Gabriel wanted to defend Cate, but couldn't see how to do so without betraying her confidence, so he shrugged and they both returned to their screens.

Several minutes later, Luciana cursed softly. "Come look at this," she said, and Gabriel went to stand behind her. As he did, he remembered that just over a week before, he and Tenoch had been right here together, looking over her shoulder. He felt a pang of loss for this determined man who'd left his past behind, only to die prematurely after all.

Tenoch had saved marked-up versions of several maps. The one on the screen showed the curve of Ventana Bay, the mass of Cerralvo Island, and the tiny islands to the east. Luciana pointed to sites Tenoch had circled. One was Hunter Araya's resort, at the tip of Punto Arena. Another was one of the Outer Islands.

"That one's outside the park. Private," she said. She clicked to enlarge the screen. The island was shaped like a horseshoe, with a long bay separating its two arms. "And look at this." She opened a file labelled "Rina Uribe," finding an interview transcript with a photograph at the top.

"She looks familiar."

"She's an actress."

But that wasn't why he recognized her. He stared at the glossily made-up face before placing it. "She was at the party. Tenoch waved at her."

"According to his notes, Rina Uribe dated Hunter for several months. Tenoch interviewed her on the phone in the morning on the day of the party. That's the same day he took the boat out on his own."

Gabriel skimmed the transcript.

"Keep reading."

One line stood out. Rina Uribe had told the journalist that if he wanted to know more, he had to go to the island. "Which one?" Tenoch had asked. She'd replied, "The one shaped like a parabola."

Luciana looked up at Gabriel meaningfully, but it took him a second to make the connection.

"Parabola. The horseshoe."

Luciana clicked back to the map.

"That's got to be the one. What's out there?" Gabriel asked.

"I've never set foot on it, but Tenoch has made our path clear."

"He has?" Gabriel asked with a sense of trepidation.

"We need to go there."

THIRTY-SIX

CATE

Just after sunset, light-headed with hunger, I grabbed my headlamp and headed down the hill through the scrub to Casa Azul. The warm light of the restaurant made a cocoon. Around me, fleece-clad, burnt-nosed hotel guests lamented the day's lack of wind. I found Gabriel with Luciana and Dario in their alcove off the dining room.

Dario was fuming over a pile of flyers, one of which he held up for me to see. In black block letters, it read:

¿Quién mató a Tenoch Gomez?

"There's no evidence of murder," he said. "Someone's trying to make trouble."

He had ripped down the signs from outside the grocery store, the pescaderia, and the church.

Gabriel was quiet. Luciana looked weary and sipped her beer.

"Is there any evidence?" Dario asked, staring at his wife. "Wouldn't Ursula have said something?"

"She's investigating. That *is* saying something."

Dario rolled his eyes. "What does Beni say?"

"I don't think his mother talks to him about her cases."

"Who do you think is putting up the flyers?" Gabriel asked.

"Probably someone from Los Barriles," Dario said. It was another town popular with kiteboarders, his competition.

"Or a concerned citizen from here," Luciana said.

"It's troublemakers driven by conspiracy theories."

His wife said, "So it's a conspiracy theory to think Tenoch was murdered, but not a conspiracy theory to think some hotel owner from Los Barriles is behind the flyers?"

We were all quiet while a waiter served a large plate of stuffed chilis.

"What happened to your arm?" Dario asked me.

"I fell off my bike."

Luciana and Gabriel both stared at my shoulder. I'd picked the gravel out of my wound in the shower, slathered it with Neosporin, and left it air-exposed for faster healing. Now I saw that perhaps I should have covered it for dinner. To divert attention, I returned to the offending flyers.

"If nobody actually knows, it seems pretty alarmist to put up signs about someone getting killed," I said.

Luciana looked exasperated. "An investigative journalist died, and it wasn't just an accident. He could have had information on—"

We all looked at her expectantly.

"—lots of different people," she said, suddenly reticent.

"Baja is not Chiapas," Dario said. "We have the lowest murder rate in the region."

"Sometimes we go straight to the least likely explanation because it seems more interesting," Gabriel said. "But a lot more people die from accidents than murder."

Very sensible, I thought. Typical Gabriel.

Then he went on: "Still, we shouldn't let that stop us from seeing the unusual thing."

"What unusual thing?" I asked.

Gabriel sighed. "Take this fish die-off. We have to look beyond the expected."

"But that's what Tenoch was writing about—fish, not gangs or drugs," Dario said. "Who would kill a guy who's writing about a scientific issue?"

After dinner, Gabriel asked me to sit on the beach with him. The hotel's low-slung mutt, Ricketts, followed us out. Of course the dog would attach itself to Gabriel. When I saw a dog, I thought of the millennia-long, uncontrolled experiment in genetic engineering that has resulted in these sentient *things*. But Gabriel just enjoyed a dog's company. Dogs knew Gabriel understood them and that I did not. Dogs—perhaps the ultimate experts on humans—always knew there was something wrong with me.

We planted plastic chairs in the sand, side by side, and Ricketts settled next to Gabriel. The moonlight shimmered on the water.

"The night of the party," Gabriel said, "Jia said you'd left before us. But you hadn't."

"Correct."

"Does Sanchez know?"

"Of course."

I heard his small sigh of relief to know that I hadn't lied to the police.

"Did you get whatever it was you wanted from Hunter?"

"Yeah," I said, a true but incomplete answer. I wasn't done with him yet.

"And what was that, exactly?"

"I thought I wanted information—to learn more about him," I said. "But I feel like he understands me."

Gabriel rubbed Ricketts's neck. "Are you going to head home now?"

"Soon." It was odd not to have Alphaneuro pulling me back. For so long, I'd had no idea where I ended and the company began.

"What's Hunter really doing here?"

I felt a dollop of suspicion in my gut. I wasn't ready to share any of what I'd read in Dr. M's file.

"He's running a resort."

"But there's more, right?"

This was Gabriel, I reminded myself. He was allowed inside my perimeter.

"He's escaping," I said. "From Dr. M, from being followed by Cleckley studies his whole life."

"You sympathize."

"Yeah."

That wasn't the only reason I sympathized. As I'd read about Hunter's company's collapse and the lawsuits against him, I kept wondering how close I'd come to ending up in the same situation. If I hadn't had Jia to keep me in line, it could have happened.

We were silent for a while. Gabriel stroked the dog's back.

"Did you talk to Hunter about energy companies?" he asked.

"Energy companies?" I parroted dumbly. How would Gabriel know anything about Hunter's pre-Baja life?

"Dario said he heard you say something to Hunter about wanting to invest in energy companies."

"Oh, that."

"So you did."

"Kind of. That was before I told Hunter who I was. I was trying to get his attention."

"And you knew that would interest him."

I couldn't see what Gabriel was driving at, which bothered me. I was used to reading him more easily.

I gave a little more. "Before Hunter came down here, that's the business he was in. Fusion energy."

I felt Gabriel freeze beside me. Ricketts looked up, his head a question mark.

"Fusion," Gabriel repeated.

"Hunter had a fusion company. It's an experimental technology, and he fell out with his investors."

Gabriel turned towards me. "What else did he tell you about fusion?"

I thought of my last conversation with Hunter. Just before I read the whole patient file from Dr. M, which at this moment I wished I'd never seen.

"He said he hadn't left it all behind."

"Listen, Cate."

I crossed my arms and my legs.

"You don't know what this guy is capable of."

"Is this Luciana's murder theory now? I thought you were on my side on that."

"Your side?"

"Wrong choice of words. But you yourself said that a lot more people die of accidents than murder."

"Yeah. Tenoch probably drank too much and fell in the water and hit his head."

"Then what do you mean by asking what Hunter's capable of?"

"I don't know yet. I just want you to be careful."

I looked at him, my arms still crossed.

"Fine," he said, startling me with the fury in that one word. He stood up. So did Ricketts. "I spent more than a year of my life asking you just to be careful, without you listening. You think I left because I couldn't deal with all the diagnostic bullshit, but you know what is way worse than whatever some brain scan said? Thinking your girlfriend might die because she puts herself in danger when she doesn't have to. Because she can't see what she's doing to anyone who loves her."

He raised his hand as though to emphasize his next words, but none came out. He stood there, arm raised, a speaker without a speech. Then his arm dropped, and he said, "I have to go."

I watched him and the dog walk back up to the hotel.

I turned back to face the sea, surprised by his outburst. He was biased against Hunter, I told myself. Either out of some misguided desire to shield me, or because he identified with the anti-resort crowd, among them Luciana. If only they understood what Hunter was really up to, they'd reconsider their attitude to him.

My gravel-torn shoulder no longer throbbed. As the day's physical pains ebbed away, I felt a wave of exhaustion, which let another question in: What if everything Dr. M had described or implied was true? What if Hunter had killed his wife for her money?

So what if he did? I asked myself. One death, and then he'd used her fortune to relaunch his fusion operation, which could save millions of lives. Most people were too squeamish to truly evaluate the greater good. Hunter saw the big picture.

And Dr. M's evidence was circumstantial. The only person who could tell me what had really happened was Hunter. Which meant I had to ask him.

THIRTY-SEVEN

GABRIEL

Gabriel and Luciana waded the lab's best panga out into the water until they were knee-deep. They hopped over the gunwales, and Beni gave them a shove into deeper water before heading to his car. His task for the day was to drive to a state office in La Paz and research property records on the Outer Islands.

Luciana pulled twice on the cord with no response, but on the third pull the engine came to life. She looked especially water-ready today, wearing a spandex top, board shorts, and neoprene shoes, her hair slicked into a ponytail. Gabriel was dressed the same way, but being bulkier, he never managed to look quite so aquatic. His polarized sunglasses were like x-ray goggles for the sea's surface, allowing his one good eye to make out the shapes and shadows underneath.

Luciana pointed the bow east by southeast and sped up until they were planing over the smooth surface of the bay. The wind was not yet awake. They buzzed past San Juan de los Planes, the long, curving beach, and the low-rise, sand-coloured architecture of Palacio Pericú. As they passed Punta Arena, Luciana slowed the panga, and Gabriel, sitting in the bow, quickly saw why. Some thirty yards off, a sleek grey body arced out of the water, followed by another and another, until the water was boiling with dolphins. She throttled down to a putt-putt.

"Reminds me of Fiji," he said, thinking of Cate in the bow of a similar boat, blue sky above, palm trees on shore, water popping with shiny cetaceans. They'd been on their way to dive in a remote lagoon, carrying tridents to spearfish their dinner.

As this pod moved southward, Luciana sped up, navigating out of the bay and into a gently rolling sea. The hull slapped the surface in a steady rhythm. To the east, a smudge of yellow grew, took on dimension, and resolved itself into separate shapes. They travelled for an hour and a half this way, until the island circled on Tenoch's map stood out sharp and real, less than a quarter mile ahead, sandy yellow against the blue sky.

Luciana slowed down. "We just left the national park."

She piloted them in closer to the island's west side, then turned to follow the shore southward. It was mostly a cliff face of yellow and grey stone streaked with white, punctuated by a series of small, sandy beaches. Low bushes and the occasional determined cactus clung to the cliff tenaciously here and there. They passed a tall, rocky islet around which a clan of sea lions bobbed and wove. They rounded a headland towards the mouth of the island's horseshoe and found themselves going against the current. That was where Gabriel spotted the first one.

"Luciana," he said, and pointed to the surface.

It floated there obscenely, one glassy eye up—pinkish scales, white flesh, and dark coagulated blood. When he looked back at her, she nodded grimly at an aluminum pole with a net. Gabriel unfastened it from the gunwale and, kneeling in the bow, leaned out to scoop up the body. Moving with care, he opened the cooler strapped in the middle of the boat and placed the dead creature into a Pyrex box inside, pausing to take a good look before he closed it. Like many of their samples, it was a huachinango with four parallel gashes on each side of its body.

He looked towards the stern and saw that Luciana's mouth was agape. He turned to follow her gaze, almost afraid to look. Just ahead of them floated more garish corpses. Three—no, five, six, eight, eleven—too many to count. The engine pushed them forward, against the current, into the mass of dead fish.

"Do you want them all?"

"Just count," she said, and he heard the anger in her voice.

He put down the net, unpocketed his phone, and took a video, a twenty-second sweep from port to starboard to capture the carnage.

As they entered a long, sunny bay, the dead fish came at them in a scattering, as though floating down a lazy river. Gabriel crouched in the bow with the net on the aluminum pole, picking up samples, sometimes two at a time, and laying them in boxes in the cooler. At the bay's midpoint, the water was nearly still. Luciana cut the engine, Gabriel put down the net, and they each picked up an oar, by silent consensus agreeing that it would be prudent to be quiet. He looked around, scanning the clear blue water with its multiple shades, the rocky land with its cacti and shrubs. A flock of California gulls cried from the cliff face, taking turns dive-bombing the water, as curious about the dead fish as the two humans. He saw no man-made structures, not even a fishermen's palapa. Besides the outburst from the birds, the splashing of their oars made the only sound.

They paddled slowly north. Gradually he noticed that it wasn't silent anymore. He looked back to Luciana; she had noticed too. It was rhythmic, a man-made sound, first muffled, then louder. They stopped paddling, but the panga continued to drift northward, gently, and then more quickly.

"The tide—"

"It's not the tide pulling us," Luciana said.

A shadow in the rock wall up ahead resolved itself into the mouth of a cave.

"Backwards, backwards," she called, her voice rising.

They both tried to arrest their forward momentum with the paddles, but the current was curiously strong. To keep control, Luciana had no choice but to restart the engine. She gave the cord a yank, but nothing happened. Gabriel's stomach lurched. The boat's drift towards the cave picked up speed. She went for it again, this time pulling so hard she fell backwards, cursing as she hit the deck. Still it didn't start. Gabriel plunged his oar into the water, paddling hard, with almost no effect. They were now close enough to the mouth of the cave that Gabriel could see how deep and dark it was. The water kept pulling them towards it. Luciana righted herself, braced her legs, and with an emphatic grunt pulled the cord once more. This time the engine sputtered to life, revving high before settling back down. She put it into reverse just as they reached the cave's mouth. The air temperature dropped and the machine noise rose deafeningly. Gabriel pushed back his sunglasses but could make out only darkness at first.

Hovering with the engine in reverse so they wouldn't be pulled in, Luciana kept them to one side of the cave and checked her depth finder. "It's getting shallower," she shouted over the noise.

He heard a rhythmic pumping, a fury of water. Listening to the sound, he imagined a printing press, an oil well, a dam. *Whoosh, whoosh, whoosh*. A windmill, a firehose, or a windmill and a firehose together. His eye adjusted to the dark.

He felt as much as heard the rasp of fibreglass scraping rock. They had bumped up against a tiny islet, and Luciana wedged the boat against it so they couldn't be pulled in any farther. She crabwalked around the hull, opening and closing lockers, and in a moment took his hand and placed a headlamp in it. They each turned theirs on and gazed into the interior of the cave. In front of them, where there should have been nothing but salt water and rock, a surface of wire mesh rose from the roiling surface to the cave's ceiling. Set in the middle of it was the machine, a giant metal drum rotating in front of them, flashing a series of blades with every turn. It furiously sucked water at its base, and from its top flung out dead huachinangos, parrotfish, and wrasses amid a spray of foam. The churning water in the cave formed a sort of whirlpool as the machine sucked and spat. Where they were, jammed up against the islet, the water wanted to pull them in, while on the far side of the cave, it rushed in the opposite direction.

Gabriel noticed a steel-grey catwalk clinging to the rock wall on the far side. Luciana, following his beam, saw it too. She used the aluminum pole to push off the islet, and the panga fishtailed wildly before finding its course. As they motored across the cave, Gabriel cowered from the reverberations of the giant drum on their port side and the flying mangled bodies splashing down all around. Some landed squishily in the boat; one hit Gabriel in the torso with surprising force. For sickening moments, the panga seemed almost still, the outboard fighting the greater power of the sucking machine. Then he felt a lurch of release, and they were on the other side of the whirlpool. They travelled under the metal catwalk towards the mouth of the cave, the water around them still frothing with death. Beyond the cave, the sunlit bay looked acutely blue.

Revving the outboard, Luciana hurled the panga into the open. Gabriel looked up and around, reorienting himself. The surrounding clifftops looked peaceful. Luciana leaned forward, her right hand on the outboard, and she didn't let up on the gas until they'd passed under the arch at the mouth of the bay and rounded the headland. She did not hug the shore as they had on their way in, but zipped straight across the sea, bow pointed northwest towards La Ventana.

THIRTY-EIGHT

CATE

I assumed the security guards thought I was a hotel guest, the way one of them waved me through when I arrived at the resort just after noon. But by the time I wound over the hill and down to the palm-lined parking lot, Octavio was waiting for me. He gestured to a golf cart. I hesitated. I thought of how he'd escorted me to Hunter's apartment the night of the party. Maybe he'd killed Tenoch out of a wish to protect his employer. What if he thought I was a threat to Hunter too?

I climbed into the golf cart beside him and sat with my body tense. We hummed quietly along the serpentine path, between low stucco buildings lined with hibiscus and bougainvillea.

"Your guests must be pleased the wind is back."

He seemed to consider that. "Indeed," he said at last.

The sea came into view, scribbled with whitecaps.

"I don't see any kites out."

"We don't have as many kitesurfers down here. Our guests have other interests."

"You do have guests, though, don't you?"

He looked at me with surprise. There had been other cars in the parking lot, but I hadn't seen any people milling around the lobby fountain or walking along the paths. The night of the party, more than half the resort had been dark, even with the power on.

We rounded a bend and came upon a swimming pool. A woman in a red one-piece bathing suit was preparing to dive in, while another read under a sun umbrella. Two men sat together talking, feet dangling into the water. As one of them looked up at me, I registered an oval face, dark hair, and light, catlike eyes.

Octavio looked at them, then back to me. "Some of our guests."

We were silent for the rest of the ride.

Hunter was waiting for me in his sea-view living room. "What a lovely surprise."

"Doesn't seem like it was that much of a surprise."

He looked boyish, cheerful, enthusiastic about something.

"How does it work? A camera at the guard booth?"

He sat on his couch and gestured for me to do the same, but I stayed standing. He spread his arms out. "That's how I knew to comb my hair and put on a shirt."

"Seems a little paranoid, out here in the middle of nowhere."

"I'm a cautious guy."

"Are you?" I moved closer to him. "You seem like more of a risk-taker." I did not want to know what I wanted to know.

"Do I?"

"You let me in."

"I don't think you're dangerous to me, Cate."

"Funny, I don't think you're dangerous to me, either. Though a lot of people seem to think you are." I moved closer to him, my questions forgotten. My libido moved in on me like clouds taking over the sky.

"A lot?" He slipped two fingers through the belt loop of my cut-off jeans.

"Dr. M, for one."

"He would say that, though, wouldn't he?"

"You were right. About him betraying you," I said.

"He'd betray you too."

"He wouldn't have any reason to."

Hunter pulled me in by the belt loop so that my waist was at the level of his face. He looked up at me. I thought about how physically vulnerable he was in that position.

"Anyone else think I'm dangerous to you?"

"No," I lied.

His fingers still firmly in my belt loop, he yanked my waist left to right, back and forth.

"Nobody you know," I amended.

"Some of your friends from the other night, maybe?"

"Maybe."

He unbuttoned and unzipped my cut-offs and yanked them down. They fell to my ankles. My shirt hung loose over my bra and thong.

"What do they think I'm going to do to you?"

"I don't know," I lied again, and kicked my shorts aside.

"I think you do know," he said.

He turned me around so that I couldn't see him, and energy shot from my groin up to my throat. With one knee, he pushed my legs apart, so that he had me straddling both of his. I saw the whitecaps out on the water. Still no kiteboarders.

"But I don't believe them," I said.

"Are you sure?"

I felt him shift. Undoing his shorts.

"Would I be here?" It came out as a gasp.

"I don't know. Maybe you would."

I thought of Joelle. What had she known? What had happened?

"Maybe you can't help yourself," he said. He fingered the outside of my thong, now damp. He pulled the fabric aside. "Sit in my lap." He guided my hips. My thighs flexed as I lowered myself. "There," he said, as his tip found me.

I slid right on, expanding into a fullness so complete it made me gasp again. His hands wrapped around me, one finger on my clit, one inside the right cup of my bra. He rested his chin on my shoulder, a perfect fit, each of us at the mercy of the other.

We lay together on the couch, his head on my chest. The breeze from the windows dried the sticky patches on my legs into crusts.

"Do you remember jumping off the farmhouse roof?"

He was silent for so long, I thought he was going to say no. But then he said, "You were the only one who would come up."

"Had you done that before?"

"A couple of times. Once I sprained my ankle, but the snow wasn't as deep."

"I wanted you to kiss me."

"You were a kid."

"Thirteen."

"What do you take me for, a psychopath?"

He looked up at me and smiled. I felt a burst of emotion from the deepest part of my brain.

"What about field week?"

I felt his nod against my chest. The waves made their slow, rhythmic sound.

"The one where Terry died," I pushed.

His body, snug against mine, tensed minutely, so briefly I could have imagined it. Then I felt another nod. I thought about how, from the position in which we were lying, with me on my back and him curled around me, he could have overpowered me in an instant. The thought reawakened parts of my body that were in repose, but I didn't move.

"What happened?"

Again that slight tensing. I wondered what was going through his head. Was he trying to remember? Calculating what to say? Had I overstepped? Did he even know what I was talking about? I stroked his hair.

"It was horrible."

I wanted so much for him to continue that, for a moment, I didn't breathe.

"I'd known Terry since I got to Cleckley. People thought we fought all the time, but we were friends."

I let myself exhale.

"We did fight, but it was like blowing off steam. It was like a hangover from when we were younger. And right then, we weren't even fighting. We were having a stupid competition about who could stand closer to the edge. I just wanted to scare him. I was going to lunge at him, kind of startle him, and grab him back. But when I lunged, he just fell. Like he'd stepped off. I didn't even know what had happened. He just plunged away."

I kept my breath steady.

"And he fell so far. It happened so fast, and then there was this crunch of breaking trees, and I could see him down there. Limp. Destroyed. I saw blood. His head must have hit a rock, and his neck was at an angle. And then his body fell down even farther while I watched. Flopped. All ragged. I knew he was dead."

Hunter's body twitched against me, like an animal in REM sleep.

"I couldn't believe it had happened. Everything around me was so normal, the trees and trail and cliff were all still there."

I pictured the boys, one on the clifftop and one down below. I felt sorry for them both.

"I panicked. I kept hiking, just thinking about what to do. And then I caught up with Willow and we waited for the rest of you."

His body had stopped twitching. He paused for a long time.

"You didn't say anything."

"Terry was dead. But I knew that if I said I'd been there when he fell, I'd be blamed. Dr. M might even be blamed."

I was silent.

"It was stupid not to say anything. But I was terrified. I thought I might end up living on a locked ward for the rest of my life."

"You couldn't let yourself be locked up," I said, soothing. I felt like I was holding a nervous animal in my palm, something that might startle at any moment and turn dangerous.

I wiped down my thighs with a washcloth in his slate-tiled bathroom. He'd accidentally killed Terry and been willing to tell me about it. I did up my shorts, tucked in my shirt. A thought nagged: If the fall had been an accident, could Hunter have ended up with Terry's Saint

Christopher charm? Sure, I told myself. The necklace could have fallen to the ground before Terry fell, and Hunter could have picked it up. I wondered what else he'd admit to, then wondered if I really wanted to know. His unboundedness was exciting, but also scarily bottomless. If you had no rules, you could justify anything.

I wanted to leave.

"You'll stay for lunch," he said when I emerged, not a question. "The chef is sending over red snapper."

"Huachinango?"

"That's right," he said—patronizingly, I imagined, as though complimenting me on my local knowledge.

I had no interest in eating, but I needed him to be at ease. I took a chair at a table next to the window. He'd put his shorts back on but was still shirtless. For all our fucking, I felt like I hadn't really taken his body in. Now I did, and was struck by how pale he remained, despite living in a Baja resort. A man who still spent most of his hours indoors.

"The last time we were together, you said you would show me what you're doing."

"My work, you mean."

"You said you hadn't left it all behind."

"We can go this afternoon."

"Go where?"

He smiled and joined me at the table. "My island."

I didn't want him to think I was afraid. "I can't go today."

"When you're ready, then," he said.

I wanted to insist that I was ready, it was just that I had other plans, but I knew protesting would show my weakness even more.

"I'm out there most days. If you come here in the morning, Octavio can arrange a ride."

"Tomorrow," I said impulsively.

"It's a date."

A bell rang and a uniformed waiter came in, carrying an enormous covered tray. He placed it on the sideboard and went about setting the table where we sat, cutlery, napkins, and all. It felt interminable. Finally, he served us our plates, each containing a whole cooked huachinango, one eyeball staring up. They were plated with rice and a green sauce like something from a culinary magazine, but all I could think of were Luciana and Gabriel's fish with the bloody gashes. Did Hunter know about the die-off? Was he messing with me?

"Shall I remove it from the bone?" the waiter asked.

"Please."

He made quick work of the body with a sharp knife, leaving me with two white boneless fillets and taking away the head and tail. The meat, removed from context, looked delicious against its green sauce, no longer a dead animal but food.

I ate a forkful, tasting the sweetness of the white flesh, the garlic and herbs of the sauce.

"What's on this island?" I asked.

"There's something I've been wondering," he said.

I washed my food down with a gulp of fizzy water.

"The first time we met, you said you were looking for green-energy investment opportunities."

"Yeah?"

He cut, chewed, and swallowed. "You never told me exactly why you thought I'd be interested, or for that matter, how you learned my new name and location."

"Didn't I?"

"I would have assumed you got your information from Dr. M, who at least knew about my company in Seattle and probably guessed I was in the general vicinity of Baja after I spooked him at that conference. But you proclaimed his innocence."

"Okay," I said. "You got me. I looked into you. A guy at my company searched the databases and figured out that Hunter Araya was probably Hunter Brandt."

"A guy?"

"A very discreet, very loyal employee at my old company," I said, suddenly knowing I mustn't incriminate Felix.

"What-all did you learn from your very discreet, very loyal employee?"

"That you'd been trying to commercialize a nuclear fusion reactor."

He shoved another forkful in his mouth and chewed. "So it wasn't exactly a surprise when I told you. I feel like maybe you acted like it was a surprise."

I opened my mouth to defend myself.

"It doesn't matter. What else did you learn?"

"You closed your company, changed your name, and moved down here."

"What else?"

"That's all I needed."

"Come to my island."

"I will."

I saw that I was not, after all, going to ask the question that had animated me most since reading Dr. M's file. The question that had sent me up into that canyon yesterday, propelled me into my car this morning, and sustained me over the forty-five-minute drive. Whether out of fear of Hunter or desire for him—or both—I'd lost my nerve.

"Why not give people their own golf carts?" I asked as Octavio whisked me by the swimming pool. The four people were gone, as though they'd been actors in a Potemkin village. I tried to remember what they looked like, as though to prove to myself I'd really seen them. A woman in a red one-piece, a man with an oval face.

Octavio chuckled. "I just didn't want you getting lost. Would you like your own the next time you visit?"

There wasn't going to be a next time, but I didn't tell him that. Octavio dropped me at my car and I refrained from peeling out with excess haste. I drove at a deliberate pace up the palm-lined drive, over the crest of the hill, and down the gentle slope until

I passed the security booth, where I slowed and waved to the black-uniformed guards, one of whom held a machine gun across his chest. The other jerked his head to indicate that I could go on my way, as if it was up to him. I felt a surge of anger to realize that it *was* up to him—on an order from Hunter, the guards would have stopped me from leaving.

I continued at a genteel velocity until the road turned and I was out of sight of the booth, then stepped on the accelerator, wildly alert. I'd been sure until now that whatever Hunter was capable of, I was safe. If nothing else, I fed his curiosity and narcissism too much for him to do me harm. That illusion fell away as I raced past salt flats and date palm plantations, slowing only when I entered the tidy streets of San Juan de los Planes. I pulled over outside a pink stucco bodega as another realization took full shape. Whether or not I was afraid of Hunter on my own behalf, I had others to protect. Felix. Gabriel. Dr. M.

I called Hunter.

"I'm getting in the boat if you still want to come out," he said.

"What happened to Joelle?"

I heard voices and splashing water.

"I was sure you were going to ask me that while you were here."

"What happened?"

"Is that why you hightailed it out of here?"

"Just tell me. I'm not the police. I'm not Dr. M. I'm not anyone. I just need to know. For me."

"I'm disappointed, Cate."

An engine started up.

"Please."

"I can't talk about that on the phone. I'm sorry, I wish I trusted you more. I feel like we were building up some trust."

"What happened to Tenoch?"

"I have to go," he said, and hung up.

"Dammit." I threw the phone into the passenger seat. If I hadn't been begging for an explicit denial, maybe he'd have given me one.

Now, finally, I felt betrayed. I'd wanted Hunter to be another proof, like me, that a brain scan and a handful of traumatic episodes were not predictive. That we could choose our futures. But he wasn't what I wanted him to be, and now he'd slipped beyond my reach.

THIRTY-NINE

GABRIEL

Neither Gabriel nor Luciana spoke all the way back to shore. Even as they were pulling the panga up the beach, they moved in shocked silence, communicating in gestures. They stored the new samples in the lab and moved on to Luciana's office, where she closed the door behind them. Gabriel collapsed into a chair—just in time, as his legs seemed to give way. Luciana was wide-eyed, the colour drained from her face.

"What is it?" he asked, because one of them had to break the silence.

She shook her head in bewilderment. "It looked like sort of a dam?"

"Do you think Tenoch got that far?"

"No. He would have capsized in the cave. But he must have made it to the mouth of the bay, because he said he found dozens of dead fish in one spot."

Dust motes floated in the sunlight.

"It's sucking fish in alive and spitting them out dead," Gabriel said. "They're collateral damage."

"But for what?"

Gabriel shook his head, confounded. "That can't be legal, right? Next to the national park?"

"Definitely not."

"We need to tell someone. Detective Sanchez?"

"Yes, but I need to think." She massaged her temples. "When

Tenoch got back from his boat trip, he said he wanted to come to the party that night so he could talk to Hunter Araya."

A knock at the door made Gabriel jump, but it was just Beni, back from the land registry office. He looked from Luciana to Gabriel and back.

"You guys okay?" He held several sheets of paper.

"We're fine, just tired," Luciana said, and sat up straighter. "What did you learn today?"

Beni glanced down at one of his sheets. "The horseshoe island is called Ballenas. My mom recognized the name—apparently our family used to go there. She said there are terns, gulls, sea lions—"

"Beni, just the business," Luciana said.

He looked up.

"The owner," Gabriel prompted.

He shuffled the papers. "Araya Holdings."

Gabriel's insides went cold.

"Araya?" Luciana asked. "Not . . . Iguaro?"

"Araya," Beni repeated.

"And you're sure it's that island?"

Beni looked down at his sheet. "Shaped like a parabola. Long bay." He gave the latitude and longitude.

Luciana furrowed her brow.

"I looked up the company registration," Beni said. "It was formed two years ago, and it also owns a desalination plant and a resort. The resort is—"

"Palacio Pericú," Gabriel said.

Beni nodded.

"Thank you," Luciana said, and held out her hand for the papers. Beni gave them to her and left, closing the door behind him.

"If Hunter Araya owns the island, he owns that machine," Luciana said. "The machine is killing the fish. Tenoch must have figured it out."

"But why kill him?" Gabriel asked.

A campaign truck with a loudspeaker went by up on the road, blaring "Light up Baja!" and "Vote tomorrow!"

"I don't know," Luciana said. "I'll call Ursula."

Gabriel's thoughts went to Cate, and whatever dangerous game she was playing out.

His chest pounded as he waited for two children to herd a flock of red-feathered chickens out of the dirt road. He accelerated as soon as it was safe, zooming past the village centre, past Oscarito's, past the giant cardón cactus in the middle of the road. He careened through the gates with the wrought-iron dolphins and screeched to a halt in the Casa Azul parking lot.

Gabriel sprinted up the hill to Cate's house, arriving at her front door out of breath. She let him in, and to his relief, she was alone.

His words came out in a torrent. "We found the machine that's killing the fish."

"Where?"

"On an island owned by Hunter Araya. And Tenoch figured it out too, or at least he suspected. He was investigating when he died."

Gabriel was breathing heavily, still recovering from his sprint up the hill. They were standing just inside Cate's front door.

"I'm so sorry," he went on. "I'm not trying to interfere, I promise. I was skeptical of the whole murder idea, but if he actually had a reason, a connection, a . . . a—"

"A motive," Cate supplied, with surprising calm.

Gabriel recognized that placid surface. Anyone else might have taken it for ease.

"Yes, a motive."

"Hunter had a wife," Cate said. "She died three years ago while the two of them were alone together, kayaking, and Hunter inherited three hundred million dollars."

Her voice was stony. The logic pulled tight like a drawstring.

"Two suspicious deaths is a lot," Gabriel said.

"Three."

He stared at her in befuddlement.

She crossed her arms and gazed at the floor. "There was another one at our school."

He wanted to hug her but had a feeling she might crack.

"How long have you known about the one at your school?"

"I knew at the time that a kid died. They told us he fell off a cliff, and I never questioned it."

"And the wife?"

"I found out the night before last, but I didn't believe it until"—she looked at her watch—"about five hours ago."

"You already knew when we saw you at dinner?"

She nodded. "I wanted to ask him about it before I said anything."

"Ask him? You saw him?"

"Today."

He reached out a hand to touch her shoulder, to assure himself that she was okay. He felt the same dizziness he'd experienced after their dive in the Haro Strait, when he found out she'd been tangled, almost trapped. "I'm really sorry. I know finding him meant—"

She cut him off. "Explain the machine."

Gabriel had a theory, developed with the help of Tenoch's file on the physicist Jean Lavalier. "Well, he needs a lot of seawater."

"It'll be nuclear fusion," Cate said, matter-of-factly. "His fusion company in Seattle got sued out of existence. Now he's doing it down here."

Gabriel stared at her in surprise. "Yeah, exactly."

"What are you going to do?" Cate asked.

"If Iguaro wins the election, Hunter will have the governor in his pocket. So we're going back out there tomorrow with Detective Sanchez."

"I'll come."

There were many reasons not to allow this. He and Luciana had a research mandate, and the detective was leading a criminal investigation. Cate had only a personal agenda.

"What do you want from him now?"

He could see her weighing what to say.

"I can help," she said. "I can communicate with him, and he'll listen."

"But doesn't he know that you suspect him?"

"He does, but he's not sure what I make of it. He might still think he can get me on his side."

Gabriel felt sorry for whatever it cost her to let go of her image of Hunter. He wanted to say no, to keep her safe. But he knew she was going to insist.

"Only if Sanchez and Luciana say okay."

They sat down on the couch, as though the conversation had taken their last energy.

"It's audacious," Cate said.

"What is?"

"Nuclear fusion. An ambition as big as the sun."

"Too bad about the rest."

FORTY

CATE

Gabriel drove me to the lab in the morning, thermos of coffee at his elbow, patch over his left eye and a dark sleepless crease under the right one. Campaign trucks plied the streets, playing their high-volume patter. Locals set up tables and flags in the schoolyard, while tourists bought fresh juice and blinked at the ruckus.

We skimmed across the turquoise water in a panga, planning to arrive at the island at low tide. Detective Sanchez sat in the bow, Luciana at the outboard in the stern, and Gabriel and I in the middle, our hands gripping the bench and almost touching. He leaned in close to my ear and told me to watch for dolphins, like we'd seen in Fiji. We passed Palacio Pericú in the distance, its architecture undulating along the waterfront like a human spine, and I wondered what Hunter was doing right now, if he was looking back at us from his art-filled living room, or if he was out on his island, unaware of our approach.

Since the day before, my feelings had been like wild animals trapped in my rib cage, shifting direction and gaining strength. Hunter had readily confessed to playing a role in Terry's death. But after that, when we'd sat down to lunch, there was a barrier between us, and it solidified when I declined his invitation to the island. As soon as he'd realized I was wary, he behaved like I'd let him down, when in fact I was the one who was colossally, crushingly disappointed. The Hunter I'd imagined, the role model and fellow traveller, didn't exist.

Luciana piloted us under a natural archway and into a long, placid bay. She took us along its eastern shore, where the rise of the land cast the water in morning shadow. Because of the rocky terrain, there were few places to beach a panga, but Sanchez knew a spot, a sandy cove exposed by the low tide. Nobody said anything when the first mangled huachinangos floated by. Despite the bodies, it remained eerily beautiful, the only sounds the occasional gull's cry and our own slow-moving vessel. Was this all Hunter's realm, a place where he hid, a place he controlled?

Luciana cut the engine and we slid onto the sand. Rocky hills surrounded us on three sides, but Sanchez swore there was a footpath, and she soon found it, beginning behind a boulder and twisting out of sight amid the streaky grey stone. We were heading for a building she'd identified in satellite photos. She wanted us to get in, document what we could, and leave.

Gabriel and I exchanged a glance. I had a different aim, but saw no need to share it just yet. I was going to find Hunter. I was going to make him confess to killing the journalist. It felt like a personal responsibility.

We set out like tourists on a day hike, with water bottles and backpacks and sun hats. The trail wound up the hillside among the cacti, and we had to bob and weave to avoid getting pricked. Soon we arrived at a ridge from which we could look down the other side. We were exposed for all to see, though there didn't appear to be anyone else around. Sprawled below us, almost the same colour as the surrounding hills, lay an enormous windowless warehouse sided in beige corrugated metal. Sitting on the valley floor, it was invisible to any passing ship. On the west side of the warehouse, left from where we stood, there were four cylindrical white towers. Beyond them, the land rose to an even higher ridge.

Detective Sanchez got out binoculars and passed them around. We identified two sets of doors into the warehouse. A rough-hewn road led away from the farther set, cutting a channel through the hills to the east side of the island, where, according to Sanchez, there was a dock for bigger boats. The closer set of doors had motion sensors above it, but there was no sign of security guards.

Sanchez led us down a path towards the warehouse, winding among tall cacti. Fine dust clung to our pants and sunglasses. When we arrived at the bottom of the hill, we were only fifty feet from the nearest doors.

Luciana looked at her watch. "The cove where we beached will be underwater in an hour and a half." She looked around at us to make sure we grasped her meaning. "If we get separated, be at the boat by eleven thirty."

We dashed across the open space. Sanchez reached for the doorknob and gave it a hard twist, and the door gave way so easily that she nearly lost her balance. We scrambled after her into cool warehouse air. As the door swung shut behind us, a siren pierced the air so loudly I stumbled.

I plugged my ears. We looked at each other, faces scrunched to fend off the repeating wail. Ahead of us stretched a semi-dark corridor with doors on either side. At the far end, I saw people in red lab coats walking by, but they weren't hurrying or looking our way. A metal staircase led upward to our left. Based on an instinct to get away from the sound and the people, I gestured to the others that we should take it.

At the top of the stairs, the landing connected to a walkway with a metal railing that ran the entire length of the warehouse, overlooking its vast floor. We crept along until we reached a large protruding cabinet, and by silent assent crouched against the wall beside it, obscured from anyone who might look up from the central warehouse floor. As suddenly as the siren had started, it stopped.

The enormous open part of the building was dominated by machinery. A dark-grey cylinder about the height and length of a semi truck stretched across the floor. A shiny silver sphere had metal tubes protruding from it, like submarines crashed into a sun. Circuit boards hung in neat rows from a warren of metal grates. The people in red lab coats moved among the machines, following pathways indicated by yellow lines painted on the concrete floor. Considering that the wail of the siren had only just stopped, they looked strangely unalarmed. They all wore industrial headphones, either covering their ears or hanging around their necks. Some had safety glasses propped on their heads.

A bearded, brown-skinned man, in a red lab coat like the others, walked to the centre of the floor and addressed those around him, but his voice didn't carry up to where we were crouched. I took him to be calming the troops, reporting on the siren like the fire marshal at an emergency drill. Was it possible they didn't know they had invaders?

"That's him," Gabriel whispered, and we all leaned in to hear. "Jean Lavalier, the plasma physicist. Tenoch had a file on him."

Detective Sanchez snapped photos and asked what we were looking at.

"The long tube makes the plasma, which you need to create fusion," Gabriel said. "It was all in Tenoch's notes. Plasma is a state of matter—like solids or liquids are states of matter. But you need unbelievably high temperatures to create a plasma and keep it steady. That was the technical challenge Lavalier was trying to overcome before he shut down his company. To make a plasma that could last more than a few milliseconds."

Jean Lavalier left the floor. Then a beep pierced the air, as loud as the siren but more staccato. There was a shout, and the workers reached for their headphones and safety glasses.

"Cover your eyes, plug your ears," Gabriel whispered urgently.

I planted my palms on my ears and squeezed my eyes shut. There was another beep, then silence. The flash of white light was so strong I could see it through my eyelids, and it was followed by a loud mechanical gasp. I opened my eyes to see the workers on the floor remove their glasses and headphones and go about their business.

We huddled in closer to Gabriel as he resumed his explanation.

"The big silver sphere is the fusion reactor. To run it, they need deuterium, and they're getting that from seawater."

"Via the fish-killing machine," Sanchez said.

"Yes. The machine in the cave sucks in massive amounts of water, and spits the fish back out dead. Those towers we saw are probably the heavy-water separator, which distills the deuterium. That would give them all the fuel they need."

I now saw Hunter's plan in its entirety. With Jean Lavalier as his chief scientist, they were really doing it. They were creating energy, actual usable electricity, from nuclear fusion. I remembered the night of the party at Palacio Pericú, the way the lights had silently come back on at the resort while the rest of the bay remained dark.

I indulged in a moment of admiration. He'd remained determined all along. Stymied by regulators and investors up north, he'd taken Joelle's life and her money and left to pursue fusion somewhere else. Somewhere he thought he could keep the law at bay for long enough to achieve success.

Those feelings rattled my rib cage again. Wanting and fury. Hunter could have been a saviour instead of another Cleckley criminal. On those two sticky afternoons together, I'd felt like we'd merged. That intoxicating fervour had seemed so self-evidently mutual. But Hunter's own feelings could have been anything, or nothing.

"We need to find the heavy-water separator," Gabriel said. "See how it connects to the machine in the cave."

Luciana glanced pointedly at her watch. It was now past eleven. They both looked to Detective Sanchez.

"Let's search for a passage to the cave," she said, and the three of them stood to go.

I said I would meet them back at the boat by eleven thirty. When Sanchez and Luciana objected to me peeling off, Gabriel overrode them.

"Don't be late," he said to me.

I grabbed Luciana by the arm as they turned to go. "If I'm late, leave," I whispered to her.

She nodded, and the three of them went back the way we'd come.

Peeking out from around the side of the cabinet, I saw that the walkway met up with another staircase at the far end of the warehouse. I was wondering how to get there unnoticed when it occurred to me to look in the cabinet. Behind the first door, I found only rolls of industrial-strength tinfoil, but in the next was a red lab coat and a pair of protective headphones. I buttoned the lab coat, hung the headphones around my neck, and set off like I knew where I was going. I was braced for someone to notice me, to look up and shout, but my presence didn't appear to register.

I planned as I walked. When Lavalier had addressed the workers, he'd emerged from a door on the opposite side of the cavernous space. If I could get to Lavalier, he'd tell me where to find Hunter. I picked up my pace, and when I reached the staircase at the far end, I turned to descend. When I was halfway down, another piercing beep split the air. I glanced over to the floor and saw workers put their headphones on, so I did the same. I had no safety glasses, but I cupped my hands around my eyes. After the blast and the flash of light, everyone started moving again.

To get to Lavalier's door, I had to go around the warren of towering circuit boards, inside of which there were three men, one operating a keyboard and two looking up at a wall of fuses. I moved fast, and when one of them glanced curiously at me, I gave him a nod as though we were colleagues. He returned to his work, but only after another quizzical look my way. It hit me that I recognized his face, but I couldn't place him.

I passed more workers, who were mostly looking at screens or each other. Twenty paces to go, ten, then five. I made the connection: I'd seen the man who'd just noticed me by the pool at Hunter's resort. Oval face, dark hair, light eyes. The resort had never housed paying guests, I realized. Just guards and Hunter's people.

When I arrived at the closed office door, I flung it open and stepped inside. Jean Lavalier abruptly stood up behind his desk. His face was grooved and tired, and he had yellowish circles under his eyes. His red lab coat hung open, showing a polo shirt and khaki trousers.

"Who the hell are you?" he asked, his hands tense on the surface of his desk.

"Cate Winter," I said, looking around. There was a second door out of the room. A bank of hard drives covered one wall from floor to ceiling, and diagrams of machinery were pinned up behind Lavalier. A computer sat on his desk, along with a geode serving as a paperweight, sliced in half to reveal a core of purple crystals.

"I know you don't work here, and you're not on today's manifest," he said. "So tell me exactly what the fuck you're doing here or I'm calling the guards."

He fingered a walkie-talkie on his desk, and I realized he wasn't as angry as he was nervous. I spoke softly to try to put him at ease.

"I'm a scientist too. A neuroscientist. I had a business, like you did."

He gripped his walkie-talkie hard, so I added quickly that I was looking for Hunter Araya.

He sneered at that. "People don't *look for* Hunter Araya. Where did you come from?"

"I came in a boat." I tried to remember details Gabriel had shared. "I heard about your work on fusion. Your breakthroughs."

He loosened his grip on the walkie-talkie and glanced anxiously at his computer screen, then at the door behind me. "You're not on the manifest. We have no visitors scheduled for today."

"I came by panga. I landed on a cove on the big bay."

"You can't be here," he hissed. "If I call the guards, you don't want to know what they will do to you."

"I want to see Hunter."

"Why?"

"It's personal."

He looked incredulous. "He keeps his own schedule."

"So he's here?"

We had a stare-down, during which I very slowly eased my way into a chair in front of his desk, figuring that if I was physically lower than him, he might feel less threatened. He did seem to relax a little, though he continued to stand, fidgety and haggard.

I decided to try a different tack. "Do you know how many fish you're killing with your machine in the cave out there?"

He glowered. "Of course we're killing fish. We built a heavy-water separator in the middle of the Sea of Cortez."

He spoke with vehemence, but I sensed his ire wasn't purely for me.

"You didn't want it here."

"We should have put it in an industrial zone where the marine life was already gone. But Araya said this was the only place where we could have the right level of secrecy."

"Do you know how many you're killing?"

"I'm too busy to worry about that. I have a deadline."

"A deadline?"

He gave an angry wave of his hand. "I told him I wouldn't do environmental mitigation."

"People are noticing."

"I told him fishermen would notice."

"Not just fishermen. Scientists. There was a journalist looking into it. Dead snappers are washing up on the beach in La Ventana."

Lavalier sat down. He looked exhausted. "Does Araya know?" he asked.

"He knew about the journalist," I said. "Who appears to have been killed. There's a police investigation."

The look that came over Lavalier's face was pure fear. I thought he might try to throw me out again.

Quickly, I asked, "Where do you and your colleagues live?"

"Araya has a hotel at Punta Arena. Most of them bunk there."

"And you?"

"I haven't left this island in seven months."

FORTY-ONE

GABRIEL

He led the way back down the stairs to the shadowy end of the warehouse. Detective Sanchez seemed calm, but Luciana was on edge. Following his hunch, they walked along the interior wall, until—yes. A heavy metal tube, about six inches in diameter and raised off the floor on struts, crossed their path, entering the main building from a hallway that jutted out at a ninety-degree angle. He peeked around the corner into the hallway. The tube extended away.

Luciana hissed his name and he looked where she was pointing. Two men in black uniforms were approaching from the far end of the warehouse. It wasn't clear if they'd seen the intruders yet.

"Hide," he whispered, and they all bolted into the hallway. It was as wide as a jetway and ended in a wall with a door to the outside. Gabriel glanced back—the pair of guards hadn't yet appeared—so he pushed through the door and emerged into the sunlight, with Sanchez and Luciana close on his heels. They found themselves in an enclosure made by a high chain-link fence with barbed wire along the top. Directly in front of them, four enormous white cylinders rose into the sky. They craned their necks. The structures towered above them, maybe three storeys tall, though still shorter than the nearest hilltops. Heavy-water separators.

Gabriel walked under the tangle of pipes at the base of the cylinders and looked up again, permitting himself a brief moment of awe. This was it, the mystery solved. He turned to look at Luciana and she nodded, but pointed at her watch. They had to go, before they were caught or the tide rose any further. He looked around for Sanchez but didn't see her. The rocky hills were enticingly close, but there were no breaks in the fence that penned them in.

"We'll have to go back through the building," he said.

As soon as they turned, the door from the hallway swung open and four people in black uniforms stepped out. One of them cried "Halt!"

All instinct, he grabbed Luciana's hand, and together they ran between two of the cylinders, under a network of white-painted tubes.

Behind them, one guard shouted to the others: "You, go left! You, go right! You, stay here!"

Gabriel's throat burned with fear. Ahead lay more pipes. He didn't know what he was running into, or which way to go.

"This way," Sanchez called, and his head whipped around. She stood at a door set into the concrete base of one of the cylinders. They made it inside, tottering in their haste, and found themselves in darkness as Gabriel eased the door shut behind him.

FORTY-TWO

CATE

"Seven months?" I asked.

Lavalier's eyes were bloodshot. "I told you, I have a deadline."

"How did you get into this?"

He let out a laugh that was more of a bark. "I made a deal with the devil."

I raised my eyebrows.

"I had a company," he said. "But you knew that already. How?"

I told him that the dead journalist had discovered his name. That the scientists trying to figure out why fish were dying had read all the articles about him.

"How did you meet Araya?" I asked.

He tented his fingers and bowed his head, then looked up. He glanced at his screen, then at the door behind me again—a nervous tic. Finally, he spoke. "My company was extremely close to creating a stable plasma. I thought my team would succeed where others had failed. But the expense to keep going was enormous. One by one, my investors lost interest." He held up his hands in a gesture of defeat. "Araya appeared out of nowhere. Showed up in Vancouver as we were about to liquidate. I didn't realize who he was at first, but he knew an extraordinary amount about what we were doing. We are a small field, you see. ITER, Lockheed, a handful of private companies, we are all aware of each other. I'd heard of Terrawave, but who was this Araya? Brandt had changed his name. When

I learned that, I thought it was a bad sign. Why would a man change his name? But after he made me the offer, I didn't care."

"What did he offer you?"

"Unlimited funds, unlimited equipment, the staff of my choice. But I had to work where he said, and I had to work to his timeline. I made some stupid promises. I said goodbye to my family. Araya did not want to deal with the regulators up north. So here we are, on this island."

"And you've made progress?"

"We've created a stable plasma."

I nodded to show him I was suitably impressed.

"We have a prototype operating at the resort. We are fine-tuning."

"And then?"

The screeching beep went off again, only slightly deadened by the closed office door. I must have winced, because he said, "You are safe in here."

"What are those?"

"It's to warn of test firings. You must not look at the generator when it fires."

The noise passed. He seemed almost relaxed now, and I was confused. Was he a leader or a prisoner?

"Do you want to be here?" I finally asked.

A mix of emotions played across his face. At that moment, the second door into the office opened, and Hunter stepped into the room. I jumped out of my chair. Jean Lavalier's face hardened, but he didn't look surprised.

"Jean," Hunter said. "Dr. Sylvain is looking for you. Why don't you go see her."

Lavalier raised his eyebrows at me in an I-told-you-so expression. Hunter had been aware of my presence all along. The physicist slowly stood and, with the stiff walk of a much older man, left the room, closing the door behind him. I felt a tingle up and down my limbs as Hunter moved to the desk chair, taking the space Lavalier had just left.

"Relax," he said. "It's not like we're going to kill each other."

Every muscle in my body was taut. Slowly, I sat back down.

"You could have come when I invited you, instead of all this drama." He spun a gold pen with one hand, one of those dexterous schoolboy balancing tricks.

I had one last chance. I considered angles, calculating how to get him to talk. I flashed back to investor meetings, to countless conference rooms, trying to get people to give us money.

"Do you know about the fish?"

"I've been in the bay. Dr. Lavalier was correct. I didn't hire him to do environmental mitigation."

So he'd been listening too. "What are you doing about it?"

"Is this really why you came here? Chased me to Baja, refused my invitation, trespassed—all because you're concerned about some dead fish? If you're trying to solve environmental problems, your energies could be spent more effectively somewhere else."

"Do you not care?" I asked, truly curious.

"Cate, I know who you are. I've read up on you since you so delightfully appeared in my life. You were a founder. You acquired competitors and laid everyone off. You basically destroyed Biogenetics by challenging their patents until they ran out of money."

"So?" That had been Jia's legal strategy, quite brilliant in my opinion. Controversial, though. It had attracted media attention.

"You experiment on monkeys, which are basically humans, and you've probably killed as many lab mice as we have fish."

"What's your point?"

That big smile. "My point is, I was starting to like you."

That touched something in me. How was it that I still cared whether he liked me? How had I started caring in the first place?

"I wasn't looking for you to like me."

"No? Wasn't that exactly what you were doing? Poor little psychopath, looking for someone who really understands?"

Sure, but I wanted my imaginary Hunter, not this one.

"You can't have it both ways, Cate. You can't want me for who I am and hate me for who I am."

"I don't hate you."

"Love, hate, anger, it's all the same. You've gone from wanting to be my friend"—he spun his pen—"my lover"—another spin—"to finding me objectionable."

"I object to murder."

He looked not even slightly fazed by my accusation. "Ours is the first nuclear fusion energy generator that will be connected to the grid. Carbon-free energy, first for Baja, then for everyone. Forever and for free. We're talking about the end of fossil fuels. The end to overheating the planet."

"You beat everyone," I said, hoping flattery would regain me some influence over him, though I also felt real awe at what he and Lavalier had accomplished. It seemed I could admire him and be angry with him at the same time.

"Those guys at ITER are a hundred years away. The bigger triumph was beating Lockheed. But if you see all this, Cate, why are you questioning me about minor losses? The fishermen, the hotels, they feel some effect. Just like those people who worked for Biogenetics before you forced them to close. It's unfortunate, but it's a communications problem."

It's a communications problem. At one point I'd said those same words to Jia and our human resources battle-axe. Told them to spin the layoffs, which they did, and our value to investors rose.

"I guess what I'm wondering is, is it worth any price?"

"That's ridiculously hypothetical. Is it worth this particular price? Yes. I know you understand having to make difficult decisions."

He still looked so at ease, and I longed to pierce his surface. See once and for all what was below. There had to be something beyond this smooth exterior. Hadn't I felt it?

He spun the gold pen. "No one has discovered a source of energy that has no environmental impact at all. Hydro kills fish, wind farms kill birds, fission has this little radioactive waste problem that bothers everyone so much."

"What about a person's life?" I asked.

Hunter sat forward in the chair, forearms on the desk now, patient. "We're talking about potentially saving billions of lives, so one person's life—hell, one hundred lives—yes, that would be worth it."

Even as I agreed with his logic, a hard wall within me said no, some things were different. "Is that why you killed Tenoch?"

He stared at me for a long time. He even stopped fidgeting with the pen and set it down on the desk.

"I had a run-in with a journalist right before I sold my company," I said. "He lied to get to me. Hid his identity. When I found out, I was angry." I mentally summoned my encounter with Nate Pryor of the *Los Angeles Times*, and the moment I found his driver's licence in the pocket of his cheap suit. I thought of how outraged I'd been, how affronted that he would try to jeopardize my sale, how immaterial he was in the grand scheme of things. I remembered the rage that had surged through me, how I'd steadied myself at the bathroom door while it ran its course. "I knew I needed to get rid of him. Somehow." As I said this, I imagined myself back at that moment, choosing a different course. "All the other ways seemed so complicated, you know? Conversations, letters, lawsuits, it all just seemed slow and tedious. It would be so much simpler if he were just"—I held up my right hand and flicked my fingers—"gone."

As I said it, I really believed it. I was making myself into Hunter, and it felt just as real to me as any other version of myself.

Hunter rolled the gold pen back and forth. "Are we playing true confessions now? I'll show you mine if you show me yours?"

"Yeah."

"So what did you do?"

I remembered the seconds I'd watched Nate sleep, how I'd rested the spike of my heel near his neck. "I was wearing stilettos. I used the heel of my shoe."

"Very va-va-voom," he said. Something changed in his eyes. An awakening. "You're more complicated than I thought."

"Tell me about Tenoch."

"Quite boring compared to a shoe. I'd gone to check on the prototype reactor at the resort, and when I came out, he was waiting. Must have followed me."

I thought of how I too had followed Hunter away from his party guests and down to the building on the water, where I'd found a locked door and then walked right into Tenoch.

"That wasn't a great choice he made, stopping me, telling me he knew about our facility out here. We had a little tussle on the breakwater. I realized a hard shove could solve the problem on the spot. Those rocks are sharp."

I stared at him. Part of me still wanted to think he was making it up in a perverse effort to impress me.

"Isn't that what you wanted to know? Now tell me more about this shoe situation. I'm very intrigued. What else were you wearing?"

"Was that before I came to your suite?"

"Just before."

"Were you trying to make me your alibi?"

He smiled. "That was just a stroke of luck. Funny how I was your alibi and you were mine, isn't it? I wonder what the detective makes of that. We could see what Dr. M has to say about your violent tendencies."

I thought back to Hunter's living room that first night. "Your doorbell rang."

"Octavio. Body found, notifying authorities, etcetera." He had a grin on his face like a pleased little boy. All through our electrifying conversation that first night, he'd known he'd just ended someone's life.

It was a relief to feel myself turn against him, my ambivalence gone.

A siren went off in the warehouse; not the shrill beep that preceded the tests, but the kind that had rung out when the four of us first entered the premises. It was muffled here in the office, and Hunter paid it no attention.

I decided to press ahead while I still had some power. "So you got rid of Tenoch because he was going to expose your facility as the cause of the fish deaths."

"We're too close to be derailed."

"And Joelle? Was that also in service of the greater good?"

He knew how closely I'd watch his reaction. We'd both been observed for so long. Doctors standing across the room or behind one-way glass, nurses and psychologists pushing dolls or blocks; later, notepads and coloured pens; later still, those damn surveys. Hunter started twirling the gold pen again, more rapidly than before. Had I crossed a line? Did he have lines?

"You've seduced an investor or two," he said. "Perhaps literally, for all I know." He smirked. "We can't do what we do without money."

I stared at him. Was he saying he'd killed her? I needed him to say it.

"Couldn't you have spent her money with her alive?"

"We didn't see eye to eye on that."

I nodded, like the decision to kill his wealthy wife sounded entirely sensible to me. "You were kayaking," I prodded. "You hit rough weather."

He sighed. "You're so keen on detail."

"I've been told I'm quite pedantic."

"It's not that hard, you know, when the person isn't expecting it." He sounded petulant.

I kept my face motionless, my expression—I hoped—still admiring. He'd done it. There was no accident. There were no extenuating circumstances. He'd just straight-up killed her for her money. He had no limits.

He said then, "I just wish we could trust each other. Do you trust me?"

"Not really."

"Smart girl."

I had the bizarre thought that I could have Hunter in my life as long as I never trusted him. As though I could trap him in a bell jar on a shelf, my special specimen. The siren blared beyond the door, but the air felt still in the room. Hunter's expression remained calm and bemused, but he changed his grip on the gold pen so that now he held it in a fist. I'd both succeeded in what I'd set out to do and imperilled myself doing it. I had the impulse to jump out of my seat, but as long as he didn't know I was aware of his intent, he might bide his time. I eyed the heavy purple geode on the desk. This was how he got away with murder, I saw. He didn't premeditate. Without planning, there could be no evidence of intent. Keeping my eyes on the pen, I talked to distract him from his whim to kill me.

"You were right," I said. "I don't personally care about the dead fish. I don't even really care about the journalist, or Joelle. But I'm not your problem. Sanchez is still investigating."

"She won't be after today's election."

"It doesn't matter. People in La Ventana are putting up flyers. Fishermen are protesting. The scientists know you're extracting deuterium. You can't kill them all."

His face conveyed nothing. I had to keep talking. But before I could, Hunter sprang from his seat and came around the desk, his right arm raised with the gold pen in his fist. I jumped back into a boxer's crouch, knocking my chair to the floor with a clatter. At the same moment, Jean Lavalier burst back into the office and the sound of the siren suddenly invaded at quadruple volume.

"There are intruders," Lavalier shouted over the siren, then looked around in confusion.

I plugged my ears. Before I knew what was happening, Hunter shoved Lavalier back through the door, followed him out, and slammed it shut. I lunged for the door and wrenched the knob, but I was locked in.

FORTY-THREE

GABRIEL

Sanchez pulled out a flashlight and led them down a metal staircase that creaked and moaned underfoot. Gabriel could see only bobbing light and shadow limbs. It grew cooler as they went down, and the air tasted of salt. Luciana softly cursed about the rising tide.

Finally, deep inside the rocky hillside, the stairs dropped them onto hard-packed dirt. There was a new noise, rushing and whispering—the sound of water. He was relieved to hear it, but only momentarily. High above them, the door opened and heavy boots clanged on the metal landing. One of the guards beamed a light down, and Luciana, Sanchez, and Gabriel flattened themselves against a rock wall. The guards conferred, and the trio waited to see if they would be chased. Then they heard more boots on metal as guards began to descend the stairs, light beams bouncing off metal and rock.

Sanchez had turned off her own flashlight, and Gabriel willed his eyes to adjust to near-blackness. The detective grabbed his arm and attached it to her shoulder, then he attached Luciana's arm to his own shoulder and they groped forward along the rock wall. The creak and clang of the metal stairs announced that the guards were getting closer.

Gabriel could only hope that Sanchez knew where she was leading them. After endless minutes of darkness, she tugged on his sleeve and had them turn and zigzag between close rock walls. The silence around them changed, becoming less echoey, and Gabriel sensed they were in a small chamber. The ground beneath them became rockier and more uneven. They couldn't hear the guards, so Sanchez risked turning her flashlight back on, and he blinked, looking around. It was a cave within a cave, with jagged walls but plenty of clearance above their heads.

They spoke in whispers, faces spectral above the weak beam.

"Did you know this was here?"

"More or less."

"Can we get out this way?" Luciana asked.

"No, but we should be able to get out by sea, depending on how well the guards know the cave. If they know we're back here, though, they can block our exit."

"We have no boat," Luciana said.

"We'll swim to ours."

Gabriel was startled. He and Luciana were strong swimmers, but what about Sanchez herself?

"But it must be—"

"Half a mile," the detective said.

The two scientists looked at her doubtfully in the bluish glow.

"You've never swum half a mile?" she asked them.

"But the panga could be gone," Luciana said. "Or Cate could have taken it."

Gabriel's insides tightened at the mention of Cate. "She won't leave without us," he said.

He felt Luciana's skeptical stare. "She should and she will."

"It's our only option," Sanchez said.

"What about the machine?" Gabriel asked.

"What about it?"

"This has to be the cave the machine is in," Gabriel said. "Otherwise, why the stairwell?"

"If the machine is on, the water will be too violent," Luciana said.

Gabriel shuddered at the thought of trying to swim in that whirlpool of death.

"Then we hope the machine is off," Sanchez said.

They heard a faint voice from outside their chamber, and Sanchez shut off her flashlight. Gabriel held his breath.

FORTY-FOUR

CATE

I pulled on the knob uselessly, trying to rattle the door in its frame. It was immovable.

"Let me out!" I yelled.

I could hear the blaring siren and Lavalier barking orders. Then running feet and people shouting. I ran to the other door, the one Hunter had come through. I shoved my shoulder against it and twisted the knob until the skin on my hand burned, but it too was locked.

I swore and looked around the room. There were no windows, just the two heavy metal doors. Beside each door was a black box to read swipe cards. I ran to the desk and began opening drawers. I found pens, paper, thumb drives, and a variety of rocks, but no swipe card. Once, so very long ago, Sissy had showed me how to pick locks. I looked for paperclips, keys, anything rigid and flat. Finally I turned to the geode on the desk. I picked it up. It was surprisingly heavy, but I could hold it, just, in my right hand. I stood three feet from the door and lifted it above my head, aiming for the knob.

The door swung open.

"Are you trying to kill me?" Lavalier asked, slamming it shut behind him.

"I'm trying to escape."

"You have a panga?"

"What?"

"A boat. You said you have a boat." He was out of breath and clutched a rectangular black hard drive to his chest.

"In the cove. But the tide—"

"Follow me," he said.

"I didn't come alone."

"I know. Your friends set off the alarm."

He went to the other door and held a card up to the black box. The lock clicked, he turned the knob, and we entered a darker room with a bank of monitors and a big window onto the warehouse floor. It had the dim sheen of one-way glass, and I knew I was in Hunter's haven, from which he could see without being seen. Outside the window, men in black uniforms herded the workers in their red lab coats into a group. The siren was still going off.

Lavalier crossed the room and unlocked another door. "Hurry," he said.

We entered another office and closed the door behind us. This one was windowless and unlit, and we crossed it too, bumping furniture in the dark, then exited into a dim hallway. Lavalier picked up speed and I followed at a jog. We came to another door, which he cracked open enough to peer through.

"We're almost to where you came in."

"You knew where we came in?"

"The south door doesn't have cameras, just motion sensors. Security thought an iguana had set off the alarm."

I checked my watch. "The tide will be up."

"We have bigger problems than the tide."

"Thank you for helping me."

"Helping you? I'm helping myself—I'm coming with you."

"What?"

"Follow me."

Lavalier tucked the hard drive to his chest under his lab coat, then walked briskly out. I followed him across the end of the warehouse, and moments later we were outside, blinking in the glare. The siren stopped.

"Just in time," Lavalier said. He looked around and up at the sand-coloured hills, then at me. "I don't know the way."

I realized how few my options were. Had the others escaped? Would the boat be gone?

I led us at a trot across the open space to the base of the hill, then began the upward zigzag through the cacti. I paused to look back, checking to make sure Lavalier was up for the climb. He was sweating but moved with determination.

"Go, go," he said.

We crested the ridge. As we descended to the cove, sandy rocks slipped from under our feet, swirling into miniature avalanches. I turned back to offer him my hand, but he refused it, instead holding his hard drive tighter as he picked his way over the unstable ground. We glimpsed the long blue bay.

"Are you sure you want to come?" I asked. He was abandoning his whole operation.

"I don't want to be his next victim. And I have no choice now that I've helped you get out."

The cove appeared below us. The tide had covered the sand and lifted the panga by a foot. It bobbed there, the line from the bow still looped around a tall rock, just as Luciana had left it. Which meant that she, Gabriel, and Sanchez were still on the island.

Lavalier and I scrambled down the last of the rocky trail, took off our shoes, and rolled up our pants. I stood in knee-deep water and held the gunwale as Lavalier climbed in, still clutching the hard drive to his chest with one arm.

I looked back up the hill. "We have to wait for the others," I said.

"They will not come this way."

"They will."

"The guards will be here any minute, and they'll turn us over to Araya if they don't kill us first. We have to go now."

I thought of Hunter and his gold pen. He'd been about to make me his fourth victim. Or maybe fifth or tenth or thirteenth. I no longer had any doubt that he would try again if given the chance. I stood in the water, holding the panga, looking up the hill for signs of life.

"Your friends can't get back this way!" Lavalier said in a burst. "The guards will be all over the plant by now. Their way is blocked. Please, we must leave the beach."

"Then how will they get out?"

Lavalier glared at me. The water tickled the tops of my knees, wetting my rolled-up pants. There was no noise but the slapping water and a gull's screech. I looked back up the hill, hoping to see the trio weaving their way down, but spotted only a lone iguana.

"We aren't leaving this island without them," I said, surprised at my own vehemence. But it was a simple decision. Gabriel wouldn't have left me, no matter what I'd insisted to Luciana. "There's a dock on the far side, right? Could they have gone there?"

"No," Lavalier said wearily. "I saw them on the monitor. They were at the heavy-water separator."

"So?"

"The guards were right behind them. They will catch them, and then we can do nothing. If we get back to the mainland, at least we can get help."

But still I stood in the shallows, hand on the gunwale. Leaving the island was the rational choice; I saw that. Lavalier stared back at me, squinting and slumped on the bench seat. If Hunter cared enough to chase after me—or, more likely, his prize scientist—he could come up and over the ridge at any moment.

"What are their other options?"

Lavalier stared into the hull and shook his head, but he did finally speak. "They might try to get out through the cave."

"The cave?"

"It's their only chance. But it's a terrible one. They'd have to swim."

"Tell me how to get there."

"It's a stupid risk for us to take. I wish it weren't so, but your friends are surely captured."

"Risk accepted. Where's this cave?"

"It's not just that. The intake will still be on."

"Explain."

He looked at me angrily. "No one can be in the water in the cave while the intake is on. They wouldn't survive, and neither would we if we tried to help them."

"So how do we turn it off?"

"It's on a timer, but"—he looked at his watch—"it'll keep running for another thirty minutes. They'll find us by then. They'll come in boats."

"We'll wait."

"This is madness," he said. "We're both dead."

FORTY-FIVE

GABRIEL

Gabriel, Luciana, and Detective Sanchez hid in silence, while just outside their grotto, two guards debated. One had a nasal voice; the other sounded baritone against the rock walls.

"How many passageways are there?" asked the nasal voice.

"We just have to be systematic," the baritone said.

"What if they left by water?"

"It's impossible."

"Or got back into the lab?"

"We would have seen them."

The voices faded and the trio sat still in the dark silence, listening hard. Gabriel thought of Cate, confronting Hunter alone. He told himself she would be okay. She was always okay. Yet he couldn't shed his fear for her safety. He was about to speak when the voices came back.

"The boss is coming," said the nasal voice.

"You stay at the bottom of the stairs," said the baritone. "I'll take the top and wait for him."

"Why do you get the top?"

"Fine, take the top, but you radio the boss."

"It's creepy down here."

"It's not creepy, it's safe shelter. Fishermen used to sleep here."

"Maybe we'll find fishermen's bones."

"Stop it."

The voices faded again. Gabriel could hear Luciana and Sanchez breathing, small, reassuring sounds in the total blackness.

"Are there really bones in here?" he whispered.

"It's possible," the detective said.

She turned on her flashlight and shone it opposite them, to where the jagged rock wall met the ground. They saw two ancient-looking wooden crates and a rough-hewn fishing net folded in a pile.

"But this was a refuge, not a burial ground. A place to stay the night." She turned off her light. "If you had fire, and some fish, you could wait out a hurricane."

"What about drinking water?"

"You collected the rain."

Gabriel thought of a cathedral to which his grandmother had taken him long ago, and the genuine relic there: a saint's brown finger bone, preserved under glass. They'd lit white candles and prayed. He felt a chill in spite of himself, and when, moments later, Sanchez got up and said she was going to reconnoitre, he felt bereft of her protective presence.

"What do you think?" he asked Luciana.

"About fishermen's bones? Does it matter?"

"Maybe they'll protect us," he said.

They were silent for a few minutes as he contemplated just how dark darkness could be.

"What happened to your eye?"

Sooner or later, people asked. Strange she was asking now.

"I was snorkelling," he said. "Near Point Lobos, near home. We went there all the time. I saw a juvenile white shark and I followed it. It bit me in the face."

"Jesus. How old were you?"

"Nine."

"You still became a marine biologist."

"A shark is a shark. You can't argue with nature."

Like you can't argue with a thousand feet of solid rock and earth above your head, he thought. Was it possible to feel both safe and claustrophobic at the same time?

"Why's Cate so obsessed with Araya?" Luciana asked.

The darkness, and the likelihood that they would never get out of there, allowed Gabriel to speak freely. "They were in school together at a place for children with"—he searched for the best term—"psychological difficulties. She was looking for a piece of her past." He paused, wishing he could see Luciana's reaction. Silent seconds of darkness drifted by.

"But now she's angry at him."

"When she found out what he did, she couldn't forgive him," Gabriel said. He wondered if that was how Cate would put it. Sin and forgiveness were part of his vocabulary, not hers.

"Because Araya killed Tenoch?"

"Yes, but more than that. It's like he personally let her down by being a murderer. That's what she can't forgive—that he's the way he is."

He heard a scuff of feet near the chamber entrance, and Sanchez was back.

"It's so hot. The machine."

"It's still on?"

"It sounds like a hundred engines."

Gabriel shifted his position, trying to find a seat where the rock didn't dig into his legs. They really were going to die here.

"There are two more guards down here, with pistols," Sanchez said. "Along with the two on the stairwell."

They were all silent as they considered their double entrapment. The idea of swimming back to the cove had seemed wildly precarious, but being stuck in this blackness felt worse.

FORTY-SIX

LUCIANA

She wondered if it was really getting hotter in the cave, or if she was just imagining it. Though she tried to remain hopeful, the idea that they were going to swim back to the cove, find their boat, and pilot it away without getting caught seemed unreal to her.

Gabriel said he wanted to see the machine for himself and slipped away. The two women speculated about the backgrounds of the guards, agreeing that at least one was local if he knew about the cave having been used as a haven. They swapped stories about snakes they'd recently seen, and hypothesized about why the road to Cabo Pulmo remained unrepaired. They stopped talking, and Luciana listened to Ursula breathe. She imagined her non-visual senses growing keener in the absence of light. She thought of animals with little eyesight. Bats, moles, deep-sea fish. She thought of Ricketts, who navigated the world unperturbed despite the fur in his eyes. She wouldn't let herself think of what it would do to Dario if she didn't come home. But now she thought of how Ricketts would react, and a tear trickled down her face.

She felt a sudden clarity about how she wanted to live if she got out.

She knew where Javi was staying. She'd known even when she told him not to tell her. During their first phone call after he'd gone into hiding, she'd heard church bells in the background, tolling a Sunday evening Mass. She'd pictured it then. Remembered. He'd taken her there in his van a half-dozen times, and they'd made love amid orange trees and crumbling walls. A place where he felt safe, an oasis that drew him like a desert animal. Like it had once drawn the missionaries who built the church of San Ignacio de Kadakaamán.

The oasis town of San Ignacio was just a day's drive north of La Paz. Reachable. Hidden. It couldn't be a betrayal to honour her own values. She needed to act now, in service of her hoped-for future.

"Ursula?"

"I'm here."

"I think I know where Javi is."

FORTY-SEVEN

CATE

I untied the line from the rock and jumped into the boat, then pulled on the engine cord to no effect. I tried again, so violently I felt a bolt of pain across my right shoulder, and this time it started. I caught my breath, took a seat in the stern, and steered us away from shore.

When I glanced back, still hoping to see the others, the hillside appeared as a single rock face, its ledges and pathways no longer visible. As I piloted the boat out of the cove, Lavalier poked around the hull. He found some old towels, wrapped them around his precious hard drive, and tucked the bundle into a locker, which he slammed shut and latched.

"What are you going to do with that?"

He looked back up at the hillside with a wary expression. "If by a miracle I can recreate what we built here, I'll have the information I need to make it work."

He carefully moved to the bow, where he sat erect, looking forward. Apparently resigned to his fate, he pointed the way to the cave when we emerged from the small cove into the long bay. The sun was directly overhead, making the water so translucent I could see the sandy sea floor. I thought of Gabriel, who had been so alarmed when he'd come to see me last night, and I felt for him having to feel for me. I paralleled the steep rock wall of the shore, travelling east to west along the northernmost curve of the bay.

"Were you really on the island for seven months?" I asked.

"And four days," Lavalier said. He turned away from the bow, opened another locker, and rummaged around.

"Did you try to leave?"

"Of course, but every time, the guards turned me around. Said I was needed for an urgent matter. That's when I knew."

"Knew what?"

"I was a prisoner. Ah!"

Lavalier procured two headlamps and handed one to me. He moved from starboard to port and opened another locker, from which he extracted a dive knife in a rubber sheath.

"This is all you have for a weapon? The guards have guns."

"It's a research boat."

"You came to rescue me in a research boat?"

Before I could devise an answer, he actually winked at me. Then I saw a fish corpse, white-bellied and gouged. I pointed to it.

"They're everywhere," I said.

A look of consternation came over his face, and he turned back to face the bow, muttering to himself.

"Almost there," he called a few minutes later.

I saw the maw. It was high-ceilinged and wide at the opening, a place where you might anchor in the shade for a picnic if the water was calm, but the surface bubbled and churned. Beyond, the cave receded into darkness and the water turned black. Lavalier peered into the void as I slowed the motor and brought us closer. Some force seemed to suck at the hull, and I felt as much as heard a thrum. I reversed the engine to keep our vessel in place.

Lavalier checked his watch and looked back into the cave. "It should be now." He shook his head and mumbled.

"What?"

He didn't answer. I backed up the boat farther, and when I was free from the pull of the cave, I turned around and began a slow circle. For a moment we pointed south, towards the mouth of the bay, towards freedom. We could leave. Lavalier caught my eye, wondering if I had come to my senses. But it didn't even seem like a choice. I turned the boat towards the cave and approached the gaping mouth again. The water still roiled. But just as I was about to make another circle, it stopped, like someone had turned off the jets. The tug on the bow and the thrum in my body both ceased.

"It's done!" Lavalier cried. "Your suicide mission can begin."

I revved the engine and a moment later we were in near-darkness, the beams of our headlamps picking up water and rock. Lavalier bobbed his head around. I caught a sheen of fish skin on the water and glimpsed a metal walkway affixed to the rock wall. Straight ahead, I saw what could only be the machine: glinting blades protruding from a wall of metal mesh.

"This is where they'll come out," he said. "If they're alive."

We heard a sound of clanging metal somewhere high above us.

"Turn off your light," he said, and we both did. I cut the engine too. Now nearly sightless, I smelled dampness and salt, heard an echo chamber of splashes. I sensed our drift, but in my disorientation, I couldn't tell which way we were floating.

For a moment, it was quiet. Then: voices, boots on metal. Sounds bounced uncannily around the cave, one moment distant and the next nearby. There was a *clang-clang-clang* far too close, then quiet. Someone else breathing.

Something hit the boat with the force of a boulder. The hull dropped away and snapped back, fibreglass and wood slamming into my bones and leaving me sprawled in the stern.

I heard "*Putain!*" from the bow, and Lavalier turned on his lamp, revealing the dark shape of a person between us.

FORTY-EIGHT

GABRIEL

He moved along the passageway in complete blackness, wary at every step, hands out in front of him. After several minutes of slow going, the stubborn darkness seemed to relent and he could make out shapes. Then he heard the unmistakable noise, growing louder as he advanced: *whoosh, whoosh, whoosh.* He heard the churning water, a mechanical hum. Suddenly he got hotter, and realized he was standing next to a wall of metal. He moved forward, rounded a corner, and saw a circle of light in the distance—the mouth of the cave.

He froze. Squinted. The far light played tricks with his eye, but he had a sense of where he was. Up ahead, running along the cave wall, was the metal catwalk he and Luciana had seen the day before. The machine hulked to his right, a tower of hot, dark steel, all shadows and angles, inside of which turned the drum that sucked in fish and spat them out.

There was a screech of metal on metal, and suddenly the machine stopped. The water fizzed and foamed and fell quiet. Gabriel was elated for a moment, then felt vulnerable in the silence. Where were the guards? He tried to peer up the stairwell, but he didn't dare shine a light.

He retreated the way he'd come, stumbling more than once. He counted paces from where the ground underfoot got rougher, as Sanchez had instructed, but despaired of finding the lip in the rock wall to mark his turn. He was sure he'd gone too far and turned around. Sharp wall, smooth wall, soft dirt underfoot. His foot caught on something, a vertical edge that seemed to stick into his path. This must be it. But he was suddenly seized by a fear of entering the wrong interior cave and never finding his way out.

A hand closed around his wrist. Terror radiated from the centre of his chest. He'd entered the other dimension he'd always suspected. He'd see his grandmother and her bony-fingered saint. He'd see the shark.

"Youngster," said Detective Sanchez. "It's me."

He gasped. His spirit reinhabited his body. She led him back into the chamber of fishermen's souls.

When he'd regained himself, he told them the machine was off and the guards appeared to be gone.

"What if they're trying to lure us out?" Luciana asked.

It seemed like a strong possibility.

"If they're gone temporarily, it could be our only chance," Gabriel said. "They'll come back with more guards and more lights."

Sanchez served as decider, and her call was that action was better than no action.

Gabriel said a silent goodbye to the fishermen's ghosts and followed the women out of the cave, his hand on Luciana's shoulder. They approached the spot where they would have felt and heard the mechanical thrum, but the beast of a machine was still off. He heard distant voices. Guards now at the top of the stairs, but none down here. An easing of the darkness. As his eyes readjusted, his companions became solid shapes.

They took off everything heavy, leaving a sacrificial pile of boots and belts. Sanchez held up a fist to their faces and counted with her fingers. One, two—on three, they ran, a silent charge towards the catwalk.

They just had to get to the end, jump, and swim. But before they reached the catwalk, there was a shout and clamour from above. He ran harder. A blast of air zoomed past his ear. A whang of metal. "They're shooting," he yelled. They were so close. He felt a pain so searing in his right thigh that he was sure he'd been stabbed, and wondered how that could have happened.

"Jump," Sanchez yelled, and he flew through the air. By instinct, he tried to pull into a cannonball. He slammed into the water and the pain ripped through his thigh like a detonation. He began to swim, but his right leg no longer worked.

FORTY-NINE

CATE

Hunter faced away from me, a black simian silhouette, balanced amidships in a wide-legged crouch. Beyond him, Lavalier's disembodied face glowed under his headlamp.

"I know you took your hard drive," Hunter growled at Lavalier, raising one arm to protect his eyes from the headlamp's blinding beam. The boat rocked. "It's in this boat," Hunter said. "Or did you bury it in the sand? Did you think you'd come back for your buried treasure?"

He inched closer to Lavalier, who braced himself against the gunwales. The boat moved with them.

"You want to leave. Give me the hard drive and go."

Lavalier finally spoke: "You'll kill me either way."

Hunter crept closer to the bow. "I won't."

Lavalier's light beam moved as he looked over Hunter's shoulder at me.

"She's not going to save you," Hunter said. "She and I are old friends."

Lavalier was right: Hunter was going to kill him either way. Hunter was taller, younger, stronger, and had no inhibitions.

But neither, in that moment, did I.

I picked up the dive knife and pulled off its silicone skin. When Hunter lunged at Lavalier, I lunged at Hunter. The boat rocked violently. When we righted ourselves, I had the blade to Hunter's throat and blocked his path.

"Not this one," I said.

He squinted and tried to look away from the beam of my headlamp, but I saw he still had a smirk on his face.

"You won't do it."

"Move and this goes in your throat," I said.

The boat wobbled. I heard noises from elsewhere in the cave.

"Come on, Cate. You didn't kill your journalist," he said, gleeful and taunting.

Footsteps and shouting ricocheted in the dark, but all I could feel was the pressure of Hunter's neck under my knife, like a secret between us. I pushed, longing for that sudden give. I tensed my arm to drive the knife up hard, into Hunter's throat.

Suddenly the pressure under the blade was gone, but there was no surrender of split skin. Hunter had twisted away, lost his balance—or jumped—and splashed into the water. The panga rocked back and I tipped over. I slipped as I tried to right myself and banged my shoulder. By the time I lifted my head, there was chaos around the boat. The white gleam of breaking water. Dead fish, living people. One coming towards the boat, one moving away, two huddled together.

I had no time to think before Luciana heaved herself over the side.

"He's hurt," was the first thing she said. She unfastened a pole from a gunwale and shoved it at me and passed a life preserver to Lavalier. "Get them," she said to me, and she took the tiller.

I braced my thighs against the hull and leaned out over the side as Luciana revved the outboard and moved us towards the two heads. The detective kicked powerfully in our direction, made lopsided by Gabriel, who had an arm around her waist. "His leg!" she yelled.

Energy rose from my belly to my throat and out through my limbs as I thrust out the aluminum pole. Sanchez grasped it. As we pulled them in, I looked around the cave, the beam of my headlamp illuminating metal mesh and the water's rippling surface. The boat rocked as Lavalier and I lifted Gabriel in, and I registered the dark, ripped cloth around his thigh.

I turned to scan the water, and in my beam saw a head of black hair breaking the surface, moving into an inlet on the far side. It went under again. My longing to stab Hunter collided with my overwhelming relief that I had not, and something inside me collapsed.

We helped Sanchez into the boat, Luciana gunned the engine, and we peeled towards the mouth of the cave.

FIFTY

GABRIEL

The agonizing throb in his right thigh cranked up a notch every time the boat hit a wave, causing him to cry out. Perhaps he could just pass out until the monster was gone, if it was ever going to go. The detective and the physicist hovered around his injury. They'd ripped his pant leg away and tied a tourniquet above the wound, and then Sanchez had poured something on it that felt like cold fire. The boat slammed into another wave and he groaned. He tried to form meaningful words with his lips. Cate's face was above his, her hands on his cheeks. She was holding him in place. When he opened his eyes, which was getting difficult, she looked right into them.

"It hurts like a motherfucker, but you're going to be okay. Do you understand?"

"Oh hey, hi," he said. He closed his eyes.

"Gabriel. Gabriel."

He opened them. She looked beautiful, familiar, strange.

"Gabriel."

Sanchez and the physicist were pressing on his leg. What was his name? Lavalier. Fighting the monster. He opened his eyes and Cate was still right there, holding on to him. He'd go flying out of this boat without her. The pain chewed on his leg.

"There's an ambulance coming, okay? We called. They'll be at the beach."

Ambulance. Sounded sensible. But so much effort. Beyond Cate's silhouette, the blue sky bobbed dizzily, an ocean upside down.

"They're going to take you to the hospital in La Paz. Do you understand? I'm going to follow in my car, okay?"

He looked up into her green eyes.

"You're going to be okay."

Ever so slightly, the pain retreated.

FIFTY-ONE

LUCIANA

Dario, Beni, and Ricketts waited on the beach alongside two paramedics with a stretcher. Luciana cut the power, slid the bow onto the sand, and raised the outboard. By the time she turned back around, one of the paramedics was in the boat, triangulating how to lift Gabriel, whose face was pale and clammy. What remained of his right pant leg was dark with blood.

Once the paramedics had carried Gabriel away and the rest of them had moved the boat to higher ground, Luciana turned to her husband. Her legs gave way as she fell into his arms and they tumbled to the sand. She held on tight enough to feel his rib cage and the heart pounding underneath it, as though he were her life preserver and she'd been drowning. "My love, my love, my love, my love," she said into his neck, thinking she would never lift her face from his skin.

"You're back," he whispered into her hair.

She was back from so much more than he knew. Not just the island, but from Javi's orbit and her own turmoil and guilt. Ricketts did laps around them.

Gradually, she became aware of the four feet near her head. Dario picked himself up first, then held out his hand to help her rise. She brushed sand from her clothes as she stood. Ursula and Beni were up the beach near the boat, having their own reunion. Cate and the physicist from the island stood in front of them, both bedraggled. His glasses were crooked, his lab coat torn, and he cradled a wad of towels in his arms.

"This is Jean Lavalier," Cate said, touching his elbow. "Can you help him? I have to go."

FIFTY-TWO

GABRIEL

The paramedics gave him morphine and hooked him up to an IV. In the back of the ambulance, his head bobbed almost pleasantly, and his right leg became a throbbing ache. As they wheeled him into the hospital, Cate was there briefly, then gone. In a surgical room, an anesthetist shot up his leg until it was utterly numb, and another doctor sewed him up. Gabriel was lucky, said the doctor, all round glasses and black eyebrows above a pale-blue mask. There was an entry wound at the back of Gabriel's thigh, and a messier exit wound at the front. But the bullet had not hit bone. They told him the muscle, with physical therapy and some luck, would eventually recover.

He woke up hours later, in a bed partially surrounded by a green curtain. His right thigh was sore, but the monster pain was gone. He was wondering if he dared move it, or touch it, when he noticed the person sleeping in the chair beside his bed and realized with an outbreak of goosebumps that it was Cate, in the same hiking pants and white T-shirt she'd worn to the island, crusted with saltwater stains and yellow dirt. It wasn't a chair made for sleeping, but she was out cold, her arms crossed and her neck tilted at an unnatural angle.

As if she could feel his attention, she took a deep breath and awoke. Her eyes, red and weary, took a few seconds to focus before finding his.

Cate had used the shower off his hospital room and found clean clothes. Now she smelled like strawberry soap.

"Come to Mexico City," he said. The morphine hadn't conjured this desire in him, but it did liberate him enough to say it.

"You have a life there, remember? A girlfriend?"

Circles bobbled behind his eyes. Penelope. She was lovely, so warm. But God, he missed Cate.

"I was scared," he said, slurring a bit.

"I'm still who I am. I'd make you feel that way again."

His face felt rubbery, and he couldn't articulate well, so he blew out air between his lips to show how vehemently he disagreed.

"I tried to stab Hunter in the neck."

Now there was a beautiful display of fireworks shooting off behind his eyes.

"You deserve someone normal," she said.

He fell asleep.

When he woke the next time, she was gone.

FIFTY-THREE

CATE

Jia came to my apartment from her new office in South Lake Union, where she'd opened her VC fund specializing in biotech. It had been four weeks since she left La Ventana, and three and a half since my own return. I'd told her over the phone much of what had transpired.

The day had been warm, but by the time the sun was dropping behind the mountains, the air was brisk. I offered her a sweater to put on over her dress before we went out onto my deck, where I poured her a glass of white wine. I wore a similar black wool pullover. When I'd opened my closet on returning from Baja, I'd been struck by the neat rows of black items on hangers, clustered in sets of nearly identical garments. Then the matching white shirts. Maybe it was time to change my uniform.

"Don't say anything," I said. "Just listen. I meant to tell you this a long time ago."

I told her everything: Being locked in the closet by my stepfather. The big fire that killed my stepbrother and mother. My diagnosis as callous and unfeeling, the brain scans, the Cleckley Institute, my years inside its walls. Eventually, my discovery of Hunter Brandt and why I'd needed to meet him. Brandt, who turned out to be Araya, and a fusion pioneer, and a murderer.

When I got to the end of my recitation, during which I'd mostly gazed at the view, I turned to find her looking at me with her mouth agape. *Here we go*, I thought.

"You always wondered why I broke up with Gabriel, but he broke up with me, after I told him what I just told you."

When Gabriel, high on painkillers, had invited me to come back to Mexico City with him, I'd been tempted. The idea was appealingly headlong, like I could just throw off my old self by diving into his life. But it wouldn't work out, I knew. I'd get him hurt, or hurt him myself. To be in one another's lives at all, we needed a safe distance.

Jia was nodding now, but I couldn't read her expression.

"Is that why you waited so long to tell me about your past?"

"No. We just got so busy. You had a lot on your plate, and I didn't want to add to the load. And then I was going to tell you in Baja but . . ."

"The guy you were looking for killed someone."

"I didn't *know* it was him," I said. "But maybe I was already afraid it was him."

She sipped her wine, then said, "You're not getting rid of me that easily."

I didn't expect the wave of relief that washed over me. I hadn't realized how braced I was for loss—to be friendless again.

Her face hardened.

"Are you angry?" I asked.

"Yeah. I thought he was such a good guy."

I was confused. "Hunter?"

"Gabriel. I can't believe he would just break up with you like that."

"You're mad at Gabriel?"

"I thought you'd gone and smashed his heart."

"You're not mad at me?"

"Of course not."

A feeling bubbled up through my torso and out my arms. Energy, leaving my body. I felt light and relaxed and suddenly sleepy. The building tops between my twenty-fifth-floor deck and the waterfront became a silhouette against an orange sky.

"Aren't you worried it will reflect on you?"

She thought about that for a moment. "You're not a psychopath."

I started to speak, but she didn't let me continue.

"Or maybe you are. Who cares? I'm not friends with a brain scan. Or a survey result. I'm friends with a whole person."

It sounded so straightforward when she said it like that. Like I could just slip free of my history and reinvent myself. And in a certain technical sense, Jia was right. I doubt I would score above twenty-nine on the psychopathy checklist if I took the test today. Maybe the Cleckley Institute had fixed me. But why had it worked for me and not others? Why hadn't it worked for him?

"Did you get what you wanted from Hunter? I mean, before what happened?"

I considered the question. For a couple of days, I thought I'd found the kindred spirit I was looking for, but Dr. M had been right: Hunter didn't have any answers for me. I still felt a twinge of longing when I thought of him, but I didn't know exactly what it was for. Information, or intimacy, or revenge.

"He shattered some delusions."

A softness came into her face. Sympathy. It made me feel squeamish, but I let it be.

"What are you going to do now?"

"There was this plasma physicist on the island whom Hunter had basically kidnapped."

"And?"

"I think he needs money."

Instead of opening the front door from the inside, Dr. M came around the side of his house, wearing gardening gloves and carrying a pair of pruning shears. He dropped them into a basket on his covered porch and led me inside. Everything in his living room was frayed—the Persian carpet, the cushion covers, the bindings on his copious books.

"Lemonade with ice?" he called from the kitchen. An April heatwave had begun.

I sat on the couch. He set a tray with two glasses on the coffee table, then left the room and came back with an ancient manila folder, also frayed, which he placed next to the tray. He sat down and took me in, as though scanning for injury.

"Safe and sound," he said.

Until now, all I'd told him was that I was back in town. Now I related everything that had happened in Baja, including the updates I'd received from Luciana and Detective Sanchez since my return. The incumbent governor, Samuel Villalobos, had won the election; it seemed that voters, though keen for a better electrical grid, had not trusted Francisco Iguaro's grand schemes. Sanchez, meanwhile, had scored two successes. She'd arrested the guard who shot Gabriel. And she'd led federal authorities to Javier Sanz, the head of Reef Pirates, who was holed up in an oasis town in the middle of the peninsula.

But she hadn't found Hunter. The day I woke up in the hospital chair beside Gabriel, Sanchez and her colleagues mounted a search of the island, ready to charge Hunter with illegal industrial activity, a way to get him into custody while they worked on proving murder. They combed the inlets and hills, and even searched the shallow sea floor in the cave. When they found a boat missing, Sanchez knew he'd escaped by sea. Between his fusion factory and the resort, he'd left a fortune behind, but absent any evidence to the contrary, I had to assume he'd gotten away with his life.

Dr. M mostly just listened, nodding gravely. His cheekbones, visible above his grey beard, flared pink a few times: when I told him about Tenoch's death, and about trying to get Hunter to confess to murder, and about Hunter leaping into our boat in the dark. By the time I stopped, we'd both finished our lemonade.

"How is Gabriel?"

"Back at work. Probably more convinced than ever that I'm hazardous to his health."

"Do you take it that Hunter killed Joelle?"

"Yeah. He seemed to be justifying his reason for doing it—that he needed her money. Like he thought I would understand."

"And he explicitly said he'd killed the journalist."

"Yeah."

"Can the police do anything with that?"

"I told Detective Sanchez. But they have to find him first."

He looked fretful, gazing into the middle distance, and I felt protective of him. I knew what Hunter had done to others, and what he'd been willing to do to me.

"And Terry," he said tenderly.

I thought of that long-ago hike. "Maybe it really was unintentional."

"I wanted to believe that. But what about Terry's Saint Christopher charm?"

"I keep wondering if Hunter could have stolen it earlier, before whatever happened between them on the cliff. Maybe he thought it was valuable."

"It's odd that he would confess to you about the journalist and Joelle, but not Terry."

"Maybe he likes the idea of me—us—being left to wonder."

"He certainly knows it will weigh on me, not knowing for sure."

We sat in silence for several moments, then Dr. M glanced down at the manila folder.

"You said something when we spoke at your party. It made me realize there was a record I should show you, if I could find it. Something to—perhaps—put your mind at ease. As it turns out, it was here in the basement, in one of the filing cabinets we moved out of the institute."

He domed his hands over the folder as I tried to imagine what it could be.

"There was a forensic investigation of the fire that killed your mother and stepbrother. It's included in the police report. We didn't keep things like this with the clinical files, out of privacy concerns."

He hesitated, then went on. “I didn’t know how your beliefs about what happened had evolved.”

I must have sat up straighter, because he held up a cautioning hand as though to warn me not to get too excited.

“It doesn’t tell you everything you’re going to want to know. But it indicates clearly that a child couldn’t have started the fire. It was electrical in nature. The wiring in the house was substandard, not up to code. It had been a hot, dry day, and at some point that night, two wires sparked by accident. In theory, someone knowledgeable about electricity could have caused that to happen. But not a child. You simply wouldn’t have known how.”

I took this in intellectually, not yet able to absorb it on a deeper level. A memory came back: the phosphorus smell of an ignited match, my head bowed together with Ezra’s, in the woods. Burning fur.

“But I did start fires.”

“Oh yes. You even tried to start one in a garbage can at the institute, as you may recall. But you didn’t start the one that killed your mother and stepbrother.”

Irrationally, I felt attacked. His arrow made a fissure in my narrative wall. Pieces of my past seemed to float away, as though I were dissolving.

He slid the file towards me. “That’s the gist of it.”

I took it with the care of someone handling a radioactive object, and without opening it, set it down beside me on the couch.

“Your grandmother obtained it from the police after they closed the investigation, and she passed it to us. About a year after you’d come to Cleckley.”

“She saw it?”

“I assume she read it.”

I thought about that long-ago day when I sat by her bed, after the fog first came over her brain. I wondered what she thought she’d forgiven me for, if not the fire. I wondered whom she thought she’d forgiven.

“I regret not giving it to you sooner. But I didn’t know—”

"You didn't know I thought I'd killed them."

"I'm sorry."

"I never said."

I put the top down on my roadster and left Dr. M's neighbourhood of century-old homes. Instead of going back to Belltown, I got on the 520 bridge and sped east across Lake Washington, towards the suburbs, the farms and foothills, and the mountains, beyond which lay Cleckley. A Jet Ski zigzagged on my right, its whine mingling with the sound of car traffic. I accelerated until I was going faster than the other cars, so that the wind stung my eyes, making them tear up. In the deafening rush of air past my ears, I started to feel something like relief. It's frightening to lose a story about yourself, but it's also a liberation.

ACKNOWLEDGEMENTS

No one writes in a vacuum. I couldn't have pulled this off without support from many quarters.

Thank you to my writing crews: Abraham Arditi, Anna Reeser, Gillian Wiley Rose, Amy Taron, and Julie Trimingham, for their wise feedback on many chapters of this book. To Allison Augustyn, Tara Conklin, Margot Kahn, and Elise Hooper for feedback, encouragement, and guidance on the project of being a writer. To Ruthie Ackerman for her empathy and endless savvy, Michelle Brower for early advice, Nicole Hardy for the mini-retreat where I read my first draft and didn't despair, and Jane Hodges and Dave Brewer for building Mineral School.

I thank my agent, Emma Parry, for her energy and vision. Rosemary Ahern for the constructive feedback. My editor, Anne Collins, and the whole team at Random House Canada, for the magic of turning a manuscript into a book. Thanks to Sue Sumeraj for the eagle-eyed copy edits and Kelly Hill for the beautiful cover and text design.

I thank John Mecklin and my other former colleagues at the *Bulletin of the Atomic Scientists*, who inspired me to learn about nuclear fusion and encouraged me to weigh the pros and (sometimes very serious) cons of exciting new technologies. I visited the Woods Hole Oceanographic Institution as a journalism fellow and the Plum Island Animal Disease Center on a reporting assignment, settings that helped inform the marine-biologist characters in this book. My years at *Forbes*, where I was lucky to work for editors Michael Noer and Tunku Varadarajan, among others, honed a fascination with business leaders behaving badly.

Also on the research front, I learned about psychopathy from works such as *The Psychopath Inside* by James Fallon, *The Science of Evil* by Simon Baron-Cohen, *The Wisdom of Psychopaths* by Kevin Dutton, *The Psychopath Test* by Jon Ronson, and *Without Conscience* by Robert Hare, the renowned criminal psychologist who devised the (real) Psychopathy Checklist. The article "When Your Child is a Psychopath" by Barbara Bradley Hagerty in *The Atlantic* helped shape my thinking about the (wholly fictional) Cleckley Institute.

I thank my parents, Linda Eaves and the late David Eaves, who, as a psychologist and a mathematician, practically guaranteed that my first novel would be called something like *The Outlier*. They were also initially responsible for luring me to La Ventana in Baja California Sur, a town and region since embedded in my heart and the setting for much of this book.

To the other friends and family who have so often fed, sheltered, and cheered me on during the long, long writing process, however baffling it may have seemed to them: Kristin Hansen, Gregory Eaves, Iou-Chung Chang, Rich Ray, Mary Jo Ray, Gina Ray, and Ben Hooker.

And to Joe Ray, my partner in love and life, who makes everything possible.

ELISABETH EAVES is a debut novelist and an award-winning travel writer and journalist. Her work has appeared in *The New York Times*, *The New Yorker*, and many other publications, and been anthologized in *The Best American Travel Writing*. She is the author of two critically acclaimed non-fiction books: *Wanderlust: A Love Affair with Five Continents* and *Bare: The Naked Truth About Stripping*. Born and raised in Vancouver, Elisabeth lives with her husband in Seattle. Learn more and subscribe to updates at elisabetheaves.com

A NOTE ABOUT THE TYPE

The Outlier has been set in Sabon, an "old style" serif originally designed by Jan Tschichold in the 1960s.

The roman is based on types by Claude Garamond (c.1480–1561), primarily from a specimen printed by the German printer Konrad Berner. (Berner had married the widow of fellow printer Jacques Sabon, hence the face's name.)